Robert C. Jenkins

**The Last Crusader**

Or, the life and times of Cardinal Julian, of the house of Cesarini. A historical sketch.

Robert C. Jenkins

**The Last Crusader**
*Or, the life and times of Cardinal Julian, of the house of Cesarini. A historical sketch.*

ISBN/EAN: 9783337097202

Printed in Europe, USA, Canada, Australia, Japan

Cover: Foto ©Raphael Reischuk / pixelio.de

More available books at **www.hansebooks.com**

THE

# LAST CRUSADER:

OR,

## THE LIFE AND TIMES OF

# CARDINAL JULIAN,

### OF THE HOUSE OF CESARINI.

*A HISTORICAL SKETCH,*

## BY ROBERT C. JENKINS, M.A.

TRIN. COLL. CAMB. RECTOR AND VICAR OF LYMINGE.

"PRO FIDE CUPIO ET VOVI MORI."

*Ep. Juliani Card. ad Eugenium IV.*

LONDON:

RICHARD BENTLEY, NEW BURLINGTON STREET.
Publisher in Ordinary to Her Majesty.
1861.

LONDON :
PRINTED BY R. CLAY, SON, AND TAYLOR,
BREAD STREET HILL.

TO

THE RIGHT HONOURABLE

## STEPHEN LUSHINGTON, D.C.L.

JUDGE OF THE HIGH COURT OF ADMIRALTY,

DEAN OF THE COURT OF ARCHES,

ETC. ETC.

## These Pages are Dedicated

IN SINCERE ADMIRATION OF HIS PUBLIC

AND PRIVATE LIFE,

AND IN GRATEFUL RECOLLECTION OF THE KIND

AND VALUED OFFICES

OF A FRIENDSHIP OF MANY YEARS.

# CONTENTS.

# LIST OF THE GENERAL AUTHORITIES

EMPLOYED IN THE FOLLOWING PAGES.

---

ÆNEAS Sylvius Piccolomini (Pius II.) Opera Omnia.

Ambrosii Camaldulensis Epistolæ.

Acta Concil. Basiliensis.

—— Concilii Pisani et Senensis. (Par. 1612.)

—— Græca Concilii Florentini. (Rom. 1577.)

—— Concil. General. Ed. Labbe, Mansi, &c.

Andreas à Sancta Cruce (in Actis Concil. Florent. ab Horatio Justiniano edit.)

Anonymi Vita Juliani, MS. in Bibliotheca Marucelliana.

D'Attichy Flores Cardinalium, S.R.E.

Benedict XIV. de Synodo Diœcesanâ.

Blondi Flavii Foroliviensis Decades.

Bessarionis Epist. ad Joannem Lascharim, &c.

Bonfinii Decades.

Callimachi (Ph.) de Monte Wladislai et de Clade Varnensi, and de Vita Gregorii de Sanocenis.

Cochlæi Historia Hussitarum.

Charlier (Gilles) ap. Baluzium (Miscellan. tom. iii.)

Dlugoss Historia Polon.

Du Chastenet, Histoire du Concile de Constance.

Eugenii IV. Epistolæ, &c.

Eggs (G. von) Purpura docta.

Fasciculus rerum Expetendarum.

Garnefelt Vita. Nic. Albergati.

Gobellini Commentaria, in vit. Pii II.

Hussii (Johannis) de Ecclesia ; Epistolæ, &c.

Juliani Cardinalis Epistolæ ad Eugenium, Orationes, &c.

Lenfant Histoire du Concile de Basle.
Maimbourg Histoire du Grand Schisme d'Occident.
Nyder (Johan.) Formicarium.
Niem (Theod.) de Schismate.
Oswald de Joh. Rokyczana, &c.
Phranzæ Chronicon. (Viennae 1796.)
Poggii Vita Dominici Capranicæ (ap. Baluzium.)
Platinæ Vitæ Pontificum.
Palatii Fasti Cardinalium Omnium.
Procopowicz, de Processione Spiritus Sancti.
Pray (Georg.) Annales Regum Hungariæ.
Panormitani Oratio ad Convent Francofurd. de Concil. Basil. &c.
Raynaldi Cont. Annal. Baronii.
Ricci (Vie de Scipio) par de Potter.
Richerii Hist. Concil. Gen.
Rosweydii de fide hæreticis servandâ.
Spondani Continuatio Annalium Baronii.
Sylvestri Syropuli Historia Concilii Florentini.
Sansovino Historia di Casa Orsina.
Seyfried Vita Hussi.
Theobaldi (Z.) Bellum Hussiticum.
Thwrocz Chronica Hungarorum.
Ughelli Italia Sacra (tom. iii. de Episcopis Grossetanis).
Vertua di Soresina La Scienza Theologica, l'eminente Scienza di
    Gesù Cristo.
Würdtwein Subsidia Diplomatica.
Wessenberg. Die grossen Kirchenversammlungen des 15ten und
    16ten Jahrhunderts.
Von den Hardt Magnum Concilium Constantiensc.

# PREFACE.

THE public life of the subject of this narrative forms one of the most animated and exciting of the episodes in the great " History of the Decline and Fall of the Roman Empire."

The few masterly touches with which the features of the life of Cardinal Julian are there drawn, might constitute the attempt to produce a more finished portrait hazardous, were it not that the sketch of the great historian contains errors as well as imperfections—errors which the impossibility of following up the separate lives of all the actors in a history of so vast a scope, made in a manner inevitable, and to which the ignorance of many of the documents relating to the fifteenth century, in the days of Gibbon, contributed not a little. It was to be expected that, instead of patiently disentangling the threads of this history, the great philosopher would merely cut the knot, and represent Julian as an interested convert, passing over from the Council to the Pope, from the selfish motives which were then too common. An early acquaintance with his letters to Eugenius from Basle, followed up by a careful comparison of the documents of that perplexing period, convinced the Author that the integrity and originality of this remarkable character had been altogether overlooked, and that both his friends and enemies had done it but scanty justice. This conviction has led him to offer the following pages to the reader, written at different times during the intervals of parochial duty, and presenting to the eye the life of Julian in connexion with those great events in the Church and in the State in which he took so conspicuous a part. The key to that life is to be found in the great principle laid down at Constance—"There can be no true union without reformation, nor true reformation without union."*

There remains to the Author only the task of making grateful mention of those who have assisted him during a work which, on account of frequent and long interruptions, has extended over many years. Among these he is able to number His Eminence Cardinal Wiseman, John Craufurd, Esq., the late Count Valerian Krasinski, Dr. Beolchi, J. B. Inglis, Esq., with others, to whom he desires to record his obligations. With this expression of them, he commends to the reader his attempt to fulfil (though in another language) the last wish of the cotemporary biographer

* Petri de Alliaco, Sermo super verba "*Laetare Hierusalem.*"

and friend of the Cardinal,—" Prego adunque chi si volesse affaticare di comporre la vita sua in Latino, lo facci, che maggiore opera di pietà e di buono exempio non potrebbo fare di quello, di scrivere una vita di si degno huomo quanto fu Messer Giuliano, exempio a tutto il mondo di tutte degne conditioni possono essere in uno huomo."*

* Vespasiano Fiorentino (ap. Ughelli Italia Sacra, de Ep. Grossetanis, tom. iii. p. 775).

*April,* 1861.

# THE LAST CRUSADER.

## CHAPTER I.

ROME DURING THE SCHISM.

THE family Cesarini, which already in the sixteenth century is ranked by Sansovino "*fra le case antiche di Roma,*" and numbered with the Savelli, the Anni-baldi, the Conti, and even with the half-regal Orsini, derived its origin from a branch of the Montanari, which had flourished in Rome during the middle ages. In the beginning of the fifteenth century, it appears first to have assumed that patronymic, which, through the two succeeding ages, has been handed down as one of the most illustrious in the nobility of Rome, and which, with the vast inheritance which followed it, merged, at the close of the seventeenth century, in the great houses of Colonna and Sforza.*

* See the pedigree of the Cesarini family, in the " Famiglie Celebri Italiani" of Count Litta, and Sansovino, " degli Uomini illustri della Casa Orsina," p. 2 (Ven. 1565). See also, for the early period of the life of Julian, the cotemporary biography of Vespasiano Fiorentino (Ap. Ughelli, Ital. Sacr. de Episcopis Grossetanis).

B

Giovanni de Montanari, who lived in the beginning of the fourteenth century, was the father of Orso, and grandfather of Andreuzzo, who, by his marriage with Paolotia Rustici, had among other children a son Orso, who, by a fortunate alliance with the rich heiress Semidea Brancaleone, laid the foundations of the opulence of the Cesarini, and a younger son Giuliano, who, as the great Cardinal Julian of the fifteenth century, was the first to establish, on a historical basis, the name which had been then so recently assumed.

Born in 1398, in the midst of that fatal schism which divided the Church first into two, and then into three obediences, and reduced Rome to a state of ruin and anarchy, which the wildest periods of the tumultuous history of the papacy had never yet witnessed, the early years of Julian, like that of his great cotemporaries, were passed under a pressure of hardship and privation, which, while it prepared him for the labours of his after life, inspired his mind with the two great influences which animated it to the very last— the longing for the outward unity of the Church as the first step to its reformation, and for the complete reformation of the Church, as the only means of its vital and permanent union.

For more than seventy years, a season which the Romans might well deplore as their Babylonian captivity, the popes, with their court, had resided at Avignon, whither their political tendencies towards France had first led them, and where the influence of France in the consistory, and in the conclave, had retained them, until the year 1374, in which, moved by the revelations of St. Catherine of Siena, though probably more deeply influenced by *ragioni di stato*, to which the disclosures of the Saint gave a religious pretext, Gregory XI. re-entered Rome and re-established the supreme power in the ancient centre of the visible monarchy; but Italy had too long been left a prey to the factions of its princes, and the tumults of its peoples, to settle down into order and tranquillity on the mere reappearance of the sovereign pontiffs. The policy of division of power which the courts of France and the empire had found to be so successful, and which gave to the one by the presence of the papal court in its own territory, and to the other by the absence of any rival power in Italy, so great advantages, was in no degree obviated by the return of the Roman court to its proper centre.

The paramount influence of France remained still in the Sacred College, while the government of the popes was impotent even in the streets of Rome. When the extravagant joys of the Romans had passed away, the real desolation of the country and ruin of the Church became more apparent than ever, and the disheartened pontiff soon found that he had done little more than transfer from a scene of comparative security to one of the most hopeless anarchy a house divided against itself—a court in which the

French and Italian parties existed in all their old inveteracy, and were even subdivided into factions of greater virulence and animosity. For while in every part of the Roman States "the pontiffs, by governing by deputy (a terza mano), had lost much of their ancient estimation and grandeur, and murders, rapine, and confusion, reigned everywhere, in Rome the confusion was still greater, and the people brought to such a state of degradation, that they suffered themselves to be led and disturbed by every slightest movement—giving occasion to one disorder after another."[*]

The great pestilence of 1348, described with such eloquence by Boccaccio, was succeeded by years of tumult, opening the way to a dearth of provisions of all kinds, which almost amounted to a famine. And although the Caporioni (or Bannerets), who had, since the residence of the popes at Avignon, usurped the entire government of the city, pledged themselves to restore it to the returned pontiff, they failed to fulfil their promise; and the tumults which filled the streets of Rome, and carried by means of violence and intimidation every measure which had the popular approval, made it even easier for Gregory to preserve the fiction of government at Avignon than in Rome itself. Wearied out with his efforts to appease the Romans, and to unite the members of the Sacred College, which numbered thirteen French to only

* Sansovino, "Historia di Casa Orsina," p. 56.

four Italian cardinals, the aged pontiff expired in the palace of the Vatican, on the 26th of March, 1378.

The scene of discord and confusion that followed was indescribable; and though the invasion of the conclave by the Roman populace is softened down by the historians of that side into a mere deputation of entreaty and supplication, that the electors would choose a Roman, and thus secure the establishment of the papacy in Italy, the evidence on the other side greatly preponderates: and it is certain that the election which followed, though canonical and unanimous to all appearance, was in no respect free, even if it were not fictitious—for it would appear, from circumstances which followed, that the cardinals themselves, in uniting their suffrages for one not of their own number—Bartolomeo Prignano, Archbishop of Bari, a Neapolitan by birth, but connected through a long residence in France with the French party in the conclave—merely designed to pacify the Romans until they could escape from their hands, and reckoned on the voluntary resignation of the subject of this forced election, who, as a strict observer of the canon laws, might be expected at once to acknowledge the irregularity of these proceedings.* He, however, not only accepted the dignity, but at once obliged them to confirm him in its possession by a due enthronization, making use, in this instance, of the very power which

* Cod. MS. Bibl. Vict. ap. Spondan.

had forced on his election—the Caporioni—whose influence he from that moment conciliated.

Of the new pontiff, who assumed the name of Urban VI., we may say (as has been said of the popes generally), "This is he of whom nothing not great; nothing not exceeding the ordinary state of mankind, on the one side or on the other, is thought or spoken." And difficult, indeed, it is to find the historical mean in such a case. But for the frightful cruelties of his after life, we should esteem him merely a severe Church reformer, an austere reviver of all the ancient canons against the countless abuses of manners and discipline which had grown up in the wildest luxuriance during the exile of the papacy—a kind of anticipation in the fourteenth century of the morose, but elevated character of Pius V.

Against the abuses which now reigned universally, he began at once to oppose himself with the greatest vehemence, but with a degree of indiscretion which is almost incredible. On Easter Monday, the day after his coronation, in the presence of his secretary, the celebrated historian, Theodoric à Niem, he publicly reproached the bishops who came thither, "for neglecting their churches, and breaking their oath of residence," upon which the Bishop of Pampeluna, his own referendary, defended his order with great boldness, affirming that on public grounds alone he came to the court of Rome, which he was ready to leave at once. A few days after, in a public consistory, which was attended by a large concourse of cardinals and bishops, he held a discourse on the words, " I am the good shepherd," in which he bitterly denounced the lives of the prelacy, and deepened the fatal impression of his first address. But his indiscretion became almost grotesque, when he received one of the collectors of the Apostolic Chamber, who was rendering him an account of his moneys, with the words, "Thy money perish with thee."

This extraordinary conduct, repeated day after day, and extended to the highest of the laity as well as of the clergy, and to those best affected to his government, and crowned at last by the most marked insults to the Duke Otho, of Brunswick, and his wife, Joanna, Queen of Sicily, led the principal number of the cardinals, under the pretence of visiting their country-houses, to seek refuge in Anagni, from which place, for security, they removed to Fondi, in the kingdom of Naples, From thence they protested to the world that their previous election was void and uncanonical, and at once proceeded to the election of another pope, in the person of Robert, Count of Geneva and Cardinal, who assumed the name of Clement VII. and was crowned before the cathedral of Fondi, in the presence of all the Neapolitan court, including Otho, Duke of Brunswick, whom the infatuation of Urban had turned from a devoted friend into an irreconcilable enemy. Thus was opened that memorable division of the papacy which, under the

name of the Great Schism of the West, separated
Europe first into two, and then three, obediences, until the Council of Constance, nearly forty years after,
restored the unity of the papal throne, but which distracted and corrupted the Western Church to a degree
which admitted of no synodical remedy, and, by the
accumulation of abuses, prepared the way for the
Reformation of the sixteenth century.

It may be questioned whether the immense collection of treatises written on either side of this disastrous
quarrel, and collected in thirty-two folio volumes in
the library of the Vatican, can throw any clearer light
upon the causes which led to so violent a division
than that which the observation of the state and
policy of the courts of Europe at this time supplies.
Indeed, if the contradictory statements of the two
secretaries of Urban VI., Niem and Gobelinus (who at
least were eye-witnesses), are a fair specimen of the
manner in which historical facts are treated on both
sides, we may conclude that the multitude of these
advocates rather confuse still further this perplexing
history, than give any means of determining its true
bearings.   So confused it was, even to those who had
the best opportunity of tracing its origin and course,
that Niem entitles his collection of public documents
and personal notes relating to it the "*Nemus Unionis*,"
dividing it into paths, by-ways, thickets, and hills
which close in one great chaos or labyrinth.

In a political aspect, the grounds of the great schism

are more distinct than they are from a religious or ecclesiastical point of view. The papal monarchy had attained its great elevation by two courses of policy, which it alternated during the middle ages with great success. The one was the union of the states of Europe in some great object of a religious character, by which their attention was drawn away from their own interests, and their strength from the protection of their own authority and the advancement of their political influence. This the crusades effected in the most remarkable degree; and the history of the papacy from the period of the first crusade until the day when Pius II. sought, in the very close of his life, to rekindle the devotion of the faithful in the same cause, proves clearly that the fear of the Turkish power was far less real than the apprehension that, in the absence of such a ground of alarm, the countries of Europe would discover their true strength and solid interests, and become less and less dependent on Rome.

The second great principle of policy, which became more and more prominent as the former became exhausted in the history of Europe, was the policy of division, so successfully carried out down to the period of the Reformation, from which time the history of the papacy as a political power may be said to have ceased. Both these paths to political power were cut off by the schism which, while it suspended all the actual authority of the court of Rome, and threw the government of the Church into interminable doubt, enabled the states of Europe, and specially the republics of Italy, to carry on their commerce, and increase their strength, to a degree unknown before. " See you not," writes Niem to a friend with whom he is sympathising on the ruin of the Church, " how the Venetians and Florentines have been lifted up during this schism, who, until it began, were in the most depressed state ? " *

In proportion, moreover, as the see of Rome had lost its influence, the power of national Churches became increased. The final appeal, in the absence of any determination of the rightful possessor of the papacy, flowed back upon the metropolitans †—the independent authority of synods revived, until the great principle of their supreme authority over the popes themselves, and their right to legislate freely for the whole Church, became established by the Council of Constance.

The indifference of the princes of Europe to the papal authority was illustrated by the fact that, though every one of them assumed the side of one or other of the disputers for the papal throne, by none it was regarded as a subject of deep importance. A difference which two centuries before would have,

* Niem (Nemus Unionis, c. xl.) Platina (in Vitâ Gregorii X.), and Johannes Marius Belga (de Schismat. et Concil. p. 1. c. i.), accuse the Venetians as being the authors of the schism, and of the dissension between the Roman and Gallican Churches.

† Würdtwein Subsidia Diplomatica. t. vii. p. 413.

beyond question, plunged Europe in a general war, left the relations of its several states unchanged. Notwithstanding the mutual citations and excommunications of the anti-popes, the princes and nobles of Germany scrupled not to form alliances with those of France who lay under the interdict of schism; and the prelates and clergy of both obediences lived in social intercourse and friendship, utterly regardless of the excommunications of their respective heads.*

Urban VI. died in 1389, and was succeeded by Boniface IX., of the Neapolitan family of Tomacelli. His rival, Clement VII. (who, following the traditional feelings of his electors, fixed his seat at Avignor), survived till 1393, and had, as his successor, the Cardinal of Arragon (better known as Pierre de Lune), who assumed the title of Benedict XIII. Meantime, the Roman throne was filled by Innocent VII. (of the family Migliorati), Gregory XII. (Angelo Corario), Alexander V. and John XXIII. (Balthasar Cossa). Of these Gregory XII. had pledged himself to resign the papacy if Benedict XIII. would do so at the same time; but the latter having fled into Spain, and there resumed his title, Gregory, who had taken refuge at Rimini, maintained his own: so that the fifteenth century dawned upon a threefold papacy, and witnessed the *verenda et abominanda Trinitas paparum* which Cardinal Pierre d'Ailly deplored at Constance.

* Niem, Nemus Unionis, c. xliv.

Such was the state of Rome in the opening years of Cardinal Julian. He had experienced from his earliest years the afflictions of his native city, and from his earliest years he longed and laboured for their relief. His indignant question to Eugenius IV. in his after life, " Am not I a member of the Church and of the court of Rome ?" had its first inspiration in the day when he saw the Church of Rome divided and its court deserted; when, under the pressure of poverty and in the foresight of the ruin of the Church from its countless abuses and hopeless divisions, he enrolled himself as a student in the University of Perugia. When we read of the city of Rome at this period, that " the houses and churches were in a state of ruin—that even the monastery of St. James, that ancient and venerable asylum of the lords cardinals, and of poor and holy men, was unable to escape destruction"*
—we may picture the state of a provincial city of Italy at this time.

It is difficult indeed to conceive how the University of Perugia, founded less than a century before, could withstand the pressure of those calamities that had desolated the Roman States, for the poverty of its students was illustrated by the fact that Julian had not the means of procuring himself a full copy of the Pandects, the very text-book of his studies and subsequent lectures on jurisprudence, and was compelled to write out with his own hand the

* Niem, Nemus Unionis, Tract. iii.

marginal glosses, a task for which he was well fitted, as (to use the words of his cotemporary biographer Vespasiano Fiorentino) "*era gentilissimo scrittore.*" While at Perugia, he resided in the house of the Buontempi family, where, by his literary talents and early promise, he soon became known to the governor of the city, Bindaccio da Riccasoli, "a literary man, and a lover of men of letters."

At his house the young Cesarini had ever a ready welcome, and to this earliest patron he dedicated some poetical essays which he composed during his university career. But these gave no interruption to the study of the Roman law, which engrossed all his time and labour, and on which from a student he became in the ordinary course a lecturer, numbering among his auditory several of the most eminent of his cotemporaries, of whom Dominico Capranica is specially mentioned, a man of stern and exalted character, the friend and companion of Julian in his after life, and elevated to the cardinalate in the same promotion.

It is easy to trace from the writings and speeches of Julian in after life, whether we take up the synodical epistles which he indited at Basle, or the subtle disputations which he conducted at Florence, how much he was indebted to this early discipline for his subsequent controversial successes. The study of the Roman law, occasioned by the discovery of the Pandects of Justinian in the eleventh century in the city of Amalfi, had formed, from that period, the foundation of the teaching of the universities of Italy, and was their only security against the progress of decretalism and the false principles of the canon law, which in the end superseded it in all the schools of Europe.

The freedom and success of the republics of Italy were chiefly maintained by the force of those solid principles which the Roman law so early engrafted upon the minds of their statesmen and even clergy,* and incorporated in the laws they established. Nor did anything tend more to promote the triumph of the civil over the pontifical law than the great schism, which, by dividing the headship and throwing it into inextricable confusion, had proved the principles and maxims of the decretalists to be as practically worthless as they were afterwards proved to be historically false and groundless.

The views of these absolutists of the Roman monarchy arose naturally out of that great phenomenon of the middle ages, which the period of Gregory VII. and Innocent III. exhibited in its fullest perfection. The Church of Rome, emerging from the darkness and confusion of the middle ages, had then arrived at the form of an absolute spiritual monarchy; and a practical expediency, if not a positive necessity, of government identified the unity of the whole Church with the unity of the presiding see.

* Of this St. Bernard complains to Eugenius III., "Et quidem quotidie perstrepunt in Palatio leges, sed Justiniani, non Domini." (l. i. de Consideratione, cap. iv.)

The great moral superiority which Rome still retained had given it a moderating influence between the conflicting powers of Europe, civil and religious, during the period in which the elements of nationality were forming, and the impressions of religious authority were the deepest and most lasting. The spiritual passed imperceptibly into the temporal, the religious into the political bond.

The chair of advice and consultation became, by degrees, a tribunal of authoritative appeal,* and this was hastened by the assumption of a legal form and system in briefs and synodical writings. †  The foundation of its imperial rank, upon which the primacy of the Church of Rome had been left by the Council of Chalcedon,‡ became too weak to bear the vast superstructure of the ecclesiastical monarchy. The supposed donation of Constantine added but little strength to the old foundation ; and in transferring the fabric of power to the higher donation of Christ himself to St. Peter, a stability and perpetuity was given to its authority, enabling it to give sanction and solidity to every other tenure of power.

The boldness of this theory, the simplicity of its plan, and, above all, the success of the forged decretal

---

* See a memoir of Bishop Ricci on Reservations, and on the Origin of the Appellate Jurisdiction of Rome. (Memoires de Ricci, par de Potter, tom. iv. p. 222.)

† Van Espen. Jus. Eccl. p. 3. t. vii. c. i. § 13.

‡ διὰ τὸ βασιλεύειν τὴν πόλιν ἐκείνην.

Concil. Chalc. Can. 28.

epistles, and their triumph over the system of the ancient canon law, which established an aristocratic rather than a monarchical government in the Church, completed the building of this visible monarchy, and suggested to later ages a new argument, derived from the mere fact of an early acknowledged and universally recognised supremacy.  The divines of the twelfth and thirteenth centuries were content to frame a theory in accordance with the facts before them; and at a time when all ecclesiastical power flowed from Rome without dispute and without obstruction, they gladly escaped from the troubled waves of controversy, and cast anchor in the decision that Rome was the proper and only source of power.  Hence arose the principles of decretalism, and the supposition of a jurisdiction " prevenient and concurrent " in every part of the Church, whereby the episcopal and every other authority were rather leased out to their occupants than held in their own right.  Upon this supposition were based all the exactions of the court of Rome, its annates and other extortions, which were little else than fines paid to the supreme pontiff on the succession to any benefice, presupposing a kind of tenancy under the papal monarchy.

To carry out this scheme more fully, the religious orders were gradually made independent of the ordinary jurisdiction, and peculiars erected everywhere, giving the popes a direct, as well as an indirect, influence in every diocese.  When, however, the monarchy was divided by the great schism, and the headship fell into endless dispute, the minds of men were dislodged from their resting-place, and found the necessity of arriving at some more rational principle of ecclesiastical order and power.

The great maxim of St. Augustine, that the keys were given "not to one, but to unity" (*non uni, sed unitati*), led them to look on towards synodical authority and determination, and to maintain that the whole Church had the right of reforming every member of its body, even though that member were Rome itself; that the ruling see was within the body, though it presided over it; and that the pope was less the "vicar of Christ" than the "vicar of the Church" of which he was only the "ministerial head."* And when the Council of Constance deposed the three anti-popes by a single act of power, the advocates of the independent supremacy of the see of Rome were left without any resting-place. "They have already" (wrote Huss, from Constance, in allusion to the epithets of Roman flattery) "cut off the head of the Church, they have torn out the heart of the Church; the all-sufficient refuge of the Church, to which every Christian ought to flee, they have made utterly to fail."

It was under these altered circumstances of the Christian world, when men were preparing themselves for this great change in the relations of this Church,

---

* Concil. Basil. Ep. Synodal. "Cogitanti." Thom. de Corsellis (ap. Ænæam Sylvium. Hist. Basil. Concil. l. i.).

and were looking anxiously for a new and firmer basis
of ecclesiastical power, that Julian returned to Rome,
where he was soon received into the family of a
still more eminent patron, Branda di Castiglione,
the Cardinal of Piacenza. The unity of the papacy
had been secured by the Council of Constance by the
election of Pope Martin V., one of the chiefs of the
illustrious house of Colonna, whose devotion to the
empire was a guarantee of the success of his mission
as the uniter of the whole Church, the builder anew of
the shattered monarchy.

Of the two great objects of the council, the restoration of the unity of the Church, and the work of its
reformation, the latter alone remained; but it was
infinitely the greater and harder : and the failure to
accomplish it at Constance was the root of the Reformation of the following century. But, to understand
clearly the position of the Roman Church and court at
this time, we are led to fall back for a moment on the
life of Cardinal Branda, whose part in these great events
was somewhat earlier, and whose influence and experience contributed so materially to form the public
character of Julian.

# CHAPTER II.

BRANDA DI CASTIGLIONE, generally called by the historians of this period the Cardinal of Piacenza, to the bishopric of which city he was nominated by Boniface IX., was a noble Milanese, brought up under the patronage of the Grand Duke Galeazzo Visconti, and was considered the most eminent jurisconsult of his age. He remained faithful in his obedience to the successors of Urban VI., until, on the failure of Gregory XII. to redeem the pledge solemnly made on his election, to hold his office only provisionally, and until a determination of the controversy should be made synodically, and in the meantime to elect no new cardinals, he renounced his allegiance to that pontiff, who at once deprived him of his bishopric and all his other honours.

In 1408 he joined the council which had just assembled at Pisa to effect the reunion of the Church, and which Balthasar Cossa, afterwards Pope John XXIII., is alleged to have hastened in consequence of his personal animosity to Gregory XII.,* and his ambitious desire to fill the throne so soon to become vacant.

The near neighbourhood of Rome, or rather perhaps the paramount influence of the cardinals and members of the court of Rome in the Council of Pisa, rendered that assembly wholly abortive in the matter of the reform of the Church, while the absolute want of executive authority, occasioned by the divided state of the secular powers of Europe, which stood aloof from a council so purely Roman in its origin and structure, deprived its efforts after the union of the Church of all their effect.

By the election of Alexander V. to the papacy, declared vacant by the deposition of Benedict XIII. and Gregory XII., against whom the council proceeded with all the formalities of the law, but who maintained their respective claims in defiance of all its acts, it left the Church in a worse condition than that in which it found it, and divided it into three, instead of two obediences.

"Thus," as the writer of the time observes, " out of all the forethought and wisdom of the men of all parts of the world who wished to make one head, they contrived to make three popes instead; truly," he adds, " there is too much reason to fear that if the Council of Constance takes place, a fourth will be made there."†

* Niem, de Vita et fatis Joan. XXII. c. xiii. (ap. Von der Hardt.)

† Theodoric à Vrie, Hist. Concil. Constat. l. v. ap. fin.

The prelates and ambassadors left in such haste at the close of the council, that the fathers found a ready excuse from entering upon the subject of reformation, which they remitted to the future council in the very cool terms :—" Whereas, our Lord the Pope, with the advice of the council, intended to reform the Church in its head and members, to which end many things have been expedited by him, and many others concerning the state and favour of the prelates and inferior clergy remain, which, on account of the departure of the prelates and ambassadors, cannot be carried on : therefore our Lord, the holy synod requiring and approving, suspends and prorogues the said reformation to the ensuing council already convoked."*

This last session was held on the 7th of August, 1408 ; and whether the new pontiff had the capacity or the will to enter upon the great work of reformation, the opportunity at least failed him ; for in less than eleven months after his election, his death left a new vacancy in the papal throne, which was filled by the election of Balthasar Cossa, who assumed the name of John XXIII.

Cardinal Branda had, as Bishop of Piacenza, taken an active part in the business (if such it could be called) of the Council of Pisa ; and his zeal in the cause of a body which (for his own advancement and for the abasement of Gregory XII.) the new pontiff

* Acta Concil. Pisan. Sess. xxiii.

had so greatly hastened, marked him out for special favour. He was accordingly included in the first promotion of the new pontiff, being restored to his bishopric, and made cardinal in 1410.

The Council of Pisa, unimportant as it was in itself, and without success in the main design of its assembly, yet was not altogether ineffectual in clearing the way for the great work of reform, which in its public sessions it passed by unnoticed. As the first occasion on which the heads of the Church were brought together, to discuss and deplore its state—as a point of union and intercourse to those great minds which became developed in the Council of Constance, and have left in the records of its acts imperishable monuments of wisdom and maxims of ecclesiastical experience—above all, as the scene in which that new theory of the Church was opened which the Councils of Constance and Basle matured, and to which alone whatever liberty remains in the Roman Church must trace its origin—we may well view the Assembly of Pisa as a necessary prelude to the Council of Constance—a fit introduction to its political and religious history. In its acts we find, for the first time, the contenders for the papacy dealt with as subjects of the Church, and not as its absolute monarchs. In the sermons preached before it, we find the first public recognition of those doctrines, which the learning and eloquence of Gerson, D'Ailly, Zabarella, and the great reformers of the fifteenth century, commended to the Council of Constance. And though the acts of the council give but a passing notice of these discourses, we can well fill up in imagination the argument of the French divine, Pierre Plaoul, in the thirteenth session, who, from the words of Hosea (i. 11), " Then shall the children of Judah and the children of Israel be gathered together, and appoint themselves one head," beautifully deduced the exaltation of the Church and its superiority over the pope.

It was in this manner that the members of the Council of Constance became prepared for their future station in that great assembly, and were stimulated to hasten its advent. The four years which intervened between the promotion of Cardinal Branda and the assembly of the Council of Constance, while they saw the abuses of the Church multiplied and its confusions increased, witnessed also the multiplication of conferences and treatises on the reformation of the Church, and increasing efforts to clear the way for the great event of the age, a free and general council convoked by an emperor, and held in one of the free cities of the West, as a guarantee of its liberty and authority.

The fears of the new pontiff, in the meantime, lest the subject of reformation should be seriously taken up, and that by a body removed from his own influence, led him to convoke a council in the Lateran— a policy which has been steadily followed by the court of Rome whenever the danger of an independent synod, held out of Italy, has threatened its security. The acts of this shadowy body were, however, rather ludicrous than formidable. In the first session, held in the Lateran church, a great screech owl, flying from the corner of the building, fixed its eyes with a frightful glare on the pope, and threw the assembly into confusion with its horrible cries. The session was prorogued, but the visit of the owl was prorogued also, for it reappeared in the following meeting, and though at last pursued and killed, the fatal omen remained ; and the council, after an ineffectual protest against the heresies of Wiclif and Huss, and the pretensions of the two other anti-popes, was dissolved almost immediately after its assembly. Of the strange incident which marked its opening, and which Nicolas de Clemangis had on the solemn testimony of one of its members, it has been pleasantly observed by an old writer, that " at length the holy dove being departed" from such assemblies, " an ominous owl overlooked the Lateran fathers, and though with much clamour they destroyed the appearing fowl, yet the foul spirit of darkness and error wrought as effectually in them as ever." *

The pope, seeing that he could no longer put off the period of a general council, strove in vain to make Italy the scene of its assembly. In a conference with the Emperor Sigismund, at Lodi, he used every in-

* Dr. Owen's Sermons, p. 227.

fluence to carry this great point, but the emperor was inflexible. To the difficulty of the cardinals crossing the Alps into Germany, he opposed the still greater difficulty of the spiritual electors crossing them to reach Italy.* With a heavy heart the pontiff yielded, and from the scene of this meeting there went forth from the emperor and from Pope John XXIII. the letters convoking the assembly of the council at Constance, on the 1st of November, 1414. The pope did not arrive at Constance until the 28th of October, having been delayed on his journey by the snow, in which, on his reaching the Adlerberg, he was completely fixed. According to Ulrich von Reichenthal, a cotemporary historian, his exclamation on this emergency was not very canonical, "Here I lie!" he cried out to his attendants, "in the name of the devil; Why did I not remain at Bologna?"† On his arriving at Feldkirch, which commands the view of Constance and the Bodensee, he somewhat facetiously prophesied his own fate. "It looks," he said, "just like a hole in which they catch foxes."‡ To ascend to the more solemn view of another cotemporary, "It pleased the supreme pontiff to go to Constance, not to judge, but to be judged;"§ but the multitude and splendour of his retinue, the amount of his largesses, and the companionship of Duke Frederic of Austria,

* Von der Hardt, vi. p. 5 and vi. p. 1. § 9.
† Ulric. Reichenthal. Chron. § 14.
‡ Reichenthal. l. c. Trithem. Chron. Hirschaug. ii. 336.
§ Theod. à Niem, Hist. Concil. Const. l. vi. dist. 4.

indicated that the conviction of the certainty of his re-election was the sole motive of his appearing in Constance, though for a short period it was prudently dissembled.

In a train consisting of nine cardinals, among whom was the Cardinal of Piacenza, and a vast number of archbishops, prelates, and doctors, he entered Constance in state, seated on a white horse, adorned with scarlet trappings, and preceded by another bearing the consecrated host. Six hundred persons were in his immediate suite, twelve hundred formed the retinue of the cardinals; besides whom there were twelve secretaries, two hundred and seventy-three notaries, and twelve hundred and seventy-two doctors. The Duke Frederic of Austria accompanied the pontiff, and increased the splendour of a procession which rather resembled a public triumph than an act of submission. Among the papal followers on this memorable occasion was the great financier and money-changer, Cosmo de Medici, the ancestor of that illustrious house, which reigned afterwards in Florence, whose rise from comparative obscurity was attributed to his connexion with John XXIII., whose simoniacal exactions and pecuniary necessities became the foundation of the wealth of the great Florentine. Other cardinals and bishops followed soon after; and by the time of the arrival of the Emperor Sigismund, on the evening of Christmas-day, with all the circumstances of pomp and majesty which belonged to the empire in the days of its greatest glory, the council numbered 33 cardinals, 346 prelates, 2,148 abbots and doctors, both lay and clerical, 564 heads of religious houses, and 1,600 noblemen, bringing up the strangers assembled in Constance to the almost incredible number of 50,000.

But a few days after the procession of Pope John XXIII., the people of Constance witnessed an arrival, whose circumstances exhibited a strange and affecting contrast to that gaudy and unmeaning pageant. Attended by his constant friend the Baron de Chlum, and a few devoted followers—" faithful found amid the faithless " of that day of self-seeking and time-serving duplicity—John Huss, whose name is too great for the epithets of earthly honour, entered the scene of his afflictions, of his condemnation, and of his cruel and glorious martyrdom. His simple and touching letters from Constance to his friends in Bohemia, and to the faithful congregation of the chapel of Bethlehem, never again destined to see his face, and to hear his words of solemn pleading and of deep though mystic piety, survive to this day, and throw a light upon the scene before us which it can receive from no other page of cotemporary history.

A few years before this, and in the beginning of that great Bohemian movement which recognised Huss as its originator and martyr, two Englishmen, followers of Wiclif, are said to have painted on the walls of an inn at Prague a picture of significant con-

trast. On the one side Christ was entering Jerusalem in the triumph of His great humility, surrounded
by the apostles, and followed by the joyful multitude;
on the other, the pope was entering Rome, surrounded
by his cardinals and with every emblem of earthly
sovereignty and secular pride. On the memorable
day which saw the reformer and his friends enter Constance, this contrast became realised in the disciple as
well as in the Master; and the thousands of strangers
who thronged the gates of Constance asking "Who
is this?" might have well been carried back in lively
retrospect to the day when the multitude uttered the
same words in the crowded streets of Jerusalem.

Soon after the arrival of the emperor, the ambassadors of the two anti-popes arrived, one or two of whom
were cardinals of the hostile obediences; and their
assumption of the cardinalitial insignia created no
little difficulty. The council which recognised that
of Pisa as legitimate, and even regarded itself as the
continuation of that assembly, could not reasonably
acknowledge even the provisional claims of those who
had been formally deprived of the papacy by the
fathers of Pisa. The jealousies which this difficulty
occasioned were increased by the mutilation of the
arms of Gregory XII., which his ambassador had put
over his house, an indignity which was believed to
have been instigated by John XXIII. himself.

The predominance of the secular power in the
council began early to show itself; and the determi-

nation to reduce the influence of the court of Rome was evidenced by the manner in which the assembly was constituted and the power of the Italian bishops neutralized.   The entire council upon its opening was divided into four nations—the German, the French, the Italian, and the English—to which (after the subtraction of the kingdom of Arragon from the obedience of Benedict XIII.) the Spanish nation was added as a fifth.   Every nation chose its own president, who was changed every month.   All the subjects of discussion were treated upon in the first instance by each nation separately.   Thence they were carried up to a general meeting of all the nations, the decision of the majority of which came before the council in its public and full sessions, in which the voting was repeated by nations, and published as a synodical decree.

The pope in vain contended against a plan which virtually cut off all his power over the body, and against which he afterwards protested as an innovation unknown to the Christian world before.*   He had reckoned on the paramount influence he possessed over the Italian bishops, whom he had increased by the nomination of titular bishops, and who all were devoted to his cause from motives of self-interest or gratitude.†  The constitution of the council he foresaw therefore as the death-blow of all his influence.

---

* Ep. Joan. XXIII. ad Wladislaum. apud du Chastenet, " Preuves de la Nouvelle Histoire du Concile de Constance," p. 316.

† Wessenberg, tom. ii. p. 117.

Nor were the cardinals less dissatisfied with an arrangement which denied them their accustomed influence as leaders and moderators, and merged them in their respective nations; in whose congregations they not only found themselves standing on the same level as the bishops and doctors, but even treated by these with such distrust and reserve that they rarely became acquainted with the subjects to be legislated upon until the decision of the nations had nearly arrived at maturity.*

It is this peculiarity in the structure of the council that gives to its acts so irregular and unsystematic a form, and makes even the admirable diary of its proceedings, drawn up by Von der Hardt, a very insufficient clue to the mass of documents relating to it, which he has collected with such judgment and assiduity. To follow its proceedings in chronological order, would be to take up and to drop one thread after another of its actual history. Our object will be, therefore, to present an outline of those leading and characteristic features, which give to the great Council of Constance such a prominence in the history of the world, as no other assembly of the kind has ever yet attained to. Of these the first in order, as in importance, is the matter of Pope John XXIII., whose cession of the papacy and flight from the council give almost a romantic

* Von der Hardt, tom. iv. pars ii. p. 140, and tom. i. pars vi. p. 431.

interest to its earlier history. After the first session, which was merely formal, and held during the absence of the emperor, and until the second, which was held nearly four months afterwards, negotiations were carried on between the nations and the pope in order to bring about his voluntary abdication of the papal throne, while similar efforts were made to give effect to the deposition of the two other claimants, by inducing them to submit to the decree of the Council of Pisa.

The fact that a proposition to open a criminal information against John XXIII. was only over-ruled on the ground of public scandal, so far alarmed the pope as to induce him to appear to enter with sincerity into these negotiations for his voluntary cession of the papacy. He even received their proposal of the nations with an affectation of pleasure, and replied with gravity that he was quite prepared to accept it if the other claimants would do the like,[*] a very safe condition, inasmuch as Benedict XIII. stoutly refused to resign either to the council or the emperor.[†] The only safety of the pontiff now lay in procrastination; and to this end he endeavoured in vain to bring on the trial of Huss in order to divert the attention of the council, and to give scope to his intrigues with the Duke of Austria. When, however, the will of the council

[*] Theod. à Niem, de Vita et fatis Joannis XXIII. l. 2, cap. 3, 4.
[†] Du Chastenet, "Preuves," &c. p. 312.

could be no longer evaded, he made a virtue of necessity, and in a general congregation held on the 1st of March, 1415, he solemnly abdicated the papacy. " How wondrous was then the joy of all present! how sublime the voices of those who chanted the Te Deum Laudamus! For not content with this, the pope solemnly convoked a session for the following day, which was held accordingly in the cathedral." "There having celebrated mass himself, with litanies, prayers, and all accustomed ceremonies, the Cardinal of Florence enjoined silence and proclaimed that the pontiff graciously decreed and accepted the form of cession which he had written. Then the pope read it, and when he came to the words 'juro et voveo,' descending from his throne, he bowed himself and knelt before the altar, and putting his hand to his breast said, 'This I do faithfully.' Then the emperor rose and blessed God, thanking the pope for his holy resolution, and that not only in word but in deed, for laying aside his imperial crown, he prostrated himself, and kissed the feet of his holiness." *

This exciting scene led on to fresh negotiations, in which the insincerity of the pope, whose grand object in this simulated abdication was to influence the emperor in his behalf, and to gain time for intrigues, became speedily apparent. He felt the pulse of Sigismund by offering him the consecrated

* MS. Victorin. ap. du Chastenet. Append. p. 309.

rose a few days after in the cathedral; but the emperor, to his mortification, instead of retaining the gift, handed it over to the image of the Virgin, and presided the next day in a general assembly for electing a new pontiff. The pope's disappointment was speedily turned into alarm when he found that the gates of the city had been closed, and from that day he meditated his escape. His constant friend, the Duke Frederic of Austria, contrived to get up horse-races and games in order to divert the minds of the strangers in Constance, and in the midst of the confusion thus occasioned, John XXIII. fled from the city by night, and arrived safely at Schaffhausen, then under the dominion of the Austrian duke.

The sensation which this news occasioned in Constance may well be conceived from the knowledge that, on the following day, the emperor thought it necessary to proclaim in the public places of the city the security and immunity of the council, and this not merely by heralds and officers, but in his own person, riding about the city with the Elector of Bavaria, and reassuring the minds of the citizens and strangers who had already began to close their shops and prepare for the general break-up of this vast assembly. Many of the cardinals followed the pope to Schaffhausen under the pretext of prevailing upon him to return, and among these was Cardinal Branda. The council itself, driven to the support of

D

its own authority, and fearing that the pope would proceed to dissolve it in the plenitude of his power, entered at once upon the work of establishing its own independence and indefeasibility, in which the great Gerson, d'Ailly, Zabarella, and the English Bishop of Salisbury, who had maintained its supremacy before the pope himself with such energy, as to lead him to complain to Sigismund of his insulted majesty, took an active and successful part.

Down to the twelfth session the council was chiefly engaged in rebuilding the fabric of synodical authority, and giving weight and vigour to those higher and more rational views of ecclesiastical polity, which formed the foundation of the liberties of the whole Western Church, until the days of the Reformation, and of the Gallican Church in particular, until the period of the Revolution, which in its natural reaction brought back the supremacy of Rome in its most unmitigated form, and made France a Roman mission rather than an independent branch of the Church.* In the twelfth session, the council not only deposed the pope, who had in the meantime, after a fruitless series of escapes from one city to another, been brought back as a prisoner to Constance, but determined that none of the anti-popes should be elected to fill the vacant throne. Cardinal Branda, who had followed the pope to

* Richer, "Histoire des Conciles," and "De Eccles. Libertate." Bishop Ricci expresses the dread lest France should, by becoming to the priests a "*pays de conquête*," become ecclesiastically a "*pays de Mission.*" (Memoires, tom. iii. p. 369.)

Schaffhausen, and was among the last to adhere to
him in the day of adversity, at length accepted the
safe conduct and invitation of the emperor, and
returned to Constance on the 20th of April, just a
month after the flight of his patron.   From this time
he took an active part in the council, and exerted considerable influence in the election of Cardinal Otto Colonna to the papal throne, which closed its labours.  Of
the three contenders for the papacy whose claims were
thus finally set aside, John XXIII. died in captivity
at Florence, Gregory XII. voluntarily ceded his claims,
and was recognised by the council as a cardinal, and
the rank of the cardinals of his promotion confirmed
by its authority.   Benedict XIII. (Pierre de Lune),
continuing obstinate in his contumacy, notwithstanding his desertion by the court of Spain, was
deposed and excommunicated; but having sheltered
himself in the fortress of Peniscola, he continued to
fulminate counter-excommunications against the council and its adherents until his death.

It was upon this accession of Spain to the obedience
of the council, that that kingdom was admitted, as a
fifth nation, to take part in its deliberations ; and this
was solely brought about by the zeal and devotion of
the emperor himself, who had undertaken a journey
into Spain, to effect an alliance with the King of
Arragon, for the completion of the unity of the
Church, and had at considerable ·personal risk travelled into France and England, in order to bring

about a peace between those countries, then engaged
in their long and disastrous wars, with a view to the
same grand object.  In the forty-first session of the
council, the last stone was put to this great work by
the election of Cardinal Otto Colonna, one of the
chiefs of that illustrious house, which had for so many
ages sustained the imperial against the pontifical
power in Italy, and who assumed on his election the
title of Martin V.

The reformation of the Church in its head and in
its members should properly have immediately succeeded the deposition of the rival candidates, but the
cardinals who dreaded the prospect of such a reform,
when in the hands of a body of unlimited power, as
well as enlightened knowledge—a body in which all
the abuses of the  court of Rome had been exposed
with so much sincerity, and denounced with such
apostolic fearlessness—used every art and every influence to put off the evil day, and succeeded in
effecting this delay by interposing the affairs of Huss
and Jerome of Prague between the deposition of the
anti-popes and the election of their successor—a
course which enables us to take up this most interesting and important of all the subjects of this narrative, as the next in order to that of the settlement
of the papal line.

For the origin of the doctrinal views which were
advocated with such irresistible power and signal
success by Huss and Jerome of Prague in the king-

dom of Bohemia, we must go far beyond the days of Wiclif and the early English reformers, between whom and the followers of Huss the connexion was much less real and influential than is generally supposed. The friends of the Church of Rome were eager and skilful in their endeavours to connect the rising rebellion against its authority with a heresy which had been already so frequently condemned; and the writers on the other side have been equally anxious to establish this relationship in order to give to the Reformation the character of an unbroken protest against the Roman Church. The Council of Constance readily adopted this connexion of the two heresies, although Huss himself declared on his examination that he had not read any of the works of Wiclif until about twelve years previously (*i.e.* 1403), and these only his philosophical writings, his works on theology not having then found their way into Bohemia.

Now, the public preaching of Huss in the chapel of Bethlehem began in 1400, and could not, therefore, have received its inspiration from the writings of Wiclif. His preaching, conducted in the Bohemian language and adapted to the popular feeling, embodied and expressed that strong religious sentiment of the Slavonian nations which, from the day of their conversion in the ninth century, had separated them in their character and sympathies from the scholastic teaching of the Church of Rome. The theology of the Bohemian Church was connected as inseparably with the philosophy of the realists as that of Rome was, at this period, with the philosophy of the nominalists; and the causes of the hostility of the leading members of the council to the unfortunate Huss are to be traced rather to the fact that he represented the realist views of the University of Prague in opposition to the nominalism of Gerson, d'Ailly, and the University of Paris, than to the religious tenets which he had advanced, and which only, inasmuch as they were based on a heretical philosophy, became in their view heretical. "And you," (exclaimed Gerson to Jerome of Prague on his citation before the council), "when you were in Paris, disturbed the university, affirming many erroneous conclusions with their corollaries, and especially on the matter of the universe, and on ideas, and many other scandalous points."*

The manner in which Huss was roused to an open resistance of the corruptions and errors of the Church cannot be better described than in his own impressive words, which carry back this great resolution of his life to its earliest period, and prove the originality and individuality of his life and mission :—

"I confess," he writes, "before God and Christ, that from my earliest age until now, I have halted between two—what I ought to choose and what to hold; whether to seek after the benefits and honours of the world . . or rather to go forth out of the camp bearing the reproach of Christ; whether to seek a quiet and

* Von der Hardt, tom. iv. p. 217, and p. 506.

an easy life, living with the multitude in peace and equality, or rather to cling to the faithful and holy truth of the Gospel ; whether to commend what almost all commend, to advise as the multitude advises, to excuse and gloss over the Scriptures, as too many men, great, famous, and learned, and clothed with every appearance of wisdom and sanctity, excuse and gloss over them ; or rather to accuse and reprove the unfruitful works of darkness, and to hold the sincere truth of the Divine Word, which openly contradicts the present manners of men, and proves and makes manifest the false brethren. . . I prayed accordingly to the God and Father of our Lord Jesus Christ, in his own most faithful words, and lifting up my Bible before him, I cried with my heart and my voice, saying, ' O Lord and Father, Ruler of my life, leave me not in the imagination and counsel of these men, and give me not the desire of mine eyes, but turn me from all the devices of the evil one. Take from me all the lusts of the flesh, and deliver me not to the ungodly and lawless men.' " *

The period for the formation of this great resolution seemed marked out by Providence in the day when the schism between the Roman pontiffs became inveterate. While, on the one side, the kings and rulers of the earth took shelter in a prudent neutrality, the bolder minds of the reformers of the Church seized the

* Hussii, " De Sacerdotum et Monachorum Carnalium Abominatione," cap. lxxviii. (Opp. tom. i. p. 578. Ed. Norimb. 1715.)

opportunity of freely preaching that word of truth which declares, " He that is not with me is against me," and could fairly denounce all the anti-popes as anti-Christs, a title which they freely applied to one another, and perhaps equally deserved. In a remarkable sermon, preached by Huss, on the words, " Stablish your hearts, for the coming of the Lord draweth near," he gives an interesting picture of his predecessors in this arduous work, and leads to the belief that he was not the first, though undoubtedly the greatest, of those who had opened the truth in all its freedom before the people of Prague.

In 1410, Sbinco, Archbishop of Prague, cited Huss to appear before a synod to account for his doctrine ; but, failing to convince him of error, or to restrain the boldness of his preaching, he referred the matter successively to the Popes Alexander V. and John XXIII. The former, in order to strike at the root of Huss's popularity, prohibited all preaching in chapels, however authorized and privileged ; but, on his refusal to submit to this prohibition, the Pope referred the case to Cardinal Colonna (afterwards Pope Martin V.), who cited Huss to Rome. But the Queen Sophia, of Bohemia, who had appointed him one of her confessors, interposed in his behalf, and with her husband, Wenceslaus, obtained leave for Huss to appear by deputy ; though his proctors were not listened to by the mortified cardinal, who, with a degree of rashness strangely opposed to the moderation of his after conduct, excommunicated not only the reformer himself, but the whole Bohemian nation. Against this the deputies appealed to the pope, who transferred the cognisance of the cause to a commission of four cardinals.

Meantime Huss remained unmolested in his work of preaching and writing against the abuses of the Church, and, on the occasion of John XXIII. publishing throughout Bohemia a bull of indulgences for a crusade against Ladislaus, King of Naples, he put up a thesis upon all the churches of Prague, impugning the lawfulness of such a publication. The doctors of law, Wolff and Lewo, with the Canon Kbel, undertook the public defence of the bull, whose arguments, from the civil and canon law, were met by Huss with the clearest proofs of its illegality from Scripture. This led on to a serious controversy, during which three of the citizens, who had denounced the papal decree, were beheaded, and Huss himself, in consequence of the interdict laid by the pope upon the people of Prague as long as he remained therein, was induced to leave the city. He found a place of refuge in his native village of Hussinetz, whose feudal lord, Nicholas (of and in Hussinetz), gave him an asylum, and in which he continued boldly to preach as before. From this retreat he published an Appeal from the Pope to the Tribunal of Christ.

The next stage of his history brings us on to the convocation of the Council of Constance, before which

Huss was cited to appear by the pope and the Emperor Sigismund, a safe conduct to and from the council having been furnished him by the emperor himself. The journey of Huss from Prague to Constance was fraught with incidents of touching interest and significance. The poor and pious clergy of the villages and towns through which he passed received him as a messenger of God, but with the sad presentiment that, when once parted from him, they should see his face no more. Even before he left Prague, one of his most faithful friends addressed him, " Master, know for certain that you will be condemned." And a poorer, but not less devoted, member of the congregation of Bethlehem, took leave of him in the words, " God be with you ! for it scarce seems possible that you will return safe, my dearest master, and most constant in the truth. May the King, not of Hungary, but of heaven itself, give thee every good thing for all the faithful and diligent teaching I have had from thee !" The same painful presentiment had occupied the mind of Huss himself, for he left in Bohemia, with a friend, in whose welfare he was deeply interested, a sealed letter, with the charge that it should only be opened in the event of his death.

The cardinals, on hearing of his arrival in Constance, invited him to appear before them, and after the conference, to the astonishment of Huss and of the Baron de Chlum, his companion, who had relied on the safe-conduct of the emperor, delivered them both into the custody of the soldiery. The latter was presently released, and made public protest against this flagrant violation of faith, of which the emperor, who had not yet arrived at Constance, expressed his disapprobation in strong terms, by letter. The cardinals insisted that faith was not to be kept with heretics, and refused to release their captive, who was passed on from one prison to another until, from the horrible state of one of the dungeons in which he was confined, and the cruelty of his restraint, he was attacked with an illness which, but for timely medical care, would have removed him from the hands of his persecutors.

His bitter enemies, Stephanus Paletz and Michael de Causis, the promoters of the suit against him, had, in the interval, made a number of false extracts from his writings, and especially from his work " On the Church," which were brought against him in the council, as he was led before it from time to time, and which formed the ground of the most subtle efforts to entangle him in some heretical formula, and, above all, to betray him into the admission of the already condemned positions of Wiclif. His violent adversaries, Gerson and D'Ailly, with great affectation of friendship and sympathy, entreated him to recant, and submit himself unreservedly to the will of the council. Unhappily, however, for the credit of that assembly, a provisional decree, which it drew up to meet this expected contingency, exists still,* in which the unfor-

* Von der Hardt, Concil. Const. tom. iv. pars ii. p. 432.

tunate Huss was doomed, in the event of his entire
recantation and submission, to degradation and perpetual imprisonment. In vain the accused insisted
that all these extracts were false—in vain he even dis-
proved one of the charges against him so fully as to
make its withdrawal a matter of necessity. The long
days of his imprisonment were spent in prayer and
meditation, and in writing devotional treatises, full of
simple and earnest piety, which still survive—defences of his doctrine and letters to his friends in
Bohemia and in the council—whose sublime simplicity, and almost inspired trust, must give them, to
every really Christian heart, a rank next to that of the
writings of the primitive age.

Among the false witnesses who rose up on this
memorable occasion, and the unjust judges who used
their testimony only as the ostensible pretext for a
condemnation already determined, the eye is enabled
to rest with pleasure on one beautiful and noble exception, in the Cardinal Bishop of Ostia, John de Bronhiac, the oldest member of the Sacred College, and
as such, the president of the council itself. This
amiable and venerable prelate visited Huss frequently,
and was regarded by him as a father. His affectionate
entreaties to submit himself to the council, and to
accept its decision, as they were dictated by a sincere
friendship, and urged in a manner which touched the
heart, were listened to by the afflicted Huss in a
spirit of grateful sympathy, though they were rejected

on the ground of imperative but painful duty. The
path of the great reformer was clear and cloudless;
the testimony of his whole life carried him on to that
last and highest testimony, which should be taken up
in glory, and carried on to eternity. The bitterest
death was but a passing cloud over such a path as
this; his mind was calm and resolute; he needed not
the earnest words of the loved, the devoted John de
Chlum, to remind him of that dreadful alternative,
" Beloved master, if you have taught errors, revoke
them; but if not, look to it lest you lose your own
soul, and the souls of many more. Do, then, that which
your own conscience dictates." Of his support in
these fearful moments he writes, " The merciful God
whose laws I have magnified was with me, and is with
me, and I trust will preserve me in His grace unto
death." Of his fixed resolve, he says further, " To-mor-
row, as I believe, I shall be purged from my sins, in
the hope of Jesus Christ, by a cruel death;" and of
his consolations he adds, " How mercifully the Lord my
God hath dealt with me, and hath been with me in
wonderful temptations, you shall know in that day
when, through the help of Christ, we shall meet again
in the joy of the life to come."

Many visited him in his captivity, and urged him to
submit to the council, one doctor even affirming that
if the council said that he had only one eye when he
knew that he had two, he ought nevertheless to admit
with the council that it was so. Well might the poor

prisoner apply to himself the words of St. Paul to the
Corinthians, and declare that "though he had many
instructors, yet he had not many fathers." But if
the visits of these false friends were tedious and
wearisome, and .those of his devoted followers in the
same degree touching and consoling, most painful
and harrowing of all were the visits of his bitter
adversary Paletz, by whose unceasing persecution
and cruel misrepresentation, the condemnation of
Huss was brought about. In his last visit to the
prison, a feeling of remorse like that of Judas came
upon him, and to the simple appeal of his victim,
" whether he would confess himself guilty if he knew
in his conscience that he was innocent ?" he replied,
" It is a hard question"—and wept—"*respondit,*
*grave est—et cœpit flere.*"* The letter which describes
this interview to his faithful Bohemians—closes with
the prayer of inspired and inspiring faith, " O most
holy Christ, draw our feeble steps after Thee; for
unless Thou draw us we cannot follow Thee ! Grant
us the spirit of Thy might, that we may be ready;
and though the flesh is weak, let Thy grace prevent,
and guide, and follow ; for without Thee we can do
nothing, far less go forth for Thy sake to a cruel
death. Grant Thou a ready mind, a fearless heart, a
right faith, a firm hope, a perfect charity, that for Thy
sake we may lay down our life mightily, and to our
eternal joy."

* Ep. Huss. i. Opp. tom. i.

On the 6th of July, 1415, after the solemnization
of mass before the whole council, Huss was confronted
with it for the last time. Then, silence having been
proclaimed by an aged bishop of Italy, and the
slightest expression of sympathy or dissent prohibited
under pain of excommunication, the preparations for
the degradation of Huss from the priesthood were
begun. But first the Bishop of Lodi, ascending the
pulpit, preached a sanguinary discourse on the text,
"Let the body of sin be destroyed" (*Destruatur corpus
peccati*), which he applied to the destruction of the
sinner instead of the sin, and brought to bear with an
almost incredible perversity against the victim of the
council's animosity, closing it with a fulsome address
to the emperor, inviting him to "destroy errors and
heresies, *and especially this obstinate heretic*," who, in
the meantime, was praying earnestly and instantly, and
commending himself to God the righteous Judge.

The sermon ended, and the allegation of the heretical articles repeated (every effort of Huss to explain
and to reply to which was at once repressed by the
soldiery), the final sentence was pronounced, and the
unfortunate Huss consigned to a commission of
bishops, to whom the repulsive ceremonies of deposition and degradation were deputed. As these in
all their stages most painfully resembled the indig-
nities offered to Christ Himself, they suggested to the
martyr words of touching significance in reply to the
maledictions and reproaches which accompanied every

stage of this dreadful rite. The words of his persecutors were meetly concluded by the commendation
of the soul of their victim to the devil, to which Huss
rejoined, "But I commend my soul to my most
gracious Lord Jesus Christ, my only Saviour." Upon
this the bishops handed him over to the secular
power; and Sigismund, addressing the Duke of Bavaria, exclaimed, "Since to us pertains the sword, take
this accursed heretic and inflict upon him the deserved
punishment of his heresy!" while the duke, laying
aside his crown, transferred his charge to the judges
of the city in the words, "In the name of the emperor
our Lord Sigismund, and by our own special command, take John Huss, this great heretic, and destroy
his body by fire!"

Attended by a vast concourse of members of the
council, soldiers, and strangers, Huss was then led
forth through the suburb of Gotleben, the scene of his
long captivity, to the place of execution, which is now
covered with the fortifications of the city; and in the
midst of prayers and litanies to Christ, was suffocated
by the rising flames, at the moment when he was
repeating for the third time, "O Jesus Christ, Son
of the living God, who suffered for my sake, have
mercy on me! Jesus Christ, Saviour of the whole
world, redeem me!" *

* The Life of Huss, by Seyfried, with the Additions and Annota-
tions of Mylius (published at Hildburghausen in 1743), has been
principally used in the foregoing pages. It contains the most careful and accurate digest of all the authorities on the subject, every

Thus closed a testimony to the truth of God, and to the power of the gospel of Christ, of which we may say fearlessly that since the days of the first witnesses of our faith it has never been equalled—a*life of severe self-restraint and consistent holiness, carried on in the midst of a corruption of doctrine and discipline such as the Church had never seen, and it is devoutly to be trusted may never see again.

The condemnation and execution of Jerome of Prague followed soon after, and presented the same features of injustice and cruelty on the one hand, and patient endurance, or rather, triumphant faith, on the other; and this completed the case of the Church and kingdom of Bohemia against the court of Rome, and opened that terrible work of reprisal against the clergy and monastic orders, of which this fatal and impolitic act of the council was the signal. Not the most eloquent of the pleadings of Huss and Jerome before the council, not the most vigorous of those discourses which the great reformer had delivered in his now silent chapel of Bethlehem, or the most impressive of those lectures which his more learned companion had read in the halls of the University of Prague, could have so indelibly traced their doctrines in the hearts of the Bohemian people as the sad and unexpected intelligence that they had sealed their testimony with their blood, and confirmed it by the evidence of so

circumstance of the life and teaching of Huss being weighed with judgment and impartiality.

E

awful a martyrdom.   In the election of an undisputed
head for the Christian Church, the fathers at Constance
had closed up a schism which existed rather in the
eye than in the heart of Europe ; by the condemnation
of Huss, it opened a schism in the very soul of the
Christian world which the Reformation of the sixteenth
century has kept open to this day.

But if the sins of commission of the Council of
Constance were thus pregnant with evils and perils
to the Church, its sins of omission were not less fatal
in their consequences.  The cardinals, who had, by
constant intrigues, put off the work of reformation—
and though they had dealt with the subject with
great vigour and sincerity in the memoirs and projects of reform which they had published from time
to time in the council, had steadily resisted its synodical treatment—made the election of Martin V. a
successful pretext for getting rid of it altogether.
Dangerous as it must have appeared to bequeathe
the principal object of their present convocation to
future councils, laden with new responsibilities and
perplexed with increased difficulties, they feared still
more its treatment by a body which had regarded
their own privileges and influence so lightly.   If their
passion for reform was great, their devotion to their
own order was paramount; and even Cardinal Pierre
d'Ailly, the most enlightened of their number, while
content to reduce the papal authority to more reasonable dimensions, claimed the representation of the

apostolic order for the Sacred College, and admitted
the episcopal only as a hierarchical degree—a kind of
culminating point of the priesthood.   This *esprit de
corps* of the Sacred College had even its martyr in the
council; for so vehement was the great Cardinal
Zabarella in his advocacy of the claims of his order
against the nations, that he died, a few days after, of
a fever brought on by the excitement of this controversial heat.

The utmost that could be gained by the nations in
the matter of reform was the adoption by the council
of five resolutions to be imposed on the future pope,
of which the first and most important was, that
general councils should be convoked at regular intervals, the next to be assembled after a period of five
years, the succeeding one after seven years from that,
and then at regular intervals of ten years.   This, as
it gave origin to the Council of Basle, and is cited
continually by the fathers of that body under its title
*Frequens*, was perhaps the most important in its
results of any of the reformatory decrees of this
otherwise fruitless assembly.   Of its doctrinal features
the most important is unquestionably the celebrated
law of the thirteenth session, which has ever since
deprived the recipients of the Eucharist in the Roman
Church of the right they had enjoyed in common with
every branch of the Church from the beginning, of
partaking in that sacrament in the integrity of its
first institution.   By this decree, drawn up in pro-

fessed defiance of the teaching of Christ and the
practice of the Church in every age, the cup was
denied to all but the celebrant, and a mutilation
which, in the first instance, was a mere corruption
of usage, became a positive and inviolable law.

This was little less than a declaration of war
against the Slavonian nations, whose very religion
seemed embodied and symbolised in the undivided
Eucharist, and who, in tradition and in practice, had
clung to this as the very palladium of their Christianity: and we can be little surprised to find that,
while an avenger of the national cause appeared in
the celebrated Zisska, an advocate of the mutilated
sacrament rose up in the Church of Bohemia in the
person of the equally distinguished Archbishop
Rokyczana.

Without entering upon the theological question in
this place, it cannot but be observed that the Church
of Rome has here discovered a total absence of that
political foresight which is its most remarkable attri-
bute. While even during the pontificate of Martin V.
the Eucharist was openly administered in both kinds
in Rome itself, notwithstanding the decree of the
council*—a circumstance which at least placed the
new usage in the rank of things indifferent—in

* This is proved from the work of Petrus Amelius, Bishop of
Sinigaglia, "On the Ceremonies of the Roman Church," in which he
mentions that he had himself seen the Eucharist thus administered
in Rome, under the pontificate of Martin V. (v. G. de Lith. de Inter-
dictione Sacri Calicis, p. 262).

Bohemia the prohibition was exacted as inexorably as though the most vital doctrines of Christianity were involved in its observance. It was natural that where such a decree was enforced, in direct opposition to the institution of Christ himself, the resistance to it should be urged as a necessary and vital point on the ground of His express command. The prohibition of the council was in direct contravention of a commandment of the Great Institutor of the sacrament, and was issued with a *non obstante* to the injunction of Christ himself. The opposition to it seemed, therefore, not only a duty, but a necessity; for what guarantee could any member of the Church of Rome possess that the entire sacrament would not be removed at last, when an integral portion of it had been taken away so lightly?

The ceremonial of the election of Pope Martin V. which closed the labours of the council, was worthy of the splendour of its inauguration. On the announcement that the choice of the electors had fallen upon Cardinal Otto Colonna, a crowd of eighty thousand persons thronged the place of election, who, separating at mid-day, returned to the cathedral at an appointed time, to witness the arrival of the emperor, in this scene of unmingled rejoicing. "The sea of people," in the words of an astonished eyewitness, "was divided again into rivers, soon to flow back and inundate the cathedral." On its return the emperor, princes, and bishops, and all the council, were merged

in the vast multitude, which proceeded with them to
the conclave to escort the newly-elected pope to the
place of his public recognition. The pontiff, mounted
on a white horse and surrounded by the cardinals,
whom perplexing intrigues and disappointed ambition,
not less than want of food and rest, had reduced to
the most wretched and emaciated state, was conducted
by them to the cathedral. On his way thither an
interruption occurred which must have reminded him
that Europe was not yet pacified, or the course
of the pontificate clear and cloudless. The Duke of
Bavaria, falling down before him, implored his aid
against Henry of Landshut, by whom he had been
wounded and despoiled. The pope could only reply
with good wishes, while Sigismund rebuked the un-
timely intrusion. After a succession of ceremonies
and consecrations, the pope elect was fully inaugurated in his office in the great hall of the episcopal
palace at Constance, an Englishman, the Prior of St.
John, Clerkenwell, holding the diadem at his coronation.

A few days after, another proof of the disorganised
state even of the territory bordering on Constance
was given in the assassination, in broad daylight, of
the Provost of Lucerne, at the instigation of the disaffected citizens. In the meantime, the grand object
of the assembly of the synod—the reformation of the
Church in its head and in its members—made but little
progress. This great work was, in fact, handed over

to the new pontiff, who very doubtfully contributed to its progress by writing a memoir upon it, which he offered to the nations. The state of every independent kingdom requiring a distinct treatment in the matter of discipline and reform, the plan adopted by the pope was that of a system of concordats, which, inasmuch as they were destitute of synodical weight, were too capable of revocation to be of any permanent advantage. The decrees published in the forty-third session on the great abuses of the age, exemptions, dispensations, annates, simony, and the general discipline of the clergy, have rather the character of reprobations of the past and promises for the future than of positive and clear prohibitions; and how ineffectual they soon became is witnessed by the increase rather than the removal of all these corruptions, which the history of the Council of Basle discloses.

Besides the danger which threatened the Church through this delay of an active and searching reformation, several lesser causes of alarm presented themselves in the council before it closed. The sect of the Flagellants, ably resisted by Gerson, the doctrine of the lawfulness of tyrant murder advocated in France by Jean Petit and a large party of his followers, the libels and injurious publications of John Falckenberg against the King of Poland, and other untoward subjects, threatened the peace of the council to the last, and gave to its closing scenes, notwith-

standing the moderation of the pope, an unseemly
and even tumultuous character. It was not until they
were menaced with excommunication that the Polish
deputies desisted from their endeavour to compel the
pontiff into a condemnation of the libellous work, and
even then they publicly recorded an instrument of
appeal to the future general council.

On the 22nd of April, 1418, after an eventful history extending over three years and a half, the
great Council of Constance was formally closed.
After a sermon on the words, "Ye now have sorrow,
but I will see you again and your heart shall rejoice,"
—a promise which seemed rather to look onward with
hope to the future council, which was summoned to
meet at Pavia, than to look back with satisfaction upon
the work of the council now at an end—the vast
assembly was dissolved, the bishops returning to their
dioceses, and the pope, with his court, to Geneva,
whence they proceeded to Rome.   Of the great
reformers of the Church who had lived to see the
grand object of their lives and labours frustrated,
Zabarella had died in the council; D'Ailly retired to
Avignon, where he continued to assist with his
writings the great cause which he had so ineffectually
maintained in the council; Gerson, the most illustrious of all, disappointed but not disheartened at this
failure of his dearest hopes, carried on his advocacy of
reform to a degree which rendered it perilous to
remain in his native country.   He wandered as an

exile through Bavaria and Austria, returning to Lyons after the death of his enemy, the Duke of Burgundy. In the solitude of the Abbey of Mölck he consoled himself with eloquently deploring the fruitless issue of the council of which he was one of the most illustrious members, and hastened, by his writings in defence of ecclesiastical liberty and reformation, the advent of that day when the one should become a reality and the other a necessity to be evaded no longer.

The suggestive words which formed a part of the ceremonial of the coronation of Martin V., when a cardinal, lighting a piece of tow on the end of a spear, exclaimed, "Sancte Pater, sic transit gloria mundi!" may well be written as the moral of the history of the Council of Constance, than which a spectacle more magnificent in all its circumstances, or more transient in all its results, has never been presented before the eye of the Christian world.

# CHAPTER III.

" WOULD that the age of Martin (not to say the age of
Saturn) could return ! " * were the words of Æneas
Sylvius to Julian, in later years, when the reign of
Martin V. was looked back upon as the Church's
breathing time, and the success of the mission of the
good pontiff, for the peace of Italy and the world,
seemed no longer even doubtful. Nor can we wonder
that this period of repose and recovery was rich in
grateful memories to those who, like Julian at this
time, were enjoying the society of the great men of the
age in the centre of the Christian world. The palaces
of the cardinals then formed the schools of advancement and improvement to the youth of Italy, and in
them the characters of those statesmen and ecclesiastics
who adorned Europe during the fifteenth and sixteenth
centuries received their formation and direction. The
residence of Julian with Cardinal Branda was at a

* Epp. l. 1. Ep. lxv.

period which was eminently calculated to enforce the traditions of his patron. Both in the Church and in the different states of Europe, events of the greatest importance, and of the most serious perplexity, were unfolding themselves with strange rapidity. Daily it must have appeared more strongly than before, that the golden opportunity of reformation and union which the Council of Constance had offered to the world had been lost for ever, and that the perils of this neglected work were becoming more inevitable. The vast and unexpected results of that great assembly, discovered in its deposition of rival pontiffs and elevation of its own authority on the basis of principles wholly new to the theories of pontifical law, must have rendered the synodical remedy in the eyes of the members of the court of Rome even worse than the diseases which so many of them had exposed with such eloquent sincerity.

From the great reluctance of Julian to accept the presidency of the future council, it would appear that the experience of Cardinal Branda had rather awakened in his mind a fear of the synodical principle than a desire to maintain its exercise. From the conflicts of the council the friends of the Church turned naturally to the new pontiff, who represented its unity, and who was pledged to its reformation of the abuses which had divided it. Unhappily, the most far-sighted of these was unable to see that the real unity of the Church was even more endangered by the progress of the great Bohemian movement than by the divided headship, which had been made one at Constance. It was enough in their view to cauterise the wound, or even to cut off the offending member; and the advocates of the council stood committed to the adoption of those corrosive remedies of fire and sword which the council itself had already applied with as little wisdom as success.

Among the older members of the Sacred College at this period was Cardinal Dominici, whose severe and uncompromising disposition represented the prevalent feeling in the strongest and most repulsive form. Under his roof, among many other illustrious men, the celebrated St. Antoninus, Archbishop of Florence, received his education. Elected to the cardinalate by Gregory XII., whose legate to the council he became, it was mainly through his influence that his patron was induced to resign the pontificate; and the council having confirmed him in all his dignities, he was enabled to take a prominent part in the election of Martin V. To him the new pontiff naturally turned as the fittest representative of the Holy See in the now distracted Bohemia, and even before he left Constance he nominated him as his legate in Germany. Cardinal Dominici returned accordingly with the emperor to become the witness of that scene of rapine and confusion which was opening in the hereditary kingdoms of Bohemia and Hungary. To the former of these Wenceslaus, the brother of Sigismund, had succeeded

—a prince who is represented by all the historians of the time as utterly deficient in every quality that could secure the respect or obedience of his people. Vacillation and cowardice marked his conduct in adversity, while his cruelties and excesses in prosperity were little calculated to conciliate the offended nationality of the Bohemians.

During the period of the Council of Constance the people of Bohemia had maintained a sullen and ominous silence. The year 1417 was memorable for a tranquillity so deep and unnatural throughout the kingdom, that it could only be compared to the calm which precédes some great convulsion of nature. That close contact between the Hussites and Catholics, which was afterwards productive of such fearful consequences, was at this time prevented by the separation of their churches and assemblies. The influential members of the Hussite faction waited for the issue of the council, and restrained by their example the more violent. After the death of Huss, the Emperor Sigismund had written to the Bohemians an apologetic letter, which, in some degree, softened the effects of the indiscreet though plausible letters of the council on the same subject; but neither the dishonour of the emperor, who had suffered his safe conduct to be violated with impunity, nor the indignation of the Bohemians, whose confidence had been thus betrayed, could be in the least degree covered by these diplomatic explanations. It is evident, therefore, that the mission

of Cardinal Dominici was one of the greatest delicacy
and difficulty, and that it required the wisdom of the
wisest and most moderate of Roman statesmen even
to delay the inevitable storm ; yet, with that absolute
disregard of every political and religious danger, which
has so often been imitated even at a period when the
Roman See was rather militant than triumphant,
Cardinal Dominici opened his campaign by an act of
violence and cruelty against those who maintained the
use of the cup in the Communion, which destroyed at
once every chance of the success of his legation.
Entering a church in the district of Slana, he threw
to the ground a chest which was placed on the altar,
and which probably contained the chalices used by the
Hussite congregation, and caused an ecclesiastic and a
layman who had opposed him to be burnt alive.   The
severities of the legate were the signal of an outbreak
throughout the entire kingdom, which proved at once
that the national feeling had been outraged beyond
the possibility of restitution, and that the court of Rome
was fatally ignorant of the extent of the danger it had
invoked.

The dread of assassination and the consciousness
of his utter helplessness in the storm he had himself
awakened, drove the legate to take refuge in Hungary,
where public tranquillity had not been so deeply
compromised, and there, we are assured by his biographers, that, notwithstanding the advice he had bequeathed to the emperor to adopt the remedies of

fire and sword against the prevailing heresy, he had
recourse to the more legitimate weapons of the Christian warfare, for he was engaged in preaching to,
and influencing the Hungarians in behalf of the
Roman rites, when he died.   On his death, which
happened in 1419, scarcely a year after he had entered
upon his unsuccessful legation, the mission into Germany and Bohemia was offered to Cardinal Branda.

This new legation of his patron was an epoch of
great importance in the life of Julian.   The high and
almost extreme opinions which the cardinal had formed
of his young *protégé* were now to be put to the
severest practical test, in a mission in which the
greatest Roman diplomatists had failed so remarkably.
If Cardinal Branda had shown on several occasions
that he was not possessed of that prudence which
formed the highest qualification for so difficult a work
as that which lay before him, the prudence and judgment of Julian on all ecclesiastical matters might yet
preserve him from the errors of his predecessors;
for to his advice he attached the most exalted opinion,
and was after heard to say that, " if the whole Church
were to fall into ruin, Julian would have been equal
to the task of rebuilding it."

On the arrival of Cardinal Branda in Bohemia, the
insurrection had assumed a definite form, and an
organised opposition to the imperial authority was to
be seen everywhere.   The success of this great national
movement (and its very nationality was the secret of

its success) was so rapid and signal, that nothing was left for the legate but to look on in hopeless dismay, and a diet held at Prague by the Emperor Sigismund opened the only scene in which the talents of the Roman diplomatist could have the slightest exercise. It would appear that, despairing of his mission to Bohemia, he retreated early into Hungary, into which the doctrines, rather than the arms, of the Hussites had penetrated. From this comparative tranquillity he was able to observe the progress of a civil war as barbarous in its general conduct, and as romantic in many of its subordinate features, as any which has ever convulsed a European kingdom. We may well, therefore, take up the opening history of the Hussite wars as its incidents of wonder and horror passed in succession before the eye of the legate.

The gathering storm which the ominous stillness succeeding the martyrdom of Huss and Jerome, and the "angry silence" of the great nobility, had so clearly augured, burst out in the very centre of the kingdom.

The followers of Huss had chosen as their general one of the chamberlains of King Wenceslaus, a member of the lesser nobility of Bohemia—John Zisska de Trocznow—while a champion of the ecclesiastical order appeared in the equally celebrated John de Rokyczana, afterwards Archbishop of Prague. The objects of these two great sections of the rebellion were different in the beginning, and grew more and more distinct as the movement advanced. The single point on which the latter contended against the Church of Rome was the denial of the cup to the laity, and this sole concession would have at once preserved them in its unity. But the general body of the Hussites, to whom the teaching of the great reformer had given a deeper thirst for change, would accept nothing short of a free and full preaching of the word of God, a secularization of the monastic orders and property, and the public punishment of all open crimes and scandals, in addition to the concession of the cup to the laity. Zisska, feeling insecure in the city of Prague, had, in 1418, built a new city and fortress at some distance from the capital, to which he gave the name of Tabor, and from which his followers received the distinctive title of Taborites. From this retreat he was able successfully to attack the Bohemian metropolis, whose weakness was fatally shown in the course of the following year.

The first news which must have reached the astonished legate on his arrival was the strange fact that, in the neighbourhood of this stronghold, an assembly of 40,000 persons of all ages had gathered together to receive the Communion in both kinds at the hands of the Taborite priests. They had thence marched to Prague by torchlight, and stood under the walls of the palace of Wissehrad, to which the wretched and helpless King Wenceslaus had retired for safety. Emboldened by the impunity of this step, and roused by the knowledge that the king, with the municipal

authorities of the city, were arranging measures of reprisal, they re-entered the city soon after, under Zisska,
and after destroying the convent of the Carmelites,
whose members had been influential in the condemnation of Huss and Jerome, proceeded to pillage and
destroy other religious houses, ending with an attack
upon the town-hall, in which the judges and senators
of Prague were consulting on the plans of opposing
them. Eleven of the senators escaped by flight, but
the rest, with a judge of the city, were cast down
from the windows of the hall upon the spears and
pitchforks of the infuriated mob below, and perished
miserably.

For several days Prague was the scene of the
most frightful disorder, and the most hideous cruelties were perpetrated against the monks and religious
orders. The reign of terror had truly begun;
and the miserable king, who would otherwise undoubtedly have been one of its earliest victims, was
removed by a sudden and strange death from the
scene of tumult and slaughter which his own cruelty
and incapacity had so greatly contributed to open.
When the massacre of the senators was related to him,
on some one observing that he had long foreseen such
an event, he flew into a violent passion, and would
have murdered the person who made the remark but
for the interposition of those present. His passion re-
sulted in a stroke of apoplexy, which carried him off
on the 16th of August, 1419. He died, as we are

told by a chronicler of the day, " with a fearful noise, as of the bellowing of a lion." *

The succession to the kingdom fell to the Emperor Sigismund, the next brother of Wenceslaus, whose endeavours to take possession of this ruined inheritance added a new element to the troubles of Bohemia. The widowed Queen Sophia, left in a state of almost hopeless peril, endeavoured to fortify herself in the castle of Wissehrad from the attacks of the Hussites, who had already overrun Prague and threatened every hour to attack the last stronghold of royalty, the scene of its ancient glories, and the witness of its present afflictions.

The palaces, churches, and monasteries of Bohemia were at this period unequalled in Europe. Æneas Sylvius who had seen the ecclesiastical glories of Italy, and even visited the then distant England, declares that no kingdom in Europe equalled this in the splendour of its monastic buildings, or in the priceless treasures of its altars and shrines. " Temples lifted up as it were to heaven, of marvellous length and amplitude, were covered with arched-work of stone. Altars placed on high were laden with the gold and silver, in which the relics of saints were enshrined. The robes of the priests were embroidered with pearls; every ornament was costly; the furniture of the very highest value; the windows, lofty and of the greatest width, gave

* Byzinii Diarium Hussiticum.

their light through glass of exquisite beauty and
admirable workmanship. Nor were these features
to be observed only in towns and cities, but even
in villages."*

In the monastery of Königssaal he tells us that
there was "a garden surrounded with walls, on
which, upon beautiful plates, the whole of the Scriptures, from Genesis to the Revelations, was written
in majuscule characters; the letters gradually increased in size as they were carried above the eye,
so that the whole could be easily read from the
top to the bottom,"—a memorable proof of the
devotion of the Bohemians to the Scriptures, but
which was barbarously destroyed. When, however, we
read that no less than five hundred and fifty of these
splendid monuments of ancient piety were destroyed
by the Hussites, we must bear in mind that a new
element of destruction had been called into existence
through the indolent incapacity of Wenceslaus,
and the utter disorganization of the government.
Brigandage had now assumed so great a boldness,
and had secured so complete an impunity, that public
security was entirely gone, and the defenceless monasteries were no less the prey of successful brigands,
whom their wealth and treasures had tempted, than
the object of the revenge of the Hussites, on the
ground that the religious orders had originated the
troubles of the kingdom by procuring the con-

* Æneas Sylvius, Histor. Bohem. c. xxxvi.

demnation of the national party. Thus, John Tysta and John Miesteczki, both members of the ancient gentry of the kingdom, pillaged and destroyed towns and villages, meeting with but little resistance from the government of Wenceslaus; and the latter is celebrated as the plunderer of the great monastery of Opatovicz, which had the misfortune to be popularly believed the receptacle of a hidden treasure.

One evening, the monks were surprised by the visit of a stranger with two attendants, coming, as they alleged, to visit the abbot. They were hospitably entertained, and were succeeded later in the evening by two others—the second arrival was succeeded by another, and yet others again—until the mysterious guests numbered thirty. With this accession of strength, they fell upon the unsuspecting monks, Miesteczki seizing the Abbot Peter Laczur, and cruelly torturing him in order to discover the place of the treasure. Unable to force from the abbot or the monks their secret, the brigands retired, carrying with them eight thousand florins in money, and sacred vessels to the value of two thousand more. Such was the impunity of crime at this period, that Miesteczki bought with his plunder the castle of Opoczno, contemptuously disobeyed a citation of the emperor, and finally became reconciled to him, without making the smallest restitution.

In the meantime, the terrible Zisska was consolidating his reign, and extending his ravages. The

cloud of confusion and slaughter which covers this
period of the history of Bohemia, is everywhere
so regular and so invariable in depth and outline,
that it is only occasionally that some new feature
of peculiar interest tempts us to continue this
digression. The work of destruction was reopened
in 1420 by the demolition of the town of Aust,
which so nearly adjoined Tabor as to render it
an object of apprehension to Zisska, its feudal lord
Ulrich de Rosenberg, of the Bohemian branch of
the great Roman house of Orsini, being a zealous
Catholic. This signal and terrible destruction of
a town, with all its inhabitants, took place during
the carnival, at a moment when every suspicion of
danger was lulled to rest, and was instantly succeeded by the attack on the fortress of Sedlitz,
where Rosenberg himself had taken refuge, and in
whose ruins he was destined to perish.

The burning of the monastery of the Servites in the
new city of Prague followed with fearful rapidity, and
the deaths of the monks of this foundation, who belonged to the noblest families of Florence and Siena,
might well be crowned by all who witnessed them
with the glories of martyrdom. Conscious of the impending danger, they proceeded, without the betrayal
of a single fear, to hold a chapter of their order, in
the midst of which the maddened Taborites burst in
upon them, and demanded them to sign the four
articles of their rebellion against the Church of Rome.

Firmly and fearlessly they protested that they would never sign, upon which their persecutors fired the building and lighted faggots to burn the monks, who died joyfully, chanting the *Te Deum* to the last, the Catholic historians affirming that their deaths were not unattended by that prodigy, so often asserted of this dreadful kind of martyrdom, and so naturally conceived by the bystanders in such a scene, the appearance of souls ascending in the flames to heaven. The destruction of the monasteries of Grätz and Königssaal, whose treasures of art have been before spoken of, succeeded; and the siege of Raby, at which Zisska, already blinded in one eye, lost his sight entirely, was added to the successes of the war, at the hazard of its future conduct.

Our narrative of conventual destruction may here be suspended, in order that we may fall back upon the fortunes of the widowed Queen Sophia, little more than a prisoner of state in the fortress-palace of Wissehrad. From the windows of this vast and magnificent pile she was able to trace the dreadful contrast of desolation and misery which every success of the Hussite arms heightened and saddened. At the close of 1419, the divided forces of the Hussites proper (Taborites), Calixtines, and Orebites were united, at the instigation of Nicholas de Hussinetz, under the very walls of Wissehrad. Foreseeing the danger, Rosenberg had with difficulty conducted the queen to a place of safety before the attack began. The

united forces opened the assault with a frightful
energy, but the strength of the garrison, and the
adoption of instruments of warfare till then unknown
in Bohemia, occasioned so great a carnage, that it was
resolved to defer the attack until nightfall, when the
darkness might favour the assailants.  That was a
fearful night in Prague, and was well described by
one who witnessed it, as "a night of much tribula-
tion and perplexity; a night of sorrow and grief, and
resembling the last day in fearfulness."[*]  Victory, as
far as the complete possession of the streets and
avenues to the fortress, and the field of battle, if such
it could be called, remained with the besiegers, and
probably another attack might have carried the place;
but a diversion against the fortress of St. Wenceslaus,
in which the Queen Sophia was believed to be still
concealed, put off for a short period the demolition of a
palace which, then at least, had not its equal in Europe.

A truce of four months, between the Hussites and the
Imperialists, occasioned by a turn of fortune in favour
of the latter, and the knowledge that the fortress had
received an additional garrison since this attack, was
agreed upon at this critical moment, the terms of it
being that either party should remain unmolested in
the exercise of their religion and in the possession of
their rights—Pilsen and some other places being
restored to the emperor.  Prague revived for a season
under this respite; the wild mob of Hussite strangers

* Byzinii Diarium Hussiticum apud Ludewig "Reliq. MSS."

retired, the senate reassembled, but the chief of the Catholic party, who had fled from the city, still feared to return. An indiscreet letter from Sigismund, in which he promised to govern on the principles of his father, the Emperor Charles IV., whose severe edicts against heresy were still too well remembered, destroyed in a moment the treacherous calm, and hostilities were renewed in the country, in which the Taborites were less successful than before. The miners of Cuttenberg hunted down vast numbers of them, and when they seized them, cast them into deep pits and wells, six hundred of them thus perishing miserably.

Sigismund, however, made use of this short interval of comparative tranquillity, by convoking a diet at Brunn, in Moravia; and to this the Cardinal of Piacenza, as legate of Martin V., was invited. It is probable that this ecclesiastic, attended by Julian, had remained with the emperor during this period, as he arrived with him and the Dowager Queen Sophia at the Diet. Except for the purpose of advising the emperor, and communicating with the court of Rome from this scene of tumult, whose real causes were far beyond the reach of Roman diplomacy, the legation into Bohemia was utterly powerless; and the only person who can be said to have profited by it was the young Cesarini, whose ardent mind seemed alone capable of grasping the meaning and fathoming the depths of this mysterious revo-

lution.  An episode of some interest, and singularly
illustrative of that spirit of bold inquiry which had
opened the Hussite controversy, and of the cruel and
impolitic means which had been throughout adopted
in order to close it, occurred to the legate and his
companion during their Hungarian sojourn.

"While I was reading the Scriptures or the sentences in the University of Vienna," are the words of
the quaint relater of this incident,* "there was just
such a heretic as you speak of to be found not far
off, in Hungary, a bachelor of arts, and a priest.  He
was, to my knowledge, so marvellously singular, and
singularly marvellous a heretic, as to be second to
none . . . . And, to cut the matter short, the wretched
man came to this, absolutely to disbelieve all the
articles of the Christian faith until they could be
proved by a natural philosopher, by a due and effectual philosophical demonstration."  After a repetition
of various heretical and even blasphemous sentiments
expressed against the rites of the Church, which led
to his capture and imprisonment by the bishop, our
informant continues: "There arrived, in the meantime, the legate of all Germany, the Lord Cardinal
of Piacenza, with three devout, prudent, and learned
professors of divinity and canon law, who visited the
guilty man in prison for his soul's health, and with
pious entreaties laboured to bring back the wanderer to
repentance.  When examined upon the various sects

* Nyder. Formicarium, l. iii. c. x.

of Wicklifites and Bohemians, which were then running their course, of Waldenses, Arians, Jews, Saracens, and every other perfidious sect, he uniformly
derided them all, but persisted in his own error."

His visitors, two of whom were Jacobus de Clavoro
and Martinus de Hispania—the third having been
unquestionably Julian—finding that to argue and
philosophize was vain against one who exhibited the
most exquisite subtlety in his replies, and even
declared himself ready to die in his conviction, contrived another plan, being more " affected towards the
soul of the poor wretch than his body. 'Let him be
bound,' they said secretly to the bishop's official,
'more. tightly; fastened to a stake, and tied with
thongs, and spending a night in this state, he will
find himself, perhaps, a little troubled in his intellect.'
This having been duly performed, these faithful soul-
surgeons * returned in the morning, wishing to see.
their invalid, who cried out impatiently, 'Prithee,
burn me, for I am ready! Why do you vex my
soul any longer?' They, however, applying sharper
spiritual remedies out of the philosophical treasures
of Egypt, showed the erring man how weak was the
human understanding, how manifold its devices, how
short its life, how false its judgment, how critical its
time, and such-like. After this, they left him, bound
as tightly as before, to meditate upon what they had

---

* The word in the original is *cyrulogi*, which I conceive to be a
misprint for *chirurgi*.

said. Returning on the next day, they found the good man inspired through the divine light." Hereupon follows a good Catholic confession, and a retirement to the convent of the Paulites, in order to carry it out without any new temptations from philosophy.

An incident like this, trifling as it is, introduces us to the spirit of the age. The severe policy of the court of Rome in Bohemia, was, in fact, only an attempt to apply to a powerful nation, capable of the most successful resistance, an argument which could only answer when applied by a host of inquisitors to a single and powerless victim.

The universal terror which the progress of the rebellion awakened, far more than the influence of the legate, inspired the members of the diet of Brunn with the most earnest resolutions of devotion, and vows to sacrifice life, and family, and property, in the cause of the emperor. Communications were opened with Prague, and Sigismund was lavish in promises and assurances to all who would return to their allegiance. Deputies arrived at Brunn to conduct the negotiation, while the Hussites, alarmed at its progress, suddenly retired from Prague to confer with their leaders at Tabor and elsewhere. A succession of barbarous executions at Breslau, by the order of Sigismund, again transferred the advantage to his enemies; and the list of terrific successes of the Hussites was reopened by the destruction of the fortress of Wenceslaus, which is said to have been betrayed to them by Czenko von Wartemberg. The exquisite chapel of St. Wenceslaus, encrusted with jasper and covered with chasings of gold, was demolished on this occasion. After this Zisska and his forces re-entered Prague, and occupied that city, whose inhabitants were now straining every nerve to defend themselves against Sigismund, who was approaching it at the head of a considerable army.

On the 30th of June, 1420, the siege of the city began. The fortress of Wenceslaus and of Wissehrad, the one commanding the old and the other the new city, being still in the hands of the Imperialists, the chances of success of an army numbering more than 140,000 men were obviously very great. But the advantages of a popular and even national cause, and the wild inspiration of a religious enthusiasm, more than counterbalanced those of position and number. Zisska was again irresistible, and on the 30th of July the emperor raised the siege and retired into Moravia and Hungary.

The victorious Hussites, whose confidence was daily increased by new successes, resolved now, with a junction of all their forces, to renew their attack on the citadel of Wissehrad. On this occasion they had recourse to the simple but infallible method of entirely cutting off the fortress from all around it, and starving out the garrison, who, after having killed horses, dogs, cats, and even rats, for food, were at last compelled to capitulate.

On the 31st of October, a day memorable also for another defeat of the army of Sigismund, who had attempted to force the assailants to raise the siege, the fortress and palace of Wissehrad were surrendered to the enemy. A few days sufficed to destroy the treasured glories of ages; and the abbey, fortress, and palace, which, since the year 683, had been the residence of the dukes and kings of Bohemia, was so utterly destroyed, that not one stone was left upon another. In the seventeenth century the site was covered by a garden of herbs—

"Et campos ubi Troja fuit."

Thus fell the ancient palace of Wissehrad, which in its accumulated treasures and venerable relics of the past was so identified with the history of the people, as well as the rulers of this ancient kingdom, as to make it a subject of just surprise that, in a movement essentially national, it should not have found protection rather than destruction. It formed the culminating point of the ecclesiastical and palatial splendour of Bohemia. Its collegiate church, founded by the Duke Brzctislaus, in the eleventh century, and enriched by the Duke Sobieslaus with all that was most costly, had received from the popes unusual privileges. It was exempt from every jurisdiction but that of the pontiff himself. The Prince and Chancellor of Bohemia were its perpetual provosts, who, as well as the dean, the canons, and even the deacons of the church, had the right to wear the mitre when celebrating mass before the duke.

The fall of Wissehrad was the bitterest humiliation and the heaviest blow that the Imperialists had yet sustained. Their last hold on the city of Prague was lost with it, while the most sacred memorials of the monarchy had perished under the very eye of the emperor, and at the very moment when he was at the head of an army more numerous, and to all appearance more devoted, than any which the energies of the whole empire had ever yet united in its defence. Sigismund in vain made wretched reprisals by ravaging the lands of the Hussites in his retreat, and laid waste among others the country of the lords of Podiebrad, an act whose only result was the exasperation of a powerful family, one of whom afterwards became his rival and sate on the very throne of which he had been ignominiously deprived.

All hopes of an accommodation with the emperor being now at an end, the people of Prague resolved upon electing another king, and directed their thoughts towards the King of Poland, a prince of the house of Jagellon. The proposition to elect a foreigner in the place of one whose foreign tendencies and character were the first causes of his rejection and final deposition, displeased the Taborites in the highest degree.

"We have hardly driven out a foreign king," exclaimed Nicholas de Hussinetz, "when you would have us call in another!"

The Calixtines were equally energetic in defence of their plan, and the difference between the two parties became so irreconcilable, that the Taborites withdrew from the city. Doctrinal as well as political disagreements threatened to dissolve a union which a great national impulse had alone consolidated, and, but for the death of Nicholas de Hussinetz, and the succession of Zisska to the undivided command of the Taborites, Sigismund might have recovered his crown. Conferences of both the great parties of the Hussites were held to remove if possible the grounds of this serious difference, and articles of faith were declared on either side, so entirely discordant, as to prove that but one point of doctrine really connected the Calixtines of Prague and the lawless inhabitants of Tabor—the right of the laity to the cup—while even this was a very slender tie in comparison with that of a common hatred of Sigismund, as representing an anti-national league, and as inspired by the denationalizing influences of the court of Rome.

The doctrines of the Taborites, which carried out to the fullest extent the mystical theory of the Church, which Huss had propounded at Constance, were essentially opposed to those of Rokyczana and the Calixtines, whose system was formed on a more scholastic model, and had been, by the influence of the University of Prague, restrained within the limits of antiquity. With the one, the wildest propositions of Wicklif were readily admitted, while with the other the concession of the cup formed the single ground of resistance to the Church of Rome and to the Council of Constance, which had for the first time authoritatively mutilated the institution of Christ. It was the observation of this essential difference that led Julian in after life, and when it devolved upon him to conduct the negotiation with the Hussites in their united character as the representative of the court of Rome, to endeavour to draw out the extreme party into admissions and declarations that might effectually separate them from the other. This skilful design, though, as we shall find hereafter, it was unsuccessful, was evidently formed on the personal knowledge he had acquired of the original differences between the moderate and extreme sections at this period.

We may observe here, that that deep dread of the progress of Hussitism, which bore so many fruits in his later life, was here implanted. The obscurity which covers the three or four years of his residence in Hungary and Bohemia may be well explained by the fact that it was the single and fruitful opportunity of learning the lesson of his future life. Every feature of that life derives light and significance from the events of which he was at this time a silent but anxious witness.

It was then that he recognised the necessity of that deep and searching reform which could alone bring back to the unity of the Church its distant and disaffected members. It was then that he first realized the truth that the Turkish empire was working its way into Europe, not so much in its own strength as from the disunion and disorganization of the European states, and the gradual relaxation of that single bond which had, from the days of the Crusades, combined them against the enemies of the Christian name.

The great Bohemian movement he naturally regarded as the most menacing of all the elements of confusion that were now threatening Europe. Its scene was the very nearest to the point of danger. Its successes were opening a path of conquest to the enemies of the Church, at a point where the Church of Rome had ever been weakest, the countries of the great Slavonian family, Eastern in their origin and sympathies, and wavering in their allegiance to the papacy since the day of their conversion by the Eastern missionaries, and their invitation, on the part of the great patriarch, Photius, to resist the tyrannical pretensions and novel doctrines of the bishops of Rome.*

The importance of connecting the eastern countries of Europe by a stronger tie to the common centre must have assumed at this time the sterner form of a necessity. And it will not surprise any one who traces the varied fortunes of the Church of the fifteenth century to find that, of the co-ordinate works of union and reformation, the latter was entered upon only as the pathway to the former— and the rule admitted and carried out, that the

* Photii, Ep. Encycl. (Ep. Ed. Montacut. p. 59.)

unity of the Church could never be real until the reformation of the Church was complete.

The year 1420 did not close before the negotiations of the people of Prague and the Grand Duke Sigismund of Poland had made considerable advancement; and the following year carried on the frightful catalogue of murder and rapine, opening with the utter destruction of the town of Commotau with upwards of two thousand of its inhabitants. Neither women nor children were spared in this barbarous massacre, which was succeeded by the destruction of the towns of Beraune and Broda, and the voluntary submission of many other cities terror-stricken at the progress of Zisska.

Meantime the scene of cruelty was reopened in Prague. The convent of noble women dedicated to St. George, of which the illustrious sister of the Burggrave of Wartemberg was abbess, was invaded by the Hussites, and on the firm refusal of the abbess to renounce her faith, she was dragged with thirty of the nuns through the streets of Prague, exposed to the insults of the populace, and, but for a timely resistance on the part of the less violent, would have been thrown into the river Mulda.

At this period the Hussites, whose arms had hitherto met with so strange a success, resolved to give it a practical direction by the assembly of a diet of the States of Bohemia and Moravia at Czaslaw, which was presided over by the great Calixtine nobleman, Ulrich de Rosenberg. The emperor thought it not beneath his dignity to consult his temporal interests by acknowledging the legitimacy of this assembly, though, after it had laid down the four great points of Hussitism, it proceeded to the solemn resolution to receive him no longer as king.

Letters of mutual remonstrance and recrimination passed between the diet and Sigismund. The one charged upon the emperor all the evils that had befallen the kingdom, and which flowed, as they maintained, from the execution of Huss, and the adhesion of Sigismund to the decrees of the Council of Constance; the other heaping upon the Hussite faction the cruelties and desolations which had ruined and dishonoured the kingdom, bitterly alluding to the destruction of the glorious Wissehrad, with its abbey of St. Peter and St. Paul, and forty dependent churches.

Neither the arguments nor the reproaches of Sigismund could delay the execution of the plan of his dethronement, and the following year witnessed the triumphant entry of Sigismund Coribut into Prague at the head of 5,000 horsemen. The nobility adhered still to the emperor, and the Taborites, with Zisska at their head, energetically opposed the election of a king. The new monarch was left accordingly to the narrow sympathies of the people of Prague—the pure Calixtines—who were unable to obtain for him the allegiance of the Bohemians generally.

The difference between Zisska and the people

of Prague, indicated in the very determination with which they had carried out a project so opposed to the principles of the proper Hussites, assumed shortly after a very serious . aspect. Everything tended to widen the breach, which in the following year (1423) broke out into open warfare. After a raid into Moravia, in which the warlike Bishop of Olmutz—more successful as a general than any who had preceded him in this strange succession of conflicts—offered him an unusual degree of resistance, the terrible leader of the Hussites advanced upon Prague, but here he had to encounter a difficulty which no amount of military skill and daring could overcome.

The national character of the movement departed from it when Prague became the object of attack, and Prague not any longer as the centre of the monarchy, but the centre of the revolution which had overthrown it. Confusion and dismay spread through the ranks of Zisska as he led them against so new an adversary. How could they carry fire and slaughter into the homes of those who had fought beside them as the joint defenders of the national honour, the joint avengers of the martyrs to the national faith? Zisska, equal to the emergency, addressed this rude soldiery in words which appealed to their former recollections, and pointed to a future which should secure them from every danger of internal division.

Mounted on a cask of beer, the blind leader of this wild host spoke to them in language of simple eloquence, as one of themselves, rather obeying their own impulse than demanding obedience for himself. "Take counsel yourselves," were his closing words, "that none may accuse me. Do you wish for peace? See only that no snare or treachery lie hid beneath it —for war? here am I with you. Choose which you will have—in either Zisska will be your counsellor."

The magic influence of the general returned as in a moment. The soldiery flew to arms. The attack was already begun when the people of Prague, under the advice of Coribut, sent a deputation to treat of peace. The chief leader of the Calixtines, Rokyczana, afterwards Archbishop of Prague, was sent to meet Zisska, and, after a long interview, the relations of peace were completed.

On the feast of the Exaltation of the Cross—a strange anniversary for a work of peace such as this —the treaty was signed. A rude monument, in the form of a vast stone-heap, was piled up to comme-morate the new alliance, and the Taborites re-entered the city as friends, and were received with every mark of honour and exultation. Turning thence into Moravia, Zisska laid siege to the town of Przibislaw; but, on the very eve of the final assault, the plague, which had broken out in his camp, attacked him with fatal virulence. "As the hand of man (writes Æneas Sylvius) had been unable to slay him, the finger of God destroyed him."

The meeting between the leaders of the two

factions, and the immediate and sudden removal from the scene of the master-spirit of this convulsive movement, makes it not inopportune to say a few words in this place of John de Rokyczana, the Calix-tine Archbishop of Prague, and of John Zisska de Trocznow, the chief of the Taborite faction.

There is in the district of Pilsen a village named Rokyczana, belonging to the Church of Prague—a village which, in the Bohemian wars two centuries after, was cruelly ravaged by Count Zdenko Leo von Kolowrat, and its wretched inhabitants reproached for the only event which has given it a name in history—the birth within its walls of John de Rokyczana, who united to the possession of a commanding intellect a singular capability of adapting himself to the circum-stances of his time. His life in all its history, from the days on which he is said to have even begged his daily food in the streets of Prague, has but one motive and one inspiration. The archbishopric of Prague, the headship of the national Church, was ever before his eye as the single object of his life.

The schism between the national party and the court of Rome opened to the crafty ecclesiastic an opportunity of rushing at the prize, while the great nobility and the partisans of the court were for a while kept back from the race. Accordingly, he espoused the cause of the national party with all the energy of a vigorous and original mind; and on the occasion of this meeting (in connexion with which his

name is mentioned for the first time) proved that he was
fit to conduct the most difficult and delicate mission.

The heads of the consistory of Prague who stood
in the way of his ambition—the equally celebrated
John de Przibram, the physician Krzistan, and Peter
de Mladonowicz — were removed from the capital
through his intrigues; and from that moment he
governed the Church of Prague with almost an absolute power. His firm adherence to Coribut, and his
employment in this negotiation, point him out as the
chief adviser of the invitation to that prince to accept
the vacant throne, as he undoubtedly was the cause of
that reaction a few years later, which sent him back
ignominiously to his own country.

At a later period we shall find him one of the
deputies of the Bohemians at the Council of Basle,
confronted with Julian himself, and sustaining his old
reputation as a controversialist and diplomatist. After
the fruitless issue of this attempt at pacification, we
find him next receiving at Prague the deputation sent
thither by the council, headed by Philibert, Bishop of
Coûtances. The acts of this colloquy were transmitted
to the council, and formed the basis of the *compactata*,
to which we shall have to revert at a later period.

This form of concord, in which the Hussites were
overreached by the subtlety of the fathers of the
council, was without doubt as much the work of
Rokyczana as of those whom he had hitherto so con-
sistently opposed. The archbishopric was the reward

of his duplicity; for, after bringing over the more obstinate of the Hussite party to the terms of the *compactata*, and obtaining from Sigismund the power of election of the archbishop and bishops for the clergy and nobility of Bohemia, his own election was immediately completed, and the end of his life seemed gained.

Rokyczana himself, in the presence of the emperor, professed his renewed allegiance to the Roman See, and received absolution from the condemnation of·the Church at the hands of the legates of the council. But the treachery of Sigismund, on his arrival at Prague, withdrew from the Calixtine leader the golden prize; and on the pretext that he did not conform to the Roman Church in those very points in which the terms of the *compactata* admitted a diversity, the emperor handed over the administration of the arch-bishopric to Philibert, the legate of the council, until Rokyczana was duly reconciled to the Roman See.

The restitution of the Roman rites and the return of the monks into Bohemia gave him an opportunity of appealing anew to those who still recognised him as their leader; and his discourses drawing from Sigis-mund threats of personal injury, he retired secretly from the city, and remained under the care of a powerful follower at Königsgrätz. The death of Sigis-mund enabled him soon after to carry on a new intrigue against the election of Albert of Austria, his son-in-law, to the Bohemian throne. But the efforts of Rokyczana were here again fruitless.

The death of Albert and the long minority of Wladislaus, his posthumous son, succeeded, and opened a new opportunity for the diplomacy of the indefatigable candidate for the archbishopric. On the election of George Podiebrad, the chief of that illustrious family which had already borne a conspicuous part in the events of this exciting period, to the vice-royalty of the kingdom, Rokyczana was established in the archbishopric and entered upon its functions, but never received the confirmation of the Roman See. To the instigation of his restless and jealous ambition the popular belief of the day attributed the sudden and mysterious death of Wladislaus, which happened soon after; and the rude rhymes of the multitude pointed against the king and the archbishop the charge of poisoning the young monarch, whose throne was presently usurped by Podiebrad, who had been intrusted with the care of the future monarch.*

But the cruelty and insincerity of Rokyczana were most clearly seen in his bitter persecutions of the Taborites, and of all who adhered to the simpler teaching of Huss. It is to this persecution, which compelled the purer Hussites to seek safety in exile, that the Church of the Bohemian and Moravian Brethren, the *Unitas Fratrum*, traces up its earlier

---

* " Auf die Erden haben sie ihn gestreckt,
    Mit einem Kuss haben sie ihn ersteckt,
    Sein Gemächt haben sie ihm durchbrochen,
    Das jammert Gott im Himmel hoch,
    Wird's nicht lassen ungerochen."

history; and by this it connects itself with the apostles of the reformation in Bohemia.

The year 1471 was fatal both to Rokyczana and to his patron, whose death, from the knowledge of his shattered constitution, he foretold as soon to follow his own. The one died on the 22d of February, the other on the 22d of March; and their last meeting formed the closing scene of that long conflict, which must have filled the minds of* both with so many bitter memories.

The dying archbishop admonished the failing king that he must soon follow him to the awful judgment-seat of God. Stung by the same remorse, and conscious of kindred crimes to which the same insatiable and blinding ambition had hurried them both, we may well conceive how bitter a commentary upon the history which we have just opened must have been read in this momentous interview. The opinion which Rokyczana entertained of the religion of his country-men he was used to express in the words, "If we could see a Christian who was one not in name only, but in truth, the very sight would move as much astonishment as if a stag with golden horns should make its appearance on the bridge of Prague." *

A character of greater levity, except in the single resolution which inspired his life, and of deeper dissi-

---

* A short but valuable biographical sketch of the life of Rokyczana is given by Oswald ("De Joanne Rokyczana Calixtinorum in Bohemia Pontifice," Altdorf. Noric. 1718), which we have here followed.

mulation of all but the hatred he bore to Rome which
had frustrated it so long, can hardly be conceived; and
in both these features it stood forth in remarkable
contrast to that of the military leader of this great
movement, John Zisska de Trocznow, whose religious
convictions, though stern and wild, were sincere and
inflexible, and whose very cruelties were carried on in
submission to a severe and vindictive morality, as was
proved in the case of the punishment of the Picards or
Adamites, a sect which aimed at the overthrow of all
the moral sanctions of society.

While Rokyczana would have readily conceded the
cup to the Church of Rome, on the condition of her
confirmation of him in the archbishopric, Zisska,
taught rather by the severe dogmatism of the Slavonian Church than by the more flexible system of the
schoolmen, regarded the assertion of the integrity of
the sacrament as a religious duty which admitted of
no compromise, and the vindication of the cause of its
martyrs at Constance as a righteous work whatever
misery and suffering it involved. The words, "Except
ye eat the flesh of the Son of man, *and drink His
blood*," imprudently applied to the Eucharist at the
moment when the very possibility of fulfilling the
second part of the condition was removed, or, at least,
but questionably satisfied in the doctrine of con-
comitancy, were dwelt upon by the Church of Prague,
in their declaration of faith, in such a manner as to
show the strength which a religious party, founded on

the resistance to the decree of Constance, might assume. That Zisska had not merely taken advantage of a popular sentiment to raise himself to his strange position, but deeply shared the feelings he understood so well, and could direct with so much energy, must be admitted by every unprejudiced observer; while none can deny him the possession of those military qualities which it is, perhaps, difficult for any but the eye of a soldier fully to measure.

The foundation of Tabor as a centre from which his operations could be carried on in every direction, appears to have been less a concession to the feudal system of strongholds, which was now fast disappearing, than a means of withdrawing those on whose support he chiefly reckoned from the strong counteracting influences of the city of Prague, which so frequently produced discord, and once serious collision, between the two great divisions of the national party. In this remarkable colony, which Pius II. (when Æneas Sylvius) visited, and describes in his "History of Europe," the party of the stricter Hussites was so organized in its religious and military plans as to concentrate the power of its founder, and to enable him to carry out his terrible warfare with the greatest suddenness and success.

The slow and cumbrous means of the Royalists, like those of the empire of which they formed a part, were but ill adapted to resist the impetuous and rapid attacks of an enemy inspired with the double enthusiasm of a national cause and a religious conviction; and the recent introduction of fire-arms gave an additional superiority to the more prompt and vigorous party. The plans of Zisska, laid with such judgment and foresight at Tabor, were carried out so suddenly and energetically as never to fail, "for he died as the conqueror in many battles (writes Cochlæus), having never been conquered in any."

Little is known of the earlier life of this remarkable man until he was appointed page in the court of the Emperor Charles IV. Probably in consequence of the brilliant opening of his military life in Poland, the period and circumstances of which his biographers are unable to determine, on the accession of Wenceslaus, he was appointed chamberlain to that king, a post from which he was able to watch the storm gathering over his country, and to prepare himself to direct it. The death of Huss, and the acceptance by the Bohemian Church of the decree of Constance, called him forth into active life, and enabled him to draw before the world the lines of a character in which the barbarous and grotesque is so interwoven with the religious and military element as to make it stand alone in the history of generalship. The blind leader of the wildest and most undisciplined hosts, with every disadvantage of personal appearance—possessing only a rude eloquence, whose chief power lay in its rough and homely appeal to the hearts of his followers—his influence over them was yet so great that, on his death, a considerable body of them refused to elect any one as his successor, and called themselves orphans, as having been deprived of a father whose loss they could never supply.

The main body of the Hussites chose a successor to Zisska in Procopius (surnamed Rasus), a chief who appears to have inherited many of those military qualifications which the first leader of the national cause had possessed in their fullest measure.

The year which witnessed the death of Zisska witnessed also the closing act of the legation of Cardinal Branda, which was the excommunication of Sigismund Coribut, who, breaking the engagement he had made at the Diet of Presburg, had entered Bohemia. His return to Rome took place soon after, and the elevation of Julian, who accompanied him to an auditorship of the Rota, opened to him that path of preferment which brought him so early to the cardinalate.

The Council of Siena, convoked in obedience to the decree of the Council of Constance, which had enjoined the assembly of a general council at an interval of five years from its own dissolution, was feebly reopening the work of its great predecessor at the period of Julian's return. Translated from Pavia, the appointed scene of its assembly, on account of the appearance of the plague in that city, it entered upon the subjects that had been bequeathed it at Constance—the reformation of the Church, and the reunion with the Eastern Churches—with so much disunion and imbecility, as to give an early pretext to the pope to dissolve it. Some of the sermons preached before it are still extant, and while they depict the Church as in the last stage of degeneracy and decay, they exhibit the state of preaching of the age as little suited to raise it to a higher standard. Ludicrous visions of St. Bridget and St. Catherine of Siena, and equally absurd grammatical and scriptural images, give a mournful picture of the ignorance of the first principles of theology which was then so prevalent, and of the degeneracy of the taste of the more educated classes before the revival of learning in the close of the fifteenth century.

The council was dissolved in February, 1424, after a miserable and convulsive existence of a few months, Cardinal Capranica being the bearer of the bull of dissolution, which summoned a new council at an interval of seven years. But though the prospects of the reformation of the Church were still so unpromising, the temporal condition of the papacy was rapidly improving, under the peaceful policy of the new pontiff.

Seven years of peace and restoration had done much towards removing the traces of that seventy years of anarchy and orphanage which Rome has ever regarded as her Babylonian captivity. But it was not less the moral than the material influence of the papacy which the wise moderation of the pontiff rebuilt on so firm a foundation. The administrative talents which he possessed in his own person were well and ably represented by those whom he selected for offices of trust and responsibility, and the court of Rome was never more richly furnished with great and good men than at this moment, when, perhaps, it needed them more than ever.

Besides the older members of the Sacred College who had taken part in the election at Constance, there were at this time in Rome Ludovicus Alemandus (afterwards President of the Council of Basle during its long contest with Eugenius IV.); the now sainted Albergati, whose success in carrying on the pacific labours of Martin V. had gained him the name of the Cardinal of Peace; Capranica, whose severe integrity and devoted fidelity to the Colonna placed him so long under the unjust ban of Eugenius IV.; and Prosper Colonna, the nephew of the pope, of whom it is said that no one could have failed to "love him, unless it were an ultra-Ghibelline." Among the older men was the venerable John de Bronhiac, the vice-chancellor, whose paternal kindness to the great Huss, at Constance, adds greatness to his own name, Cardinal Branda, and Cardinal Condolmieri, afterwards Pope Eugenius IV.

To these members of the college, one was soon to be added whose name is better known in England than any of his contemporaries, Cardinal Beaufort, or, as he was then generally called, the Cardinal of

H

Winchester. To this prelate, who was included in the large promotion made by Martin V. in 1426, the legation into Bohemia, now rendered additionally difficult by the failure of Cardinal Branda, was confided. The new legate, whose zeal to promote the interests of the court of Rome with his nephews, King Henry V. and the Dukes of Bedford and Gloucester, as well as the success with which he had carried on an ecclesiastical negotiation of another kind, had pointed him out as fitted for a mission of still greater difficulty, entered at once upon the command of the large forces which the empire had placed at his disposal for carrying on the Hussite war. The failure of the previous mission had left no other resource than an appeal to arms, in which the Bohemian cause, from its very nationality, was ever more fortunate than in diplomatic warfare.

The terrors of the insurrection had now extended far beyond its first field, and the most flourishing towns of Saxony and Lusatia soon fell a prey to the ravages of the Hussite arms. The sad fate of the town of Lauban, in Lusatia, as it has been more circumstantially described than many others, may enable the reader to estimate the misery and ruin which followed the successes of these desperate marauders through all their career. That town forms one of the six municipalities of the Margraviate of Upper Lusatia, and the Taborites having carried their work of plunder and massacre through the neighbouring country of Silesia, attacked it on the 15th of May, 1427, under

the command of Diedrich von Klüx, a Lusatian nobleman, a headship which shows that the Bohemian
disaffection had spread among the higher classes of
Lusatia also, and formed part of a general Slavonian
movement against the German population. The inhabitants of the neighbouring villages had taken refuge
in the town, in order to escape the cruelties of the
Hussite invaders ; but notwithstanding the courage
and vigour with which, under the command of the
Burgomaster Conrad Zeidler, they repelled the enemy,
driven into confusion by the death of their leader,
they fell back into the town, whither the infuriated
Hussites pursued them.

On the 16th of May, the place was taken by assault,
and a frightful massacre, not only of its defenders, but
of the helpless women and children, who had fled for
refuge to the churches, succeeded. In the great
church, whither the priests and scholars had betaken
themselves for sanctuary, and which was crowded
with miserable suppliants, singing the *Salve Regina
Misericordiæ*, in the vain hope, if not of a miraculous
interposition for their rescue, yet of touching the
hearts of their persecutors with pity for their utter
helplessness, the murderous assailants hewed down
all without mercy, till a stream of blood flowed
through the building. A priest of the church,
Jeremias Grolle, mounting the tower, addressed
energetic words to the brave townsmen, who defended
themselves so vigorously, that in every direction a

Hussite and an inhabitant of the town were seen fallen together, or engaged in a hand to hand conflict. The unfortunate patriot was soon, however, dragged down from the place of his momentary security, and torn to pieces by horses in the market-place. So utter was the destruction of those who had taken refuge in the church, that the escape of a scholar who had concealed himself under the surplice of a murdered chorister is recorded as almost a miracle. After the Hussites had left, the survivor of the massacre found a piece of bread, on which for three days he contrived to support himself, and having escaped this calamitous day, lived to become altarist at Löwenberg. The demolition of the nunnery of Lauban, and the slaughter of the nuns and the women and children, who had taken refuge with them, followed, nor did the Hussites relinquish the place until the work of desolation was complete.

Four years had scarcely passed away since this fatal attack, when the town again fell a prey to the Hussite marauders, who were vigorously, but in the end vainly, resisted by Bernhard von Uchtritz. On this occasion the church was again the scene of a frightful slaughter, the guardian Johann Crone and eight monks being slain before the high altar. These details of cruelty and rapine were repeated in every part of Bohemia and Germany, in which the successes of the Hussites enabled them to act out their sanguinary warfare, and make it easy to fill up the picture of anarchy and confusion which the empire was now exhibiting, wherever the Slavonian element was to be found.*

Cardinal Beaufort, to whom the legation into Bohemia and Germany was now confided, had learned from the failure of Cardinal Branda, a far more experienced diplomatist, that the season of negotiation in that distracted country was at an end, and that nothing but the most prompt and vigorous military action could bring back the reign of law and order. The date of his appointment as legate was the 16th of February, 1427, and he lost no time in opening the crusade, which was first published in his own diocese of Winchester, from which he hastened to the seat of war. From Mechlin he communicated with the pope, and received an encouraging reply. The rapidity with which he raised a large army from every part of Germany gave the sure promise of ultimate success.

The forces which were thus collected, were divided into three corps—the Saxons and troops of the Hanseatic league formed the first; the contingents from Franconia, Thüringen, and Lüneburg, under the Elector of Brandenburg, formed the second; while the third was supplied by the electorates of Bavaria, and the Palatinate, and the free cities of the bench of Swabia. Entering into Bohemia, they encamped respectively at Commotau, Egra, and Tausch.

* These details are given by Carpzovius in his " Ehrien tempel der Ober-Lausitz," and were derived from the MS. annals compiled by the Burgomaster, Christopher Wiessner, in the seventeenth century, and preserved in the Town-hall of Lauban.

The Hussites in the meantime, foreseeing the
danger, had prepared for it by a work of reconciliation between the two great factions of the Taborites and Calixtines, whose divisions had already
been far more fatal to their arms than the greatest
successes of their adversaries.    Sigismund Coribut
had been dismissed from Prague, deserted alike by
all, and thus the chief element of discord was removed.    The city of Meissen was the scene of the
first encounter of the rebels and the imperialists,
who were bent upon regaining this important position.    The siege had already commenced, and the
success of the legate, with the vast resources at his
command, seemed to be inevitable, when, for some
unexplained and even yet inexplicable cause, the
army of the besiegers took to a sudden and shameful
flight.

Probably, the best and most reasonable solution of
the sudden defection, that so frequently rendered
abortive the energetic and for that period gigantic
efforts of the imperialists, who had gathered the
flower of the armies of Europe into this strange
battle-field, may be found in the nationality of the
Bohemian movement, and in the terror which its
wild successes and savage features had inspired
throughout Christendom.    The spirit which had
animated the crusades was now passed away, and
the folly that sought to evoke that spirit against
Christians, and had drawn forth the sublime denun-

ciation of Dante, had tended to hasten the day of its
utter extinction. The publication of the crusade of
Martin V., though it succeeded in enlisting one of the
largest armies hitherto collected in Europe, could not
keep it together in the face of a religious influence
like that of Hussitism, which was rooted in national
sympathies, such as Rome could never awaken in the
day of her greatest power.

The renewed success of the Hussites, whose cause
seemed to be providentially sustained against that of
united Europe, led the emperor again to have recourse
to diets and diplomacy, and to strive to put in motion
the cumbrous machinery of the empire, whose executive power had ever, from its very complication,
been so weak and difficult to direct in the hour of
danger. Again was a diet summoned at Nuremberg,
to concert immediate and vigorous measures for
crushing the hitherto successful rebellion. To this
diet, Julian, now nominated a cardinal deacon, with
the title of St. Angelo, was accredited by Martin V.
as his representative, combining the offices of legate
in Bohemia and president of the general council,
which, in pursuance of the celebrated decree " *Frequens* " of the Council of Constance, was shortly to
assemble at Basle.

But scarcely had he arrived at Nuremberg, when
the afflicting intelligence of the death of his patron
reached him. His twofold mission seemed abruptly
closed. Upon one portion of it, that of legate into

Bohemia, he had entered with that eager zeal which his devotion to an active life, and his strange predilection for a military activity above every other, made so natural to him. Upon the other he had entered not only with hesitation, but with actual repugnance. Even when he accepted it, and was congratulated by his friends upon his double appointment, before he left Rome, he loudly complained of this part of his office, and to none more loudly than to the successor of Martin V., Cardinal Condolmieri, and to the Cardinal of the Holy Cross (Albergati), who both " condoled with him," as he himself affirms, " with parental affection on the assignment of such a province to him."

As some days had elapsed between the announcement of the election of Eugenius IV. (Gabriel Condolmieri) to the papal throne, and the confirmation of him in his legations by the new pontiff, he began to indulge the hope, that at least the presidency of the council had been delegated to another member of the college. But it was not long before the dreaded appointment arrived, and Julian found himself confirmed in both his offices, while Eugenius, as if to increase his embarrassment, urged upon him the necessity of the immediate assembly of the council, apparently viewing that as the most important part of his commission. All that the legate possessed at this moment was the discretion to give priority to the one subject or the other, as either appeared to him to be the more urgent. It was natural, therefore, that notwithstanding the pressure from Rome, he should give priority to what was now of paramount importance, and should at once address himself to the reconciliation of Bohemia. Such a course was necessary even to enable the council to fulfil the most difficult part of its labours, and to make it an effective instrument in restoring the religious peace of Europe.

Julian took advantage of this interval to press again on Eugenius his entreaties to be absolved from a charge which he so much dreaded, and prayed the pope to transfer to another the presidency of the future council. Meantime, he opened the diet of Nuremberg by the publication of the bull of Martin V., authorising a crusade against the Hussites, and proposed a large and judicious plan for the future campaign, which, after its adoption by the diet, he communicated by letter to John Hoffmann, the energetic Bishop of Meissen. The letter itself runs thus :—

" ' There must,' saith the Apostle, 'be heresies, that they which are approved may be made manifest : ' ' for gold is tried in the fire, and acceptable men in the furnace of adversity,'—men who offer themselves as a wall for the house of the Lord. O grief ! the abominable heresy of the Wiclifites and Hussites of the kingdom of Bohemia, surpassing in cruelty the heresies of every former age, has prevailed in our day. Yea, it hath filled their hearts with such obstinacy and rage, that, even as the deaf adder that stoppeth her ears, they hear not the words of the Church, their mother, and heed not her holy doctrine, insomuch that they seem to be inflexible to the labours, the arguments, the gentleness, the entreaties of those who would bring them back.  And, besides their pestilent doctrines, which proclaim every kind of blasphemy, they have utterly put off the feelings and the nature of men, and, becoming as it were brute beasts, pant for the spoil and for the very blood of Catholics.  Their crimes and sacrileges against God and man, against the sacraments and temples consecrated to God—their murders, their rapines, their zeal for the destruction of every earthly institution—are so notorious and conspicuous to all, that to recount them severally were indeed superfluous.  In arms and in violence is their only trust—by fire and sword alone do they seek to defend their errors.  And, above all, thirsting for the blood of Catholics, they murder and burn all who will not assent to their errors with savage cruelty, hideously mutilating them, and afflicting them with manifold torments.  How shameful and ignominiously they handle the divine sacrament of the Eucharist, which, with profane feet, they tread down into the blood of the slain—how inhumanly they break and burn the images of our Lord Jesus Christ, and of the most glorious Virgin, His mother, and of all the saints—how they destroy churches and oratories from their very foundation, it were too tearful to relate.

"Against such an insane and armed heresy the

Catholic princes are most justly and meritoriously rising mightily in arms and warfare. For to them the power of the sword hath been granted by God for the punishment of evil-doers, and for the praise of them that do well. Wherefore the most Serene Prince, and illustrious Lord Sigismund, by the grace of God, King of the Romans, of Hungary, and Bohemia, etc., desiring, as the defender and advocate of the Church, utterly to root out this pestilent heresy, having assembled in this city of Nuremberg the reverend fathers and illustrious lords, the electors of the holy Roman empire, the archbishops, bishops, princes, dukes, counts, barons, and ambassadors of the cities, we ourselves being present, unanimously took counsel and resolved, for the defence of the faith, that on the feast of the nativity of St. John the Baptist next ensuing, a strong and powerful army gathered together from every part of Germany should assemble at Weyden, on the frontiers of Bohemia, to advance (with the favour of God) into Bohemia in due course for the extirpation of the heretics, if they should refuse to return into the bosom of the Church.

"But since pious prayers and supplications were ever wont to prevail more than arms, we ought to imitate the holy Moses, who prayed for the people while they were fighting, and as long as he held up his hands to heaven caused them to prevail, and when he dropped them again to yield. Follow we also the example of the Levites, who, by the sound of the trumpet, animated the people to battle. Let us pray, then, without intermission, suppliantly and devoutly, and, with tears and prayers, implore of God, through his grace, that our Catholic army about to contend for the house of the Lord, and for the salvation of his people, may obtain victory over the enemies of the faith. Let us, moreover, exhort these warriors of the faith, these wrestlers for Catholic truth, by sermons, by admonitions, and by the examples of their ancestors, not to suffer the sanctuary of the Lord to be polluted by wicked enemies. Let us arm ourselves, let us strengthen those whom we invite with the saving sign of the life-giving cross, and with spiritual graces and gifts, so that they may confidently and successfully defeat the enemies of God and man.

" Wherefore we (as we are bound), wishing to fulfil with all diligence the commission laid upon us by the Apostolic See, and desiring that this holy work may be joyfully completed, by these presents, do exhort, advise, and charge you, and in virtue of your holy obedience lay the strict commandment upon you, that without delay in all cathedral and other collegiate and con-ventual churches, as well as in all parish churches of your city and diocese, you do solemnly pray, and set forth and proclaim the word of God, and the apostolic indulgences to the exhorting and awakening of the faithful on every Lord's day and festival during the approaching campaign ; and that you will ordain and depute discreet and fit priests with the power of signing

with the cross, and absolving and doing all such
other things as are contained in the apostolic letters,
according to their form and tenor, whereof I send
you an authentic transcript, under our seal and official
signature.

"Given at Nuremberg, in the diocese of Bamberg,
A.D. 1431, ninth indiction, 20th day of March, and in
the first year of the Pontificate of the most holy Father
and Lord in Christ, Eugenius IV."

The diet of Nuremberg, whose resolution on the
Hussite war was thus promulgated through the
empire, carried on its discussions under the presidency of Sigismund himself for as many as eight
months. The very prolongation of its sessions, and
the fact that more than two months elapsed between
its assembly and the publication of the letter of the
legate, leads to the belief that the unanimity here alleged
was not arrived at without much preliminary difference
of sentiment. We are told on very good authority that
the emperor was himself at the head of the dissentient
party, and strongly urged upon the princes the im-
policy of the expedition of which Julian was the
energetic advocate. Sigismund wisely saw the
danger and complications which even a successful
campaign against his own subjects would bring with
it to the empire, and that success in such a cause
would not only make an irreparable breach between
himself and his people, but tend to the exaltation of

the princes of the empire, and of the court of Rome
at his expense.  His natural policy, as well as his own
feelings, urged him to resist the warlike counsels of
Julian, and even when they prevailed, to make a private attempt to conciliate his Bohemian subjects.
Passing to the frontier town of Egra, he sent on two
of the gentlemen of his court to propose terms of
accommodation.   Their overtures were well received
by the Calixtines and Taborites, and all except the
Orphans, from whom, as the obstinate opponents of
all reconciliation, they met with determined hostility.
The other factions agreed to send deputies to the
emperor, who gave them several interviews, but without arriving at any successful conclusion.

At this critical moment, the discovery of the hostile
plans that were now matured in the diet, and the news
of the preaching of the crusade throughout the empire, awakened in the Hussite ambassadors a fear of
treachery, too natural to those who remembered how
easily the safe conduct of Huss had been cancelled,
and the oath of the emperor broken.   Abruptly leaving the scene of the diet, they returned to Prague,
uttering only reproaches and accusations against Sigismund, asserting that upon the Catholics alone the
blame of this furious warfare would rest, which they
themselves had vainly endeavoured to terminate.

The military predilections of the legate, supported
in this instance by his experience of the fruitlessness of
negotiation, even when entrusted to the most prudent

diplomatist, not only prevailed over the open opposition of Sigismund, but overruled the ill-concealed disinclination of the majority of the princes of the empire. With a selfishness more than ordinarily shortsighted, they refused to look upon the war in their federal character, and maintained that its expenses should fall upon those who were most immediately to profit by it, and especially upon the Elector of Saxony. On the part of these, however, it was properly rejoined that the war was for the defence of the empire and of religion itself. The closing scene of the diet of Nuremberg completed the triumph of the warrior over the diplomatist. In a full assembly, and with every circumstance of pomp and solemnity, Cardinal Julian delivered into the hands of the Margrave of Brandenburg and his sons, the blessed banner of the crusade; and the ancestor at once of the great Frederic, and of that not less glorious, though less warlike successor, who so lately filled his throne, received the symbol and accepted the mission of a crusader against the children of the same faith, and the confessors of the same Cross.

In the meantime, Julian, who employed the intervening period in publishing the crusade in the district around Nuremberg, seems to have had at least a misgiving that his warlike counsels had been premature, and that the duty of exhausting every peaceful means had not been fulfilled before the sword was drawn. The day of the appointed meeting of the allies had already passed away without finding them assembled,

and while he was awaiting the signal for the opening
of the campaign with that impatience which was so
natural to his ardent mind, he addressed to the Bohemians these last words of pathetic entreaty—words
whose tones of peace and love harmonized ill with the
notes of warfare, and the noise of the instruments of
death, out of the midst of which they were uttered :—

" Julian, by the grace of God, Cardinal Deacon of
St. Angelo in the Holy Roman Church, and Legate
of the Apostolic See throughout Germany.

" Of all the things which we desire from our heart
this is the highest and the chief, that the celebrated
kingdom of Bohemia may return to the one faith and
to its ancient obedience to the holy Roman Church.
For if this were indeed to come about, not only the
salvation and bliss of the soul, but peace, rest, and
every other good, would doubtless flow back upon the
kingdom in as large a measure as they did before this
confusion and innovation began.   But in order that
this may be fruitfully accomplished, I am applying
myself with all my strength and in virtue of my office
to this one point—for this alone I exercise my mind,
and to this devote my life—that the citizens of this
kingdom may see with their own eyes the fervency of
my anxiety for their salvation, the sincerity of my
desire to deserve well at their hands; yea, to that
extent, that if need be I am ready to welcome death
itself for the name of Christ.

"But since we have found that those who scatter evil seeds pretend (in order to detach the minds of the inhabitants from peace and concord) that our Christian forces are led by us into your kingdom to overturn it, to fill it with rapine, slaughter, and burnings, to its utter and irreparable destruction—taking due consideration hereof, and willing to remove from you this groundless suspicion—we thus make known to you that we have brought together our Christian forces only to appease your controversies and to conciliate peace among you, to restore sacred rites fallen into disuse, to confirm the relations of peace and quietness with you, to renew and upraise the name and glory of God, which this disorder has diminished, and finally to reduce everything into a certain order, if only the inhabitants agree to reject that confusion already alluded to, and their change of government, and join themselves to us as they did before by ties of social and political alliance.

"We exhort, therefore, and with the deepest and most heartfelt love we implore, all Bohemians of either sex and of every age to return to the faith and conversation of their ancestors, who agreed with us, and in no way whatever to depart therefrom.

"We assure the Bohemians that they may all freely return to the holy Roman Church, and that they need entertain no fear whatever either for their persons or for their property. For these our Christian forces have never injured, either in life or in property, a single

I

one of those who sought again the bosom of the
Church their mother, and suffering from constraint or
injury betook themselves thereunto ; and we solemnly
promise you that you will be welcomed by them so
tenderly and lovingly that not even the slightest point
of enmity will be visible between you.

"Let not, therefore, him who seeks to live in the
fear of God, and to escape these troubles, fear to
become reconciled to us ; for such as this may look
for every office of Christian love from our forces.
Nor do we doubt that the Bohemians, when they are
reconciled to us, and see our benevolent feeling towards
them, will return thanks to the great and good God
for having put this grace into their hearts, and that the
only ground of sorrow that will remain will be the
thought that for so long a time and for so slight a
cause they were separated from us.   Return, then, to
the breasts of your mother the Church of Christ.   Do
not bring her even a yet greater grief, who already
groans and pours forth tears, and expects with ardent
love the returning of her children, who, having asked
for the portion of the inheritance which fell to them,
have wasted it in riot in a far country, and whom
hunger and every other ill has overtaken.

"Return, dear pledges of love, return to us ; we will
go forth to meet you ; we will embrace you ; we will
put upon you the new garment ; we will slay for you
the fatted calf ; we will call together our friends and
our neighbours, having found the sons we had lost,

and make joyous festival with them. What is it that
our fellow-citizens and brethren still fear? Were we
not born of the same mother? were we not renewed
at the same font of holy baptism? Do we not partake
the same Christianity? do we not unite in acknowledging the same Mediator and Redeemer, Jesus
Christ? Have we not the same word and sacraments?
do we not embrace the same Scriptures? What, then,
hath alienated you from us? Who hath been able to
separate the children from their mother? But a little
while ago you exceeded all nations in faith and piety;
now you are pursuing Christians themselves with fire
and sword. The piety you showed erewhile you are
now changing into cruelty.

"Were it not better for us who are signed with the
sign of the cross to fight against the Turks and Saracens, those most bitter of the enemies of the Christian
name, than to attack our Christian brethren, to the
inevitable destruction of our religion, and to the
depopulation of your own territory? We do it unwillingly; we are compelled; unwillingly and with
tears we advance in arms against you. But since
necessity demands it, and the love of our neighbour,
most inhumanly persecuted, spoiled, slain, by the
Bohemians, requires it, we cannot sit silently with our
hands closed, nor connive at the destruction of the
temples and houses of prayer in which God is invoked
and his worship celebrated, at the breaking and
burning of the images of Jesus Christ, of the Blessed

Virgin, and of all the Saints, at the torturing with
manifold torments of the Catholics, at the treading
under foot of the venerable sacrament, and the plunder
and ruin of all the countries around.  O! with how
great misery and destruction have they filled their
own kingdom of Bohemia, Austria, Hungary, Silesia,
Misnia, Bavaria, Franconia, and the adjacent countries,
—or, I should say, rather, continue to do to this day,
—so that it is grievous even to speak of?

"By this iniquity and these crimes, strange to
human nature, we are roused; not that we seek war
against you, but fight in defence of Christians, and of
our neighbour, for our salvation.  We are consoled at
the number of those Bohemians who are displeased at
this state of disorder, but, while they think with us,
are so oppressed by tyrants as not to dare to remove
it.  It is to free all those who are thus piously disposed
in the Bohemian kingdom, and to punish those who
love and promote this state of confusion, that we have
justly taken up our arms.

"What then, knowing this our zealous affection
towards you, can ye say?  What can you fear for
yourselves?  We bring you peace, we offer it to you,
if there are any among you to accept it.  And as we
have offered you peace, the guilt of war cannot be
laid to our charge, but to those who will not accept
it, and would be wise above measure, all which errors
arise from that evil spirit˙ the enemy of mankind,
who is envious of this kingdom lest it increase in

faith, and love, and righteousness. Yet you ought not to embrace a strange and foreign teaching, nor suffer yourselves to be borne to and fro by every wind of doctrine—a danger which you will easily escape if you embrace the immoveable column of the Christian Church and cling thereto.

"And think not that these few among yourselves have a deeper knowledge than the whole world and the universal Church of Christ, both of the present day and in the ages that are past. What can soldiers, burghers, rustics, and other illiterate persons teach you? Can these excel in understanding the doctors who have gone before or who still remain, not to speak of universities and colleges in which the Holy Scriptures are assiduously treated upon? Will you rather believe two or three men, I know not who or what, than so many doctors, masters, and learned persons, to whom, as they lived so many years before them, not even the suspicion of hatred or contention can attach itself? Look at St. Augustine, who says that he would not believe the Holy Gospel itself if it were not accredited by the Christian Church. Many evangelists have written gospels, but because the Christian Church, which under the guidance of the Holy Spirit does not err, bids us read only four, we receive those only, and withhold our faith from the rest. The same is taught us by all the doctors of the Church with one consent, who will have us keep to the faith which the true Church teaches us.

" To the same Church our Lord and Saviour Jesus
Christ hath promised His Holy Spirit to lead it into
all truth, to preserve it, and to remain with it eternally.
I could produce countless sayings of the Holy Fathers
to the same effect, but these I omit lest I should be
too prolix, and repeat in fine that all Bohemians who
betake themselves into the bosom of the holy Roman
Church may obtain, according to this our promise, a
full and perfect remission of their sins, and pardon
for this guilt in all clemency, tenderness, and love,
yea, in all that a son can ask of a father, or certainly
expect from him.

" May our Lord Jesus Christ, who has redeemed and
bought us for Himself with His most precious blood,
vouchsafe to the Bohemians and endue them with
such a mind that, believing with us, they may embrace
one faith to the good of their own souls and the
peace and glory of their most worthy kingdom.

" Given at Nuremberg on the third of the nones of
July, 1431."

To a letter such as this, the very simplest of the
Bohemian recusants might have given a very profound
reply.   A community in which, as Pope Pius II. himself tells us, the very women knew far more of
Scripture than the priests of Italy,* might well be
expected to reply at least to the religious part of the
cardinal's appeal with vigour and success.

The answer which they transmitted to the legate is

* Æneæ Sylvii, De Dictis Alfonsi Regis.

one which indicates a masterly hand—probably that of Rokyczana himself, if not of Peter Payne, the English Hussite. There is a vein of irony running through the opening passage in which the Bohemians suggest to the cardinal that he cannot but be aware that many salutary precepts were delivered by the Lord Jesus Christ while upon earth, and that the chiefest among them were these, that the sacrament should be distributed in both kinds, that the Word of God should be freely taught, that open and notorious sins, even when done under a pretext of religion, should be punished, and that the administration of public affairs should be taken out of the hands of the clergy. They charge the Roman Church with having deserted the principles of Christianity, and the clergy with having implicated themselves in secular matters and neglected their religious duties.

They maintain that they have simply taken up the cause of Christ after vainly seeking for a hearing from a general council. They forcibly advert to the argument of necessity alleged by the legate, and urge the far greater necessity of teaching and observing the precepts and institutions of Christ, than of obtaining the aid of armies gathered from every part of Europe to force back the Bohemian nation into the obedience of the Roman Church.

They then proceed with as much ease as freedom to deal with the *petitio principii* involved in the latter portion of the cardinal's appeal. They peremptorily

refuse to admit either the legate or the witnesses
whom he cites as the judges in a cause which the
Eternal Word of Truth alone can determine, reminding him of the words, " If an angel from heaven
preach unto you another gospel than that which I
have preached let him be accursed." Human opinions
frequently err in such a case. They desire to reconcile
themselves with the Roman Church by reconciling
that Church with the Scriptures. They point to the
obvious contrast between the methods of Scripture
and the warlike measures with which they are now
threatened, and they significantly remind the legate
that if he had come to them as St. Peter to Cornelius,
he would be received as he was; the ministers of
Christ among them would have rejoiced greatly, and
have killed not only the calf of the parable but the
stalled ox, and have called together their friends and
their neighbours to rejoice with them.

"If you weigh these things well (they conclude),
you will see the reason why we, baptized as we are with
the same baptism as yourself, but exercising the faith
of Christ not with the lips only, but in the life, are
separated and drawn away from you. Wherefore we
pray you to hear us as a brother, and as the world is
near its destruction, to associate yourselves with us
and tread with all your heart in the footsteps of our
Lord Jesus Christ and his disciples. For by this
means the Christian people shall live peaceably here
in tabernacles of hope, and shall come to everlasting

bliss hereafter." Given at Prague in the mouth of July, 1431.

The day for opening the campaign had now arrived, and Julian, at the head of probably the largest army which the empire had ever before collected, moved towards the border-town of Egra. A hundred and thirty thousand men, gathered from every part of Germany, might seem a force sufficient, at least in number, to crush the rebellion of Bohemia, wherever it might show its head. But it wanted the unity and the clear object, as well as the courage and discipline of its now experienced adversary. Its leaders were divided among themselves, and the soldiery looked with indifference upon a cause which could give no inspiration of ardour or courage even to those who were most interested in its success.

The Bohemians, whom the presence of their great general, Procopius, inspired with the highest confidence, and who, by the fusion of the three parties which divided them, for the sake of their common defence, had proved the possession of a more solid unity than that of the hosts who were assembled for their destruction, were not slow in discovering their vantage ground.

The Imperial Army, whose commissariat appears to have been as defective as its discipline, fell at once upon the prey before it; and the villages and towns which lay in the course of its march were mercilessly plundered and burnt. So great was the eagerness

with which the soldiery entered upon their work of
pillage that the consciousness of the presence of a
powerful and dreaded enemy seemed lost altogether.
While they were besieging the town of Tachow, Procopius approached the place with so great a stillness and
secresy as to escape detection, and to cause such
alarm, when his presence was known, that the besieging army fell back on Tysta, which they ravaged with
a barbarity worthy of the cowardice that had prompted
their retreat.

While they were encamped there, the news that the
enemy had followed them, and was fast approaching,
occasioned a panic so wild and universal that the entire camp seemed broken up in a moment. So suddenly and completely did this vast armament melt
away that it seemed rather a preconcerted plan than
an unforeseen misfortune. The scene was strange and
stirring. On the one side generals and princes de-
serting their posts, and the soldiers dropping away
from their ranks; on the other, the energetic legate,
"faithful found amid the faithless," riding from rank
to rank, and from man to man, encouraging, persuading, reproaching, and even shaming them into
fidelity to the cross they had taken; appealing in one
breath, and in every possible form, to their religious
devotion, their patriotism, their fears of temporal loss,
their peril of eternal salvation. Every motive was held
up to them in vain—their courage as Germans, their
pride of a warlike ancestry, their zeal as Christians,

their faith as crusaders, their honour as men,—all were gathered up in the few sentences of exhortation which were multiplied by Julian on this occasion.*

Blending together in himself the characters of the priest and the soldier, between which his whole life was so strangely divided, he sought to kindle the hearts of his crusaders with the fires of religious zeal and of patriotic devotion; but the potency of a blessed banner and a consecrated sword had passed away with the age of the earlier crusades: and though the spectacle of an ecclesiastic urging on an army to a war of faith might excite wonder and admiration, it had ceased to awaken sympathy. The labour was a hopeless one, and the sagacity of the legate must have traced this bitter humiliation of the greatest Christian host that had ever assembled to those political divisions in the empire from which the Church of Rome had already suffered so much, and which, in the day of the Reformation, gave occasion to the greatest and most irreparable of her losses.

This failure of the last attempt to reanimate the crusading army, which is described by Æneas Sylvius (probably on the authority of Julian himself) as so sudden and signal as to be wholly inexplicable, is qualified by Theobaldus, who derives his authority

---

* The set speeches which are put into the mouth of Julian by Theobaldus exhibit too much of the elaborate skill of the historian to enable us to regard them as the exact report of what took place at emergencies so sudden and under circumstances so confused as these. I have therefore given rather the substance than the words of these addresses.

from the Bohemian chroniclers.  For a brief space, according to his statement, they rallied; but the panic returned with the approach of the Bohemian army, and the slaughter was so great that eleven thousand of the crusaders perished on that fatal day, the legate escaping by flight, and leaving in the hands of the enemy the papal bull authorising the crusade, his cardinalitial hat and mantle, together with the cross and other insignia of his legatine office, which were kept and exhibited afterwards at Tysta, where they were to be seen as late as the seventeenth century.

The Archduke of Austria, who had brought up his forces to support the army of Julian, when he heard of the flight of the cardinal, turned off his men into Moravia, which he so far reduced as to extort from the inhabitants the promise to submit without reserve to the decrees of the approaching council.  Julian, returning to Nuremberg, where the Emperor Sigismund awaited the result of the campaign, loaded with the bitterest reproaches the princes of Germany, to whose cowardice and disunion he traced the disasters of the imperial force.

The dreaded alternative of the council was the only resource which now remained to the baffled legate, and the success of ecclesiastical diplomacy had been made so doubtful by the premature appeal to the sword, that it became necessary for the emperor to assume the style of an apologist, and to disavow that hostility which he had (perhaps unwillingly) sanctioned, while he invited to the council now assembled at Basle the irritated malcontents of Bohemia.

" We exhort you," are his words, " and advise you to appear in the council. There you will find the Reverend Father in God the Lord Cardinal Legate of the Apostolic See, and our Vicar, the most Illustrious and Serene Margrave of Brandenburg, whom we have charged to protect all those who come to the council to explain their faith, and to aid and sustain them; to confirm, moreover, all that shall be agreed upon, and to take all pains to convince you how fully your hereditary King and Lord is disposed to gratify your wishes and to advance your interests."

Before we accompany Julian to the Council of Basle, our attention is called back to Rome and to the political changes and altered influences which the accession of Eugenius IV. to the pontificate opened upon the Church and the world.

# CHAPTER IV.

NEVER had a more auspicious day dawned for the Roman pontificate than the 11th of November, 1417, on which the controversies and conflicts of the Church were closed with the announcement which till then had but an uncertain sound, "*Papam habemus*"—no longer the pope of a schism or a faction—no longer a mere pretender to a disputed throne, but the elect of all Europe, whose representatives, with a marvellous unanimity, concurred in the choice of Cardinal Otto Colonna. Centuries of party triumphs had not witnessed so great and unmixed a joy as that which hailed the conclusion of the great work of restoring the unity of the Church in the person of its head. So great was the wonder and delight of the multitude, that, for a long time, they could not even speak, while the joy of the emperor took a more loquacious and practical form. "Overflowing with delight, and regardless of his dignity, he entered the conclave, and gave thanks to all for having elected so great a man, and one so necessary to the all but perishing state."*

It would appear as though Martin V. had been the elect of the emperor, even before he was that of the council, and that the concessions which were made by the co-electors, who had been appointed by the council to act with the cardinals, in order that an Italian cardinal should be chosen, were not altogether unconditional. From a state of almost hopeless disunion, they arrived at so sudden an unanimity in the choice of Cardinal Colonna, that the known predilection of the emperor can hardly have been without its influence. For not only on the ground of his belonging to that illustrious family, which had ever maintained the cause of the empire in Italy, and had become as positively identified with it in interest as it was traditionally connected with it in origin,† but on the far higher ground of the prudence and moderation with which he had balanced the conflicting interests, and overruled the factious dispositions of the council, the desires and even the necessities of the emperor could not have been satisfied by the election of any other.

Even the powerful cardinals of the contrary faction seem to have acquiesced in these feelings, and no member of the college was more influential on this

---

* Von der Hardt, tom. iv. p. 1483.

† The house of Colonna and that of Hohenzollern are believed to be of the same origin, while that of Orsini has its German representative in the Bohemian Counts of Rosenberg.

occasion than Cardinal Giordano Orsini, whose later conduct stood in singular contrast with his disinterested generosity as the elector of a Colonna.

Faithful to the principles which had placed him on the throne, Martin V. maintained to the last the determination to keep aloof from every feud of party or family; and his sudden departure from Constance before the arrival of his uncle, Count Frederic Colonna, and his refusal to remain in Germany after the dissolution of the council, though greatly urged by Sigismund, may be traced to his anxiety to escape even the suspicion of a political leaning. When, from being pronounced "the poorest and the simplest of all the cardinals,"[*] he became to be considered "the richest and most tenacious of popes," he still received the same character of wisdom and moderation, even from those whose jealousy had been awakened by the unexpected change. And when, after thirteen years of an enlightened government, such as Rome had rarely witnessed in the most vigorous ages of the papacy, and certainly has never seen in the period of its decrepitude, the good pontiff was struck with apoplexy, the confusion and dismay which reigned in the city, and spread throughout the Church at the news of so irreparable a loss, may readily be conceived.

To the one great work of building up a solid peace not only in Italy, but throughout Europe, the reign

---

[*] "Der ärmste und einfältigste Cardinal."—(Windek, Vita Sigismundi, c. lxxvii.)

of the pontiff had been dedicated, and if he failed to
satisfy the expectations of those who looked at his
hands for the Reformation of the Church, as well as its
union, he had so strengthened the central power as to
give it, at least, the means of entering successfully
thereafter upon that great work which he had left
unaccomplished.

On the question of the priority of the reformation
or the union of the Church the sentiments of the
emperor had differed from those of the council from
the first.   Sigismund foresaw with that shrewdness
which he was so little able to exercise in his relations
with his own subjects, that when once the election
had taken place the claims of the reformers of the
Church would be set aside, or deferred to the more
convenient season.   With this conviction, he had
urged the importance of the reformation of the Church
as the only safe guide to its reunion.

Against this the cardinals, who were the least
interested in the work of reformation, and whose
power and prosperity had grown up so rapidly in
the anarchy of the schism, reclaimed with energy and
success.*   Having with them the French nation in
the council, which was indebted to the schism and to
the abuses of which Avignon had been the centre for

---

* "Hæ autem taxationes ecclesiarum. . . . reservationes ecclesiarum, etc. in Avenionensi curiâ, ipsâ illic remanente, pro majori parte
initium habuerunt.   Quia *non poterat quilibet Cardinalium illius tem-
poris statum tenere regalem nisi talibus lucris undecumque venirent, quotidie fulciretur.*"—(Gerson de Reform. Eccl. cap. 17.)

K

its undue influence in the conclave, and over the
papacy itself, they had carried the question of
priority in favour of the election to the papacy; and
Sigismund, when urged to press upon the newly-
elected pope the great work of reformation, retorted,
with just severity,[*] "While we were insisting that the
work of reformation should be done before you proceeded to the election of the pope, you would not
acquiesce, and would have a pope before the reformation was accomplished. Lo, now you have a pope,
and we have one also. If you want to expedite the
work of reformation, go to him. For the question no
longer interests us as it did then, while the see of
Rome was vacant."[†]

Thus the election of Martin V. sealed up the question of reformation, and the pontiff entered upon his
work of restoring the papacy without finding it
necessary to redeem the pledges upon which it had
been obtained. The pacification of Italy, the restoration of peace between France and England, the
rebuilding of the ruins of Rome, the union of the
empire in the crusade of Bohemia, these, and many
other features of his reign, have constituted him the
greatest benefactor the Roman Church has ever had in
the long line of her monarchy, while in the convocation of the Council of Basle, to complete the great

---

[*] Gobelinus Persona. (Ap. Von der Hardt, tom. iv. p. 1503.)

[†] To promote this feeling of contentment Martin V. had given to
Sigismund a year's tenths of the whole empire, and concluded concordats with Germany and France.

work which was left unfinished at Constance, he proved,
at least the desire to reform that Church, whose unity
and strength he had restored.

Had he survived to fulfil this desire, the world
might have never witnessed the renewal of that
schism which his prudent policy had closed up, and
his successor might have inherited the proud title
which was inscribed on his cenotaph in the church
of St. John Lateran, "*Temporum suorum felicitas.*"
Yet with all these qualifications Martin V. did not
escape the charge of nepotism, and of enriching the
great family of Colonna at the price of all his earlier
pledges, and to the disappointment of the just expectations of Europe.   Not only had he erected
principalities and obtained fortresses for his house,
thus laying the seeds of its future troubles, and
contributing fatally to the restoration of the anarchy
of the schism, but had advanced his nephew Prosper
Colonna to the cardinalate, which he had pledged
himself to restore to its best estate, and even to
foreign dignities and benefices which the weakness
of the sovereigns of Europe had enabled him to grasp
at anew.

At the age of fourteen Prosper Colonna fulfilled
the prophecy of his name, by obtaining the Arch-
deaconry of Canterbury, and a permission to hold
other benefices to a certain amount in Europe—
while he held also the dignities of cardinal and
archdeacon of the Roman Church.   The immense

wealth which had flowed back upon the Roman
chancery after the accession of Martin V., indicating
the renewed prosperity which had been secured to
Europe by the settlement of the papacy, taken
together with the fact that all the strongholds of
the Estates of the Church were in the hands of the
Colonna, awakened in the cardinals of the Venetian and
of the Orsini interests the utmost jealousy and alarm.

The sudden death of the pontiff gave them an
opportunity of checking the progress of a power
which might otherwise have brought into complete
subjection to itself all the minor factions of Italy.
Of the Venetian members of the college, the youngest
and most promising was Cardinal Gabriel Condolmieri the nephew of Pope Gregory XII., who had
filled several offices of trust under Martin V.   He
had inherited from his uncle that hatred of the
Colonna and affection for the Orsini, to which the
very choice of his name when elected to the Papacy
significantly pointed.   For as Eugenius III. had
raised to the cardinalate the first of the Orsini
family who attained that rank, so Gabriel Condolmieri,
when through the influence of another Orsini, he
took possession of the papal chair, assumed the
name of Eugenius IV., and failed not to carry out
all the traditions of the faction to which he had
attached himself.*

* V. Wessenberg's " Grossen Kirchenversammlungen," &c. tom. ii.
p. 340.

The ·cardinal electors did not, however, proceed to their work without a vigorous attempt to regain the power which they had lost during the reign of Martin V., who, as he owed his election less to the cardinals than to the deputies of the council, who had been in this instance associated with them, was enabled to enter upon the papacy unfettered by a single pledge. Before they proceeded to choose his successor, the fourteen electors pledged themselves mutually by oath, that whichever of them should be elected should for the future insert into the papal briefs the words "*with the consent*," instead of "*with the advice*" of the cardinals—that no new cardinals should be elected but with the consent of the College; that the half of the patrimony of the Church should be assigned to their body; and that a general council should be held at the time and place fixed by the Council of Constance. The second of these conditions was probably the ground of the unjust treatment of Cardinal Capranica, to which we shall have occasion to advert presently, while the other three appear never to have bound the conduct, whatever claims they may have had upon the conscience, of Eugenius.*

The family of Colonna had foreseen the difficulties that were likely to arise on the death of Martin V.,

---

* Raynaldi Annal. ad. an. 1431. n. 5 and 6. A MS. of the original diploma is to be found at Vienna. Its opening words are, " In qualibet monarchiâ tam ecclesiasticâ quam mundanâ." (See Würdt-wein Subsidia Dipl. tom. viii. præf.)

in the separation of his personal accumulations from those which belonged properly to the pontifical treasury.   As soon, therefore, as they heard the news of his death, they delivered up the castles and forts which they held in the name of the pontiff, and handed over to his successor a vast sum which, no doubt, faithfully represented those public funds of which they were the depositaries.

But the jealousy of the Cardinals Orsini and Conti, who took advantage of the absence from Rome of some of the most eminent of the friends of the Colonna, and above all of the Cardinals Cesarini and Capranica, was dissatisfied with this reasonable sur-render of place and power.   Eugenius, too short-sighted to perceive the dangers into which he was being led on, lent a ready ear to the tales of peculation and embezzlement of which the Colonna were accused, and with a rashness which is almost incredible, ordered into custody all the high officials of the court of his predecessor, on the mere suspicion of their concealment of a portion of that money upon which there was a public claim.

In this insane course he was urged on, not only by Cardinals Orsini and Conti, but also by Stephen Colonna who, probably on account of some difference arising out of the division of the property of the late pope, had sided with the opposite faction.   To him the imprudent Eugenius gave the not unwelcome but most dangerous office of seizing the vice-chamberlain of Martin V., only enjoining him to take him into custody and bring him into his presence without tumult or indignity of any kind.

This injunction was so wantonly and purposely broken that it is questionable whether the emissary of the Pope had not at heart rather the embroilment of Italy in a new civil war, than the advancement of the interests of his master. The unfortunate chamberlain, Oddo Poccio, was dragged like a felon into the presence of Eugenius, and even maltreated and plundered by the soldiers who were sent to take him.

In a moment the eyes of the pope were opened to see the dangers he had so recklessly invited. But nothing could repair the injury he had done to the family of his predecessor or to the security of his own succession. Remonstrances and even threats were vainly heaped upon the treacherous emissary, but these were even yet more fatal, as they drove him to the camp of his own family, and enabled him successfully to propagate the report that Eugenius had determined to extinguish the very name of the Colonna. Upon this strange announcement which, though it came from one so little to be trusted, gained ready belief from the experience of the earliest days of the new Pontificate, the Prince of Colonna and all the retainers of that almost regal family flew to arms, while Cardinal Prosper Colonna hastened from the city to join their ranks.

At such a moment there was little chance that any

of the friends of Martin V., least of all those whom he had elevated to the cardinalate, would receive the merest justice, not to say mercy, at the hands of Eugenius. We have seen, indeed, that among the earliest acts of that pontiff was the confirmation of Cardinal Julian in his Legatine office, in Germany and at the Council of Basle, but the conduct of the pontiff to his friend and pupil, the good Cardinal Capranica, proved that it was rather with a view to keep him away from Rome than to give him any real authority elsewhere, that Cesarini received this apparent mark of confidence. Capranica, who had not only enjoyed the instruction, but had shared the friendship of Julian since the days when he was a reader of law at Padua, had been created a Cardinal by Martin V., *in petto*, on an understanding that he should not be so pronounced until the lapse of two years, except in the case of the death of the pope, on which event he should take his place with the other electors. This compact had been sanctioned by an oath to which Eugenius was himself a party.

On the death of Martin V., Capranica hastened to Rome, but being dissuaded from asserting his claim to the conclave, waited until the election was over and preferred his claim to the new pontiff. When, however, he found that Eugenius was putting him off from day to day, and was evidently listening to the suggestions of the Orsini faction, who proposed even to take him into custody, he hastily left the city and retired to Monfalcone. Thither the papal emissaries were

sent to capture him, but he eluded them by flight.
The pope, mortified at his escape, continued his vindictive course by depriving him of his benefices and
estates, and planning even against his life. On this
he appealed to the Council of Basle, which, after
hearing from him an eloquent exposition of all the
wrongs and cruelties which for three years he had
endured from the implacable Eugenius, solemnly
restored him to the cardinalate and reinstated him in
all his rights.*

In the meantime the party of the Colonna began
to re-assert its influence in the college, and the admitted merits of Martin V. and his house roused into
action those who had derived their elevation from him.
" The whole senate began to burn with envy and
hatred."†

Already the narrow escape of the pope from an
attempt upon his life by poison had warned him of
the terrible elements of danger which were concealed
under the peace which his predecessor had bequeathed
him ; while a conspiracy, headed by the Archbishop
of Benevento, a Colonna, and providentially discovered
just in time to prevent its execution, proved that the
hostility which the pope had so rashly invoked by his
earlier acts was as powerful as it was implacable.
In his misfortunes he looked towards the emperor,

* Poggii Florent. Vita Card. Capranicæ, Baluzii Miscell. l. iii.
p. 266.
† Blondi Hist. Decad. iii. l. 4.

whom he had urged to come into Italy for his coronation, and whom he sought to conciliate by hastening
the assembly of the Council of Basle.   For Sigismund, who had never forgiven the dissolution of the.
Council of Constance before it had fulfilled the pledges
of reformation for which it was assembled, looked to
the approaching council as the only available instrument for the pacification of Germany.

From the affairs of Rome we return to the proper
theatre of our history, the empire, whose relations
with the Church were so naturally and unfavourably
influenced by the fatal policy of the new pontiff.   We
left Julian at Nuremberg, engaged in laying before
the emperor and the diet the humiliating history of
the reverses of his last campaign.   Among the most
anxious and interested of his hearers were the deputies of the faithful from Bohemia, who could only
look from so disastrous a past into a future of utter
despair.

The sanguine and undaunted legate, who had been
the first to reckon on the military campaign as the
only remedy for the spreading disease, was now the
first to fall back upon the council from which he had
hitherto augured so little good.   " As I saw no other
remedy left " (are his own words), " I animated and
encouraged all to remain stedfast in the faith, and
to fear nothing, since on this very account I was
going to the council where the whole Church would
assemble."   The panic at the successes of the Hussites

was so universal at this moment, that it needed all
the resources of a mind as fertile in persuasion as
Julian's to restore the slightest degree of confidence.

The zeal of the legate was well responded to by the
nobles of Germany, who felt themselves deeply dishonoured by the late defeat, and attributed all to the
princes of Germany, whose miserable divisions and
signal cowardice had occasioned that great disaster.
They were eager to go forth again, alone, and without
any payment, as mere soldiers of the faith, if a subsidy could be raised for such a purpose. " I answered
them," writes the legate to Eugenius, " by encouraging them in this holy determination, telling them
that I would write to your holiness about it, by whom
I fully hoped this subsidy would be paid, but urged
them at the same time to come to the council, for
whether by your holiness, or by the council, such
a subsidy should without doubt be raised. When
I heard their words, I lifted up my hands to heaven,
thanking God who, in so great an extremity, did not
forsake his Church."

It appears that no answer whatever was sent by Eugenius to the letters which Julian " wrote again and
again " on this important offer. The domestic troubles
of Eugenius are the only apparent reason for this otherwise inexplicable silence ; and as for a subsidy, the
state of the Roman treasury, from which the vast
accumulations of Martin V. had in the first six
months of the reign of Eugenius melted away, *mira-*

*bili profluvio,*[*] was sufficient to render the appeal of Julian as unaccountable to Eugenius as the silence of the pope had been to the legate.

As late as the 30th of June, the pope had been eager and urgent for the immediate departure of Julian to Basle; but no sooner had he determined to proceed thither, than the desires of Eugenius cooled down; and whether the change arose from that suspicious habit of mind which is so conspicuous in all his conduct, or from the sinister influence of the Orsini party, to which Julian himself alludes so frequently in his first letter from Basle, it is clear, that from the first moment that the council became a reality, he had resolved on the perilous attempt to suspend its sessions, and to transfer it into Italy. To this end he used all his influence with Sigismund to persuade him that the pacification of Italy was the first and necessary step to the restoration of the peace of Europe,[†] and endeavoured to draw him into Italy under the pretext of his coronation.

From the real necessity of uniting the conflicting members of the Western Church, he turned to the chimerical project of a reunion with the Eastern Churches. He persuaded himself that the Hussites, as already condemned, had no claim even to an

---

[*] Blondi. Hist. Dec. iii. 1. 4.

[†] Hence, among the instructions to the legates of the council is the following,—"Item, si perdat vestra Majestas istud regnum Bohemiae. . . . non recuperabitis per istos et Ytaliam sed Ytaliam facilius per Alamanniam et Bohemiam."—(Würdtwein, tom. vii. p. 10.)

audience from the council.   He evaded the question
of reform, denied its urgency, and pointed to other
means as better adapted to the pacification of Europe.
These grounds he alleged as moving him to issue a
bull, empowering the legate to dissolve the council,
and to summon another at Bologna, over which he
would preside in person.   This bull was dated the
12th of November, and was immediately transmitted
to the emperor, and to the president at Basle.   The
emperor replied with energy and determination, inva-
lidating, by the most solid arguments, the allegations
of the pope, and demanding the immediate and
unconditional suppression of the bull of dissolution.

The reply of the cardinal-president is too valuable
and important a document to be presented to the
reader in any other words than those in which it is
conceived.   It would be difficult to find any writing
which more completely represents the originality of
the character of its author, and the military and ecclesiastical spirit which animated his public life, often in
rapid alternation, and sometimes in ill-omened conjunction.

"Many things (he writes) compel me to speak
freely and fearlessly to your holiness; the peril of our
faith's overthrow as well as that of the ecclesiastical
order, a withdrawal of obedience from the apostolic
see in these parts, yea and the darkening the very
name of your holiness itself.   Nor less does the love
which attaches me to your holiness and by which you

are animated towards me compel me to take this
course.   Wherefore I will speak with great confidence,
following the words of St. Ambrose to the Emperor
Theodosius, 'No one uses greater boldness than he
who loves affectionately.'   Nor will I spare, if need
be, severe words, since (as says St. Bernard) 'true
friendship sometimes reproaches but flatters never.'
And it is necessary to know the danger that we may
consult afterwards what is to be done.   Unless I
acted thus I should seem guilty of sacrilege and
unfaithfulness to God and man.

"But before I approach the embassy of my
reverent father Parentinus, I beseech your holiness
to bear with me while I relate some of the events
which have passed away, and which may have
escaped your memory, lest it should be believed
that I came here more eagerly than I did.   The
whole Roman court is, I think, aware how distressing
to me was the legation to the council.   No one
visited me at that time to whom I did not very heavily
complain of it, and above all to your holiness, then
in the lesser orders, and to the most reverend the
Cardinal of Bologna, who both sympathized with
me that this province had been assigned me.   For
inasmuch as I went willingly on the mission into
Bohemia I went unwillingly to this, on account of
much which I then feared would happen and already
begin to experience; yet I should not have feared
if this duty had been enjoined me by your holiness.

I arrive at Nuremberg; word is brought me of the departure from the world of my lord Martin, of blessed memory; and as no instrument had arrived confirming me in the presidency of the council, I deemed that this heavy yoke was removed from me. But God, for my many sins, suffered me not to be without affliction.

"The emissary Cuntzo arrived soon after and presented to me that bull which had already reached the hands of many even out of the court of Rome. When I saw it I was distressed beyond measure, and although I was importuned by several to come hither, I wished first to know your holiness' desire in so great a matter, especially as you had been so recently elected. Twice or thrice, and by my own messengers I announced this, and entreated with many prayers that this cup might pass from me; and because I thought myself much better fitted for the Bohemian expedition than for the council, I besought instantly that another might be deputed to preside here. And I remember to have written so strongly on this subject that I sometimes feared to give offence to your holiness, by seeming to refuse that labour after your promotion which I had undertaken in the pontificate of another.

" When I had gone over Germany preaching the cross against the Bohemians, on returning to Nuremberg I found Leonardus de Piscia with instructions

for me to come to the council—if I could do so
without prejudice to the Bohemian expedition. The
same was enjoined me in the letter of the Bishop
of Cervetere on the part of your holiness. But
although I was earnestly requested by many to go
to the council, thinking that I should act more
usefully by entering Bohemia with the army, and
especially as I had heard of but few arrivals at
Basle, I determined to prepare myself for the expedition ; and lest any one should insinuate against
your holiness that you wished to neglect the council
of Basle, which was appointed by former councils
and by your own predecessor, I sent as my deputies
John de Polemar an auditor of the Rota, and John
de Ragusio, telling all that when the business in
Bohemia was settled, I would myself go to Basle
in obedience to the commands of your holiness.
This I immediately announced to you, and received
in the letter of the Bishop of Cervetere your approbation and applause for what I had done.

 " The misfortunes which succeeded in Bohemia, fell
out as it pleased God they should. And when, from
the flight of the army, all the people were at the
utmost pitch of terror and alarm, I (as I saw no
other remedy left), animated and encouraged all to
remain stedfast in the faith, and to fear nothing, since
I was, on this very account, going to the council
where the whole Church would assemble, and in
which a remedy would be found against the heretics

sufficient to resist and to extirpate them. I said
the same at Nuremberg in the presence of my lord
the emperor, and the greater part of the barons
and nobles of Germany. With this too, I encouraged
the ambassadors from the faithful at Pilsen and
Egra, giving them the hope of assistance through
the council. And, indeed, so great was the alarm
of all the population, that it was necessary to do thus.
Let no one, therefore, wonder that I exerted myself
to make all either come or send to the council; for
it was necessary to obviate so many and so great
dangers by finding some quick means of providing
assistance. And, indeed, the mere report of the
council retained many, and even now retains the
states bordering on Bohemia, from joining the rebels.

" The nobles and warriors of Germany who were
in that unfortunate expedition, urged me at the same
time, charging the flight to their princes alone, and
offering again, with a much larger army, to return
the ensuing summer into Bohemia, where they resolved
to conquer or to die. They wished none of the
princes of Germany to be present with them, but
themselves alone to elect that commander, whom,
by long experience, they might judge best qualified.
Nor did they ask more of the Church than the
payment of their common expenses alone, not exceeding, I should think, 30,000 ducats. I answered
them by encouraging them in this holy determination,
telling them that I would write to your holiness

L

about it, by whom I fully hoped this subsidy would
be paid, but urged them at the same time to come
to the council, for whether by your holiness or by
the council, such a subsidy should without fail be
raised.   When I heard this, I lifted up my hands
to heaven, thanking God, who in so great dangers
did not forsake His Church.   For this report and
expectation was bringing to life again the hearts of the
soldiery, already almost dead, and animating them to
resist the heretics.   I wrote directly to your holiness
by the Abbot of Perugia, I wrote again and again.
I thought that when so great an offering on the
part of the army, and such a confederation of
Christendom was made known, the Apostolic See
ought to sell its crosses and chalices and instantly
meet it.

"But now almost five months are gone, and I
have received no answer; but a power is sent me
to dissolve that council in which resides the only
hope of defending the faith and the Church in these
parts.   Yet was it for this very reason that I was
induced to come hither, that if perchance no assistance be provided by the court (of which I have
now no slight fear), some might at least be provided
here.

"My lord the Archbishop of Cologne incited me
besides, for in the retreat from Bohemia he persuaded me that nothing could be of more service
to the expedition than to engage the Duke of Bur-

gundy, whom he knew to be well affected towards
it.   On this account the archbishop said that a
general subsidy should be imposed, which it appeared
would be best levied in the council all present and
consenting.   And it might reasonably be expected
if a great multitude of prelates had flowed together
hither, on considering the dangers now impending,
that no one would have opposed the grant not only
of the subsidy of the tenth, but even of a greater
tax, which might have been exacted without difficulty
afterwards, since it would be imposed in so different
a manner from that of Martin V., the payment of
which, excepting in Italy, was resisted.   A letter,
moreover, which was sent by some Baron of Bohemia
to Nuremberg after the retreat of the army, incited
me to come hither, affirming that that kingdom
could not be conquered by arms, but by concord
and treaty.   To whom I returned an answer that
since a council of the whole Church was being now
celebrated in Basle, the Bohemians should take care
to send thither their plenipotentiaries, since nowhere
better than here could such a treaty be entered upon.
To this end they should have a safe-conduct, and
whatever else was necessary.

"Besides this, the corruption and derangement
of the clergy of Germany induced me to come hither,
for from this cause the laity are beyond measure
indignant against the ecclesiastical order.   Greatly
is it to be feared lest on this account (if they reform

L 2

not in the meantime) the laity may be excited to turn upon the whole clergy in the manner of the Hussites, as they openly threaten to do. And this corruption it is which produces so great a boldness in the Bohemians, and gives a colour of reason to the errors of those who specially inveigh against the immorality of the clergy. Wherefore, even if there had been no general council convened already, it would have been necessary to hold a provincial one, by means of the legation in Germany, for the reformation of the clergy. For it is really to be feared, that unless that body corrects itself, even after the extinction of the Bohemian heresy, others will rise up.

"Your holiness' wish having been considered as well as the above named reasons, who will not consider me in a manner compelled to come hither? But, furthermore, there arrived a letter from your holiness, dated June 30th, in which I am expressly commanded to come hither, in these words: 'We will and command you, when you have fulfilled the Bohemian charge, whose termination is expected, to direct your steps presently to Basle, for the celebration of the council, and there make timely provision according to the injunctions and ordinance of the Council of Constance.'

"But some one perchance will say, 'You have been too diligent in this matter.' A strange thing this! to be accused of diligence when sovereign pontiffs are wont to say, 'We commend your diligence in the Lord.' But stranger far, for that diligence to be blamed, which is exerted in the extirpation of so pestilent a heresy. It was not my wish to deserve that malediction of Holy Scripture, 'Cursed is he that doeth the work of the Lord negligently.' And hence it did not appear to me that your holiness wished me to dissemble or to act negligently in so holy a work. Nay, I was bound to hold the contrary opinion, from having ever known you in all things pertaining to God's honour and the defence of the Church most ardently zealous. But if I be indeed commanded to act with dissimulation or insincerity, I should freely answer, 'Let this burden be laid upon another, for I have resolved never to act the part of a dissembler.'

"Your holiness requires me to make timely provision according to what has been enjoined me, and I know of nothing enjoined me in the bull of Martin, except that I should act with diligence. This the necessities of the Church demanded, and still demand. And I thought that a diligence of this kind not only became so holy a labour, but even brought great honour and glory to your holiness, since as your messenger and minister, and in your name I did all these things. If, therefore, I have done anything, diligently as I was acting in behalf of Christ and for your holiness, I rejoice, yea, and regret.that I did it not yet more diligently. Let whoever will condemn me, I care not; it is enough for me that neither God

nor your holiness condemn me.   Nor yet let any one
allege that this, my diligence in the matter of the
council, was only of recent origin, for the whole
world is witness how ardently, how almost beyond
reason, I laboured for the extinction of this heresy.
Let my reverend lord of Piacenza be asked with
what ardour for three years I have pursued this work
with him.

"What I afterwards did at Rome is known to
the whole court and to your holiness.   This I have
not related for my own praise, but lest any should
imagine that this zeal had come upon me recently
or for any other than the real cause.   And if this
diligence was displeasing to any of the heretics, the
court of Rome ought most particularly to commend
it, since the Hussites desire nothing more eagerly
than utterly to wipe out and extinguish the name
and authority of the Roman Court and of the Apostolic
See.

"Now I come to the embassy of Parentinus, concerning the prorogation and translation of the council.
Oh, that I had been at court; oh, that the dangers
here existing were known there! then, without
doubt, such an embassy had been never sent.*   Its
very rumour has already produced great scandal and
disquiet; how, then, will these be increased when its
effects actually take place?   How far wiser would it

* This is a plain allusion to the fatal influence of the Orsini,
which has been mentioned before.

have been to intimate these plans first to me who am here, that your holiness, well advised of all the circumstances, might afterwards weigh them more maturely; for how can a plan be justly arranged when the case and all its circumstances are unknown? Hear, then, patiently the scandals that must ensue, and how near the consequences of this step will bring us to a total ruin of the faith.

" First, the Bohemians are called to this council. The letters summoning them I sent to your holiness on another occasion. Every one approved this measure as salutary and necessary; for arms having been so long employed in vain, another way was to be tried. Our letter has already arrived at Prague, and the people of Prague reply to those of Egra as is contained in the inclosed letter. We hope that they will come. But if the council is dissolved, what will the heretics say? Will they not turn upon us with insolence and increased effrontery? Will not the Church confess herself conquered by not daring to wait for those whom she herself has summoned? Oh, to how great confusion will the Christian religion be put hereby! For by this flight we shall sanction their errors and condemn our own truth and justice. Will not the finger of God be seen in this? Lo! a host of armed men has often fled before their face, and now the whole Church flies in like manner. Neither arms nor arguments can overthrow them. It will seem a manifest miracle of the Almighty, proving their opinions to be true, and ours to be false. Oh, ill-fated Christians! oh, faith of Catholics deserted by all! Soldiers and priests alike desert thee, none dares to stand up in thy behalf. But will not the sacrilege be laid to his charge who was the cause of this council's dissolution? There is none that will not revile and traduce the Roman Court, which produced so great a confusion of our faith.

"In the second place, will not all the faithful, knowing that the said heretics have been summoned to the council remain thunderstruck, and thinking our faith false by reason of the flight whereby we prove that we dare not defend it, will they not follow the heresy of the Bohemians? especially as the latter have oftentimes already, and now very recently disseminated through Germany libellous documents, containing about thirty articles contrary to the faith, and particularly directed against the ecclesiastical order, fortified, moreover, by many authorities of Holy Scripture and the fathers of the Church, in which they expressly assert that our clergy not having the means of answering them, will escape the opportunity of doing so by not giving them audience. What then will the Catholics say, if, when that audience is arranged, we fly? And let your holiness advert to this fact, that the great majority of these articles are directed against the Apostolic See, and towards the depreciation of the

Court of Rome.  Furthermore, directions have been
sent to all the universities to send the most reverend
doctors and masters they have to this place for the
purposes of the council.

"Thirdly, since it has been everywhere published
that this council is called together for the extirpation of the Bohemian heresy; how much confusion
and ignominy must accrue to the Church if it leaves
its chief purpose unaccomplished?  How great a
danger of evident overthrow impends the Church,
who will not naturally reflect?  Woe to its wretched
ministers wherever they may be found!

"Fourthly, what will the whole world say when
it perceives this?  Will it not judge the clergy to
be incorrigible and anxious to remain always grossly
in their corruptions?  So many councils have been
celebrated in our time which no reformation has
succeeded—men were expecting some fruit, at least,
to follow from this.  But if it be thus dissolved,
they will say that we only mock God and man.
And when all hope of our amendment is taken
away, the laity will deservedly rush upon us in
the manner of the Hussites; and this public report
actually warns us will be the case.  Men's minds
are now as it were pregnant—already do they begin
to cast forth that poison with which they will destroy
us—they think that those who murder and rob
the clergy offer a sacrifice to God; since they will
be deemed plunged in the depths of evil, they will

seem to have become hateful to God and to the
world. And as even now there is but a very slight
reverence paid them, then it will be altogether
withdrawn.

"This council was a kind of link which attached
the laity to us; but when they find all hope failing
them, they will relax all the reins of their conduct
in the severity of their persecution of us. Ah! what
honour will it then be to the Court of Rome to
have disturbed a council gathered together for the
reformation of the clergy? Assuredly all the odium,
all the crime and the shame will be transferred to
it as the cause and the author of so many evils.
Ah! reverend father, be it far from your holiness
to enable any one to say hereafter that you were
the author of so great a calamity—of your hands
will the blood of all who perish thereby be required.
Of all, one by one, will you have to give account
before the strict tribunal of God; what will you
say then? what reason will you then be able to
produce? If against him who offends one of the
Church's little ones so fearful a judgment is threatened
by God, what will be the portion of him who offends
the whole Church together? And to speak without
reserve, so greatly have all been scandalised by the
mere report that I know not what may happen if
it be (as I trust it never will be) realised. Already
they say, 'We trusted that this was he who should
have redeemed Israel.'

"For God's sake abstain from so great an offence; even if you knew that this council will be your destruction. Suffer not yourself to be branded with so indelible a shame, suffer not so great a scandal to ensue. If in your youth, if at every period of your life, if both before and after the cardinalate you have ever shewn the signs of integrity and holiness—if you have ever been the nourisher of virtue and the enemy of vice, how much more ought you to be so now, when you are become God's vicegerent upon earth? But if this take place, even if your whole after-life were like St. Peter's, men would never believe it so to be, they would think it to be all hypocrisy. Henceforth no hope nor faith will be placed in any man, if your holiness permits so great a stain to remain upon yourself.

"Fifthly, it is announced that this council is assembled to establish peace between the kings and princes of Christendom, because the bull of Martin, of which copies were spread everywhere, commands the convocation of the council for this object among others. Already kings and princes are invited, and especially those of France and England, who have been so long warring together. Some preparation towards this has been already made, concerning which I have on a former occasion written to your holiness, inasmuch as I have charged the Archbishop of Cologne to go into France to the assistance of

the most reverend lord of the Holy Cross (Albergati).
I have written, also, to him in answer to an announcement, that if any place were chosen to which
ambassadors might be sent on both sides, it would
be very desirable to send thither a solemn embassy
on the part of the council.

" And let not any one ask why it was necessary
that the council should intrude itself, since my lord
the cardinal of the Holy Cross was sent for this
very purpose; for this plan was held expedient
by all and is commended even by himself,—finally,
whatever is done here is done in your holiness'
name, and yours will be all the praise and merit.
Again, did not my lord Martin first send the cardinal
of the Holy Cross, and then give him a power to
negotiate peace between the Christian princes?
Whatever be the result it may be profitable, but
cannot be injurious.

" Sixthly, the King of Poland, the Duke of Lithuania,
and the Prussians have been written to, in order
that they may be induced, in the meantime, to
suspend their wars; an embassy has been offered
them to treat of peace, and a letter to this effect
has been sent to the bishops of Poland; will not they
consider themselves deluded? How many evils ·may
ensue from that war, I have on another occasion laid
before your holiness. For it is even to be feared
that the one may call in the Tartars and the other
the Bohemians to the destruction of Christendom.

"Seventhly, at this time the metropolitan city of Magdeburg has expelled its archbishop and clergy, and the citizens already are armed with chariots after the manner of the Bohemians, and it is said that they have sent for a Hussite captain; and what is greatly to be feared, is, that that city is in league with many cities and communities of the same party. The city of Passau, which is under the government of the bishop, has, likewise, expelled its bishop and erected engines of war against his fortress. Both these cities are adjacent to the Bohemians, and if they unite themselves with these, as there is great reason to apprehend they will do, they will draw in their train many others. Both have been urged to suspend their warfare. And if any controversy remains between the parties, the council offers its mediation to terminate it, and in other respects so to provide that the citizens themselves may be in the fullest measure contented. An ambassador, moreover, has been sent to Magdeburg to bring about this plan of peace, by writing to the lords and communities adjoining, urging them to interpose their authority also. The same course will be pursued towards Passau when the ambassador has returned. Furthermore, since there is great discord between the city of Bamberg and the bishop and chapter, a discord which is beyond measure perilous from the nearness of heretics, the council is exerting itself to interpose in behalf of peace, and summons both parties who have already come. If, however, the council be dissolved, these discords cannot be removed, but will be increased, and many other cities and towns will fall into the same state.

"Eighthly, by the advice of the Archbishop of Cologne, the Duke of Burgundy has been solicited, and a letter has been sent to him to ask him whether he will accept the command of this expedition against the Bohemians, since he appeared to be very well fitted and disposed towards it; and it is but a short time since he has made a truce for two years with king Charles, the tenor of which expressed his motive thereto to be, the desire to devote himself to the extirpation of the Bohemians, as he was solicited by me. Already he has replied to me, that he wishes to send hither ambassadors to bring about the matter. If the council be dissolved we shall lose this most useful means, and the prince himself will be exasperated against the Church, by which he will say he has been twice deceived. See how wonderfully all things are arranged for the overthrow of the ecclesiastical order. Therefore the most extreme and exact diligence has been, and is deservedly exhibited in order that all prelates should flow together, hither, to impose upon the whole Church, with unanimous consent, some considerable subsidy for this object, exceeding the tenth, if need be. This, if imposed in the council, would be raised without difficulty, which was not the case in the time of Martin.

A copy of the letter of the Duke of Burgundy I send enclosed herewith.

"Ninthly, the officers and nobles of Germany have offered to lead next summer into Bohemia a most powerful army, if only a subsidy be granted them to liquidate their general expenses, as aforesaid. And as four months have elapsed since I announced this to your holiness, first by the Abbot of Perugia, then by many letters, but have had no reply—and they sent to intimate to me by the Master of the Teutonic Order that unless by the octave of St. Martin I could give them an assurance of such subsidy they would dismiss the project of their expedition—I wrote to them, by order of the council, and sent an ambassador, promising them again the same subsidy. I wrote again yesterday, and solicited them, through the two ambassadors, to follow up so holy a work, again promising the same subsidy. Perhaps it may not be obtained from the court, therefore I hastened and hasten the assembly of the prelates, that if it be not obtained from the court, it may be obtained here.

"But if the council be dissolved, in whose name this requisition and this promise also has been made, what will they say? Will they not discontinue the work which they had begun? And this will be of the greatest injury to us by giving an excess of boldness to the heretics, while our own party, deprived of their last hope, will be inspired with fear and distrust, and will be compelled to conclude a peace with the heretics. The mere hope they now entertain is of the greatest benefit, even if nothing follow from it, since it keeps men from uniting with our adversaries. But what is, perchance, worse, will not the whole army and nobility of Germany, seeing themselves deluded and deceived by the Church, be exasperated against the clergy, and, as they are already prepared to do, spoil and persecute them everywhere? How will they open their mouths to gainsay them? 'We were willing,' they will exclaim, 'to expose our bodies and our property for their defence, but they, whose cause we undertook, refused even to give the smallest contribution towards it.' Truly, truly, this is to put a sword into their hands, and to give them an express license to attack the clergy even more violently than the heretics.

"It was not enough, it seems, to have the Bohemians as our enemies, but we must gratuitously add to their ranks this vast multitude of secular nobles. When this is related through the world, will not others applaud whatever these military leaders may do against us?  Will not others, also, be in the end inflamed and incensed against us?

" Behold in how great dangers we are, dangers which to say the truth, we have raised against ourselves. And I shall be everywhere denounced, whose letters, written with my own hand, conveying the promise of this subsidy, are in the possession of these very officers. Assuredly that I may obviate these dangers, that I may not be the cause of this overthrow of the whole estate of the clergy, but may altogether avoid it, I will labour with all my might to influence the prelates who are here to contribute to this subsidy, since, with their counsel, I essayed all this. And if I cannot bring it about, I have resolved to die rather than to live in dishonour. I will go, perchance, to Nuremberg, and put myself into the hands of the nobles there to do with my body as they like, even if it be to sell me to the heretics. My innocence, at least, shall be clear to every one. Behold the reward which awaits my zeal and ardour for the defence of the Catholic faith!

"Sure I am that when your holiness hears this you will determine otherwise; you will even provide otherwise, since eventually all the responsibility, and every mark of infamy, will rest on the Apostolic See and your holiness. How unexpected was this event! I deemed that your holiness would send me the required subsidy, and word is brought to me that I am to dissolve the council. And if your holiness alleges the war we have had as a reason, I reply, that if wars were still raging—even if you were certain to lose Rome, and all the patrimony of the Church—we ought rather to come to the relief of the faith and of the souls of men, for whom our Lord Jesus Christ died, than to that of citadels and walls. Dearer to Christ is one soul, not only than the temporal patrimony of the Church, but even than heaven and earth; for

M

neither heaven nor earth were made after His like-
ness and image, nor was it for them He died. Your
chiefest office, most holy father, is to save souls, following the steps of Him who said, 'I am not sent but
unto the lost sheep of the house of Israel.' I say not
that the temporality of the Church is to be neglected,
but that the salvation of souls is to be valued far
higher.

"But some one, perhaps, may say, 'Who laid it
upon you thus to bind yourself to these soldiers, or to
enlist the Duke of Burgundy?' I answer, the
evident danger of the subversion of the faith; for
unless some hope had been held out to them they
would have withdrawn themselves altogether. Since
I was appointed legate for the extirpation of this
heresy, it seemed incumbent upon me to adopt every
means whereby its extirpation might be effected.
Furthermore, inasmuch as I am his messenger who
is the vicar of that Great Shepherd who laid down
his life for the sheep, I justly indulged and still
indulge the hope that he will not refuse, at least, to
lay down some money for so great an object. To
this is added the consent of the fathers of the council.
But if, perchance, your holiness cannot give the
required assistance, suffer me, at least, with these
of the council to find some method of providing it;
otherwise, I perceive that the faith and ecclesiastical
estate will perish remedilessly.

"Tenthly, since after the retreat from Bohemia

many nobles and cities adjacent to Bohemia have
entered upon truces with the heretics, to prevent
others from doing so these of the council have sent
two persons of consideration through Austria, Bavaria,
Franconia, Misnia, and the states bordering upon
Bohemia, to exhort the people and their rulers to
remain firm in the faith, and since the council is
convoked for this very reason to give them the hope
that it will, at all events, apply some remedy for the
extirpation of this heresy. And some who were
already meditating the negotiation of truces with
the heretics hearing the report of the council, in the
hope that some conclusion might be arrived at against
that heresy, have desisted therefrom.

"If the council is now dissolved, will not the
people of Germany, seeing themselves not only
deserted but even deceived by the Church, make
agreement with the heretics and become more hostile
to us than they? Alas, alas! how great a confusion
threatens us! Our end is inevitable! Already I perceive the axe is laid at the root; the tree is bending
to its fall; it can stand no longer. And while it
might have stood by itself we are hurrying it down
to the earth. At least, let him who will not grant
assistance to the faith, abstain from offering it obstruction. See how many evils, how many scandals,
will follow from such a dissolution?

"And even granting that none of those benefits
which are foreseen from the council follow from its

continuance, yet if it be dissolved all will say, 'If it had not been dissolved so many and so great benefits would have ensued,'—and all this will be imputed to your holiness, nor will you ever be able to wipe off this stain. Suffer it, then, to run that course which it has begun under the sanction of other former councils and of your predecessors, and which has been approved by your holiness' own letters. And although it be said that such prorogation and translation of the place is for a good object, that elsewhere from your holiness' presence greater benefits may accrue, no one believes this, for they say, 'We were deluded in the Council of Siena, again we are deluded in this. A legate is sent, bulls are sent, and, nevertheless, a change of place is demanded and a prorogation.' What hope can then be entertained?

"Moreover, holy father, the scandals which have been detailed cannot be removed by such a prorogation as this. Ask the heretics whether they will postpone for a year and a half the dissemination of their poison. Ask those who are scandalized at the corruption of the clergy whether they will in the meantime let their object be superseded? Lo! this heresy is budding daily; its followers daily seduce the Catholics or forcibly oppress them. They lose not the least moment of time. Daily new scandals arise from the disorganization of the clergy, and do we, notwithstanding all this, temporise in our plans of remedy? Let us do what must be done, now—and

let what is more than that be left for a year and
a half.   I fear that in a year and a half's space,
unless we provide otherwise, a great part of the clergy
of Germany will be ruined.   If this rumour that the
council is dissolved be but spread throughout Germany,
of a surety all the clergy will become a spoil.   Is
your holiness so changed?   You wrote to me to come
hither and make opportune provision according to
what was enjoined me in the Council of Constance.
This I have taken care to do, but if your holiness had
this intention of so soon dissolving, it had been better
not to have begun.   What can your holiness fear, seeing
that you live so holily, that others ought rather to fear
you than you them.   Of a truth, great astonishment
has seized all who have heard these things.

"And that I may not suppress anything that is said
hereupon, some fear that, perchance, severe and pro-
tracted illness may not permit your holiness to consult
as maturely as was requisite.   Martin V. sate on the
papal throne for fourteen years, and nevertheless commanded a council to be held.   And as I remember
your holiness to have twice answered when asked at
different times by me what you wished me to do,
'Do what is right,' I am thrown into a kind of
stupor of mind when I hear such things as this.
Your holiness was wont to be of a firm and consistent
mind, and now you have made a sudden change
without any extreme circumstances to account for it.
Whatever may be the excuse offered for it, men will

not believe that the motive is good; they say, ' If he
cannot come himself by reason of his infirmity, let
him send more and more cardinals; let him send other
men of the highest eminence: this is not the first
council which has been celebrated in the absence of
the supreme pontiff.' Of the security of the place they
allege that there can be no doubt; for the citizens
have pledged themselves to defend the council from
every adversary and in plenary form as at Constance.

"But I hear that some are alarmed lest the temporality of the Church should be taken away in this
council. A strange fear, and one which could only
be entertained if this council were celebrated by
those who are not ecclesiastics. But who is the
ecclesiastic who would consent to such a resolution,
inasmuch as it is not only against the faith but would
redound to their own injury? Who, moreover, of the
laity would entertain it? None, or the very fewest
possible. And if perchance there should be some
princes to send representatives, they will send for
the most part ecclesiastics who would in no wise
give their consent to such a proposal. Nor will those
few laymen who are to be in council have a deliberative
voice when the affairs of the Church are under discussion. And I think that hardly ten secular lords
altogether will be present here in person, and possibly
not even five.

 "Furthermore, I do not think that this council will
be greater than those of Pisa and Constance, and

yet not even in these was the question, whether the temporalities should be taken from the Church, agitated. From the Passion of our Lord to this day, I reckon that about a hundred councils have been held, but in not one of them was this question discussed. How can it be feared, then, that the temporality may be taken away in this? Nor yet was there ever any lawfully assembled council in which the Holy Spirit permitted anything opposed to the faith to be determined. Why is the contrary to be feared in this? This is to distrust the Holy Spirit. I fear that what happened to the Jews will happen also to us. They said, 'If we let this man go, the Romans will come and take away our place and nation.' So also say we, 'If we let this council be celebrated, the laity will come and take away our temporality.' But as, by the just judgment of God, it fell out that the Jews lost their place because they would not dismiss Christ, so by the just judgment of God it will befall that, as we would not let this council take its course, we shall lose our temporality. Would that we may not lose therewith our bodies and our souls! When God wishes to bring any calamity upon a people, He first disposes them not to understand and not to consider their dangers. This seems now to be the case with ecclesiastics, whom I often maintain to be blind, for they see the fire and nevertheless run towards it.

"'This sound of the dissolution of the council has

an evil omen, engenders suspicion, irritates men's minds. Strange indeed! I find that councils have ever strengthened, defended, increased the power and the liberties of the Church; and now we fear that they must needs take them away. But admit that a decree should pass taking away the temporality. The danger to the faith is at least greater if the council be dissolved as was more clearly shown above. But, perchance, the authority of the supreme pontiff will be prejudiced in some manner or other; I do not deem that any one will consent to what is against the canonical sanctions and the decrees of the holy fathers, nor would the Holy Ghost permit it. Never would any council have been celebrated if such a fear as this had invaded the minds of our fathers as it invades our own. But even if we retain this fear, why oppose no remedy to it? Why, to avoid one evil do we seek to incur a greater? Here is, then, the remedy. Let your holiness send some of the most reverend lord cardinals and other as notable prelates and as well affected to the Apostolic See as can be found, well affected moreover to the universal good. Let your holiness give all possible favour to this council and promote it as much as possible. Write to it kindly letters, exhorting the fathers to the holy works they propose, offering yourself, &c. All that the council asks of your holiness, courteously grant. Strive to procure money for the moderate subsidy of the soldiery of Germany.

"Besides this, let your holiness reform whatever remains to be reformed in the court, as you have praiseworthily begun. Write also to these of the council, that if there is anything which they judge requisite to be done by you for the good of the Church Universal, you are ready to do it with all your power. When they see and hear this, sure I am that even if they had a bad disposition towards you they will change it, and will not only study to preserve the authority of the Apostolic See but to increase it : because the more powerful and vigorous the head is, the more will the members be advantaged, since greater will be the the energy that is diffused throughout them. But if they see the contrary, for instance, the dissolution of the council, then they will be offended, and the consequence will be that whereas they were before lukewarm, such an announcement will make them quick and fervent.

"And in truth, when the day before, the citizens, of this place assembled in the public congregation in the presence of Parentinus, and complained of the suspicion which had arisen on the dissolution, and sought for the application of a remedy for this scandal, all the members of the council turned in a manner furious and armed themselves to persevere more boldly; and as far as I can collect from their expressions, are prepared to endure anything rather than recede. They said much, not indeed against the reputation of your holiness, which from your

acts at every period of your life, they greatly commended, and for that very reason thought it unlikely
that this should proceed from the mind of your
holiness.

" Added to this, let your holiness carefully reflect
that besides the dangers which have been already
enumerated, another danger greater than these hangs
over us, that, namely, of a schism, of which I have
exceeding fear, if your holiness perseveres in this
plan of dissolving. Those here will never consent
either to a prorogation or translation, for, as they
said at the time, the decree of Constance expressly
prohibits both. They seemed, moreover, expressly
to protest that the procuring this is to obstruct the
extirpation of heresy, the reformation of manners,
and the peace of the Christian people, and hence
is to foster heresies, sins, wars, and enmities. The
deep significance of this I beg your holiness to
consider, For God's sake, suffer not yourself to be
thus persuaded, for I fear a discord in the Church of
God. I fear that the time is approaching of which the
apostle writes, that ' there must first be a falling away.'
I plainly perceive that for me or for any other to
attempt to dissolve the council, or to change its place
without their consent, were but to invite them to seize
and stone me as a heretic, yea, to tear me to pieces
with their teeth. If any one desires my death let
him send me to Prague, or to the Turks, where I shall
die as a Catholic. In defence of the faith I desire,

and have resolved to die; but not in this manner, to the scandal of the universal Church. If your holiness is pleased that I should be no longer your legate, let this be intimated to me, and after this letter and an answer from your holiness, I will immediately resign the legation. Nay, it will even be more grateful to me for this province to be assigned to another, since I find myself here exposed to many labours, and cares, and difficulties, both of mind and body. I will return to Rome, if this is your pleasure, and remain with greater quiet; and there I trust to be as acceptable to your holiness as any other. But, and in this I supplicate at the feet of your holiness with many tears, do not seek my ignominy and scandal, and not so much mine as that of the faith, and inasmuch as I am bound in behalf of the faith to these military leaders, find the means of fulfilling my obligation. Otherwise, even if I labour no longer as legate, at least I will labour in the council as a private person, that the fathers of the council may grant the aforesaid assistance; but if I cannot effect this, before I can be branded with such infamy, I will put myself into the hands of the soldiery at Nuremberg, as I said before.

"I have now said enough. Let your holiness discuss everything in the best manner, consider my past life, and ask yourself whether you have found me a liar or faithless. God, who will be my Judge, is my witness, that if I had been begotten from your own body, I could not more faithfully advise you. Whatever I have said springs without doubt from the fountain of that overflowing love which I have for God's honour and your holiness. If anything, perchance, has been expressed more keenly than becomes me, be it ascribed to that filial devotion and ardent charity which considers not the dignity of him who is addressed, but is borne along by the impulse of love beyond measure and degree. When the house is on fire the servants may be permitted to cry out and shriek, and if their lord is asleep to awaken him without reverence. Nevertheless, I most humbly ask pardon if in anything I have erred in this letter.

"After what has been detailed above, Parentinus announced a message from the court, and handed me a certain bull giving a faculty of dissolving the council; before which I was empowered to appoint a place with the advice of the council, for another to meet at an interval of ten years. He affirmed that he had nothing touching the council but this : but made some observations upon it to myself and others, which, for the honour of the episcopal rank, I would that he had left unsaid. And because at first many were offended at him, by his own advice I publicly excused him, saying that concerning the conduct of the council he had nothing, but that that rested with me, and that they ought by no means to fear since he would do nothing respecting it. Even he himself had said to persons of high authority, that he should deem that he was making a sacrifice to the devil if he did anything for the dissolution of this council.

" And because all entertained evil suspicions of your holiness on account of this report of dissolution, lest they might think that your holiness was bringing it about for bad purposes and without some motive, by the advice of the aforesaid Parentinus, I read the bull in question to some of the principal members of the council. They answered and said that since your holiness was moved by reasons which were not true, and you were not truly informed of the fact, and were ignorant of the inconveniences and scandals which might accrue from such a dissolution, to the faith and the Church, they desired to send an ambassador to your holiness, who might fully inform you of everything, persuading themselves that after hearing him you would determine otherwise; and that they would by no means assent to this dissolution before they had informed your holiness of that which was true in fact.

" They said, first, that the cause which was expressed in the bull—to wit, that some of the townspeople about Basle were infected with the Bohemian heresy, and were persecuting the clergy—was untrue, for they are all faithful, and nothing of the kind is heard of in these parts. Nay, the citizens of Basle are all good Catholics, and defend and protect the clergy. The second cause, that there was not a safe access on

account of the war between the dukes of Burgundy
and Austria, this is also untrue; for a truce has been
made and no one has ever been injured or spoiled
when on his way to the council. Wherefore, as these
are mainly the motives of your holiness, they pronounce the bull surreptitious. The approach of
winter they do not admit to be a sufficient cause
of dissolution, for those who wish to come do not on
account of the season put off their journey.

" They say further, that this council, so solemnly
instituted, ought not to be omitted on account of the
Greeks; and count it absurd that for the sake of the
doubtful reduction of the Greeks it should be permitted that Germany, which is now and always has been
faithful, should fall away into the heresy of the Bohemians. And this they say is greatly to be feared unless
a remedy is speedily applied; and as to this song of
the Greeks, its burden is now of three hundred years
ago, and is renewed every year. They add that both
objects, inasmuch as they are good, may be accomplished, the one now at the appointed time and the
other in a year and a half's time; that all will gladly
approach the latter subject, the former having been
well completed by that time.

" And much else they say on this matter. On the
point of your holiness' presence, they say that if you
cannot for the alleged reason be present, considering
the danger of the faith and of the ecclesiastical order,
this council, in which is your holiness' legate, and to

which more might be sent, ought not, therefore, to be neglected; and that though Pope Martin asserts in his bull of convocation that he cannot come in person to the council by reason of his known infirmities, nevertheless he enjoined its celebration. Again, the same treaty of the Greeks was pending with the same pope, yet notwithstanding he commanded the council to be assembled. I have held frequent communications with Parentinus on all these points; and though he seems altogether disposed towards the dissolution, nevertheless he said that he had not come but to confer with me on the subject, and that he would be guided by my advice and do according as I should write to your holiness. Nay, I should have even written much sooner to your holiness had not he induced me to wait. After this, early one morning, he precipitately departed without any mention of his purpose to me, and gave out that he was going to Strasburg to exact from a certain collector money due to the apostolic chamber. But now they say here that he was seen to go towards Constantinople.

"I was greatly astounded to find myself treated herein with such dissimulation, considering all that he had said before. I had unsuspectingly trusted him in everything: I grieve that matters of faith are treated and confounded with such mockery. There remained here a young doctor who had accompanied him, who showed me a twofold document; one in which your holiness dissolves the council, another in which you give Parentinus himself a power of dissolving it. I asked him to show me the original letter, since I found him so often to change, and heard so many false and fictitious statements, that I was in a manner compelled not to believe him : up to this time he has not shown it me, but now says one thing and then another. I asked him to go to Parentinus, that if he had anything in his directions he might put it off for two months, until I had consulted your holiness upon it. Unless I see the original letter, I will not believe it; for it does not appear in any way consistent for the dissolution to be entrusted to me, and a choice of a place for the future assembly of the council to be made by it before its dissolution, and at the same time for your holiness to have already dissolved it at Rome, especially when this is expressly opposed to the tenor of the decree of the Council of Constance, in which it is provided that during the month preceding the dissolution of the council, a place shall be fixed upon for the future council with its own consent and approbation. But what was the need of all this mystery? Why were not these things clearly expressed to me? It is a token that confidence is not placed in me. But all this I patiently bear.

"The fathers of the council have altogether resolved to remain here and to continue the council, and to send a person of eminence to your holiness within two days.—I see a door open to great scandal and

confusion in the Church of God. . I see Him already
brandish his sword over· us, the axe is laid at the
root of the tree, the scourge is at hand. Sure I
am that your holiness cannot see the extent of the
offence, or you would rather have died than assented
to it. For God's sake, then, oppose the only possible
remedy which seems to me to be both easy and
proper, and let your holiness write back that as you
were not fully informed on these matters, therefore
you had thought fit to prorogue the council for the
general good for a year and a half's space.

"But since you have heard these things you have
resolved that the council should take its course and
deign to command Parentinus, if he has any power of
dissolving, not to put it forth. At least, holy father,
let your holiness defer it till the month of July,
because by that time the inconveniences and scandals
which now obstruct us will have ceased; the invitation (namely) of the heretics and of the military
leaders for all these arrangements will have been
by that time completed. Some regulations, moreover, may have then been framed for the reformation
of the clergy of Germany, and promulgated there;
and thus something, at least, will seem done, nor
can any blame be then laid upon your holiness,—and
this, indeed, which could not now be done without
scandal and with effect, might then be done more
honourably.

"Holy father, all your holiness' faithful servants

are grieved beyond measure at these things, especially
the archbishops of Treves and of Ratisbon who are
now here. It seems to them and to all that a
perpetual brand will remain herefrom on your holiness and the court of Rome; all will ever denounce
it, the universal church will be publicly and seriously
offended, and your holiness, in one moment, will
lose that reputation of integrity and sanctity which
you have acquired during so many years.

. "May I ask, holy father, what your holiness or the
court of Rome apprehends? Am not I, also, a
member of the Roman church and court? have I
no interest therein? wherefore then are these things
concealed from me? I wither at the thought; con-
fide in me, I pray you, if there is any cause of fear.
Lo, I swear by Him who liveth for ever and ever,
that as far as God permits, I am ready to die and to
go to prison for your holiness. Put off your design
for this short time; there can · be no excuse for
refusing this, for a council to treat on the question
of the Greeks cannot in anywise be impeded thereby;
and further, if you wish, your holiness can convoke
one at Bologna, not only in a year and a half but in
two years' time.

"If, notwithstanding all this, your holiness will not
be turned from your purpose, deign for the love
of Christ to provide the means of freeing me from
the obligation entered into with these generals.
For if your holiness will not give the aforesaid

subsidy, nor these of the council give it either, I am bound, as I have said, to go to Nuremberg and put myself in the hands of these leaders. Rather will I die in their prisons than be the breaker of my promise. If the unbelieving Regulus, for his promise's sake, feared not to return to the Carthaginians, neither will I, who am a Christian and am bound to them for the faith's sake, fear to return to them.

"I know not at this time what I can say more; I have done and do as much as I am able; I can do no more than weep and lament the scandal that I fear must follow from this dissolution. But it is not my transgression, it is not my iniquity; 'I am weary of my crying, my throat is dried.' Do thou, Jesus Christ, aid thy church which thou hast founded with thy most precious blood! I advise your holiness that on my departure hence, or resignation of the presidency, the council will of its own authority create a president. To the instructions touching what has hitherto been done here, I answer fully in the inclosed paper; all that is done has been done in accordance with the dispositions of the common law, the form of the councils of Pisa and Constance, and the bull of Pope Martin, with the consent, moreover, of those who are here."

"Thus," to use the words of an eminent writer of the modern Roman Church, "spoke this great prelate, who had a single eye herein to the truth and to the

interests of the Church."*     Of the perfect authenticity of this letter, which Spondanus has sought
to discredit, but with a criticism as impotent as
his frequent appeals to the revelations of St. Bridget
are infatuated, we need say no more than that it
is found in all the earliest and most authentic manu-
scripts of the acts of the council, including those
at Basle, at Vienna, and in the Harleian collection,†
and above all in that of the College of Navarre,
written by the very hand of a person present in
the council.   While, as incorporated by Pius II. in
his history of the later acts of the council, in justifi-
cation of his continued adherence to that body, it
stands upon a foundation of authority which the
conjectures and assumptions of Spondanus can never
in the slightest degree disturb.

* Abate Vertua da Soresino "La scienza teologica," tom. xi. part
p. 80.
† No. 826.

# CHAPTER V.

JOHANNES DE POLEMAR, an auditor of the Rota in Rome, and Johannes de Ragusio of the order of Friars Preachers, had arrived in Basle about the middle of July, 1431, as the deputies of Cardinal Julian. Few of the prelates had then arrived, for the crusade in Germany as well as the hostilities between the Dukes of Austria and Burgundy, rendered the access to Basle difficult and even dangerous. The commissioners had nevertheless held several preliminary congregations, in which they prepared the way for the public sessions of the council. About the middle of September, the arrival of the cardinal from Nuremberg gave a new impulse to its assembly,* and the gradual accessions to its ranks before the close of

---

* His letter of invitation to the University of Cologne, beginning " *Quum necessarium sit instanti tempore*," is dated Sept. 17th. Julian took up his abode near the church of St. Leonard's, where he appears to have remained during his sojourn in Basle. A document signed by him in 1436 is dated, "Basileæ, apud S. Leonardum in ædibus solitæ residentiæ memorati cardinalis."

the year enabled the president to inaugurate its public
sessions in the December following. The interval
was employed in renewed negotiations with the
Bohemians, and in the endeavour to bring about a
reconciliation between Burgundy and Austria, an
object whose importance is urged upon Eugenius in
the letter of Julian, which has already been laid before
the reader.

On the 15th of October, he addressed another
letter to the Bohemians, inviting them to the council,
and promising the freest and fullest consultation of
their differences with the Roman Church, and of the
means of their re-union. This letter he transmitted
to the emperor by Hamman von Offenburg, a senator
of Basle, and Johannes Gelhusius, Abbot of Maulbrunn, who found Sigismund at Feldkirch in the Tyrol,
upon the point of passing on to Rome, for the cere-
mony of his coronation. The emperor forwarded this
invitation together with an urgent letter of his own,
disavowing the hostile sentiments which the popular
belief attributed to him, to the chiefs of the Hussite
party at Egra, who returned a dignified and vigorous
answer. They defended their "honest disobedience"
to himself and the see of Rome, on the high ground
of their supreme allegiance to God, and declined an
invitation which appeared to them only an insidious
method of depriving them of that religious freedom
which they had so successfully asserted against the
united force of the whole empire.

The letter of Julian was, as ever, earnest, persuasive, and full of professions of the most exalted charity. "It will be permitted you," he writes, "to speak freely your religious opinions, to consult, and to propose methods of union. We have heard that you have often complained that an audience such as you require has never been conceded to you. This subject of complaint will henceforth exist no more ; you shall be heard in future publicly, and as often as you desire. On this account we pray and entreat you with all our heart and with all our soul, in the name of the Holy Spirit, to delay not entering by the fair and great door which is now open to you, and to come in all confidence to the council. And though we have provided for the security and freedom of every one in the council, in case you should nevertheless be restrained by any diffidence herein, we are ready to give you a safe conduct full and sufficient for your journey hither, your sojourn, and your return, and will grant you in the name of the universal church everything that can contribute to the safety and liberty of your deputies. We pray you to choose these wisely, and to send pious, mild, and conscientious men, humble in heart, peace-makers, and disinterested, and such as ' seek not their own, but the glory of Jesus Christ.' "

The minds of the fathers, occupied as they were by the Bohemian negotiation, were soon distracted by the affairs of Rome, where the hitherto confused

conduct of Eugenius was assuming the definite policy
of hostility to the council and a resolute determination
to dissolve it before it could enter upon its reformatory
labours.

While the legate was anxiously expecting letters
confirming all that had been done, and promising
even pecuniary aid, an emissary of Eugenius brought
with him, at the close of November, a bull, authorising,
on various pretexts, the dissolution of the council, and
the convocation of another for a future day at Bologna.
The bearer of this fatal document was Fantino
Valleresso, a Venetian, who had been recently translated from the Bishopric of Parenzo to the titular
Archbishopric of Crete, which he represented in the
Council of Florence.*

The reader will recall the bitter complaint made by
Julian, of the duplicity and inconsistency with which
this ecclesiastic carried out his mission. First, he
assumed almost a legative character, then that of an
ambassador, then reduced his pretension to that of a
mere adviser and consulted with the legate and the
council. He had in his possession other bulls and
instructions, which came to the knowledge of Julian,
and awakened in him the deepest alarm. The mystery
and dissimulation which reigned in the Councils of
Eugenius rendered it impossible to foresee the nature
of his policy, or to guard against its dangers except by

* He is called sometimes "Episcopus Venetus," at other times,
" Parentinus."

the vigorous and independent action of the council. With these convictions he wrote the letter which, on account of its recapitulation of the events which hastened his progress to the council, has been already given, and while anxiously awaiting the result of the mission to Egra, entered energetically upon the work of establishing the council upon a solid and indestructible basis.

The first public and general session was fixed to be held on the 14th of December, on which day, after mass of the Holy Ghost had been solemnized by Philibert, Bishop of Coutances, and the prayers and antiphonies proper to so great an occasion chanted with all the pomp of the Roman ritual, the Cardinal President, in full pontificals, delivered an eloquent and fruitful discourse on the words of Isaiah (c. lii. v. 11), " Be ye clean that bear the vessels of the Lord "—" in which," say the acts of the council, " he exhorted all to purity, cleanness, and integrity of life, with much judgment and unfeigned charity." Then were recited that decree of the Council of Constance—the celebrated decree *Frequens*—under which this of Basle had been assembled, the bull of Martin V. convoking it, and appointing Julian to preside over it, and that of Eugenius confirming this convocation and appointment. Upon the basis of these decrees the council passed several resolutions asserting its own authority and indefeasibility.

In the meantime the news of the attempted disso-

lution had roused not only the indignation of the
council, and of the senate, and people of Basle, but,
passing rapidly on through France and Germany, had
everywhere drawn forth bitter remonstrances against
the party of Eugenius, and earnest addresses of
encouragement to the body whose existence was so
prematurely threatened.   The University of Paris sent
letters in January, 1432, urging the council to the
most determined resistance, while the Cardinal of St.
Eustachius complained of an appearance of too great
leniency towards the pope.   The possible necessity of
suspending him from his office was openly canvassed,
and an anonymous writer went so far as to prove that
such a sentence need not be preceded by the usual
proof of contumacy.   At the same time came forth
other writings proving the legitimacy of the position of
Julian as president of the council, notwithstanding the
attempted dissolution.*

Nor did the cardinal himself act unworthily of the
spirit of his memorable letter.   He assumed the
highest spiritual powers of his office, as appears from
the licence he gave in the name of the council to the
University of Cologne, to choose a confessor for giving
absolution in the cases reserved by the pope to himself alone.†   Eugenius had, meanwhile, received from
the Emperor a letter of remonstrance against his

* All these are referred to by Würdtwein as extant in the Imperial Library at Vienna.  (tom. viii. præf.)

† This concession, beginning, "*Benigne sunt nobis illa concedenda,*"
is also at Vienna.  (Würdtwein ut sup.)

intended *coup d'état,* couched in language which must have seriously alarmed, though it failed to deter, the venturesome pontiff from his dangerous project. After destroying with a few touches of his pen the web of pretexts with which Eugenius had concealed his real motive, the Emperor enjoins him to go in person to Basle, and at least to send an immediate revocation of his bull of dissolution. Eugenius, however, was inexorable, and the formal bull of dissolution was issued only four days after the first session of the council. All Europe reclaimed against the fatal act, which recalled the disappointment of the council of Siena, and threatened a renewal of the great schism, at a period when the dangers of Europe were so greatly increased. The kings of France and England had seconded the remonstrances of the Emperor, but the weight of opposition seemed only to increase the obstinacy of Eugenius.

But the discouragements which the council had met with from the court of Rome, were greatly relieved by the prospects of success which were already opening upon their embassy to Bohemia.

In consequence of the interviews of the emperor with the Hussites, it had been arranged that a congress of the deputies on the part of the council and on that of the Bohemians should be held at Egra, in order to promote the great object of an immediate negotiation with the council itself. On the side of the council the celebrated Dominican, Johannes Nyder,

and the abbot of Maulbrunn were associated in this
embassy with Philibert, bishop of Coutances, Johannes
de Polemar, and Henry de Toke, a canon of Magdeburg, who took a conspicuous part in it.

On the 25th of April they arrived at Egra, and
were joined on the 8th of May by the deputies from
Bohemia, who were addressed at the residence of the
elector of Brandenburg by Henry de Toke on the
words, "Peace be unto you." After several conferences the following points were agreed upon as the
conditions of their acceptance of the invitation of the
council. First, they claimed an entire freedom in
going, staying, and returning; next, the liberty and
right of determining, on the ground of Scripture
and antiquity, the controversies pending between
themselves and the Church of Rome; . thirdly, the
right of celebrating divine service according to their
own usages without hindrance or ridicule; fourthly,
they stipulated that until their arrival the council
should not be continued; fifthly, that it should be free
and open to all; and lastly, that its headship over the
pope should be maintained. These preliminaries being
admitted, the deputies of the Bohemians, after returning to Prague, proceeded to the council to obtain the
confirmation of them, and to procure a safe conduct in
a proper form.

This first stage of success led the cardinal to address
a second letter to Eugenius, even more vigorous and
decisive than the former one, in which he continues

and enforces the arguments of that eloquent appeal with the skill of an accomplished canonist and the zeal of an enlightened churchman.

" Now at least," he takes up abruptly the thread of his former letter, " the whole world will know whether your holiness hath the bowels of fraternal love and the zeal of the house of the Lord; whether you are sent for peace or for discord, to gather or to disperse; whether you are that good shepherd who layeth down his life for the sheep. Behold, already the door is opening through which the lost sheep are to return to their own fold. Behold, already there is hope in the gate that the Bohemians may be reconciled. If your holiness even now assists and promotes this work as you are bound to do, you will obtain glory both in heaven and earth. But if (which can upon no ground be believed) you endeavour to obstruct it, all will accuse you of impiety; heaven and earth will unite against you; there is none who will not forsake you. For how can they follow him who, when by a single word he could restore peace and tranquillity to the church, refused to speak it? But I begin to hope better things, and to believe that now your holiness without any excuse will favour this council with your whole mind, and give thanks to God that for so worthy a purpose this assembly has not departed hence. Behold the legates of this holy council, in replying to us from Egra, announce with joy and exultation how, through the grace of the Holy Spirit,

they have entered into a firm engagement with the
ambassadors of the Bohemians, (those namely of
Prague, of the Orphans, and of the Taborites; among
whom there were present the generals of this people,
especially Procopius,) to this effect: that a solemn
embassy of all the States of the kingdom should come
to the Council of Basle upon a safe-conduct being
transmitted to them according to a stipulated form,
which shall be done without delay. With wondrous
joy, and hands upraised to heaven, this holy assembly
rejoiced thereat;—for our ambassadors allege that
this treaty was made with such exceeding charity, and
that they saw and conjectured so much while with the
Bohemians, that they justly conceived the greatest
hope of their reduction, and at length departed from
Egra after embracing them tenderly and with tears of
joy, the Bohemians themselves urging them to hasten
as much as possible this business. They related that
many things occurred in this negociation of such a
kind, that if any one wept not for joy when he heard
them, he would show himself but coldly affected to
Christ. On three out of the four articles they appeared to make no difficulty: on the fourth (the
communion under both kinds), there is a hope that
they will follow the judgment of the council. Who is
there that can now dare to advise your holiness to
persevere any more in your intention of dissolving the
council? Even if it had never been convoked, for so
great a hope and so great a necessity it ought to be

convoked now and in this place.  How praiseworthily
would your holiness act were you to dismiss your
care for Italy and everything else, and come hither in
person even if it were necessary to travel in a carriage.
The temporal care and defence of the patrimony of
the Church may be provided for amply by legates and
vicars.  The true patrimony of the Church is to gain
souls.  For the Church is not a heap of stones or
a pile of walls.  Christ did not constitute you the
guardian of castles and walls, but the shepherd of
souls; and therefore that which is more necessary and
dearer to Christ ought to be done in your own person,
and the rest by deputy.  It was thus the apostles did,
who, that they might more freely addict themselves to
the preaching of the word of God, appointed seven
who should serve tables and minister in inferior
matters.

"I hear that, through the grace of God, your
holiness improves in health from day to day.  And if,
as it is said, you now visit some churches on foot,
perchance on horseback, you will be able to come
hither.  You could not come to a more useful
business or one better becoming your office than to a
place whence innumerable blessings are expected to
proceed.  Let your holiness reflect in what labours
Christ, whose vicar you are, St. Peter whose successor you are, and the rest of the apostles and
sainted pontiffs exercised themselves; and as you
have succeeded them in office, succeed them also
in life.

"But if your holiness refuse to come hither, I advise you, for so great a good, to send the majority of the most reverend cardinals of the Roman court, and to charge all the prelates to come hither. Withdraw not, obstruct not (as it is reported you do), those who desire to come, but rather encourage them so to do. Believe me that love alone impels me thus to advise you, separate not yourself from your members; cherish your sons as a hen doth her chickens under her wings. If even you send no one for this purpose, at least say this one word—I will that the Council of Basle be held. For at this time another piece of intelligence has reached us, on account of which your holiness ought altogether to desist from the dissolution. The reverend father, the archbishop of Lyons, has written to the council, and to me also, that the prelates of France have assembled in the city of Bourges, and there, after a long and accurate examination, they concluded that the council is lawfully assembled here, and that it is necessary that it should be celebrated here and now, and that the prelates of France ought to join it.

"The motives and reasons by which they were led to this conclusion he has also forwarded; I believe that a copy of them has been sent to your holiness by others. Wherefore, then, can you delay any longer? You have endeavoured as far as you could by messengers, letters, and various means, to draw away the prelates; you have laboured with all your might for the dispersion of the council. Nevertheless, as it seems, it increases daily, and as the prohibition becomes more absolute the opposition of every one becomes more vehemently inflamed. Is not this, I ask, to resist the will of God? Why do you provoke the Church to indignation? Why do you irritate the Christian world? Deign, I entreat you, so to act as to obtain the love and favour, not the hatred, of the world. Exceedingly must it be offended at hearing these things. Do not suffer yourself to be led away by any one who would insinuate into your mind a fear where there can exist none, or persuade you that this is not a legitimate council. I know that I shall offend your holiness by seeking to prove that it is. But it is better that I should offend a little in words and profit in deed. Thus the physician applies to the sick man the burning cautery, and heals his wound. Nor can the medicine profit unless its taste be bitter.

" In this persuasion, I will not fear to lay open the truth, that knowing it, your holiness may more piously consult for the Church and for yourself. Whether this council be rightly constituted or not depends upon the Council of Constance. If that was a true council, so is this. Yet no one seems to doubt whether that was legitimate, or hesitates to receive what was there decreed. For if any one were to affirm the decrees of that council to be invalid, he obliges himself to the conclusion that the privation of Pope John made upon the strength of its decrees is invalid also. But if this be invalid, neither does the election of Pope Martin hold good, made as it was while the former yet survived. If Martin was not pope, neither is your holiness, elected as you were by cardinals created by him. No one, therefore, is more deeply interested in upholding the decrees of that council than yourself. And if any one of its decrees be called in question, on the same grounds could all the rest of them.

"For the same reason the decrees of all the other councils must fall, for if our faith in one council is shaken all the rest are shaken with it, as St. Augustine argues, and is contained in the ninth distinction, in the chapter *Si ad Scripturas*. Thus the faith and all the mysteries of the Church will give way if a doubt is entertained of one single council lawfully constituted. Now by the Council of Constance a decree was passed beginning *Frequens*, in which it is appointed, that the first succeeding council shall be at the expiration of five years from its dissolution, and the next in seven years' time from that. Accordingly, five years after the termination of the Council of Constance, that of Siena was celebrated, after whose termination, seven years having elapsed, the celebration of this council is begun. To what end, therefore, is this expressed in the bull of dissolution among other reasons, that the seven years is now passed? Seeing that it was requisite that it should elapse before the celebration of the council, these

words, in seven and in five years' time, meaning, in
legal acceptation, that all the divisions of time contained in them are completed and the term of them
waited for. Hence it was necessary for seven full
and entire years to pass before this Council of Basle
could be opened, as a full period of five years had
passed before the opening of that of Siena. But
some one may say it ought to have been celebrated on
the first day after the expiration of the seven years,
else the council must expire too.

" But it may be obviously replied that it is not contained in the chapter *Frequens*, that unless it is begun
on the first day the power of celebration is at an end;
nor can this be deduced either from the words or the
intention of that law. It only provides that it should
be celebrated after the seven years—accordingly,
whether it is celebrated on the second or third day—
on the first, second, third, or fourth month after the
seven years, the chapter *Frequens* is satisfied. For
when the first day arrives then the power of celebrating begins; but before that it does not. Afterwards,
however, it is not prohibited, nor is this opposed by
the fact that in the chapter *Frequens* the expression is
inserted 'in the five years immediately ensuing,' which
seems to be repeated in the case of the seven years'
period also. Since it is not meant that the celebration
is necessary punctually on the first day after the seven
years, but the words immediately following are only
placed there lest another seven years' period beyond

o 2

this should be supposed, although that word *from* (de) was clear of itself—for when we speak simply of seven years we understand those which are nearest to us—this addition was made, then, for greater precision.

" Add to this, moreover, that even if, in the chapter *Frequens*, there had been inserted after the words 'immediately following' any such words as these— without delay, presently, continuously, or instantly, or words synonymous; still they ought to be interpreted with some slowness and some interval of time, and as speedily as was practicable, as such words are expounded by lawyers and doctors. For they are extended and contracted according to the subject matter, and the various circumstances of things. It is in every way incredible that it could have been the intention of the legislation considering the length of the journey, the difficulty of preparing for a business of this kind, and the many obstacles that may occur in it, to limit the time so strictly to the first day as to make the legal existence of the council dependent upon this condition. For if we pursue these subtleties we must have it not only on the first day, but at the first moment, yea, the first second after the seven years' period.

" But, since words are to be taken in their general meaning, such an interpretation is strange and unwonted. And if any argues that in this case there would be a prorogation, which is prohibited in the same law, I reply that he who thus affirms neither understands his own meaning, or the value of words. For that is not prorogued which is begun in the second or third month, but is rather a continuation or execution of what there is already a power to do. For if it had been a prorogation, then, since a prorogation has the nature of a former delay, it could not begin before that period to which prorogation is made. But this is not true in the present case. For, although the council was not begun in the first month, but in the second or third, it is not to be concluded from this that it could not be begun in the first. But, if there had been a prorogation to the second month, then it could not have been begun in the first. For instance, I promise to give Titius a sum of money after Easter, he cannot exact it before Easter, but after Easter he can; and, even if he does not, I do not cease to be bound; and, although he does not exact it till the second or third month, it is not therefore understood to be postponed, nor does it follow that I could not be compelled to pay in the beginning, which would not have been the case had there been any postponement. The nature of a prorogation is this, that it must be declared before the lapse of the first term; after that it is not properly a prorogation, but a new convocation, a continuation.

" And if it is said, 'Can it then be put off for a long time?' I answer that herein we must abide by the judgment of the Church, which, having considered

the different circumstances, will determine the due
season; for it is for her benefit and advantage that
this power of celebrating councils was instituted.
For how would it be if, in the place of its celebration, when the period arrived, the plague were to
supervene, or a siege, or anything of the same kind,
which might continue for three or four months? if,
moreover, the pope had not, in the meantime, changed
the place of assembly, according to the form of the
chapter *Frequens*, and, on account of these obstacles,
the prelates could not come on the first day to the
appointed place? or if any of the prelates, coming to
the council, were taken prisoners by the way, who
otherwise might have arrived there on the first day
and earliest moment?—shall it be said that for this
reason the power of holding the council has expired,
and that when the obstacle was removed, and the
prelates had arrived, the council could not be celebrated? This surely would be very absurd, and, too,
injurious to the Church of God. In our case, however, there was a sufficiently just reason for the delay
of the prelates beyond the beginning of the term.
For when it was approaching, on the 20th of February, Pope Martin died, on which account the prelates might reasonably doubt whether there was any
impediment to the council. At the same time, they
waited to see if any should come thither in the name
of the pope, lest, without an apostolic president, they
should remain in the place in vain. The legate, how-

ever, who was appointed to the council, and whose presence was expected before he prepared himself for his journey, did not arrive at the council at the appointed time, but went to Nuremberg to pursue the extirpation of the Bohemians, according to the injunction of Pope Martin, which charged him to go thither before he went to Basle. The same legate was oftentimes importuned by the emperor, when in Nuremberg, to go to Basle to celebrate the council, according to the power given him; but he replied that he was unwilling to go before he had the consent of the new pontiff.

"This, therefore, was the cause of the delay of the prelates. Nor can these prelates be reprehended for suspecting that Pope Martin was not willing to hold the council; for they feared to put themselves in a position of inconsistency and contradiction, and had reason to entertain such a fear from what had happened in the Council of Siena; and much was said at the time which indicated suspicion. I remember it to have been told me that some had said that I was come into Germany to disturb the council. It was also the view of Pope Martin that, although the council was not opened in the beginning of March, the power of celebrating it had not expired; for when the period of the council was at hand, he wished me to go towards Bohemia, before I went to the council, of which wish the consistorial bull of dissolution makes mention.

"But why need I prove this from any other source than your holiness's own letters? In your letter, dated May 31, and therefore long after the appointed term, which letter was actually presented to me three months later, you command me to hasten the affair of Bohemia, whose close was shortly expected, and direct my steps towards Basle, to celebrate the council, and there to provide opportunely according to what was enjoined me, and ordained in the Council of Constance. You even repeat this in the bull of dissolution, brought me by Parentinus, whose words are these : 'We gave our instructions to your discreet excellency,* by reason of the non-assembly of the prelates at Basle for the celebration of the council at the period of your visit to the part of Germany, to direct your attention in the meantime to the expedition against the Bohemian heretics like-wise entrusted to your care, and thence to proceed to the city of Basle, the place of the said council, there to preside in our and the Church's name.'

"What, I ask, is clearer than this? If any doubt remains, by the tenor of this letter it is obviously removed. And if it is alleged that neither Pope Martin or Eugenius could give validity to the council by writing such letters, since that would be a pro-rogation, an act prohibited by the chapter *Frequens*, I answer, that it is not a prorogation, but the execu-tion of a legitimate power, or rather a declaration that

* Circumspectioni tuæ ... dedimus in mandatis.

it is not necessary to celebrate the council precisely in the beginning. Moreover, it is not a prorogation, because a prorogation must be before, and not after the period in question; for if after it, it would be rather a new convocation, and a new question would arise; and if it be said it could not be convoked anew, then it may be objected, How then can the convocation of the Council of Bologna be legitimate? And if it be affirmed that the new convocation of the Council of Bologna has force because that of Basle has been dissolved by your holiness, then I have this difficulty: if it was dissolved, then it must have existed as a council, for deprivation pre-supposes possession; but if it was a council previously, then (as will be proved below) it could not be dissolved without the consent of the council. What can be said in reply to this?

"To illustrate it still farther:—On the very day of the appointed term, or before, the Abbot of Vezelai having assembled for this purpose the officials of the great church, and certain other prelates and men of consideration, made a solemn protestation to the effect that the time for celebrating the council had arrived, and that he was come to Basle to require all present, until the rest of the council arrived, to treat and confer together; and of this a public instrument is in existence. Within a month's time came the ambassadors of the University of Paris, and began to treat of the things pertaining to the council,

even writing to the emperor, and to other princes of
Germany, to send representatives to the council, which
letters I then saw. Nor does the fewness of members signify, for where there is authority, a great
number is not required, according to the words of
Christ, " Where two or three are gathered together
in my name, there am I in the midst of them ;" in
virtue of which councils are held. Now, therefore,
your holiness must see more clearly than light itself
that the aforesaid objection is sufficiently frivolous.

Again, why is the dissolution made if the council
is not in being? Wherefore, on no ground can it be
doubted that the council is legitimate, and canonically
assembled; and, perhaps, scarcely any council can be
found sustained by so many authorities as this is,
confirmed as it is by the two preceding Councils of
Constance and Siena, and by two Roman pontiffs.
I hear that, among other things said of me at Rome,
it is alleged by some that I could not call the prelates
to come to the council, because in the bull of Martin
this clause was not added. I am exceedingly amazed
at this objection. In the first place, I did not alone
call them, but I and those who were here assembled
in the council. A marvellous thing! Pope Martin
gave me a power of extirpating heresies with the
advice of the council, of pacificating kingdoms, of
reforming the manners of every order of the Christian
community, and dare they say that I am not empowered to cite? The power of judgment and of

condemnation is given to me, and have I no power of citation? The jurisconsult would say, he to whom jurisdiction is entrusted, receives therewith a power to do all which the exercise of that jurisdiction requires. But how can the aforesaid things be done, unless the prelates and others come hither?

"Again, why is it said in the chapter *Ego enim (de jurejurando,)* 'being called to a council, I will come,' if there is no power of calling thereto? By whom is the summons implied to be sent, unless by the council, or by him who presides therein? The whole 18th distinction speaks of nothing else than this, that bishops summoned to a council and not coming are liable to excommunication and suspension. Let such read the book of the councils of St. Isidore, and they will find in many councils that the prelates were called by the council. It now remains for me to speak upon the point whether the dissolution is of force. Again I am afraid to speak, fearing to irritate your holiness, but love constrains me. For perhaps your holiness believes the dissolution to be of force, and, therefore, persists therein; wherefrom since many scandals must ensue, my conscience urges me to remain no longer silent. In the first place, the chapter *Frequens* appears to imply that it is not of force. For if a prorogation is prohibited, which is less, far more is a dissolution, which is greater, for it is a greater act to do away than to defer; by proroguing you defer, by dissolving you do away. Those here say, also, that the aforesaid constitution *Frequens* would be thus easily rendered abortive ; since immediately the council was begun it might be dissolved without accomplishing anything, as they say was done at Siena, and say farther, was done by your holiness on this occasion upon sinister and false information. They allege, moreover, that the aforesaid dissolution evidently tends to the overthrow of the faith, the ruin of the Church, and the confusion of Christian people, and that, therefore, it ought not to be done, and cannot be obeyed. They affirm further that the said dissolution could not be made, opposed as it is, by a decree of the Council of Constance, since in those things which pertain to the faith, to the extirpation of the schism, and to the reformation of the Church in its head and in its members, every one, of whatsoever rank he be, even the pope himself, is bound to obey the statutes and ordinances and precepts of every general council, and unless he obeys may be punished, &c. So, to be able to pass a law against any one, to be able to punish the disobedient, these are manifest tokens of a superior power in those in whom the law commands, ordains, or punishes. To be bound, moreover, to obey, to be subject, and to submit, are signs of inferiority in the aforesaid cases. Therefore in them, since the pope (as they say) is inferior to a council, which was, indeed, proved in fact (since for one of the three cases the council deprived Pope John, and for another deprived Benedict) he cannot dissolve it; since an inferior, in that wherein he is inferior, cannot bind and loose, as appears from the chapter *Cum inferior* (de Ma. et Obe.), and other similar laws. Nor can he repeal the law of a superior, otherwise it would involve this contradiction, that he is bound to obey and yet not bound, since he can dissolve. But how could he obey any ordinance or statute of a council if he could take away and annul that very ordinance or statute? This council, however, is assembled for the extirpation of heresies, for the negociation of peace, for the reformation of manners; and in its first session it ordained and resolved that it ought to devote itself to these objects, and that any one occasioning an impediment, dissolving, proroguing, or changing this council, ought to be severely punished, and proceeded against as a disturber of the public peace, &c. If, however, it can be dissolved, it is evident that the said ordinance is infringed. Hence it must be admitted, as a necessary conclusion, that if it can be dissolved the said decree of the Council of Constance has no force. And this is proved by another argument. No one doubts that if an accusation of heresy were to be brought against any pontiff, he could not dissolve the council; because if he could dissolve it, he could not be judged, which is contrary to the chapter *Si Papa* (40 dist.). And as it is in the case of heresy, so must it be in the two remaining cases; for these three are made equal by the Council of Constance. The council and the chapter *Si Papa* speak the same doctrine on this single point. And (as I observed before) the council approved this opinion in its acts; for on account of the schism it deprived Pierre de Lune; and on account of his depravity of life, it deprived Pope John.

"And if there be found any laws which say 'the chief See is not judged by any one,' and 'let no one judge the chief See,' they must be understood with these three qualifications; first, in matters of faith, provision is made in the chapter *Si Papa;* the other two are provided for by the Council of Constance. Otherwise, if that rule *Prima Sedes,* &c., be understood without any exception, then the chapter *Si Papa,* and the decree of Constance, would be false. And if the former had added to the case of heresy these two others, no one would have doubted this view. Let no one, therefore, doubt the decree of the council, which was made with the papal authority, and represents the whole Church. And if it be said, 'In councils it is always understood "the papal authority excepted,"' I answer, that is true when the person of the pope is not specially included; but if it be specially included, then it could not be excepted, as that would savour of contradiction.

" These things have I said, holy father (God is my witness), with disquietude of mind. But I am compelled thus to speak, that your holiness may desist from your dissolution, that I may prevent infinite evils from arising in the Church of God. If your holiness could see the pure mind and clean conscience, and integrity, with which I write this, you would embrace me of your exceeding love, and regard me, without doubt, as a son. I have said often, and say now, and protest before God and man, that if you change not your designs, you will be the cause of schism and infinite calamities. May Almighty God preserve your holiness in the prosperity of a virtuous man; at whose feet I humbly prostrate myself. Basle; on the fifth of June."

Among the distinguished members of the Roman Church, who had already arrived at Basle, was Cardinal Branda, the earliest patron, and now the most energetic supporter of Julian in his arduous work. His presence and authority contributed much to preserve the identity of the council in feeling and labour with the great assembly of Constance. During the earlier session, in which the controversy with Eugenius was opened, and the great principles laid down at Constance were re-established, the Cardinal of Piacenza took an active part; while the influence of his name, not only in the council but at the court of Eugenius, is proved by the fact that five of the cardinals whom the authority of the pope

had retained in Rome* nominated him as their
representative at Basle.† The bull of dissolution,
which must have reached Basle at the end of
December, had no other result than to animate the
fathers with a still greater zeal in behalf of their
own authority as the representatives of the Church
universal. In the second session (February 15,
1432), they renewed the decrees of the fourth and
fifth sessions of the Council of Constance, on the
supremacy of a general council over the see of
Rome, as a preliminary to the citation of Eugenius,
to appear at Basle in person, or by deputy, to answer
for his late proceedings. The third session was held
on the 29th of April, and the fourth on the 20th of
June, in which, as the time of Eugenius' citation
had not expired, nothing further was done in
regard to the pope than the decree (which his
alleged infirm health rendered opportune, if not
necessary), that in the event of a vacancy in the
papacy, his successor should be chosen in the council,
and that the election of new cardinals at the present
moment should be prohibited, as well as the recall
of any who were incorporated with the council.

In the fifth session, held on the 9th of August, the
council appointed proctors and judges to examine into

---

* A paper entitled "Mandatum factum Romæ Cardinalibus
Cortesanis nomine Eugenii Papæ de non exeundo urbem" (February 30th, 1432), is among the MSS. at Vienna.

† "Procuratorium," &c. dated July 25th, 1432 (Würdtwein,
tom. viii. præf.).

such matters of faith and doctrine as might be referred to it, and fixed a period of three months as the term of their office. Appeals to the court of Rome against any of the members of the council were prohibited in the same session.

In the meantime there had arrived at Basle, from the court of Rome, Andrew, Archbishop of Colosse, the Bishop of Magelona, and Antonio Sanvitale, an auditor of the Rota, as the proctors of Eugenius, who were admitted to an audience with the council in two general congregations, held between the fifth and sixth sessions. Finding the spirit of the council to be so thoroughly roused that the attempt to defend the act of dissolution would be in the highest degree perilous to their cause, the prudent ambassadors confined themselves to general and trite propositions on the power and functions of the pope, on the dangers of the threatened schism, and on the necessary loss of the unity of the Church whenever the unity of the presiding see was disturbed or endangered. " Who could hope for the union of the Greeks when the unity of themselves was at an end ? or the admission of a headship which they would themselves have made impossible ? And as for the Hussites, they were already condemned at Constance, and needed rather the execution of the law than a new hearing." Thence they passed on to the old arguments of Roman absolutism, and finally offered, on the part of Eugenius, some place for the assembly of the council in Italy, where

P

the work of reformation, as well as union, could be entered upon under the direction of the pope himself.

The scene which presented itself in the council at this moment cannot be better described than in the words of its reply to the Imperial Commissioners at Mentz, in 1439. "In this Council of Basle (they write), at the time of the first attempt to dissolve it, there were present seven of the most eminent of the cardinals of the Roman Church, manfully defending that doctrine of the authority of councils which was declared at Constance, and insisting that no dissolution of this council can have any vigour either at the present or any future time without the consent of the council itself; and, in conjunction with the rest of the fathers, they composed and published to the whole world many solemn decrees upon this subject. Moreover, in a synodical reply, they replied with great authority to the orators of Eugenius, who desired to maintain his bull of dissolution, 'We had rather die than yield ignominiously to so great an error. This article, which is now in question, relates to faith, and cannot be neglected without peril of salvation. If Eugenius refuse to hear the Church, he must be unto us as a heathen and a publican.'" *

The synodical reply of the council, addressed to the whole Church, so closely resembles in style and diction the letters of Julian, as to point clearly to him as

* Resp. Concil. ap. Würdtwein (tom. viii. p. 56.) Init. "*Rem gravissimam.*"

its author. In it the great principles of Church authority opened out at Constance are re-affirmed and carried on to their legitimate conclusions. The extravagant demands of the advocates of Eugenius in defence of the papal claims are met with the assertion that, "though the pope is the *ministerial* head of the Church, he is not greater than the whole Church; otherwise, if the pontiff should err, as has often happened, and may yet happen, the whole Church would err, which is impossible. And though he be the head and chief prelate of this mystical body, he is, nevertheless, within the body, and would not, in such a case, remain the head of it. The body, therefore, contains the entirety, both him who is called the head, and all the other members." From this doctrine the council advanced yet another stage in its later sessions, in which the title of the popes as vicars of Christ is reduced to that of vicars of the Church, while on the ground of this delegated power is built the right of the Church to depose a pope on the charge of public scandal, as well as on that of heresy.

There are many points in this remarkable state-paper, which must give it the highest interest to all who would place the Church on a sounder basis than that of an irresponsible autocracy. Opening, as it does, by disclosing the ruinous state of the Church before the time of the assembly of the council, from which alone it looks for a remedy, it upbraids Eugenius for cutting off by his precipitate hostility the last hope of restoration. "If (are its words) against him who offends one of these little ones, God hath threatened so terrible a judgment, what, think you, shall be the case with him who has offended the universal Church?" Then, touching the grievances which Eugenius retorted against itself, in rather a lighter vein, it asks, "Who would not be amazed if the one who strikes the blow should say to him who is so stricken, Why do you strike me? when such language belongs rather to him who receives, than to him who gives the blow?" Then the delicate question of the un-changeableness of the papal decision is somewhat rudely approached in the words, "Nor ought the pope to be restrained from such a course by shame or any other human motive, since the Roman pontiff, when he sees the error of anything that may be suggested to him, or finds that he has done some-thing tending to evil, is accustomed immediately to revoke it, and even acquires the greater glory and honour from this very change." The idea of the dissolution being remedial instead of destructive, is met with another stroke of humour: "What should we say if when the sick man asked the physician to cure him, he should straightway kill him, in order to avoid the trouble of applying remedies?" The fears which kept Eugenius from Basle are met by simply reminding him of the hostile armies at his own door, and a rumour that the principal work of the council, the pacification of Bohemia, had been delegated by Eugenius to a single individual (the Archbishop of Gnesen), and transferred from the representatives of the whole Catholic Church, is mentioned with indignant surprise. Finally, the determination is expressed in the most emphatic terms to resist the "pretended dissolution ;" and the charge of heresy on the ground of resisting the Roman pontiff, thrown back upon himself in the words, "If he be accounted a heretic who takes away the supremacy of the Roman Church, how much greater a heretic must he be who denies that that Church, in which the Church of Rome is contained and presides (continetur et præest) hath jurisdiction over all Churches and all men?"

Such were the noble sentiments of ecclesiastical wisdom and freedom, which the fathers put forth to the world in defence of their resistance to Eugenius, and with which they ratified and in a measure authenticated the letters of their great president, and gave a synodical weight to the doctrines he had expressed as an individual. But while the contest was thus raging at Basle, a sympathetic movement of another kind had occurred at Avignon—that city of ill omen to the court of Rome, recalling so many recollections of the schism and suggesting so many dangers of its renewal. The French and Spanish cardinals had still too many thoughts of affection, too many lingering desires after the scene of their former reign, to enable the pope to look without the most lively apprehension to any sympathy between the council and the people of Avignon. The old proverb, "*Ubi papa ibi Roma*," might yet regain its former hold, and the presence of a pope elected by the whole Church restore the place of the former exile of the papacy to more than its ancient position, while it gave back to France that real supremacy of which the election of Martin V. had deprived it. Eugenius had appointed his nephew Cardinal Francesco Condolmieri as his legate at Avignon, but the people of that city resolutely refused to admit him. This unpopular appointment having led to tumults and bloodshed, the council, at the prayer of the city of Avignon, appointed a legate of its own, the Spanish Cardinal Carillas, of which act, as of an unheard of usurpation of the papal rights, Eugenius complained in a letter of bitter remonstrance. The appointment of the new legate, who belonged to the creation and obedience (as it was called) of Benedict XIII., recalled the memories of the great schism of the west, and was a bold defiance of Eugenius in a principality which had hitherto belonged as exclusively to the see of Rome as any of its Italian legations, and might well be regarded as the most ominous of the indications of an approaching convulsion.

The eighth session of the council was little calculated to allay the apprehensions of the court of Rome, for the formal proceedings which had already been opened against Eugenius, began therein to assume a judicial aspect; a term of sixty days being accorded him for withdrawing the bulls of dissolution which formed the ground of his citation. This delay was no less opportune to the council than to Eugenius, as the time of the long expected visit of the Bohemians had now arrived. Those men, whose names had so long been the terror of the civilized world and the reproach of the armies of Europe, were now for the first time to enter peaceably into an imperial city, the guests of an assembly of ecclesiastics, whose warfare was of so different a nature. Crowds of wondering citizens, among whom were seen many of the members of the council, poured forth to meet them as they approached the city, and proved the intense interest and excitement which their arrival had awakened. Every one of them was the subject of some tradition of terror, but in Procopius, the great successor of Zisska, the interest of the multitude had its centre. Men, women, and children filled the doors and windows of the city as they entered the streets of Basle, one pointing out one, and one another of these terrible guests. The national dresses of Bohemia, so new to western Germany, the savage expression of countenance, the eye fierce and determined—

everything, in a word, that caught the attention
of the bystanders—gave freshness and reality to those
scenes of horror of which they had heard so much,
and in which few families of Germany had not taken
part or suffered bereavement. Nor can we doubt
that scarcely less interest was felt by the more
intelligent, and above all by the members of the
council, in the religious leaders of this great movement, and specially in the Archbishop Rokyczana,
upon whose influence the results of the coming
negociation so much depended.

A few days after their arrival, they were admitted
to an audience by the council, and the conference
was opened by Cardinal Julian, who, in a graceful
but ill-judged address, set forth the claims of the
Church, and appealed to the affections rather than
to the reason of the sturdy dissidents. Unhappily,
they remembered too well how soon the "voice of
the charmer" had been succeeded by the noise of the
instruments of death—how soon the invitation, "Return, dear pledges of love," had been changed for
the sword of the crusader—to enable them to listen to
the words of a welcome in which their cause was so
evidently, though so insidiously, prejudged. Their
reply was solid and consistent. They denied the
charge of disobedience to the Church, which the
president had unwisely insinuated; they alleged that
they had been condemned unheard at Constance;
they denied that they had taken away any part of

the faith of the Church, or dishonoured any of her doctors. All that they had done was based upon the Scriptures, and to these they feared not to appeal.

On the 16th of January, 1433, they proposed to the council, in a public audience, the four articles which have already been exhibited to the reader, and selected four deputies to conduct the advocacy of them. First, the Archbishop Rokyczana was employed in defending the communion of the laity under both kinds, which formed the distinctive controversy between the Calixtines of Prague, of whom he was the representative, and the modern Roman Church. Three days were occupied on this question alone; after which, Nicholas Pelzrimowski, a Taborite priest, contended for two days in behalf of the correction and suppression of public crimes and offences, the neglect of which had summoned the followers of Zisska to that terrible work of vengeance which neither the arms nor the diplomacy of Europe had been able hitherto to arrest. On the conclusion of this argument, Ulrich, a priest of the Orphans, vindicated and demanded the free preaching of the Word of God. The case of the Bohemians was closed by Peter Payne, an English Hussite, who impugned the right of the clergy to the possession of secular property and power.

These discourses have not reached our time, though the answers of the advocates of the council have been carefully recorded and appended to its public acts. The first of these opponents was Johannes de Ragusio, who answered the arguments of Rokyczana during eight forenoons. Upon him followed Gilles Charlier, Dean of Cambray, who for four days replied to the second Hussite advocate, and was succeeded by Heinrich de Kalteisen and Johannes de Polemar, who each took up three days in impugning the positions of the third and fourth of the Bohemian deputies.

Far, however, from being persuaded by these replies, the deputies returned with still greater zeal and prolixity to the defence of their cardinal points, Rokyczana again leading the way by refuting, for six days, the discourse of Johannes de Ragusio.

But before the questions were thus re-opened, the cardinal-president, by a skilful, though unsuccessful stratagem, endeavoured to divide the forces of the adversary. Knowing that the Bohemian delegates represented, at the very least, three distinct parties, and that the only grounds of their union in a common hostility to the Church of Rome were the four points for which they were then contending; observing, moreover, that one of them cited Wiclif as an evangelical doctor, he called upon the deputies to say, whether they admitted the celebrated propositions of that reformer which had so often been condemned, and, finally, by the Council of Constance itself. He knew well that the Taborites, as the stricter followers of Huss, would readily assent to the heretical propositions, and thus compromise themselves with the Calixtines of Prague, by whom they were eagerly repudiated. The deputies were, however, too clear-sighted not to discover the design of this transfer of the battle to a field in which they must so soon be divided and lost. They replied, therefore, that they had appeared at the council to propose and to defend, on behalf of the Bohemian nation, the four articles they had already propounded, and those only; and resolutely declined to enter upon any other question.

It had now become evident that their mission was fruitless, and that it had only opened another and a still more intricate chapter in the history of this long and eventful controversy. Private conferences succeeded public disputations, but the hope of a final settlement was as distant as ever. Eventually, it was determined that a commission should be sent into Bohemia, to return with the deputies, and there, in the centre of the scene of conflict, should feel about for some path of union which the collective wisdom and penetration of the council had been unable to discover at Basle.

The absence of Sigismund from Basle at this critical juncture, while it revived the worst suspicions of the council, deprived it of the best chance of removing those differences which had as deep a root in political animosities as they had in religious convictions. A remarkable paper of instructions to the ambassadors of the council at the court of the emperor is still extant, which opens to us very clearly the mind of the fathers at this moment. " You shall relate," are its words, "that if his majesty had been here, the Bohemians would have remained longer, and, perchance, some method of peace might have been discovered. It is believed, also, that if his serene highness would proceed quickly to the council, the Bohemians, hearing of his approach, would send another embassy hither, and might be more easily reduced, at the intervention of their lord, the king." From this expression of hope, the ambassadors were at once to proceed to the disclosure of the fears of the council. "You shall then boldly explain how that the holy council has heard with the greatest wonder the intelligence which his serene highness has lately communicated to it, that he has come to an agreement with the pope on the ground of his approving of the council, whereas it is manifest to every one who has seen the bull of the pope that he has in nowise approved of it; nay, as far as lies in him, has, by that very bull, endeavoured to destroy the foundation and authority of the council."

The attempts of Eugenius to draw over the emperor to himself on the occasion of his coronation, are then exposed, his motive being alleged to be, simply to detain Sigismund in Rome in order to prevent the council from taking judicial proceedings against himself, which, in the absence of the emperor, it would be less likely to initiate. The ambassadors are therefore instructed to urge him to remain at Siena, if he is still there, or if he has arrived at Rome, to hasten his departure thence with all speed.

After reverting to the political importance of the Bohemian difficulty, and the necessity of making the reduction of that kingdom the ground-work of a general pacification of the empire, the council again presses upon the emperor the danger of any appearance of union with the pope, and the fatal injury which their own body must receive from the very rumour of such an agreement. Upon all these grounds they urge the necessity of the immediate presence of Sigismund in the council.* It would appear by these instructions that the pope had misrepresented to the emperor the relations between himself and the council at this period, with a view of drawing him to Rome, where through his personal influence he might induce him to consent to its translation into Italy.

Eugenius, though his own policy was always marked by the most fatal inconstancy and vacillation—timid in the hour of danger, and vain-glorious in the day of relief—was yet most skilful and most successful in turning to account the weaknesses or excesses of others. His early associations in the great mercantile community of Venice seem to have given to all his diplomacy, so to speak, a Venetian character— and hence the fathers at Basle complain of his earliest communications to them, that they were "so full of safeguards and involutions, that they seemed rather to

---

* Avisamenta ad Sigismundun ex parte Concil. Basil. (Würdtwein, tom. vii. p. 1—17),

be the bargains of merchants on worldly goods, than the conventions of ecclesiastics on the things of the Church."*

Sigismund had already promised the fathers by letter that he would never receive the crown at the "hands of the pope until he had given his sanction to the proceedings of the council—that he would sooner return uncrowned to Basle, than prejudice its interests in any way."† But the desire to receive the crown of Lombardy at Milan, and that of the empire at Rome, to deck himself with the symbols of a power which in Italy, as well as in Germany, was fast falling into weakness and contempt, prevailed over the mind of the emperor, and was readily turned to advantage by Eugenius.

In every respect, such a journey was a political failure. The Italian princes looked upon it with jealousy and suspicion, while Germany, upon whose free cities even more than its princes, he relied for support, viewed the emperor's overtures to the pope as too likely to end in a general council in Italy, and a denial of those reforms for which, since the day of their neglect at Constance, the empire had become more than ever clamorous. It is possible that Sigismund might have set before him the pretext, though he could have hardly entertained the opinion, that his presence in Rome would be as beneficial to the

*. Concil. Basil. Congreg. June 16th, 1433.

† Mansi Concil. tom. xxx. pp. 103—4. "Avisamenta Concil." (ap. Würdtwein, tom. vii. p. 4).

interests of the council as the fathers themselves believed it to be detrimental. If, however, he had ever entertained such a thought, it was soon lost in the cold reception and the ill-concealed triumph of Eugenius.

The ceremonies of the coronation were no sooner over than the emperor discovered his error, and the pope his miscalculation of its results. His recantation followed close on his frailty, and in a letter to the council from Rome he renewed his allegiance to it in stronger terms than ever, vowing to remain faithful to it until death. The fathers replied in becoming terms of gratitude, and in their ninth session reciprocated the imperial devotion, by taking the emperor and all his estates and interests under their special protection, annulling and abrogating every act which the pope or his partisans might institute against him. Sigismund had contrived to extort from the pope, before his coronation, the promise to send legates to the council, and this promise Eugenius fulfilled, but not in the sense in which the emperor had received it. Instead of having full powers to authorize the proceedings of the fathers hitherto, the legates were simply empowered to ratify the selection of some place for a future council.

In the ninth session, held on the twenty-second of January, 1433, the citations against Eugenius began, which were renewed in the tenth session, held on the nineteenth of February.

The resolution of the fathers to proceed to the last extremities became now more and more apparent in every stage of their progress. Already it had been openly maintained that a sentence of contumacy was not necessary before the work of deposition was proceeded with,* and the "*auferibility* of the Pope," which was justified by Gerson at Constance, had become an admitted doctrine at Basle. In the eleventh session the fathers entered again upon the defence and explanation of the great synodical provisions of the council of Constance, a subject which the second letter of the president to Eugenius had so ably cleared from the sinister interpretations of the court of Rome. They construed the words *nullatenus prorogetur* of the thirty-ninth session of Constance, as a prohibition so absolute as to leave the pope no ground of defence for his illegal dissolution, and determined that the council could not be dissolved or translated but by the express consent of two out of the three divisions of classes and deputies of which it was constituted. The twelfth session of the council was held on the fourteenth of July, and after a recapitulation of the injuries which Eugenius had inflicted on the Church, granted him at the earnest interposition of Sigismund a further term of sixty days to withdraw his obnoxious bulls, and to reconcile himself to the council; otherwise the sentence of suspension and deposition from

* An anonymous tract to this effect is in the MSS. of the library at Vienna (v. Würdtwein, tom. viii. præf.).

the papacy must proceed. A copy of this decree was forwarded by Sigismund to Rome by a confidential messenger, and affixed to the very gates of St. Peter's.[*]

But the greatest, though the least conspicuous, of the acts of this memorable session, was the re-institution of the fourth and fifth canons of the Council of Nice on the freedom of the election of bishops, a remarkable proof of the zeal of the fathers for the restitution of the primitive laws of the Church. Eugenius, intrenching himself behind "the plenitude of his power," satisfied himself by simply annulling the decrees of the twelfth session, and making public the former of those bulls of dissolution which had hitherto been merely placed in the hands of the legates, and promulged the second of them in the following month.

Sigismund in the meantime had recourse to every art of deprecation both with the pope and with the council, putting forth to the one every plea for delaying its extreme measures, and to the other the most urgent entreaties to withdraw the decrees of dissolution. He beseeches the pope by letter to "come with all speed to the aid of the Church, already in the struggle of death, and only waiting for extreme unction;" while to the other he assumes in person the character of a mediator.

On the 11th of October he arrived at Basle, and was received with due pomp and solemnity by the

[*] Mansi Concil. xxx. 46, 47.

Q

fathers, who went to meet him on his approach to the city. On the 16th he took his place in a general congregation, at which a lively and energetic argument was conducted between the Archbishop of Spalatro, the envoy of Eugenius, and Cardinal Julian. The president dwelt with his usual point and felicity upon the absolute necessity of a reform in the Church, and upon a general council as alone able to enter upon the task. The dangers which would follow the submission to the papal decree are pointed out no less clearly; while the charge that the council had hitherto acted prejudicially to the holy see is met by the assertion that every one of its steps had been taken with a view to the elevation of the spiritual interests of Rome and of Christendom.

On the 7th of November the council met again, and the controversy with Eugenius was re-opened. The patience of the fathers hardly survived the expiration of the term they had already allotted to the pope for his entire submission. At the intercession of Sigismund it was, however, prolonged to another period of sixty days; after which the sentence of suspension was to go forth. In the meantime three formularies of adhesion to the council were offered to the pontiff, one of which he afterwards embraced. The state of desertion in which his impolitic course in Italy had now left him, the open support which was given to the council by the Grand Duke of Milan, and the threatening attitude assumed by the republic of Venice—while the presence of Sigismund at Basle shut out the last hope of imperial support—all these had left Eugenius in a state of such utter helplessness that an uncondi-tional submission became a necessity.

But ere we turn to the act of pontifical submission which made the opening of the year 1434 so memorable in the annals of the council, we are led to dwell for a moment on that important restoration of diocesan synods in the same session, which is at once the greatest monument of the wisdom of the fathers, and the greatest proof of the ,weakness of that Church for which they so wisely though ineffectually legislated.

Falling back upon those earliest precedents, the fifth canon of Nice and the second of Constantinople, the Council of Basle enjoined in this decree the regular assembly of provincial and diocesan synods at least once a year. We can bestow no greater praise upon this important act of the council than to affirm that it is in every respect worthy of that better period whose traditions it embodied anew. Had such a law been faithfully obeyed, any reformation from without the Church, like that which the sixteenth century witnessed, would have been rendered unnecessary by the gradual renovation of the whole body from within. In vain did the Council of Trent, whose reformatory labours have been very ill appreciated or even under-stood by those who have rejected its doctrinal defi-nitions, re-enact this important law. "This pearl of its reformatory decrees (as a great writer of the

Roman Church has said in our own day) lies in the dust."*

It is memorable that the decree on diocesan synods was carried by those of the inferior orders in the council, and that to Cardinal Julian, as their head, supported in this instance by only five of the episcopal order, the Church was indebted for this signal victory over the prejudices of the hierarchy.† A similar opposition was given by the bishops to all those decrees which tended to curb the pride or ambition of the episcopal order. The confirmation by the court of Rome of a law thus carried, gives an implied sanction to the right of presbyters to a decisive vote even in general councils—a right which is based on the fact that in the apostolic and primitive councils, the three orders of the Church had a full and free representation. This appears by the signatures attached to the earlier synods, as those of Arles and Rome (under Symmachus) in which priests and deacons, without any mention or indication of a mere delegated authority, attach their names as present and consenting parties. The right survived in the middle ages in the cardinals and mitred abbots, who exercised not only a deliberative but a definitive power even in general

* Wessenberg (Bishop of Constance), "Die Grossen Kirchenversammlungen des 15ten und 16ten Jahrhunderts," tom. iii. p. 472.

† See the speech of Johannes de Segovia, in the History of the later Sessions of the Council, by Æneas Sylvius (Pope Pius II.).

councils; and though the extreme advocates of the episcopate have endeavoured to explain this on the ground that jurisdiction was transferred from the episcopal order in these special cases, this shifting of the qualification from order to jurisdiction is not only contrary to every principle of ancient ecclesiastical jurisprudence, but fatal to the very cause for which they contend.

While the year 1433 was thus crowned with a work of reformation worthy of the best ages of the Church, the dawn of 1434 was made no less memorable by the submission of Eugenius, and the revocation of his bulls of dissolution. "Hereby (exclaims Bossuet) he renders honour to the Council of Basle, and to the universal Church which that council represented. Hereby he places it above himself, since, in deference to its commands, he revoked the decrees which he himself had published with all the authority of his see." But it was not without strange misgivings and even deep suspicion that the fathers of the council accepted this reluctant surrender. The insincerity of Eugenius had been too often experienced to enable them to disband their fears or suspicions as long as the slightest doubt or ambiguity remained. When the admission of the legates of Eugenius, and their incorporation into the council, came under discussion, it was observed that there was a discrepancy between the date of the bull of adhesion to the council as given in their instructions, and the date of the original bull, "whereupon some of the fathers began to suggest that the adhesion of the pope was rather verbal than real." On this Sigismund (who appeared, nevertheless, to share their suspicions) observed pleasantly that "the council ought to act like a good physician, who even out of what was poisonous could make a sweet potion by mixing wholesome herbs therewith."*

The bull of reconciliation (in which the name of Cardinal Giordano Orsini has so prominent a place as to lead to the belief that he was in this instance the special adviser of Eugenius) declares that "the general Council of Basle from the time of its commencement has been, and is still, legitimately continued, and ought to have always the same continuation and prosecution as though no dissolution had ever been made." It pronounces the said dissolution to be null and void, and proclaims the intention of the pontiff to give full effect to the synod in its progress with all devotion and affection. In proof of this good-will two out of the three briefs which had been published in Eugenius' name are formally withdrawn, and the third (beginning *Deus novit*) which was disavowed by him, is annulled with them, to satisfy the desire and for the greater security of the council. The bull bears date on the 17th of January, 1434.

---

* Responsio per unum ex Oratoribus Concilii in Diœtâ Nurem-berg. (Concepta sed non exhibita), Würdtwein, tom. vii. p. 220.

Four legates had been commissioned by Eugenius
to associate themselves with the president on this
act of reconciliation by the council, Cardinal Albergati, the Archbishop of Taranto, the Bishop of Padua,
and the Abbot of St. Giustina, who were formally
received in the sixteenth session held on the 5th of
February. Before, however, they were incorporated
with the council, it was resolved that a solemn oath
of fidelity and devotion should be exacted from them
according to the terms of the fourth and fifth sessions
of the Council of Constance. This condition, after
much hesitation and discussion on the part of the
legates, was at length acceded to, and in the seventeenth session (April 26th) they were admitted to
their precedence in the council, but not until the
fathers had still further protected themselves against
any interruption or delay of their reformatory labours,
by a resolution that the new legates should not have
any coactive jurisdiction over their synod. In this
session the emperor again took part in state, and the
reconciliation between the pope and the council was
inaugurated with all the pomp that imperial ceremonial could give. On the 19th of May Sigismund
retired from Basle.

After the departure of the emperor the great question of the Reformation of the Church was entered
upon with a boldness and energy which indicated the
consciousness of the support of the secular power, if it
did not even point to its instigation. For in the

twentieth session the long-disputed question of annates received its synodical settlement, and that greatest of the abuses of the court of Rome was encountered, not with the delicacy and reserve with which it was approached at the Council of Constance, but by an absolute decree of prohibition.

At a single blow one of the principal resources, not only of the Roman see, but of several of the great electoral bishoprics of the empire, was cut off. The remarkable exaction which was thus summarily extinguished was no less than the payment of a year or a year and a half's income of every ecclesiastical benefice, from a bishopric to a simple parochial cure, to the Roman chancery. It is believed to have originated in the fees which it was customary to pay to the see of Rome on the institution to any benefice or dignity,[*] and especially on that for the *pallium*, which had accrued to the papacy as early as the pontificate of St. Gregory the Great, but which that eminent man had abolished in a synod held at Rome, by which all such payments were pronounced to be simoniacal.[†] Pope Urban continued this prohibition, but permitted the voluntary oblations of those who received institution or investiture, a practice which remained until the voluntary offering grew up into a customary fee, and in the time of Clement V. the translator of the ponti-

---

[*] De Marca de Concordiâ Sacerdot. et Imperii, l. vi. c. 10, Würdt-wein, Subsidia Diplomatica, tom. vi. præf.

[†] Regist. l. iv. ep. 55.

ficate to Avignon, this charge reached such extravagant proportions, that the Council of Constance was compelled to reduce them by ordering a reassessment of every benefice in order to relieve the Church in some degree of so intolerable a burden, or, at least, to adjust it more evenly.

This recognition of the principle of the tax naturally failed to satisfy those who regarded it as a simoniacal abuse. It was a poor expedient to make a new rating for the purposes of such a tax, when the legality of the tax itself was disputed. The Council of Basle, less tender in the treatment of these venerable corruptions, swept away in a single decree every fine, fee, and impost of the Roman chancery, leaving only the regular legal expenses of writers, abbreviators, registrars, and the other officials of the court. We should commit an injustice were we to fix this great abuse on the court of Rome exclusively, though the example of the reigning see originated and contributed so much towards retaining it. The great primates of France and Germany derived a considerable income from the same exaction, and the Archbishop of Mentz was not less vigorous than Eugenius himself in his remonstrances with the Council of Basle on this sudden exhaustion of one of the chief sources of his income. His appeal was so successful, on account of the moderation with which his taxation of benefices was drawn up, that up to the close of the last century, the diocese of Mentz retained this relic of the abuses of an earlier age.

Reservations, another of the great abuses which the council undertook to deal with, were properly prohibitions addressed to ordinaries forbidding them to fill up an actual or expected vacancy, and retaining it for the pope himself. To the person pre-elected to fill the vacancy, this reservation became a *grace expectative*, a term which expresses, in another form, the same singular usurpation.

The commission of cardinals appointed by Pope Paul III. in 1538, and which included the honoured names of Contarini, Sadolet, and Pole, proposed the extinction of all these abuses, and their report still remains as a monument of their own wisdom and zeal, and a proof of the feeble and paralysed state of that Church, which was incapable of acting upon the advice it so eagerly sought. The golden maxim there laid down, " *Redditus sunt annexi beneficio ut corpus animæ*," strikes at the root of that corrupt system which, by the subtlest inventions, had drawn away to the Roman chancery so rich a portion of the endowment of the churches of Europe. A valuable memoir of the deputation, *Ad pias causas*, presented to the senate of Venice as late as 1769, describes these abuses as then in the fullest vigour. " There still remains a large field (are the words which close this important paper) for the existence of all that disfigures the patrimony of Christ and of the poor, and which has given so many grounds of complaint in the last general councils. The rules of the chancery, plurality of benefices, frequent translations, resignations in favour of particular persons, coadjutorships with promise of future succession, commendams, resignations in curiâ, annates, canonical dispensations, and manifold abuses deplored by the piety of the faithful, and prohibited by the ecclesiastical laws, flourish still."*

Eugenius no sooner heard of the resolution of the council against annates, than he dismissed an envoy thither, to protest against it, and at all events to demand some compensation to the see of Rome for the threatened loss of one of the chief means of its support.

This request drew from Julian an eloquent and memorable address, in which he defended the conduct of the council in this matter, and refused in its name to rescind the decree protested against; promising at the same time to consider the claim for compensation put forth by the papal deputies. "What have we done?" he exclaimed; "hear, I pray you, and consider with me. We have decreed that benefices and holy orders should be conferred without money. Is this, I ask, a crime and a sacrilege? Did not our Saviour lay upon us this necessity, when he said, 'Freely ye have received, freely give?' What have we done further? We have decreed that spiritual things should not be dispensed by any pecuniary compact, agreement, contract, or negotiation. For even Christ himself, seeing this done in the house of God, having

* Vie de Scipion de Ricci (par de Potter), tom. iv. p. 283.

made a scourge of small cords, fired with a holy zeal, drove thence all buyers and sellers, and overturned the tables of the money-changers.   And while He declared His hatred against other sins in word only, this sin He severely chastised with his own hand. What have we done?   We have determined that spiritual things shall be dispensed without the intervention of money.   And St. Peter, the first Vicar of Christ, who understood the mind of the Lord by daily converse, when Simon Magus offered money for a spiritual grace, abhorred, cursed, and repelled him, saying, 'Thy money perish with thee.' "

But while the work of the reformation of the Church in its head and in its members, was thus proceeding at Basle, the affairs of Eugenius and the state of Rome had assumed a new and most serious aspect.   The policy of the pope towards the states of Italy had been like that towards the council, of the weakest and most irritating nature.   The details of his quarrels with the Grand Duke of Milan and the republics of Venice and Florence, as they are given us by one of the most devoted of his advocates and negotiators,* show that the meanest intrigues and endeavours to sow discord among the many enemies he was creating for himself, were Eugenius' sole reliance at this period.   But it was in vain that he sought

---

* Blondus, the historian, gives the fullest particulars of the Italian events of this period, in many of which he took part. (" Pontifex Episcopum Recanatensem Florentiam, *nosque* Venetias simul mittit," etc.)

money from the great mercantile communities of Venice and Florence, to carry on this difficult policy, for even Bologna, from which he might more reasonably have expected the needed assistance, had been lost by a successful revolt.

While he was thus wasting time at a distance, he overlooked the dangers which surrounded him in Rome itself, which were daily becoming more imminent. In the very heart of the capital the Grand Duke of Milan found his strongest allies in the injured Colonna, while the fear lest the pontiff, by being drawn away to Basle, would disappoint the hope of a council at Rome,—had excited the minds of the multitude. The burden of constant warfare, the want which was felt everywhere, and the prospect of utter ruin unless the government were wrested from the hands of Eugenius, had been aggravated by the reckless conduct of Cardinal Francesco Condolmieri, the nephew and chamberlain of the pope, whose unfeeling reception of the grievances of the people of Rome drove them into an open revolt. The multitude rushed to the palace of the pope, demanding a change of government, and claiming the favoured nephew as a hostage until their demands were fulfilled. The earnest remonstrances of Eugenius and his pathetic deprecations were alike fruitless in this moment of resolute action, and Francesco Condolmieri was snatched from the arms of his uncle, who himself became a state prisoner in his own palace. Cardinals Orsini and

Conti, who had all along been the ministers and
advisers of the pope in his infatuated course of mis-
government, were only just able to shelter themselves
from the storm they had raised.   Conti, in disguise,
" entered a boat, near the Flaminian gate, and escaped
along the river to the mole of Hadrian," while Orsini
betook himself to one of the strong fortresses of his
family, under the protection of his brother.*   The
pope had recourse to the same  ignominious flight,
but not before it had become much more difficult and
dangerous.   In the disguise of a monk, and accompanied by a single attendant, he ventured in a boat
in the direction of Ostia, but had hardly got beyond the
city, when a volley of arrows and stones announced
the discovery of his flight, and disclosed the extent of
the danger from which he had had so narrow an escape.

About ten days after this event, the Council of Basle
held its eighteenth session.   This was entirely occupied with what might seem at the present moment
the superfluous work of re-enacting the great laws of
the Council of Constance, which had already been
insisted upon and re-enforced in the earlier sessions.
The occasion of this return to a subject so completely
wornout as this, appears to have been the suspicion
which the forced reconciliation of Eugenius had still
left in the minds of the fathers, and the doubt they
had, whether these earlier sessions were adopted in
good faith, and not with some secret reservation or

* Blondi Hist. Decad. iii. l. 4.

plan of future disavowal. To this end it was important that the newly incorporated legates should be committed to their ratification, and that no element of synodical or papal authority should be wanting to the consolidation of those principles upon which the whole of the previous acts of the council were based.

The affairs of Bohemia having been brought as near to a settlement as the influence of the council could bring them, by being entrusted to a commission having the fullest powers to conclude a final arrangement of them, while the conflict with Eugenius had been closed by his unqualified submission, the fathers entered upon the third of those great works which they had undertaken to accomplish —the union of the Eastern and the Western Churches, at once the hardest and the most fruitless of all. But before we enter upon this third act of the council, it is necessary to fall back upon the previous pontificate, during which the negotiation originated.

The idea of the re-union of the Churches at the moment of the redintegration of the papacy in the person of Martin V., appears first to have presented itself to Eugenius himself, then Cardinal Gabriel Condolmieri, one of the ministers and most influential friends of the pope.* His knowledge of the East in early life, and the proximity in which the

* "Summa dictorum Nicolai de Cusa" (Würdtwein, tom. ix. p. 5.)

Churches stood in the Venetian republic, which formed, as far as was possible, a neutral ground in the long controversy between the East and West, had naturally led him to contemplate this union at an early period, and to view it as a means of giving new life and energy to the papal power, weakened as it was by so long and fatal a schism.

The attention which had already been awakened in the West to the literary riches of Greece, and the thirst which had been excited among the higher ecclesiastics by the public teaching of men like Chrysoloras, who numbered among his pupils at the Council of Constance, Cardinal Zabarella and Ambrosius Traversari, afterwards the most influential friend and confidential adviser of Eugenius, tended to familiarise the public mind with what might then be termed the great Eastern question, and on the ground of a political necessity to introduce the project of an ecclesiastical union.

The Council of Basle, which, as it had a single eye to the reform of the Church, regarded with suspicion every object which stood in the way of, or might distract the attention of Churchmen from that single aim, had looked upon this plan of re-union with suspicion and secret disaffection from the beginning. They regarded it as a mere shadow, in the pursuit of which they would lose the great substance of reform, while to Eugenius it would prove a cover and a pretext for the intrigues he was carrying on against themselves.*

The view which was taken of the union of the Churches by the Eastern court, greatly resembled that in which the fathers of the council regarded it, though it was prudently dissembled by the emperor and his ecclesiastics. No one believed in the possibility of a council in which both Churches should deliberate freely, or conclude fairly on the serious points of difference which had separated them for so many centuries. The fact that recourse was never had to this project of re-union, until some necessity on the side of the Eastern court or reason of state on that of the court of Rome, rendered the introduction of it useful to both, marked it out clearly as the suggestion of political expediency rather than the obedience to a religious duty.

The historian Phranza, the near connexion of the imperial family, overheard a very significant conversation on this subject between the emperor Manuel Palæologus and his son John. The question of a council having incidentally occurred—" My son," said the venerable monarch, " I know firmly and truly from the very midst of their hearts, that these infidels are in great perplexity, from the fear lest we may come to an understanding and union with

* " Deus novit... quantis modis laboravit (Papa) ut ipsos (Græcos) ad se traheret ut sub umbrâ Græcorum sua compleret desideria." (Resp. Synodal. ad invectivam Gabrielis quondam P. Eugen. Oct. 1439).

the Western Christians. For it seems to them that in such a case, some great evil will befal them from the Western powers through us. Exercise, therefore, great care and watchfulness in the matter of a synod, and above all, whenever it is necessary to alarm the infidels, but never attempt to carry out the plan itself. For as far as I can read our own people, they are not sufficiently agreed among themselves to find out a scheme and method of reunion, or of peace and concord, unless, indeed, they contemplate the conversion of the Western Churches to the faith which they held with us at first; but this being impossible, I almost fear that a worse schism may ensue, and thus we shall only expose ourselves to the infidels."

To this wise advice, almost prophetic of the future of the Council of Florence, John Palæologus gave little heed, and as he left without caring to reply, the king, turning to Phranza himself, continued—"My son thinks that he is very well adapted for the government, but not, as I think, for such a time as this. For he has in view and imagines grand schemes, such as are fitted to the prosperous days of our ancestors; but in the present day, as things press upon us, the empire needs rather a steward than a king. I fear that, through his proceedings and plans, our house will decline." *

The occasion of this remarkable conversation (which

* Phranza, l. ii. c. 13.

Phranza passes over in silence) appears, from the minute historian of the Florentine union, Syropulus, to have been the overture made by Martin V., at the instigation of Cardinal Condolmieri, to Manuel Palæologus and to his son, to carry out the project of a synod of the East and West. Eudæmon Joannes, an ardent promoter of this policy, had been sent to Rome to congratulate the pope on his coronation, and had entered into a close intimacy with Andreas, Bishop of Rhodes, a Greek ecclesiastic, who had been tempted to go over into the camp of the Latins, from whom he received his titular bishopric as the reward of his conversion. The readiness with which Martin V. listened to their arguments, and entertained their plans, was manifested by the letters which he immediately addressed to Manuel and John Palæologus, and to the Patriarch Joseph, who had just been preferred from the see of Ephesus to the patriarchate of Constantinople. The reply of the two kings and of the patriarch, after indicating the assembly of a free and universal council as the only method of effecting the reunion of the Churches, alleged the necessity of its assembly in Constantinople, and the right of the Eastern emperor to convoke it.

At this period, however, the convocation of the Council of Siena, which the decree of the Council of Constance had rendered imperative, led to the remission of the whole subject from the pope to the council, while the dangerous state of Manuel Palæologus, who was seized with paralysis, at the same time, interposed a corresponding difficulty and delay on the side of the Greeks.

The pope had entrusted this delicate negotiation to Antonio Massa, a Franciscan monk, who, in an inflated address to the emperor and patriarch, and the great officers of the Eastern court, had prejudged the entire controversy between the Churches, by claiming for his master the titles of "Lord upon earth, successor of Peter, the anointed of the Lord, the lord of the universe, the father of kings, the light of the world." The reply of the emperor and the patriarch to this oration was of a very moderate and practical nature. Constantinople was still urged as the place of meeting; the presence of all the Eastern prelates was not held to be essential in order that the decrees of the future synod might have force and legitimacy, while the poverty of the imperial treasury appealed to the generosity of the pope to provide the requisite means for the sustenance of this great assembly. The Latins endeavoured in the meantime to draw over the minds of the Greeks to their favourite scheme of a council in Italy, the pope pointing to his own advanced age as the reason for immediate action in a matter in which his successors might be so differently affected from himself.

Notwithstanding the misunderstandings that arose between the emperor and the legates of the pope, and the far more ominous difficulties which the disaffection of the patriarch to the project of a council in Italy occasioned, the negotiation was proceeding with a rapidity which few Roman questions have ever exhibited, until the death of Martin gave it a serious interruption. The imperial legates, who had only just started when the news arrived, returned home and were ill received by the emperor, who hurried them back to carry on their work with the newly elected pontiff.

But Eugenius, with the pontificate, had assumed a new nature as well as a new office. He was no longer the conciliator of Churches and kingdoms, but a fierce absolutist both in religion and politics. He received the ambassadors with the angry inquiry, " Why Patras had not been restored to its bishop? " and " How they could ask a synod of him until it had been thus restored?" The legates, after vainly explaining and remonstrating, left the pope impressed with the conviction " that he touched the matter of the synod carelessly, and as it were with the tips of his fingers." He wrote, however, by them to the emperor, promising that a synod should be convoked in Italy.

It is difficult to account for this very impolitic discourtesy of Eugenius except on the ground that the interested motives of the Eastern court had now become transparent, and that the opportunity for claiming an equivalent in favour of Rome had accordingly arrived. It is highly probable, moreover, that the fact that the emperor had sent ambassadors to the Council of Basle to open a negotiation there, even before the deputation to Eugenius had returned to Constantinople, had mortified the new pontiff, and led to this unexpected reception. However this might have been, the news of the assembly of the Council of Basle, and of the adhesion to it, not only of Sigismund, but of all the Western powers, created a profound sensation at the Eastern court, and awakened an immediate desire to enter upon so new and promising a field.

An embassy to the council was at once despatched, consisting of Demetrius Palæologus, the Abbot (afterwards Cardinal) Isidore, and John (called Dissypatus or Bisconsul, from his having twice filled a consular office), who was a son-in-law of the emperor. These were authorised on the part of the emperor and the patriarch to promise that the entire strength of the Eastern Church and court would be ready to join itself to the council, in order to form an œcumenical synod in whatever place might be selected by that body. Eugenius, whose conflict with the council had now begun, sent off an emissary in all haste to the emperor, to avert, if possible, this threatened defection to the ranks of his opponents; and the diplomatic warfare which had so long been carried on between Rome and Basle was transferred, with increased bitterness and subtlety, to the neutral ground of Constantinople.

The emperor, who had received from the ambassadors to the council a description of their reception, which surpassed all his expectations, and had found that it represented all the political strength of Western

Europe, gave his entire support to the plan of a junction with the fathers of Basle; while the patriarch, with a natural leaning to the ecclesiastical element, and as natural a dread that he might be carried to the very end of the world—at which his geographical ignorance had fixed the scene of the council's labours—and that in the pursuit of a very doubtful object, clung to the pope and the promise of a synod in Italy.*

The council lost no time in following up the deputation of the Eastern court by an embassy to Constantinople, of which John de Ragusio and Simon de Fiero were the leading members. While at Constantinople, where they assisted in certain religious processions, connected probably with the projected union, the report that Eugenius had again dissolved the council led them to write to the president to ask for information on the subject.† Their letter is dated on the 10th of March, 1436; and this enables us to form some chronological connexion between the documents of the council and Eugenius, and the narrative of Syropulus, which during the controversy become more than usually complicated, and often contradictory.

In the meantime the success of the deputies of the council with the emperor was so complete that the

* Syropul. sect. ii. c. 25.

† MS. Vindobon. Cod. Can. 69. f. 11. "Joannis de Ragusio et Simonis Fierum legatorum Concil. Bas. Literæ ad Julianum Cardinal. Cæsarinum (ut videtur) petunt sibi certa renuntiari de concilio quod dissolutum fuisse fama attulerat; et late describunt piissimam quandam supplicationem Cpoli habitam." (Würdtwein, tom. viii. præf.).

patriarch was filled with despair. Gathering together
his cross-bearers, of whom the historian Syropulus
was one, he complained that the monarch had altogether gone with the fathers at Basle, and that they
should be led thither at last. At this critical moment
the indiscretion of the council in its preliminary decree
again turned the balance in favour of Eugenius. "The
fathers," it alleged, "having hastened to reform the
new heresy of the Bohemians, were now about to
obviate the old heresy of the Greeks."

In the face of such a document as this, where was
the promised freedom of the projected synod? What
justice or equality could the Greeks expect from those
who had already judged and condemned them with
the revolted Bohemians? Well might the representatives of the council have said of their own proposals
of peace what they said so happily of Eugenius—
"Would that his benign answer had been less like
that of Joab, who, taking the beard of his companion
Amasa, and giving him the kiss of peace, stuck his
sword into his bowels and killed him.*

In vain the delegates of the council were called
upon to alter the offensive proeme. Though they
professed to treat it as a mistake of the copyists—an
interpolation which they could not account for, alike
without authority and without meaning—they dis-
claimed the power and declined the responsibility of

* "Responsio per Unum ex Oratoribus (C. Bas.) concepta sed non
exhibita." (Würdtwein, tom. vii. p. 197).

altering a single word.* After many fruitless conferences, they proposed at last to draw up a new preamble to the decree, and to obtain for this the sanction of the council.

In the meantime, and in order to quiet the apprehensions of the Eastern bishops, the emperor suggested the composition, on their part, of a new introduction, and the eventual selection between the two forms of that which was most agreeable to the feelings of all. The new introduction of the Latins, however, so fully satisfied the Eastern court, that it was at once adopted, though another question of still greater importance appeared in the distance. What if the projected union should turn out a failure? and how, in this case, would the stipulations of the decree be affected? The representatives of the council replied to this, that whether the union were effected or not, the return of the Eastern court should be equally secure and honourable. Upon this assurance, the decree was formally drawn up and transmitted to the council by Henry Mancer, one of the deputies.

The legates of the council took advantage of this delay to effect the conversion of the patriarch to their views, who, from the beginning, had been most eager to accept the papal overtures, and looked with natural suspicion upon a body whose relations with the papacy had become so anomalous, and whose derivation from the pope-deposing Council of Constance

* Syropul. Sect. ii. c. 29.

awakened a natural alarm in one of the same order. And here the emissaries of the council succeeded so well in misrepresenting the true relation between Eugenius and the fathers at Basle, as to bring over the patriarch to their side, and to induce him for the first time to enter heartily into the projected union.*

The ambassadors of the council were not, however, alone in this field of subtle diplomacy, for Eugenius was represented in it by Christopher, Bishop of Corone, who studiously propagated among the Greeks the news of the dissensions which were reigning at Basle, and of the schism which was opening between the council and Eugenius. Not only had he succeeded hitherto in detaching the mind of the patriarch from the synod, but had been apparently equally successful in influencing the mind of Joannes Dissypatus, whom the emperor was about to send, as his plenipotentiary, to the council. The ambassadors of that body, who were not unaware of the intrigues of the papal emissary, endeavoured to extort from him the concurrence of his master in their negotiations with the Eastern court, which, after some tergiversation, he was compelled to promise.†

On the arrival of Dissypatus at Basle, in the beginning of February,‡ he had an audience with the council, and, after delivering his credentials and

* Syropul. sect. ii. c. 38.    † Ibid. sect. iii. c. 36.

‡ Panormitani Oratio in Conventu Francoford. (Wurdtwein, tom. viii. p. 128).

describing the good-will of the Eastern court towards
the projected meeting of the Churches, opened the
question of the place in which this great work of
union was to be accomplished, and of the means that
had been prepared for the conveyance of the Eastern
court. To this, Cardinal Julian made answer, that
the naval preparations were already completed, and
that the cities of Basle or Avignon, or some place in
Savoy, had been chosen as the scene of the future
council.

On this, the ambassador protested strongly that the
Greeks would, on no account, undertake so long and,
to the aged prelates who were to take part in the
council, so perilous a journey; that they had believed
the Savoy mentioned originally, to include only the
Italian dominions of the duke, although, as it was
enumerated among the places agreed upon out of
Italy, it was difficult to maintain this ground. The
representative of the Eastern court insisted further on
the absolute necessity of the pope's personal presence
in the council, from all which it was evident that he
was seeking occasion, " or had been suborned by
some other influence, to find for the Greeks an
opportunity of receding from their agreement with
the council."* The fathers, who suspected the source
from which these unexpected protests and reclamations
had arisen, met them with a determined resistance,
until, on the 15th of February, Dissypatus read and

* Panormitan. p. 130.

delivered a formal protest, drawn up in Latin, which was introduced by Eugenius into the bull which he put forth soon after, confirming the acts of the recusant minority at Basle.

The language of this protest is so singular, as to prove that it was the composition of the ambassador himself, though there cannot be the shadow of a doubt that its inspiration was from Eugenius,* and possibly also from the patriarch, whose special delegate he is said by the pope to have been.† He begins with saying that he has been sent by the emperor " *ex multis respectibus et specialiter propter quatuor,*" the first being to announce the readiness of the Eastern court and prelates to fulfil their engagements ; secondly, to entreat the fathers to fulfil their own in their full integrity and with due punctuality ; thirdly, to see whether the place selected were among those named in the preliminaries, and convenient both to the Greeks and to the pope, the necessity of whose presence and concurrence he so dwells upon, as to make it appear that he represented the interests of Eugenius not less than those of his proper consti-

---

* Panormitanus mentions, with just suspicion, the fact that the protest was written "not in Greek, but merely in Latin," and notes the significant circumstance, that the Eastern delegate insisted on the presence of the pope *in person*, whereas the original compact added the alternative, *or by his representatives*, as a proof that he had received his instructions from Eugenius. (Würdtwein, tom. viii. p. 129).

† Eugenii Bulla " *Salvatoris et Dei nostri*," ap. Justiniani Acta Concil. Florent. p. 7.

tuents; fourthly, he is commissioned to examine the vessels procured for the use of the emperor and prelates. He then protests that they have chosen a place " to which the pope will never come, nor send his legates "—a clear indication that he was receiving instructions from Eugenius, whose change of mind with regard to Avignon, which was actually his own suggestion, he could not otherwise have known.*

The pope had generally expressed himself to the council as " very little solicitous about the place of union, so that the union were only effected ;"† and Avignon, as immediately subject to his jurisdiction, would have naturally been the best substitute for Rome or Bologna. But whether the resistance of that city to his authority, and the refusal to receive his legates, still rankled in the memory of the pontiff, or the fear that its selection was the prelude to a new schism, and threatened a new headship of the Church, as well as a new scene for the council, Eugenius soon disavowed his fatal suggestion, and nothing but a council held in Italy could now satisfy his desires.

The zeal with which the citizens of Avignon had come forward with the funds to meet the engagements of the council, and the fact that they alone had

---

* Panormitan. p. 126.

† See the reply of the legates at the Diet of Nuremberg, " Concepta sed non exhibita " (Würdtwein, tom. vii. p. 192). This is a very important document, as the fact of its non-publication in the diet sufficiently indicates. It is conceived with much more truthfulness and candour than is generally exhibited by such diplomatic productions.

responded to this urgent invitation of the Church out of all the cities of Europe, must have awakened in the suspicious mind of Eugenius the fear of ulterior designs, and of the interested motive of making Avignon again the centre of the papacy. This fear he betrayed in the inhibition which he laid presently on the people of Avignon from raising money, in order to fulfil their contract with the council;* and having thus disabled them from completing their arrangements within the thirty-two days appointed, he has the modesty to make this failure the ground of setting aside the choice of the council, and pro-ceeding to a new election.†

Dissypatus, instead of returning at once to Con-stantinople, proceeded to Bologna, to Eugenius, and having given him his protest as the groundwork of his bull of translation of the council, induced him to send vessels to bring the Eastern emperor and prelates to Italy, so as to anticipate the designs of the council.‡ It chanced that the papal triremes arrived first at Constantinople, and the emissaries of Eugenius represented themselves as bearing the credentials of the council as well as of the pope, by which successful falsehood they brought upon

* "Difficultates per Ambasiatores motæ" (Würdtwein, tom. vii. p. 269). Nationis Germanicæ Responsum ad Literas Stephani Palatini Rheni. (id. tom. vii. p. 299).

† Justiniani Acta Conc. Florent. p. .10

‡ Syropul. sect. iii. c. 5. Theophanis Procopowicz Archiep. Novogrod. Historia Controversiæ de Processione Sp. Sancti. p. 94 (Gothæ, 1772).

Eugenius and his party the bitterest reproaches of the fathers at Basle, who recognised in this masterpiece of duplicity the crown and completion of the Eugenian policy.*

The return of Dissypatus and his colleague at this critical moment contributed not a little to this unexpected triumph. For they brought the readily credited news that the pope and the council were reconciled, that the sessions at Basle were at an end, and every obstacle to a synod under the papal presidency and in Italy removed. Dissypatus was extravagant in his zeal to propagate this strange intelligence, and the arrival of Cardinal Albergati as legate from the pope, contributed to the success of these misrepresentations.

The address of the German nation to the Palatine of the Rhine affirms boldly, not only that the ambassadors of the pope assumed to represent the council, but that they were actually fortified with letters to which the seal of the council had been surreptitiously affixed.† The history of the subsequent rifling of the chest in which this seal was deposited, in order to attach it to the act of the minority, in which Cardinal Julian was himself implicated, indicates the too great probability of this dishonest proceeding. The successive stages

---

* Panormitan. Propositio ad Electores facta (Würdtwein, tom. vii. p. 103).

† Würdtwein (tom. vii. p. 300).

of the diplomacy of Eugenius, which was crowned
at this point with so complete a success, may be
thus briefly recapitulated.   By his attempted dis-
solutions and transfers of the council to Italy, he
had compelled it to regard its very existence as
identified with its permanence at Basle, or at the
very least with its continuance in some city out
of Italy.   He had himself accepted and sanctioned
the resolution of the council to remain firmly at
Basle, until the Eastern court should arrive at the
port which might be selected for their landing,
and thus contrived to paralyse the action of the
fathers until that period when the success of his
own diplomacy should render it utterly fruitless.
He had by "glosses" and misrepresentations, of
which Dissypatus was a most convenient channel,
led the Greeks to raise difficulties on every one of
the cities out of Italy, which had been included
in the first schedule of their agreement with the
council, suggesting that Savoy only referred to the
possessions of the Duke of Savoy in Italy, whereas
it was enumerated in the decree as one of the places
that might be chosen *out* of Italy.*   Finally, when
the last stage of the negotiation had been arrived
at by the guarantee of the requisite funds by the
citizens of Avignon, the pope interposed to prevent

* Difficultates per Ambas. motæ (Würdtwein, p. 263).  In this
important paper the course of Eugenius' policy, and his plans of
dividing the council against itself, as well as detaching it from
the Greeks, are well discussed.

the fulfilment of the terms of the promised loan, although the suggestion of Avignon as the place for the future council had come originally from himself,* and by anticipating the council at the court of the emperor, completed his great political work by an act of duplicity which has probably but few parallels in history. On the faith of this "false legation" the emperor and the patriarch prepared for their anxious journey.†

At this point our attention is recalled to Basle, and to the solution of the interesting but difficult question, how far the immediate subject of our narrative was implicated in these transactions. The only clear and consistent narrative of the proceedings which led to the final schism at Basle, and the retirement of the legates, is the address of Panormitanus at the diet of Frankfort, which was replied to by Nicolas de Cusa in a counterstatement, or rather argument, which took three days to deliver. The "sum of his discourse" has alone reached us, and though it contains nothing to invalidate the historical statements of Panormitanus, it may be regarded as a faithful representation of the causes and motives which led Julian to that apparently sudden change of purpose which, with some writers is the greatest reproach, with all, is the deepest mystery of his life. It may, indeed, be reasonably

---

* Oratio Panormitani (Würdtwein, tom. viii. p. 126).

† Syropul. sec. iii. cap. x.

S

believed, that at least the facts of this statement were derived from the president himself.

Up to the arrival of Dissypatus, and his protest in the general congregation, held on the 15th of February, his loyalty to the council remained un-shaken. For, notwithstanding all the denunciations of the orator against the choice of Avignon, and his allegations that the path of union would be irremedi-ably cut off by its adoption, Cardinal Julian ad-ministered the oath to the deputies of the council, who were about to proceed to that city to receive the first instalment of the loan.[*] Between this and the general congregation of the 23d of February, in which the final arrangements were made for the payment of it, the relation between the council and the president had become materially changed. He had been invited to take part in this congregation —an invitation which itself indicated a difference of opinion already springing up on the subject of the present discussion—but excused himself on the ground that he could not concur in the schedule of places "in so far as it related to Avignon."[†] The arrangements with the representatives of that city were made accordingly in the absence of both the legates, though the assertion of the advocate of Eugenius that they were made " unknown to them " [‡]

---

[*] Würdtwein, tom. viii. p. 130.
[†] Panormitan. ap. Würdtwein (tom. viii. p. 134).
[‡] Summa dictorum Nicolai de Cusa (Würdtwein, tom. ix. p. 8).

is refuted by the clear and full statement of Panormitanus.

The negotiations opened at Avignon assumed, however, so suspicious a complexion as to lead at once to
the belief that the final nomination of that city would
reopen the warfare with Eugenius, and perhaps inaugurate a new schism at a moment in which the great
object of the reunion of the Christian Church seemed
to be so near its accomplishment. The very eagerness
which the people of Avignon—the city of the exiled
papacy—had shown on this occasion, the ominous
absence of its principal citizens at the court of the
king of France at the very moment of the arrival of
the ambassadors,* the inflexible resolution of Eugenius
and of the Eastern court, and the increasing exasperation of the council, must have awakened in the minds
of all its more moderate members the gloomiest apprehensions for the future.

The colleague of Julian, Juan de Cervantes, the
cardinal of St. Peter, maintained at this critical
moment a perfect neutrality—" *Neque hos neque illos
laudare solebat.*" †   He was able to retire into a more
private life from a conflict in which Julian was compelled to take an active and decisive part.   For "it
was evident to all the world," as his ancient biographer
affirms, "that he would have been himself chosen to
fill the throne which by the deposition of Eugenius

---

* Panormit. (l. c.).      † Æneæ Sylvii Ep. xxv.

s 2

would so soon become vacant.* For him, therefore, no place of neutrality could remain; nor can we wonder that he looked anxiously for a pretext for setting aside the election of Avignon, and closing with Eugenius on some place in Italy in which the disunion of the Western Churches might be concealed from the eyes of the Eastern world.

The inability of the citizens of Avignon to complete the payment of the loan within the time prescribed, and the acceptance by the ambassadors of a moiety only, with a security for the payment of the rest, suggested to the Archbishop of Tarentum, the devoted adherent of Eugenius, the idea of breaking the compact on the ground of the non-fulfilment of its main condition. This suggestion was eagerly adopted by the legates, and the question was mooted hereupon, whether the council should proceed to a new election, or should confirm the choice of Avignon. The subject was remitted by the council to the committee on the reunion of the Churches; but before it was decided therein the legates resolved at once to offer a new schedule, naming Florence or Lyons as the place of the future council. Accordingly, in the twenty-fifth session, after the confirmation of the decree offering Basle, Avignon, and Savoy as the future meeting-place of the council, an official authorized by the legates ascended the pulpit, and read a counter-decree, in which Florence, Udino, or any other suitable place

* Vespasiano Florentin. (ap. Ughelli Italia Sacra).

in Italy, were substituted for the places nominated by the majority.

A scene of strange and hopeless confusion ensued. The majority, including the Cardinal of Arles, and all the prelates of inferior rank, together with the lay-members of the council, inflexibly adhered to their resolution, while not less pertinacious, though standing almost alone, were the two cardinals, who, in the end, seceded from the body of the council, and carried on the negotiation with the Greeks as though its representation had been centred in themselves alone.

Julian continued, however, still to carry on his office as president, and to take his place in the general congregations, anxious, if possible, to obey the solemn resolution of the council by remaining in Basle until the arrival of the Eastern Court in Italy, and, during this critical interval, to promote the work of union, or at least, prevent an open rupture with Eugenius. This retention of his presidential office secured to him the custody of the official seal of the council, which he refused to attach to the decree of the majority without sealing also the counter-decree of the minority. In consequence of this refusal the acts and proceedings of the council remained for some time without official sanction.

Yielding at length to the solicitations of its members, the seal was, by common consent, confided to the care of a commission, consisting of Cardinal Cervantes, Alphonso Bishop of Burgos, and Nicholas,

Bishop of Palermo, better known as the great Canonist Panormitanus. The two former were Spaniards by birth; the last, as representing the King of Arragon, was connected officially with the same country, and all of them well qualified to mediate between the French and Roman parties which divided the synod. To them Julian appealed in order to obtain the seal of the council to the decree of the minority, but his application was at once rejected.

This led to an outrage, which forms a strange and painful contrast to the legal and dignified conduct which the legate had hitherto maintained. His secretary, Bartolomeo de Battifero, with others of his domestics, succeeded in breaking open the chest in which the seal had been deposited, and attached it to the schedule of the minority.* How far Julian was implicated in this transaction it is difficult to determine; but the Archbishop of Tarentum was found to be so deeply involved that he was immediately placed under arrest, but soon effected his escape to the court of Eugenius. A correspondence he was holding with the pope was intercepted by the council, in which the state of affairs at Basle is thus significantly sketched: —"Your holiness may believe me that even when the

---

* These facts, asserted by Panormitanus, and not in any particular denied by Nicolaus de Cusa in his reply, are further confirmed by a MS. in the Imperial Library at Vienna, described as a fragment of the Acts of the Council, containing "testimonies to prove the surreptitious scaling of the decree concerning Florence and Udino" (Würdtwein, vol. 8).

Greeks arrive, it will be difficult for us to depart hence without a schism (*scissura*). I perceive my lord the legate to be most firmly resolved at the time of their arrival, to transfer the council, and to fulminate censures against the rebellious, who will be twice the number of the other party."* The treacherous prelate must have already reached the Roman court when Eugenius received the official notification of the act of the minority, which he eagerly ratified, accepting the selection of Florence or Udino, and confirming it in a public consistory.

The rupture between Julian and the council was now irremediable; and yet he never appears to have surrendered to any other his presidential authority, employing it in order to carry on his unsuccessful work of mediating between the parties in the council to the very last. As far back as the 20th of December, 1437, he had eloquently appealed to the wisdom and moderation of the fathers, in order that they might rescind their monitory against the pope on his engaging to revoke his bull of translation of the council. He pointed out, with his accustomed force and persuasiveness, the necessity of showing to the Greeks that they were not making the union of the whole Church the pretext of a still more hopeless schism in their own body. He proffered the mediation of Sigismund, the great defender of the council, as at

* "Difficultates per Ambasiatores motæ" (Würdtwein, tom. vii. p. 269).

once acceptable to Eugenius and to themselves. He exhorted them not to exhibit to the Greeks the humiliating spectacle of men who were seeking union with strangers, while they were falling into disunion among themselves. Finally, he implored them "in all humility, and adjured them by the terrible tribunal of Christ, and that dreadful day of judgment in which, willing or unwilling, they must give an account of all their thoughts and deeds, and in the name of the Redeemer, the Lord Jesus Christ, who, coming into the world, proclaimed peace, conversing in the world, preached peace, rising from the world, spake peace to his disciples."

From the first he had rested in the conviction that the influence of Sigismund was alone able to prevent the threatened schism, and that some plan of reunion might be effected, either by a mutual compromise, like that entered into between the emperor and the electors, or by a direct mediation on the part of the emperor himself.* Great, then, must have been his consternation to find that, at the very moment he had urged the acceptance of this mediation on every ground of political necessity, and even religious duty, Sigismund had been summoned away from the long and weary conflict, having expired at Znaym, in Moravia, on the 9th of December.

This intelligence, succeeded as it was by the arrival

* Responsio ad Oratores Regis Romani (Concepta sed non exhibita, Würdtwein, tom. vii. p. 216).

and representations of Dissypatus, must have strengthened, if it did not even originate, the determination to
throw himself and the moderate party in the council
into the balance against the majority. As soon as the
news of the embarkation of the Eastern court arrived
at Basle, Julian, accompanied by only four prelates
and his own attendants, set forth towards Venice, the
place of their expected landing, resting at Mantua on
his way. To the latter place he would naturally be
led, in order to consult at this critical moment the
head of the Gonzaga family, the near relative of the
late emperor. From Mantua he proceeded to Venice,
in a mixed public and private character, which a
contemporary historian describes in the words, " He
went to visit the emperor and the patriarch, and went
as the legate of the Council of Basle."*   In this light
he was received at Venice, both by the Greeks and by
the Venetian government, which accorded him the
same honours which had been bestowed upon Cardinal
Albergati as the representative of Eugenius.

The controversy on the place of the future council
was here renewed in another form; the Doge Francesco Foscari urging the claims of Venice, the papal
party contending for Ferrara, while Julian would
appear, from his sudden return to Mantua, to have
suggested that city as the safest scene of the future
synod. The eloquence of the Eugenian advocates, and
especially of the celebrated prior of the Camaldules,

* Sanuto.

Ambrosius Traversari, had been hitherto vainly spent
in the effort to bring him round to their views.    The
latter seems to have been specially commissioned by
the pope for such a purpose, his letters to Eugenius
making frequent mention of his labours for the cardinal's conversion.\* On one occasion he writes,
"Sometimes I entertain a hope, sometimes I despair
of his conversion."   On another he says, "We cannot
be sanguine, and yet cannot despair of it."

The return of Julian to Mantua† must have frustrated these hopes ; as it proved that whatever might
be his ultimate decision, it would not be on the ground
of any change of purpose or conversion, but from those
free and independent convictions which had been
growing up in his mind since the time when the
reconciliation between the pope and the council had
become impossible.   It was not till the 11th of March,
1438, that he formed the determination to join the
Greeks and Eugenius at Ferrara ; and the surprise and
delight of the papal court at the accession of so great
a man to their ranks proved that it was an unexpected
not less than a welcome event.‡

The egotism of the Eugenian party eagerly claimed
as a conversion what was really the natural develop-

----

\* Ambrosii Traversarii Ep. p. 400.

† "Cardinalis Sanctæ Sabinæ Mantuam reversus est " (Justiniani
Acta Concil. Florent. pars ii. coll. i.).   See also Sanuto (ap. Raynald
ad ann. 1438).

‡ "Atque ut magis exultet S. V. adplicuit Cardinalis S. Sabinæ
paratus et promptus pro tuâ sanctitate, si ita sit, opus intendere"
(Ambrosii Traversarii Ep. p. 58).

ment of those great principles of ecclesiastical policy
upon which Julian had acted from the beginning; and
this claim has been too readily admitted by historians
of every creed. While, however, the advocates of the
pope were thus rejoicing over the immediate fruits of
a successful duplicity, that vigorous and impulsive
mind, which had guided the intellectual strength of
Christendom in the freest and most enlightened
council that had assembled since the apostolic age, was
preparing itself for a future of more enduring triumph.
The long and dreary night of schisms and controversies
seemed now far spent, and the day of strength and
reunion was at hand.

How sublime was the prospect now opening upon
an earnest and sanguine mind! The restoration of
the Church to its first beauty and integrity—its reformation by the recovery of its first estate, and of
that spirit which made it one in Christ—the overthrow
of the infidel and the enemy of the Church by a
warfare of whose glories the earlier crusades would
become but a faint prophecy—the extension of the
power of the papacy over all Christendom, and the
restoration of the episcopacy to its pristine beauty
under the one universal patriarch—these were the
most prominent features of this vision of things to
come.

We cannot wonder that, with such a view before
him, the great reformer of the Church at Basle laid
down the work of reformation to take up that of union;

and while keeping still, as the rule of all his labours, the truth proclaimed at Constance, "There can be no real union without reformation, nor true reformation without union," fell back upon the work of union when that of reformation became impossible. To one who regards his course from this point, every stage of his transition from Basle to Florence will become clear and consistent. Everywhere we shall recognise a careful provision for the exigences of the Church, formed from the matured experience of its past dangers, and a disinterested zeal which, in an age of selfish intrigue, was as naturally misrepresented as it was wilfully misunderstood. The insinuation of Gibbon is at once confronted by the fact that if Julian had not sought the peace of the Church rather than his own aggrandisement, he might have grasped at this moment the papacy itself, and wrested from Eugenius that authority under which he was content to close a life of brilliant but unrequited service.

# CHAPTER VI.

THE Greeks, who had embarked amid conflicting rumours of the reconciliation and renewed hostility between the pope and the council, arrived at Venice in a state of indescribable division and perplexity. All that they believed in common seems to have been that whatever party they attached themselves to would be immediately and necessarily joined by the other. It was difficult for them to conceive the possibility of a continuance of the prolonged hostility between Eugenius and the fathers at Basle after they had added themselves to the ranks of either. Those who clung to the promises of the council looked eagerly for the arrival of Julian, of whose independent position at this moment they knew nothing, and whom they believed to be still the zealous advocate who had opened the negotiation with them at first. They accordingly urged the emperor to withhold his acceptance of the invitation of Cardinal Albergati, who had arrived at Venice as the legate of Eugenius, until the return of Cesarini. The prepossessed monarch replied with impatience, " Come at once to the point, and trouble not yourselves about the cardinal."*

The arrival of the Marquis of Ferrara in Venice and that of Cardinal Albergati were hailed by the Venetian court with great joy. The venerable Doge Francesco Foscari, whose name has descended in poetry as well as history, received the papal ambassador with the greatest devotion, even condescending to bear his train in public. The scene which this city of waters presented at this memorable period was in the highest degree picturesque and exciting. Moving amidst an astonished multitude eager to witness the arrival of the illustrious strangers—the canals and the surrounding sea covered with boats and gondolas, through which the state-barge of the doge slowly made its way to the vessels which conveyed the emperor and his train, one of which was laden with the sacred vessels and chalices of the great church of St. Sophia, without which it was deemed that the magnificence of the Eastern ritual could not be worthily represented before the Western Church—the procession exhibited a stateliness and solemnity which reminded the bystander that it was not a mere secular pageant that he was witnessing, and that something more than a worldly triumph was expected as the result of this day of joyful meeting. In the contemplation of this scene, in which the setting glories of the Eastern empire, surviving its power,

* Syropul: sec. iv, cap. 17.

were poured for the last time upon the Western world, the historians of the day are lost in wonder and admiration; the despot Demetrius gravely exclaiming, "Methinks it was of this place that the prophet wrote, 'God hath founded it upon the seas, and prepared it upon the floods!'"

As soon as the imperial train arrived near enough to the city to recognise the palace of the doge, the cathedral of St. Mark, and the stately palaces and churches that surround them, appearing one after another to fill up the glorious prospect, their enthusiasm began. Passing up the grand canal, they beheld the Rialto crowded with an eager multitude, whose acclamations burst over them as they recognised the banners of the Republic and of the Eastern empire floating in the breeze together, perhaps for the first time in so close and propitious a union. At this moment the admiration of the Eastern court reached its highest point, and found vent in the exclamation that "the earth and the sea had become a heaven."*

The pageant of the day of arrival being over, and the members of the Eastern court suitably lodged, the more tranquil and diplomatic part of the ceremonial began, which was brought to a speedy close by the determination of the emperor to adopt the place and plans proposed by Eugenius. He reached

* The account of the despot Demetrius is given by Phranza, and is repeated almost verbatim, but without his name, in the introduction to the Greek acts of the council.

Ferrara, where the pope, with his court, was awaiting him, on the 4th of March, the patriarch, who travelled by water, not arriving there until the 8th.

At about the same interval, after the arrival of the latter, Cardinal Julian entered Ferrara, and was received by Eugenius with the liveliest emotions of joy. The public reception of the Eastern court at Ferrara was not inferior in magnificence to that which it had experienced at Venice. But so extraordinary an event as the meeting together of the heads of the Eastern and Western Churches had been, unfortunately, but ill provided for in the ceremonial books of either; and the claims of reverence which were advanced by the pope so startled the patriarch that the very opening of the congress was prophetic of a disastrous termination. It was announced to the Eastern primate, at the preliminary communication, that he was expected to kiss the foot of the pope. At this demand the aged prelate, in the words of the Eastern historian, " was horrified." In vain had Traversari, the tried friend of Eugenius, endeavoured to avert this danger: " Let it not move you" (he had written to him) "to be called by the patriarch, 'Brother,' for the Church of Constantinople is second to Rome, and an inveterate and not newly assumed habit may be readily pardoned." It was a pity that Eugenius needed, and a still greater pity that he neglected, such advice. He continued, however, to press his foolish demand, until his pertinacity and resistance of the Eastern prelates gave it a formidable importance. "And on what grounds," exclaimed at length the indignant patriarch, "does the pope make this demand? or which of the councils has sanctioned it? Show me whence he derives it, and where it is recorded. Albeit he is the alleged successor of St. Peter, we are not less the successors of the other apostles. Did those apostles kiss the feet of St. Peter? who ever heard of such a thing?"

His final determination not to leave the vessel by which he had reached Ferrara until the offensive claim was withdrawn, compelled Eugenius to give way. A reception in the pope's private chamber, in the presence of the cardinals only, and the substitution of the cheek and hand for the foot were at length agreed upon, and Eugenius was prevented from repeating in public a scene which Rome had too often witnessed, and which Bishop Cuthbert Tonstall so quaintly describes when (in 1505) he beheld Pope Julius "standing on his feet whyles a noble manne of great age dyd prostrate hymselfe uppon the grounde and kyssed his shoo, whyche he stately suffered to be doone as of duetie," adding : " where me thynke I sawe Cornelius the centuryon capytayne of the Italyon's bende, spoken of in the tenth chapiter of the Actes, submyttynge hym selfe to Peter and moche honourynge hym; but I sawe not Peter there to take hym up and to byd hym ryse, sayenge, 'I am a man as thou arte,' as saynte Peter dyd

T

saye to Cornelius; so that the byshoppes of Rome do clymme above the hevenlye clowdes, that is to saye, above the apostels sente into the worlde by Chryste."[*]

A still more difficult question, involving in a deeper degree the controverted question of the papal supremacy, succeeded this. How were the seats of the prelates in the council to be satisfactorily arranged? How, without pre-determining this controversy, which was one of the subjects of discussion, could the pope and the patriarch, as well as the emperor, be satisfied with the seats assigned them? The event proved how difficult was the solution of these questions. And though the prudence and eloquence of Julian were now bestowed upon the cause of Eugenius, the relative position of the seats was a subject of eager altercation, which greatly delayed the session of the council.

The synod was opened on the 9th of April, 1438, when the instruments of its convocation were published and ratified in full session. The Greeks, though pressed by the Latins to enter immediately upon the regular labours of the council, resolutely urged the propriety of waiting for the arrival of the fathers from Basle, who, they imagined, upon the knowledge of their arrival and of the opening of the synod, would hasten to take part in its debates. All that the Latins could prevail upon them to do was

[*] Sermon preached before Henry VIII. on Palm Sunday, 1539.

to meet them in preliminary conferences, in which the subjects of difference were privately discussed, and plans of reconciliation suggested.

This period of suspense was, however, not un-favourable to the cause of the Latins; for not only was the strength of the adverse party worn away by the long delay, and their dependence upon the papal court made more complete, but an opportunity was gained for sowing dissension among the principal advocates of the Eastern Church, which facilitated more than any other cause the success of the Roman diplomacy. Of the leading prelates on the side of the Greeks, Bessarion, Archbishop of Nice, and Marcus Eugenius, the Archbishop of Ephesus, were the most conspicuous in rank and talent. Regarding one another, it is probable, from the very first, as rivals, the seeds of jealousy were very easily sown in their minds, and Julian, who, in this interval, entertained both of them at his table with much hospitality and cordiality, was not a little instrumental in dividing these champions of the adverse party.

The patriarch, justly suspecting that too intimate a social intercourse with the chief advocates of the Latin cause might lay the foundation of a deeper union, and must in any case endanger his own position as the spiritual head of the Eastern Church, forbade the acceptance of the cardinal's invitations by his bishops and officials. On this ground the grand chartophylax, and the historian Syropulus, his principal cross-bearer, were compelled to decline the invitations of Julian. The learned and philosophic Bessarion had been, however, unable to resist the friendly importunities of one in whom he found so kindred a spirit, and such congenial tastes; and the intimacy which began on the ground of philosophy, soon found a firmer basis on that of religious inquiry.

The great Platonist, accompanied by the profound Gemistius, the Nestor of the Greeks in the council of Florence, whose name is hardly ever mentioned but with the epithet " the wise," was engaged in solving questions of moral philosophy at the table of the cardinal, while the severe and dogmatic Ephesius had hitherto resisted this dangerous hospitality. At length he also was prevailed upon to overcome his scruples, though his conversation, unlike Bessarion's, who appears to have been acquainted with Latin, if not also with Italian, even at this early period, was conducted through an interpreter. The object of Julian in these pressing invitations appears at once in the fact that he took the earliest opportunity of urging Ephesius so far to commit himself to the project of union, as to address. a panegyrical letter to the pope, applauding his design, and encouraging him to carry it on to a successful issue.

Ephesius, who suspected that the real object of this suggestion was rather to commit him to a policy which he had so energetically opposed, than to strengthen the inclinations of the pope, which needed no such stimulus from without, hesitated before he could be prevailed upon to entertain it. But when the persuasions of the Bishop of Mitylene were added to those of his host, he consented to draw up a paper which should be presented to the pope, after having been first transmitted to Julian. Julian, with a breach of confidence which throws a just suspicion upon his previous conduct in the matter, showed this writing to the emperor, whose indignation was at once awakened against Ephesius, as having ventured to write on subjects upon which he had not as yet even spoken. In the first excess of his anger, he brought the matter before the patriarch and the assembled bishops, and proposed that condign punishment should be inflicted on Ephesius by the judgment of the whole synod. Bessarion here interposed, and urging the scandal that such an exposure of one of their brethren would occasion before the Western Church, prevailed upon the emperor to pass over an offence, which it is too probable he might himself have originated.

It is easy to trace in this incident the source of that severe hostility to the future union, and utter distrust of Julian and of Bessarion himself, which animated the future conduct of the indomitable Mark of Ephesus. Nor can we fail to observe this at the same time as one of the earliest stages of that moral declension in the course of Julian, which was at once closed and expiated in the dark page of the Hungarian legation.

The business of the council was now opened in preliminary conferences, in which it was proposed to lay out a scheme for the public sessions, and to come to a kind of non-official understanding on the subjects of controversy, and the methods by which they were to be treated.

These conferences were prefaced by Julian himself, who after many encomiums on the design of the union of the Churches, and the zeal of those who had come so far to effect it, inquired whether some plan had not been already proposed in a synod at Constantinople, and earnestly desired that, if so, it might be communicated to the Western Church. Ephesius, in reply, denied that any scheme of the kind had been adopted, and invited rather the propositions of the other side. The Greeks had come ready for the fullest discussion of every difference, but not committed to any project of union beforehand. Julian replied to this at some length, urging the view that the present conferences were the proper opportunity of discovering a medium of union—dwelling on that word with a peculiar emphasis and unction.* The eloquence and persuasiveness of Julian is confessed by the Eastern historian to have had so unpleasing a contrast in the ruder sentences of Ephesius, that it was found desirable to entrust the second reply to Bessarion, whose eloquence surpassed in this instance that of the Western advocate, and who met his importunate inquiries for some

* τῇ τῆς μεσότητος λέξει ἐπιφυόμενος. Syropul. sec. v. cap. 6.

method of union with the only words worthy of such an occasion, " We have no method of union but the truth. As we have the truth with us, we shall have that as the means of our union—we know no other. For we cannot find any other means of union than the truth."

The attempt of Julian to anticipate in these private conferences the work which (as the Greeks properly insisted) belonged exclusively to the public sessions, and thus to make these latter the mere ratifications of a union already completed, rather than the exhibition of an open warfare on questions whose history was almost unknown to the members of the Western Church, though skilfully repeated and eloquently sustained, was for the present at least unsuccessful. The great and vital controversy, that on the procession of the Holy Ghost, was regarded by the emperor as one too sacred and primary to be even touched but by the synod itself. And this determined withdrawal of the main difference from a mere subordinate treatment, left only two of the minor controversies, that on purgatory and on the primacy of the Pope, within the scope of these preliminary conferences; for the principal remaining question, on the use of leavened or unleavened bread in the Eucharist, as it related to the highest mystery of faith, was placed by the emperor in the first class, and with that on the procession reserved for a more solemn and synodical decision.

After four conferences had been held without any
practical result, the Latins selected, out of the controversies offered them, the question of Purgatory, as
that on which first to break ground with the Eastern
Church.*

It devolved upon Julian to lay down the doctrine
of the Roman Church, which he did in the following
terms :—

"After their departure out of this life, those souls
which are pure and free from stain, as the souls of
the saints, immediately depart into bliss.  But the
souls of those who have fallen into sin after baptism,
and have afterwards sincerely repented and confessed,
but have been prevented by death from fulfilling the
injunctions laid down by their spiritual adviser, or
from producing worthy fruits of repentance for the
satisfaction of their own sins—such souls as these are
cleansed by the fire of purgatory, some speedily,

* One is surprised to find it asserted by modern Roman controversialists that the question of the existence of purgatory formed no
part of this dispute, but only its nature,  For Cardinal Giustiniani,
in his notes on the Acts of the Council, published by authority in
Rome, asserts two questions to have arisen out of this subject,—
" *An purgatorium sit ?* " and " *An pœna ignis corporei ibidem sit ?* " and
admits that the council decided only the former of these questions,
the latter being still, according to Bellarmine and Suarez, an open
question (Acta Concil. Florent. p. 327).  The celebrated writing of
Marcus Ephesius on this subject was directed against the *existence*,
and not the *nature*, of purgatory.  " *Rejiciunt Purgatorium*," writes
the learned Goar in his letter to Nihusius (an. 1647) of the Greeks of
his day.  The question is fully and learnedly treated by Diecman in
his treatise "De Ecclesiarum Orientalium et Latinæ in Dogmate de
Purgatorio Dissensione " (Stad. 1671).

others slowly, according to the measure of their guilt, and, after this purification, depart into bliss. But the souls of those who die in deadly sin, or with the stain of original sin unremoved, pass immediately into punishment." This he affirmed to be the doctrine of the Roman Church on purgatory, which he pursued with great diffuseness and logical order, adding at the close, " What I have said and alleged hitherto has merely been by way of preparation and introduction to the words of the Master of the Palace, John of Spain (Joannes de Ragusio), who will speak and propound the matter well and from its first principles, according to the judgment and wisdom that is in him, and will engage with a sufficiency, which I altogether disclaim for myself, in the controversy on this doctrine."*

To this statement Ephesius replied in somewhat general terms, expressing surprise and gratification that the difference between the Roman view as expressed by the cardinal, and that of the Eastern Churches, was so much less than it was popularly supposed to be. After a few words from Ragusio, the conference closed, the following one being occupied with the statement of Ephesius in reply to the Latin advocates, in which he sustained the doctrine of the Eastern Churches on the ground of Scripture and tradition. After the disputation had thus proceeded for some time without any promise of success,

* Syropul. sec. v. c. 13.

it was determined to draw up the statement of both sides in writing, the reply of the Greeks being entrusted to Ephesius and Bessarion.

This opened a fatal rivalry between the two prelates; for the emperor, like James I. at the Hampton Court conference, assumed to act as the moderator and critic in this assembly of divines, and pronounced a strong judgment on the comparative merits and defects of both performances. Ephesius, to whom he adjudged the first place on the ground of argument, had introduced trivial and unnecessary allusions in support of it—such as the story of St. Macarius interrogating the skull of an infidel and receiving an answer from it—an argument which the emperor very prudently foresaw would occasion derision rather than conviction on the part of the Latins; while Bessarion, though less clear and forcible in his arguments, had introduced the subject with an elegance and propriety far excelling the method adopted by his rival. The emperor concluded, therefore, that a fusion of the two treatises would best answer the object in view—a scheme which he commanded to be carried out by the writers themselves, under the auspices of the "wise" Gemistius. The schism between the two great advocates of the Greeks was completed by this injudicious proceeding.

The result of this wedding together of the arguments of Ephesius and the diction of Bessarion was, however, the production of a controversial writing so clear and admirable, that we have, perhaps, little reason to regret the circumstances of its origin; for there are good grounds for believing that the treatise thus produced was none other than the remarkable writing, *De Purgatorio Igne*, which was published by Salmasius in the Appendix to his work on the " Primacy of the Pope," while the document to which it is the reply is given by Cardinal Giustiniani in the " Latin Acts of the Council."* While this controversy was going on, the increasing necessities of the Greeks, the carelessness and levity of the emperor, who was spending in the pleasures of the field that season of preparation which every hour was becoming more momentous and more precarious, the alarming intelligence which was daily arriving of the progress of the Turks towards Europe—everything, in a word, was warning the Eastern court of the perils, while it was convincing them of the fruitlessness of this ill-timed visit. And yet so general was the apathy of the Greeks on the subjects of the gravest importance, and so puerile the interest excited by the most trifling intrigues and incidents of the moment, that it was left for the Latins to press on the work of the synod, and to hasten the period of its public sessions. After many conferences and consultations, they at last succeeded in fixing the day for the formal opening of the council. On the eighth of October,

---

* Salmasii de Primatu Papæ, Lugd. Bat. 1645 (ap. p. 65). Horatii Justiniani Acta Concil. Florent. p. 285.

Bessarion, Archbishop of Nice, gave an eloquent inaugural address to the assembled fathers, which was echoed in the following session by the Latin Archbishop of Rhodes, on the part of the Western Church. The third session introduces us to Mark of Ephesus, by whom the real business of the synod was opened. His argument was begun on the ground that, as the words "and from the Son" had been inserted into the creed by the Latins, and had thus developed a doctrine which was new to the Christian Church, and unrecognized by its earliest councils—viz., the procession of the Holy Ghost from the Father, *and from the Son*—it devolved upon the Western Church to establish the legality of the addition, as well as the truth of the doctrine it embodied. Taking up his position on that great decree of the Council of Ephesus, which prohibited every change or addition of any kind to the creed which had been completed at Constantinople, and fixes it as the inviolable rule of belief, and test of orthodoxy, the Eastern advocate planted himself impregnably on the legal ground of the argument; a ground hitherto utterly unknown to the Latin controversialists, who, in the profound ignorance of the sanctions of antiquity which reigned in the West since the separation of the Churches, had confined themselves altogether to metaphysical speculations on the doctrine of the procession itself. The Latin Archbishop of Rhodes followed in defence of the Roman Church, and an interminable argument was carried on for several sessions on this ground; an argument through which it would be needless to conduct the reader, as here it rather rested upon minute technicalities than embraced the whole subject of the double procession— the real doctrine at issue between the Churches. It will be sufficient to remind him, while tracing his path through the tedious but ingenious debates of the Ferrara-Florentine Council, of the necessity of keeping in view, not only the two great divisions of the argument as legal and doctrinal, but also the two branches into which the legal argument itself was subdivided.

The first ground of this argument was the intention of the legislator, as discovered from the construction of the law itself; the Greeks arguing that its terms excluded all addition whatever, verbal and formal, as well as doctrinal and substantial; true and orthodox, as well as false and heterodox ; the Latins maintaining that it was only designed to exclude an addition contrary to, and destructive of, the truths it embodied and involved. This led them into the assertion of a principle of development in Christian doctrine, strongly resembling that propounded by Dr. Newman, not only in its nature, but in the method of its advocacy, which was conducted by the Archbishop of Rhodes, and the Provincial of Lombardy, through the first seven sessions. The second part of the legal controversy was entered upon by Julian himself in the

ninth session, the ground being, not the outward construction of the law (which by this change seemed
abandoned to the Greeks), but the meaning and
qualification given it by the circumstances which
preceded and attended its promulgation.  The great
object of the Latins throughout was to hurry on the
Greeks to the discussion of the doctrine involved in
the addition, for which point of the argument alone
they were prepared.  For by reason of the utter
ignorance of the ancient laws of the Church into
which the whole of the West was thrown, the introduction of the legal argument caused a consternation
among the Latin advocates not to be described.
Photius, the great Patriarch of Constantinople, had in
the earlier days of the controversy been urged by the
bishops of Italy to save them from the tyranny of the
see of Rome, by which (as they described) the "sacerdotal laws were insulted, and the ecclesiastical
sanctions were overthrown."*   But time, while it
taught them to submit to the yoke, taught them
also to forget these "sacerdotal laws" and "ecclesiastical sanctions" so utterly, that when they were
recited in the Council of Florence, many of the Latins
then present declared, according to the testimony of
an eye-witness, that they had never known the true
grounds of the separation of the Eastern Churches
from them, nor had heard them from their doctors.†

And, indeed, the writings of Aquinas, on which the

* Photii Ep. p. 59.        † Syropul. sec. vii. cap. 19.

Latins founded their principal hopes of converting the Greeks to their views, and from which they drew their principal arguments, indicate an entire ignorance of those legal grounds on which the Eastern Church so securely rested. When, therefore, they could no longer elude the arguments derived from the Ephesian decree, they endeavoured to enlarge the scope of it, so as to divide the forces of the Greeks over a wider and less definite field.

From this concession the advocates of the Eastern Church were led to make that further one, upon which rested all the hopes of the Latins, and consented to pass from the legal argument to the doctrinal one, and to lose themselves in the interminable mazes of a theological controversy, or rather of a metaphysical inquiry into the properties of the Divine existence, and the nature and manner of a spiritual emanation.

It is not our purpose to weary the reader with these interminable disputes, but rather to show the part which Cardinal Julian took, not only in the deliberative, but also in the diplomatic treatment of this difficult controversy. His political course was not less skilfully directed here, than it had been before in the better task of reforming the Christian Church. On the first discovery of the strong position assumed by the Greeks in the great prohibition of Ephesus, he made the same desperate effort to dislodge them, which Cardinal Humbertus had made in the eleventh

century, alleging that the *Filioque* had an ancient and
original existence in the creed of the Church universal,
or at least an existence prior to the separation of the
Churches, and that, therefore, it was not sufficient to
cause their separation now.  To support this, he
produced a Latin manuscript in which it existed, and
wrote eagerly for a Greek manuscript, which belonged
to Nicolas Cusanus, in which he declared he had
detected the word *evidenter et ad oculum abrasa.*\*

But the movement, though well conceived, failed at
once.  For not only did the Greeks disprove the
existence of the word, but the Archbishop of Rhodes,
and the principal advocates of the Latins, admitted
candidly that the word had been added by the Roman
Church, and that it devolved on that Church to defend
its conduct herein.  Upon this he entered with zeal
upon the course which the Archbishop of Rhodes and
the Provincial of Lombardy had taken, and strove with
them to prove that the *Filioque*, though an addition in
form, was not an addition in the sense implied in
the Ephesian decree.  He sought in the words of
the canon—which to the prohibition against adding
or detracting, annex the words " but declaring "
(διασαφοῦντες) " that the Holy Ghost is Lord "—an
argument to prove that only what was contrary to
the faith was prohibited, and that explanations or
elucidations were permitted by the council. But the
counter-arguments of the Greeks were so clear and

* Ambrosii Traversarii Ep. p. 976.

forcible, that the necessity of enlarging the field of battle must have appeared as evident to Cesarini, as it did to Bessarion, Archbishop of Nice, who confesses even after his election to the cardinalate, that the victory at the first was on the side of the Greeks, and that the Latins had produced no argument of weight or solidity, until the speech of Cesarini, in which the second ground of the legal argument was entered upon.* It was not until the ninth session that Julian drew off the forces of his adversaries to a new point of defence, and took up his position in the history of the prohibitory canon, and the circumstances which led to its promulgation.

The attempt to lead the Greeks away from the legal to the doctrinal argument having hitherto failed, it became necessary at least to extend the field of argument, and to consider the law, not as standing alone, and existing in an absolute and independent form, but as qualified and explained by the circumstances under which it was enacted, and having rather a relative than a positive existence. Thus he endeavoured to limit the operation, and relax the stringency of the law in question, and to prove that the Roman Church had not violated its spirit; and thus also he prepared the way for the still greater change which was afterwards made from the question of the legality of the addition to that of the truth of the doctrine it conveyed.

* Epist. ad Alexium Lascharim. (Acta Concil. Florentini, Horatii Justiniani, p. 399.)

U

"The question," he said, "arose out of the prohibition
of the Council of Ephesus, which the Roman Church
understood to exclude only those additions which were
contrary to the rest of the creed, but which in the
sense of the Eastern Church excluded all additions
whatever. But rightly to interpret the law, required
the consideration of the circumstances under which it
was enacted. In the present case, Charisius, a pres-
byter of the Church of Philadelphia, had prayed for
the protection of the council against Anastasius and
Photius, disciples of Nestorius, who had excommunicated him for not receiving a creed which they had
imposed upon certain schismatics, whom they were
commissioned to reconcile to the Church. Against
this unauthorised exaction, Charisius appealed to the
Council of Ephesus, then fortunately sitting, which,
after condemning the conduct of Anastasius and
Photius, put forth a law of general application,
prohibiting the composition or exaction of any creed
other than that of Nice (or Constantinople) under any
circumstances, or for any cause whatever.

Julian argued first that as Charisius in his appeal
delivered, according to invariable custom, a statement
of his own faith, differing in form, though not in
substance, from that of Nice, which statement was
received by the council, their subsequent law was
directed solely against professions of faith differing in
substance from the great standard of the Church. He
maintained secondly, that the prohibition against the

private entertainment of another faith showed that it was intended merely to exclude doctrines contrary to those of Nice. The words *ne liceat sentire*, when connected with those *ne liceat conscribere*, indicated, he alleged, that such was the meaning of the decree. But if in opposition to this it were urged that Charisius, as a private person, might put in a creed verbally different from the Nicene, yet that the Church could not publish any other, he referred to the universal scope of the words "Let no one offer," &c. Furthermore, if the decree excluded truths, not expressed but implied in the creed, from being held together with it, all private persons were under an anathema, for they all believed in such implicitly conveyed doctrines—for instance, the eternity of God's existence, &c. His third ground of argument arose from the additions of the council of Constantinople to the Nicene creed, which he contended were equally unlawful if this decree made that creed an unalterable standard. He next argued from the intention of the Legislator, which was directed against a contrary faith, and not a verbal difference. Fifthly, he produced as an argument the permission given by the Council of Chalcedon to Pope Leo, to put forth the same faith in other and explanatory terms, when he was accused of having broken the law in question by so doing. Lastly, he alleged the case of Dioscorus, who, while holding Eutychian opinions, nevertheless professed his belief in the Nicene creed, and sheltered himself under the prohibition of Ephesus; where the synod ruled with the bishop of Mitylene, who held that this canon gave him no protection.

He concluded a speech, which may be safely affirmed to be the most acute and eloquent defence of the Latin cause that had been hitherto published, with an urgent appeal to the council to pass from the subject of the addition to that of the doctrine itself. If it were a truth, he insisted that it should be everywhere received; if erroneous, that it should be as universally rejected.

But, notwithstanding the skill of the cardinal, which gave so fresh a complexion to a subject whose every fact and argument had been exhausted in the controversial heats of six centuries, he could but imperfectly conceal the dilemma in which this addition of the *Filioque* had placed the Roman Church. For either the doctrine was implicitly contained in the rest of the creed, or it was altogether a new article of belief. If the former were true (as the advocates of the Church of Rome maintained), the addition was plainly as unnecessary an intrusion as the θεοτόκος was held to be by the Council of Chalcedon. If the latter were true (as the Greeks asserted), the addition was as obviously illegal. In either case, the see of Rome had usurped an authority inherent only in the Church universal, and that not by an open act, but by a course of secret and sinister conduct.

The circumstances of the law, moreover, however

they might illustrate the determination of the council in the particular case of Charisius, could not limit the scope, or qualify the meaning, of that general law, to whose enactment they only gave occasion. As many other cases come within its terms, and are comprehended in its design, the single case which led to its promulgation cannot affect its bearing on all other cases in which the creed of the Church universal is violated or superseded.

In the twelfth and following sessions, an argument between Marcus Ephesius and Julian, on the questions raised in the speech of the latter, was conducted with great earnestness and obstinacy. One explanation was adduced after another till the patience of the council was exhausted by the pertinacity and prolixity of the inflexible combatants ; and the Greeks, worn out by endless disputations and fruitless delays, began to show symptoms of submission to the desire of the Latins to pass from the addition to the doctrine. Bessarion, who confessed afterwards that his conversion to the Latin views took its rise in the discourse of Julian, was almost the only prelate who advocated this change, so fatal to his own party. The emperor, anxious only for those temporal succours which the slow progress of the council was detaining from him, neglected, on this question, the opinions of the appointed advocates of the Eastern cause—even of the learned Gemistius, whose wisdom had become proverbial. The patriarch, aged and wearied out, acquiesced in the desires of the impatient monarch; and, with a proviso that the former ground might be entered upon again at a future time, it was resolved to proceed to the discussion of the truth of the doctrine, that the Holy Ghost proceeds " from the Father and the Son."

The new argument was, however, destined to be opened upon new ground; for the plague, having broken out at Ferrara, it was no longer thought safe for the labours of the council to be continued in that city. An adjournment was, therefore, determined upon from Ferrara to Florence, which was published in the fifteenth session, and both parties made immediate preparations for the journey. The passage of the Roman and Eastern courts to Florence was characterised by the same magnificence that had marked the arrival of the Greeks at Venice and Ferrara; and this pilgrimage of the council delayed its sessions until the 26th of February, 1439.

They were reopened by Cardinal Julian, who, having succeeded in his great object of shifting the ground of argument, was further successful in changing the method of conducting it. He had urged from the beginning, but hitherto without effect, the expediency of carrying on the discussion in open session, instead of in private conferences. And this plan was now adopted, delegates being appointed on either side, and the defence of the Latins opened by John, the Provincial of Lombardy, the indefatigable champion of the Roman cause. The doctrine of the Procession of the Holy Ghost, opening so wide a field to the speculations and transcendentalism of scholastic philosophy, was now introduced on the strength of certain passages of St. Basil, St. Epiphanius, and St. Athanasius, and further supported by arguments derived from scholastic sources. But Ephesius replied to these with so much solidity and pertinence, that nothing was left to the Provincial but the passages he had produced from St. Basil, on which alone the council was occupied for seven sessions, " as if," writes a learned primate of the Russian Church, "that holy synod had met together for no other purpose than to judge St. Basil." We are compelled to admit, with the same writer, that " there was here a miserable neglect of the Scriptures, and an utter ignorance of the principles of theology, which is the chief cause of all evils."*

It happened in the course of the twenty-third session, as the Easterns were groping through the pages of the fathers in their search for a pretext and a point of union with the Latin Church, a ray of light broke in upon them from an Epistle of St. Maximus. In this it is admitted orthodox to say that the Holy Ghost proceeds "*from* the Father *through* the Son;" but notwithstanding this, it is maintained that the Father is the sole source of the

* Theophanis Procopowicz, " De Processione Spiritus Sancti," cap. ii. sec. 25.

Divinity, the cause (αἰτία) of the Son, who is begotten by, and of the Holy Ghost, who proceeds
from Him. A clue to union seemed here to present
itself in the ambiguities of the prepositions *from* and
*through* (ἐκ and διά), when used on so mysterious a
subject. The Greeks at once grasped at it, and
offered to unite with the Latins upon the basis of
this definition. The Latinizing prelates, as may be
seen from the writings of Bessarion and Joseph of
Methone, contended that the two words had precisely
the same force and meaning—a proposition which
Ephesius and the strictly orthodox party resolutely
and with reason repudiated.

In the meantime, the emperor, wearied out with
these endless debates, on which so much time had
been fruitlessly spent at a period which was in the
last degree critical to his empire, commanded Ephesius
to abstain from appearing in the council for the future,
fearful lest the skill of the Ephesian metropolitan
should be brought to bear against the new scheme of
union, upon whose success he built so much. Accordingly, in the twenty-fourth session, the Latins had an
uncontested field, the forced absence of Ephesius
giving the Provincial an opportunity of parading his
old arguments with more than usual confidence, and
even of expressing the wish that Ephesius had been
there to reply to them. To this the emperor made
answer, that it was in obedience to the imperial desire
to put an end to these prolix debates, and not from

the fear of being unable to take his former part in them, that Ephesius had absented himself from the council. The Provincial, continuing to take undue advantage of the clear field which was thus given him, received a second check from Isidore, the primate of Russia, and afterwards cardinal, who said, " He who runs a race alone, and contends alone for the prize, seems to be a conqueror; and he who disputes alone, with none to answer, may seem, in like manner, to have put forth an unanswerable argument."

After this time there were no regular sessions of the council, but merely private meetings and congregations on either side, according to the more effective plan of the emperor. In these conferences and private interviews Julian became more active than ever in urging, persuading, and remonstrating with the emperor and his clergy. His negotiations terminated in the appointment of delegates on either side to treat of a plan of union on the ground of the definition of St. Maximus. The Latins were, however, dissatisfied with the use of the word *through*, and endeavoured to lead on the Greeks into the admission of the doctrine in their own terms. A series of statements and definitions being given and required on both sides, and the Latin and Eastern delegates having mutually satisfied each other, though not without considerable and serious disagreement having been occasioned by the exacting spirit of the former, the controversy was

formally closed by each of the Eastern prelates and
doctors being called upon to deliver their judgments.
The patriarch's was given first, who pronounced that
the Holy Ghost proceeds from the Father through the
Son, eternally and substantially, as from one principle
and cause. But at the same time he did not suffer
the introduction of the words, " and from the Son,"
into the creed, or the alteration of any of the rites of
the Eastern Church. The emperor's definition of his
views was rather eulogistic to the council than strictly
theological, but he carefully qualified it with the
proviso of the patriarch. Next, Isidore, as the representative of the patriarch of Alexandria, delivered
his judgment in similar terms, and was followed by
Bessarion, who, in a more decisive form than had been
yet employed, admitted the doctrine of the Latin
Church. But when it devolved on Anthony, Bishop
of Heraclea, on Dositheus of Monembasia, Mark of
Ephesus, and Sophronius of Anchialum, respectively
to pronounce their decision, they utterly rejected the
views which the rest had embraced, and inflexibly
maintained the doctrine of the Eastern Churches.
The despot Demetrius, the brother of the emperor,
had withdrawn from Florence not only to avoid
signing the act of union, but to discountenance it as
much as possible ; but the Bishop of Mitylene and the
remaining prelates acquiesced in the sentiments of the
majority.

At a subsequent meeting an instrument was drawn

up expressing the desire of the Eastern Church to be united with that of Rome upon the conditions proposed, and this was forwarded without delay to Eugenius. Regular articles of union were then framed, which were approved of both by the Eastern clergy and the pope and cardinals, who, on the completion and ratification of these preliminaries, rose and embraced their Eastern brethren with a great show of joy and much mutual congratulation.

Eugenius, eager to take advantage of the present favourable disposition of the Greeks, endeavoured to extort from them the declaration of their belief in purgatory, a doctrine which, since the preliminary conferences in which they so steadfastly resisted and so ably protested against it, had remained untouched. The spirit which had animated this resistance was now worn out and enfeebled by fatigue and delay, and the exactions which had been submitted to on the greatest of all their differences with the Western Church, so disheartened the Eastern prelates, that they were little prepared to reopen an inferior controversy. The only question on which they seemed disposed to make any stand was on the manner of consecrating the Eucharist, which, in opposition to the Roman doctrine of the intrinsic efficacy of the words of the institution (vis verborum), they held to be effected by that solemn invocation (ἐπίκλησις) of the Holy Spirit, which is so distinctive a feature of the Eastern liturgies.

As, however, they had received no permission from the emperor to treat on either of these subjects their conferences were rather of a private character; and during their progress a new gloom was cast over their fatal visit to Italy, by the death of the patriarch Joseph. This, from his great age and increasing infirmities, had been long expected. The venerable head of the Eastern Church expired suddenly on the evening of the 10th of June, 1439, while he was at supper, and a very few days after he had made his formal declaration on the union.

The Latin party, eager to claim his authority in behalf of all their extortions from their now almost passive opponents, put forth a document which professes to be a declaration of his dying sentiments in behalf of the Western Church. The spuriousness of this paper, which the advocates of the Eastern Church have ever regarded as too contemptible for serious refutation, is evident on many grounds. It is unmentioned by Syropulus and by Andrea Santa Croce, the Greek and Roman historians of the council, the former of whom would have been compelled, in the defence of his cause, to have invalidated it had it been in existence, while the latter could not have failed to dwell upon it as the greatest triumph of the Roman court. The patriarch's death is by both described as too sudden to give any opportunity for writing it, though the Roman historian mentions that before his death he subscribed the

schedule on the procession of the Holy Ghost, which
had been already agreed on, and which gives us a
ground for believing that the document in question
was ingeniously substituted for it, as a pious fraud,
by the Latinizing party which surrounded the patriarch.
But the crowning argument arises from the date
of this last testament, which is June the 9th; the
same Greek acts which contain it describing a conference between the patriarch and his clergy on the
11th of the same month. The two historians of
the council before cited agree in fixing his death
on the evening of the 10th, so that in every point of
view this document, protesting to be written just
before his death, is inconsistent with the facts.

An incidental proof of its spuriousness may be
derived from the statement of Andrea Santa Croce,
that while purgatory and the other questions remained undecided (*hác difficultate stante*) the patriarch was seized with a severe paroxysm of disease,
which took him off the same night. Now, had he
known how readily and satisfactorily the patriarch
settled in this last testament all the disputed
questions that remained, he could not have thus
described the present state of the controversy, or
asserted (as he does afterwards) that the death of
the patriarch "further delayed this matter," which
would have rather, if the disputed document be true,
greatly helped it on to a complete settlement ; nor yet
would Eugenius, when these questions were entered

upon, have failed triumphantly to produce it, instead of coldly and generally praising the good disposition of the deceased prelate towards the union. The importance of this document, if it were genuine, has rendered it necessary to show some of the grounds upon which we are bound to pronounce it a forgery.

After this melancholy. event, the remaining differences of the Churches were reopened and briefly discussed, the Latins manifesting the eagerness of men who are led by one concession to grasp at another, the Greeks betraying the carelessness of those who, having parted with their most valued possession, give up one by one all their inferior treasures from mere weariness and perplexity. Even that most sacred point of difference, the use of leavened or unleavened bread in the Eucharist, which was reserved by the emperor with such anxious solicitude, was surrendered without a struggle, and a controversy whose history fills a volume * was closed in a careless line.

At length a general instrument of union was drawn up, and transcribed in Greek and Latin, containing the definition of the procession of the Holy Ghost from the Father and from the Son, as from one principle and one inspiration. On the 6th

* A German divine, J. Gottf. Hermann (pastor of the church of Pegau, in Saxony), has devoted an entire volume, full of the greatest learning and research, to the history of this single controversy. (Hist. Concertatonum de Pane Azymo et Fermentato, Lips. 1737.)

day of July, 1439, after the celebration of a solemn
service in the church (afterwards the cathedral) of St.
Mary, in Florence, Cardinal Julian solemnly recited
in the one language, and Bessarion in the other, the
celebrated act of union, which opens with the first
words of the letter of reconciliation from Cyril of
Alexandria to John of Antioch, inviting heaven
and earth to join in the celebration of this peaceful
triumph—" *Laetentur cœli et exultet terra.*"

The means which were employed to induce, or
rather to compel, the members of the Eastern Church
to add their signatures to a document so subversive of
the principles of their faith, and of their boasted
adhesion to the traditions of the Church, were worthy
of the occasion. Promises and bribes on the part of
Eugenius, and compulsion and intimidation on that of
the emperor, alternately urged them on to that sub-
scription of which they afterwards so bitterly repented.

The secret history of this strange negotiation is given
by one who was an unwilling witness of it—Syropulus,
the grand ecclesiarch of the church of St. Sophia, and
the minute historian of this fictitious union. The two
last of the Byzantine historians, Phranza and Ducas,
the one connected by marriage and the other by blood
with the imperial family, pass over this eventful visit
of the Eastern court to Europe with a brevity which
shows either that the Council of Florence possessed in
the East but little influence and authority, or that
they were anxious to touch as lightly as possible a

subject so fraught with melancholy and humiliating reflections.

The arrival of the imperial court at Constantinople, amid the tumult of eager inquiries that broke forth from the multitude assembled to witness its debarcation, completed the humiliations of Florence. Proud anticipations of victory and success were in every heart and upon every tongue. Deep, therefore, and bitter was the mortification of the anxious crowd when, with the one noble exception of Ephesius, the broken-hearted prelates confessed that their convictions had been betrayed to their necessities, and that though they returned in greater poverty than ever, they had lost withal the inheritance of their faith—proving themselves (as Ducas somewhat naïvely observes) even worse than Judas, who, when he repented, was at least able to bring with him the thirty pieces of silver, the price of his betrayal.

The domestic affliction of the emperor, in the death of his wife, was lost in the universal flood of sorrow and remorse, and in the terrible prospect of the overwhelming calamities which awaited the empire. Yet the apprehensions of future ruin were insufficient to screen from the minds of the distracted citizens the humiliating events of the past, for which they held that "fire was kindled against Jacob, and anger also came up against Israel."[*]

A sincere, but too late, retractation crowned the

* Ducas, cap. xxxiii.

bitter repentance of the Eastern Church. In a synod held in the great church of St. Sophia, in 1450, the act of union was solemnly and irrevocably cancelled, and the final and most inveterate of the separations of Eastern and Western Christendom completed. The Council of Florence fulfilled in its day the mournful office which the Council of Trent sustained in a later age of the Church's history, confirming and establishing, perhaps for ever, a schism which it had been called together to heal. Bessarion and Isidore, who had contributed so much to this specious but hollow reunion, were rewarded with the cardinalate; from which the former would have been elevated to the papacy, but for a timely appeal to Italian nationality from one of his too envious colleagues. The tide of emigration of noble and learned Greeks flowed on with them towards Italy; and the results of the Florentine Council were to be traced rather in the world of letters than in that of divinity—rather in the revival of philosophic learning in Western Europe than in the importation of the mystical divinity of the Eastern Church.

Meantime Eugenius, flushed with the success of his religious diplomacy, invited other proposals of union from the sectaries of the Eastern Church; and the same year which witnessed the election of an antipope by the Council of Basle disclosed projects of union with distant bodies of Christians, which scarcely at any other period would have been recognised by the

Church of Rome. Cardinal Julian, mindless of the strange events which were taking place in that distant body, which was once the theatre of his own achievements in the cause of the liberties of the Christian Church, devoted his undivided attention to the reconciliation of the Armenians with the Church of Rome. For this purpose, in company with Albergati and other men of learning, he held frequent conferences with the deputies of that nation, which terminated in their acceptance of a statement of the faith of the Roman Church, very minutely drawn up and signed, in February, 1441, by Eugenius and twelve cardinals. From the absence of his own name from this final settlement of a negotiation which he had himself conducted, we are led to suspect that Julian had just before left Florence for Rome, whither, in 1442, the council was itself transferred.

The union of certain Jacobites or Monophysites with the Church of Rome was then effected. This was brought about by the zeal of Albertus à Sarthiano, who had long represented the court of Rome in the Eastern world. This ecclesiastic had drawn the attention of Cardinal Julian to the distressed state of the countries of Palestine, and claimed in their behalf the intervention of the court of Rome. There can be little doubt that he prevailed upon certain members of these separatists from the communion of the Eastern Church to obtain the protection of the Western powers, by placing themselves under the spiritual rule of the

Roman pontiffs, and thus to shelter themselves by a timely alliance from the storm which overhung the Eastern Church, even in Europe, and whose effects they had already experienced.    The fact that the supplementary proceedings of the Florentine Council, or rather of the Western remnant of it, received no countenance in the East, and are even unnoticed in the records of the Eastern Churches, indicates that they were little more than a theatrical representation before the European powers of the results of that celebrated union of the Churches, whose fictitious character was becoming daily more apparent—a pageant to celebrate the triumph of Eugenius at the very moment when a stranger had invaded the pontifical throne. For the long threatened deposition of the pope, and the election of a rival pontiff, had been now accomplished.    Amadeus, Duke of Savoy, who had changed the scene of his life from the field of battle to the retirement of a hermit on the banks of the lake of Geneva, was invited from the hermitage to the papacy, in which he was solemnly installed by the fathers of the Council of Basle.    And, though the act was, under the present circumstances of the Church, rather one of desperation than of conscious power, the memory of the past gave it to the mind of Eugenius an aspect of danger which prevented him from looking upon it without the most gloomy apprehensions.    Hastily calling together a consistory, he opened his anxiety to the assembled cardinals, and

x 2

received from Julian so new a view of the cause of
his fear, as to enable him to look upon it with entire
indifference.  The council, in truth, had become the
mere wreck of that which had once resisted the
supreme pontiff, and had so signally defeated his
attacks on its authority and independence.  The
Cardinal of Arles still retained the presidency; but
the support of the secular power, which had so
successfully backed the presidency of Julian, was
now withdrawn, and the laity generally, wearied out
with this unnecessary conflict, ceased to take interest
in the anathemas and counter-anathemas of popes and
councils.

A body which had once numbered in its ranks
hundreds of mitred ecclesiastics had now dwindled
down into the mere shadow of its former greatness.
To the loss of Cesarini, Cervantes, and Capranica,
was added that of the Archbishop of Palermo, better
known as Panormitanus, one of the greatest canonists
of that and of every age.  He had been the very soul
of the council in its later history, and the powers of
his mind were fortified by learning so extensive and
profound, that his name alone carried with it an
irresistible authority in the ecclesiastical world.  As
none had been more active than he in furthering the
citation and suspension of Eugenius, his defection to
the pontifical party was looked upon with the greatest
amazement.

Nor had defection been more active in thinning the

ranks of the council than death. The plague, breaking out at Basle, cut off Ludovicus the Prothonotary and the Patriarch of Aquileia, and brought to the very verge of the grave the celebrated Æneas Sylvius, afterwards Pope Pius II., the most influential and remarkable of those who carried down to a later period the traditions and the policy of this memorable age, and with whom they may be said to have become extinct. He had accompanied Cardinal Capranica to Basle, and was appointed soon after secretary to the council, where his talents recommended him to the patronage of the Emperor Frederic III., who made him his secretary. He remained in the imperial household until his election to the cardinalate by Nicholas V., the successor of Eugenius, and not many years after (the short pontificate of Calixtus III. intervening) was elected to the papal throne.

But while the Council of Basle had thus died out, the Council of Florence had well fulfilled the mission which the policy of Eugenius had assigned to it, of restoring the power of the papacy through the stately machinery of a synod, and bringing about a union sufficiently specious to dishearten the adherents of the opposite faction. "Under the shadow of the Greeks," to use the words of the fathers themselves, he had carried his designs against them—or as the Eastern emperor described his object in the preliminary conference—"The pope does this not so much for necessity's sake as for the report which will be spread

in Basle and everywhere that an œcumenical synod is
assembled and in full work, whereby himself will
be advantaged and the Council of Basle will be
diminished."*

Julian, whose contempt of the factious proceedings
of the council after his departure was never for a
moment dissembled, had throughout regarded this
negotiation as the means to a greater end—that of
bringing the Eastern empire under the protection of
the rest of Christendom.  Nor could he have seriously
devoted himself at so critical a moment to the absurd
and chimerical projects of union which succeeded the
departure of the Eastern court, had he not regarded
them as bearing on this great political object.

But ere we altogether pass away from the Council
of Basle, the imperishable monument of the wisdom
and of the zeal of Cardinal Julian, we are led to trace
some of its more important results on the future
history of the Church.  While the acts of that great
assembly discovered the previous errors and neglects
of the ecclesiastical order, the failure to enforce them
hurried on a far greater movement than any which
was contemplated in the most turbulent periods of its
later existence.

The courts of France and Germany in vain appealed
against the suppression of those reformatory edicts
which illustrated at once the grandeur of the design
of the council and the weakness of its executive power.

* Syropuli, Sect. v. cap. iii.

The celebrated letter of Martin Mayer to Pope Pius II. on behalf of the German empire, and the constant reclamations of the French monarchs, were not, however, without their ultimate fruit; and the long disputations which were occasioned in Europe by the strife between the council and Eugenius led to a state of neutrality which far better than any other promoted that freedom of thought which had been awakened at Basle and Constance. The advocates of this neutrality, which was not only profitable to ecclesiastical inquiry, but also to the interests of the powers of Europe, wearied out with the long warfare of popes and councils, maintained the lawfulness of suspending all decision between their conflicting claims until the assembly of a future general council, and in the meantime asserted that every metropolitan might erect in his own province a tribunal of final appeal. "It is evident," to adopt the words of a contemporary writer on this subject, "that by reason of this neutrality the Christian religion is divided into as many parts as there are heads of these exempted persons."* When we remember that the first step of the reformation in Germany was the appeal from the pope to a future council, and the first stage of our own the recovery of the rights of metropolitans, we shall be prepared to acknowledge not only that the suppression of the reforms of the Council of Basle was the immediate cause of the reformation of the sixteenth

* Tractatus de Neutralitate (ap. Würdtwein, tom. vii. p. 413.)

century, but that the first principles and impulses of that greatest of all religious movements may be traced to the enlightened assembly which received its inspiration from the zeal of Cardinal Julian.

# CHAPTER VII.

THE return of Julian to the Eternal City, the scene of his earliest associations and of the only repose which his life of tumult and distraction had ever enjoyed, enables us to stay for a moment, and but for a moment, the rapid current of our narrative.

. For the first time since his legation into Bohemia as the representative of his patron Martin V. he was now permitted to re-enter the city of his birth and the scene of his early affections. There is something refreshing in being able to dwell upon the shortest season of rest and tranquillity in a life so hurried and tempestuous as his was; and this residence in Rome, though short, was one of comparative repose and serenity. He was now enabled to cultivate the society of those learned and eminent men whom the union of Florence had secured to Rome, especially Bessarion and Isidore, both now elected to the cardinalate.

The riches of Eastern philosophy and the literature were now being opened out to Europe, and it may well be doubted whether any one contributed more to this revival of learning and science than the great Cardinal Bessarion, who was once nearly elected to the papal throne. Many converts of wealth and rank had already made their homes in Italy, and as the fall of the Eastern empire became more and more inevitable, the desire to obtain shelter in the West grew stronger and more urgent. By the learned and illustrious society which filled Rome at the close of Eugenius' pontificate, the public mind was well prepared for that great intellectual change which the days of Leo X. matured rather than began; and the platonism of Bessarion anticipated, if it did not even inspire, the philosophic tastes of a Bembo and a Sadolet. In a congenial society like this Julian might well have desired to linger; but his repose was rudely broken by the claims of inexorable duty, and the perils of eastern Europe called him back with renewed energy into the field of active labour.

The affairs of the kingdom of Hungary were already developing many causes of serious apprehension to the court of Rome, and to these his mind was now directed with the same ardour with which it had before been directed to those of Bohemia, as he himself declares in a letter to Æneas Sylvius written at this period. The death of Sigismund, which we have before shown to have exercised so great an influence over his conduct as regarded the council and Eugenius, opened in the hereditary dominions of the deceased emperor many difficulties and causes of political anxiety. His son-in-law, Albert, Duke of Austria, had been nominated his successor in these kingdoms, but he did not enter upon their government without experiencing the resistance and disaffection of the Hungarian nobility, by whom, as a German, he was considered a foreign intruder.

An insurrection soon after his accession to the throne, arising from the same national jealousy, proved that the tenure of it was as doubtful as the acquisition of it had been difficult. An attack of dysentery, brought on probably by anxiety and fatigue, relieved him from the cares of his new station by removing him from the scene of them; and shortly after his death his wife Elizabeth gave birth to an heir who received the name of Wladislas. The infant prince, after his coronation as King of Hungary, was placed under the guardianship of Frederic III. who had succeeded Sigismund in the empire. But in the interval between the death of Albert and the birth of Wladislas the nobles urged upon the queen the importance of contracting another marriage, pointing out Wladislas, King of Poland, as worthy of her choice. The queen permitted them to send an embassy to the Polish prince to open this delicate negotiation, but stipulated that if in the meantime she should give birth to a prince this permission was to be considered withdrawn. Before the ambassadors reached Poland the news of the birth of

Wladislas was brought them, but they failed to
fulfil the promise they had given in such a case,
and proceeded with their negotiation. Nay, they
even went so far as to offer the crown of Hungary
to the Polish prince, and invited him to take immediate possession of it. He accompanied them
accordingly without hesitation to Buda, where he
was solemnly crowned by the same archbishop who
had officiated but a little while before at the coronation of his more legitimate namesake.

The emperor, who adhered firmly to the cause of
legitimacy, which was ably sustained by the partisans
of the queen and her infant son, strongly resisted
the new claim to the throne of Hungary, while the
court of Rome, viewing a long minority in that
kingdom as perilous to the whole of Europe, of which
it formed the key, advocated the cause of the elder
Wladislas as one of necessity. A civil war was thus
begun in which both the imperial court and that of
Rome were too deeply interested to be qualified to
become mediators, and which threatened to divide
and dissipate the forces of Europe on that very
battle-field upon which they should have united to
check the alarming progress of the Turkish power.*

The legation into Hungary was at such a moment
of primary importance as well as of the most perplexing difficulty; and to this Cardinal Julian was

---

* Æneæ Sylvii Europa, c. i. Epist. 81, ad Leonardum Episc.
Patavin. &c.

without delay appointed. In the year 1443 he entered upon this new scene of exertion and danger; but before his departure he received from Eugenius the bishopric of Frascati, a preferment which seemed rather given in acknowledgment of his services in defence of the Roman court than as their peaceful and final reward. The addition of this new pastoral care could but remind him with renewed force of the contrast in which his sacred office already stood with that upon which he was now preparing to enter; and while he laid aside the spiritual weapons he had wielded at Florence to resume in Hungary the temporal sword he had so unsuccessfully drawn in Bohemia, his fatal predilection for the camp was again conspicuous. We have to lament, moreover, that there was not merely a change in the manner and weapons of his warfare, but even in the principles for which he fought; while we approach a period of his history so fatal to his reputation and to his life as that to which we have now to lead on our reader—"Dishonorably obscuring hereby his later days," observes Count Litta, in his animated sketch of the life of Cesarini,* "he provoked his fatal destiny."

As the objects of his policy became more extensive and difficult, his mind became more sanguine and unscrupulous in their pursuit; and at the present moment, the great work of uniting Christendom

* Famiglie Celebri Italiane (Fam. Cesarini), Fasc. v.

against the Turks, which, till the close of this century, was the very soul and secret of the policy of the court of Rome, and that chiefly through his own ardent inspiration, had thrown all the objects and principles of his former life into the background. The vastness of his plans and the conviction of the necessity of carrying them out seem to have entirely absorbed his mind. That conduct alone seemed good which was favourable to the leading policy and ruling idea of his life—that alone evil which obstructed or opposed it. When he left the clearer atmosphere of Basle, and the influence of that great republic of free and vigorous minds had ceased to exercise itself upon his own, he entered upon a scene of intrigue and casuistry at Florence which at once unfitted him to resume the station he had left, and prepared him for a still more fatal degeneracy.

His noble and apostolic conduct in resisting the encroachments of the papal power was first gradually relinquished, then looked upon with a suspicious dread, and finally openly repudiated. " I admit," were his words at Vienna, when this now distasteful subject was pressed upon him, "that I have said and written what you allege; but departing from the truth I erred. . . You followed me when I erred, follow me then when I advise well."* This advice the rising courtier to whom it was addressed (and who was none other than Pius II. himself) was

* Pii II. Bulla Retractationis.

led to adopt; and the same advice he offered at a later period to the University of Basle, in the memorable words " *Æneam rejicite, Pium recipite.*"

It is seldom, however, that such a recommendation has been followed in the case of any great man who, having invited to a new and untrodden path, attempts to call back his followers into the beaten track. Even those who are unfit to lead acknowledge, in their very imitation, the truth that "that is most valuable which is individual, which is marked by that which is peculiar, and characteristic in him who accomplishes it."* The bull of Pius and the advice of Cesarini follow their earlier writings with so halting a pace, that they seem but the apologies of age and decrepitude for the sincere zeal and intrepid activity of manhood.

The first object of Julian on his arrival in Hungary was to settle the minds of the people in their adhesion to Eugenius, the schism occasioned by the election of Felix V. having given a dangerous pretext for disaffection to those who, from political causes, were alienated from the court of Rome. Then, finding that the only method of pacificating the kingdom was to effect a matrimonial alliance between the widowed queen and the usurping Wladislas, he addressed himself with his usual diplomatic zeal and skill to this difficult task. Frequent were the interviews he had with the queen on this subject; and the

* Dr. Channing " On Associations."

motives he urged for such a union were such as,
had not her maternal feelings been dignified by the
sense of her duty towards her people and in a confidence in their zeal for her person, would have
speedily commanded her acquiescence. The protection of her son (which Julian urged, as making
this alliance a duty and a necessity) she confided
to the justice of God and the loyalty of the Hungarians. She yielded, however, at length, rather to
the importunity than to the arguments of her advisers,
and assented to the marriage on these conditions:
that Wladislas was to abdicate the throne he had
usurped, and to become the regent of the kingdom
during her son's minority, or until he should die;
that an ample dowry should be secured her; the
claims of Hungary to Podolia and Wallachia relinquished; and certain lands belonging to Hungary
transferred to the kingdom of Poland for defraying
the expenses of the projected war. These conditions
were readily accepted by Wladislas, but the Hungarians and their great general Hunyiades demanded
terms which should be less injurious to the interests
of their country. Julian modified them, but without
success. He then proposed a conference between
the queen and the Polish prince, but this was equally
unsuccessful in accomplishing the much-desired object.
An amnesty was the only result of this singular
interview, but the terms on which it was accepted
did not transpire.

Almost immediately afterwards the queen was seized with an acute internal disorder which closed her life so strangely and suddenly, that the suspicion that she was poisoned rooted itself deeply in the minds of all her subjects.* But the cause of her son did not materially suffer by this calamity; for Giskra, her faithful and active general, still vindicated it with the same zeal as before, and the Emperor Frederic was uncompromising in his resolution to maintain the cause of his helpless ward.

In the meantime the zeal of the cardinal legate was absorbed in the endeavour to avert the possibility of a treaty or even suspension of hostilities with the enemies of the Christian name. Wladislas, devoted as he was to war, and knowing that the field of battle was the proper theatre of his skill, had, notwithstanding, at the present moment, a just apprehension of the value and importance of maintaining peace until the troubles and distractions of Europe should be tranquillized. On the side of the Turks the desire for peace was no less deeply felt; and the successes of Hunyiades, and the ardour of the young king to continue and complete them, induced them to hasten the negotiation of a peace with Wladislas. Julian, whose arguments and entreaties derived an irresistible force from the warlike

* Vitus Arnpeck, a cotemporary writer, attributes her death—but without sufficient reason—to Wladislas, whose whole life is far above the imputation. (See Hieron. Pez. Scriptores rerum Austriac. tom. i. p. 1,254.)

Y

propensities of the young king, failed not to urge upon him the vital importance of an immediate and uncompromising resistance of the Turkish power, painting in vivid colours the perils of Europe, especially his own kingdoms, and the hopes it entertained of him at this critical juncture. To his fervid eloquence was added the subdued, though deeper appeal of the despot of Servia, who, as a despoiled prince and bereaved father, called upon Wladislas to assert and avenge his cause against those who had deprived him of his country and of his children.

The success of these urgent entreaties was complete; and animated with the thought that the dangers of Turkish diplomacy were now removed, the cardinal undertook a mission to the emperor at Vienna, accompanied by the orators of the king, the Dean of Cracow, and Laurentius de Hedervara, palatine of the kingdom. Frederic, who had just returned from a progress through the Rhenish provinces, received them coldly, and with marked aversion to the object of their embassy, which was to arrange conditions of peace between himself and Wladislas. The two orators were such violent partisans of the Polish monarch, that it was with great difficulty that Julian made them agree on any terms of peace with the emperor. A truce of two years' duration was finally determined upon, in which it was stipulated that the two monarchs should refrain from every act of hostility against Hungary and Austria respectively.

This temporary agreement is mainly to be attributed to the prudent chancellor of the empire, Caspar Schlick, who anticipated from it the most beneficial results. "For," he writes to Julian at this time, " as from a little war a great one arises, so from a short peace there may spring a more enduring one. In this two years' time we may hope that men's minds will be softened, a forgetfulness of injuries will supervene, commerce and communion will produce intimacies from which, please God, an universal concord may be found to arise."*

On the return of the cardinal from Vienna, the king determined to open the campaign without delay.† After several days spent in public prayers and religious solemnities, the army left Buda, and marching on slowly, in order to give the inhabitants of the districts which it traversed an opportunity of joining its ranks, arrived at the confines of Wallachia and Bulgaria. Here the king received an accession of troops, headed by one of the Bulgarian chieftains, with whose assistance he succeeded in capturing several towns; and finding that parties of the Turks were lying in ambuscade in the neigh-

* Epist. Æneæ Sylvii. ed. Nuremberg. 1496, Ep. 169.
† The authority for this part of our history is the work of Philip Callimachus, " De Rege Wladislai seu de clade Varnensi" (Aug. Vindel. 1519.) He was nearly a cotemporary of those who took part in these transactions.

bouring woods, he encamped on the farther side of
the river Morave. From this encampment, Hunyiades,
with a chosen body of men, made an effectual inroad
into the interior of Bulgaria, and took the town
of Sophia. After frequent successful enagagements
with the enemy, he returned to the camp to Wladislas,
who resolved to lead forth the entire army. Being
advised that Carambus, the Turkish prefect of Asia
Minor, was coming to the defence of the Sultan
Amurath, he depopulated and laid waste the southern
country of Bulgaria through which the Turkish
general must pass. As the allies advanced, animated
with their uninterrupted success, it was rumoured
that the Turks were lying in ambush in a strong force
near the town of Nissa. Hunyiades undertook to
fall upon their ambuscade by night, but they anticipating this movement retired to some distance from
the town, of which Hunyiades took immediate possession; gaining intelligence that the enemy were
returning and had encamped at no great distance,
the indefatigable Hungarian again planned a noc-
turnal surprise. The light of the moon enabled him
to draw up his men in perfect order before the
enemy was aware of his approach, and the attack
was contrived with so much energy and decision that
flight was almost as impossible as defence.

The victory of Hunyiades was as easy as it was
signal, and the number of the slain very considerable.
To the success of this vigorous movement a very

remarkable personage contributed not a little, whose
name has descended to posterity in close connexion
with that of the great Hungarian. George Castriot
(better known under the name of Scanderbeg) was
the son of a prince of Epirus, who had been deprived
of his country by the Turks, and kept with his
father at the court of Amurath as a hostage. His
two brothers had been despatched by the tyrant, and
his own great courage and promise, from which
Amurath expected much future benefit, was the sole
cause of his preservation from the same fate. On
his father's death, finding that he was still kept in
the same ignoble thraldom, he secretly resolved to
free himself from so intolerable a yoke. By a skilful
stratagem he recovered his liberty and that of his
Epirots, and, taking advantage of the successes of the
Christian arms, assisted them in effecting the humiliation of that power from which his family and country
had suffered such cruel injury.

The army of the allies now passed onward into
Thrace, but the prospect of the journey over Mount
Hæmus, which was now before them, and the entire
failure of their provisions and other resources, compelled them seriously to meditate breaking up the
campaign and returning homewards. The voices of
Julian and the despot of Servia were loudly raised
against this submission to the pressure of circumstances, but the time of deliberation was unexpectedly
shortened by the enemy, who, from maintaining a

defensive system of warfare, entered upon active hostilities and attacked the allied armies with vigour and decision. The battle was long and well sustained, but terminated in favour of the Christian forces, who among their prisoners numbered the Turkish general Carambus, whose name has been already mentioned. Thirty thousand, according to the despatch forwarded by Wladislas to the Emperor Frederic, fell on the side of the enemy in this encounter—a computation which Æneas Sylvius justly suspects as exaggerated " in the fashion of the Poles, who of great things talk still greater."* But although the confidence of the allies was increased by this victory, their hunger was unappeased, and their threatening necessities had no better prospect of relief than before.

The king reluctantly submitting to an influence which was beyond his control, began his return from the scene of his successful crusade. After painful and tedious marches, which were continually interrupted by parties of the enemy, the victorious army reached Belgrade, and thence proceeded to Buda, where it was received with great pomp and rejoicing. The public entrance of the allies into the Hungarian capital had almost every feature of an ancient triumph; the captives and the spoil went before them, the soldiers of the crusade commanded by Cardinal Julian being ranged between these and the rest of the army. Wladislas did not re-enter his palace

* Epist. 81.

before he had offered public thanksgivings for the
success which had attended his arms, in a cause which
was looked upon so eminently as the cause of the
religion of Christ.

In the beginning of the following year embassies
and deputations from all the powers of Christendom
arrived at Buda, to offer congratulatory addresses to
the king on his late achievements. Not the least
zealous of these in the demonstrations of their joy,
and in urging the necessity of continuing the war,
were the representatives of Eugenius. They were
ably seconded by the legate and the despot of Servia,
who brought forward all the motives that could
influence a prince whose warlike propensities received
so high a sanction from his religious zeal. But a
powerful counteracting motive presented itself in the
wasted and disturbed condition of his two kingdoms,
Poland having been devastated by the Tartars, and
Hungary divided with factions and menaced by an
invasion from Giskra and the untiring partisans of
the young prince on its Bohemian frontier. The last
danger rendered it necessary to negotiate a peace with
the legitimatist general for two years; but the claims
of Poland were not so easily dealt with, the public
voice demanding the return of the king with even
greater importunity than Julian and the Hungarian
nobility urged the prosecution of the war. The latter,
however, again prevailed, and after a diet held at
Buda, it was resolved to invite the co-operation of

all the allies, and to enter immediately upon a new campaign.

When intelligence of this determination reached the Turkish court, Amurath, seized with consternation, hastened to open a negotiation with his warlike adversary.*    After some delay his ambassadors obtained an audience of Wladislas, who, yielding rather to the necessities of his own kingdom than to their arguments, agreed upon conditions of peace of which the fundamental stipulations were the cession by the Turks of all their European conquests except Bulgaria, and the release of captives on both sides, especially the sons of the despot of Servia.    A day having been fixed upon for the surrender of the cities and countries to be ceded by the Turks, a peace was finally concluded between Wladislas and the sultan, which was to last for ten years.    The oath by which this treaty was ratified was taken by the Christians on the Gospels, and by the Turks on the Koran, constituting it on either side a convention of the most solemn and paramount obligation.    And as if this were not enough to complete its sanctions, the Eucharist itself was added, and, in spite of the warnings and protests of Gregory de Sanocenis and other bishops, the very ark of the Christian faith was, for the first time in the history of the world, offered as a pledge for the security of the infidel.†

---

* Æneæ Sylvii. Europa, cap. v.
† See Callimachus, l. 2, and Æneas Sylvius (Europa and Ep. 81).

Scarcely were the ratifications completed, when letters arrived from the Cardinal Admiral Condolmieri, from Hunyiades, and from the Emperor John Palæologus, of a character tending most fatally to unsettle the mind of the king. His destiny pointed him out as the champion of the Christian cause, and his successes hitherto seemed to give a divine sanction to the mission which he had so enthusiastically entered upon. To the fulfilment of this high destiny his friends and allies urged him on, and before them all, and while they were watching with admiration and cheering with their applause his victorious progress, he had suddenly withdrawn from the conflict and deserted those whom he was leading on to a new harvest of glory. Every eager response to his invitation to the war seemed now to reproach his inconstancy, and to cover with shame his retreat from the exalted position in which this hitherto successful crusade had placed him. Instead of the tranquillity which follows the honourable settlement of an anxious warfare, he experienced the chilling remorse of one who has made a fatal and perhaps irretrievable concession. The reaction of the ardent mind of the king was too violent to need any impulse from those around him. His repentance was as sudden and complete as it was deep and bitter; and Julian, who had watched its course with a keen discernment, until it reached that point at which it most needed the direction and most easily admitted the influence of

another, at last opened his mind to the king, after
vainly endeavouring to associate in his counsels the
high and upright bishop Gregory de Sanocenis, who
with Hunyiades had insisted that though faith was
not rashly to be reposed in such an enemy, when
once given it ought on no account to be broken.

Turning to the king and to his counsellors, who
were in a state of doubt and desire which too well
prepared them for his fatal casuistry, he spoke as
follows : * " I would that we had altogether abstained
from entering upon that treaty which seems to have
been concluded with the Turks, though I hope it will
prove to be void and of no effect.  Not that we need
admit that any right or religious compact would be
broken if we should still prosecute the war, but because in giving and accepting these conditions we
have wasted a good deal of the season best fitted for
its prosecution.  I should have opposed it in the
beginning but I saw that your minds were too bent

---

* Bonfinius (Rer. Ungar dec. iii. 1. 5) gives a different version of
this address to that of Callimachus, but on many grounds we may
regard the latter as the more accurate version.  The Jesuit Rosweyd,
on the strength of Bonfinius's narrative, endeavours to exculpate
Julian altogether from the breach of faith which has so darkly
clouded the reputation of his later years, but with so little satisfaction even to himself that he is obliged to add, " Age vero, sint è nos-
tris qui opinati fuerint censuisse unum Julianum perfidis Turcis non
servandam fidem, quid hoc ad causam de quâ agimus ?  An privati
hominis error constantem ecclesiæ labefactabit fidem ? " (*De fide
hæreticis servandâ*, p. 152.)  Unfortunately the "privatus homo"
was here the papal legate, and the confirmation of the act, probably
even the origin of it, is to be traced to Eugenius himself.

upon peace to give me the least hope of raising them
to energetic action by my influence.

"Besides this, I knew that all which has been
this day announced on the facilities of carrying on
the war in Europe, while the Turks are implicated
and detained by a war in Asia, would very soon
transpire, and I rather chose to wait until you could
believe it on the authority of others, than by un-
timely declaring it to risk the suspicion that I had
feigned the intelligence and was boasting only of my
own vain desire. Now, however, since the confirmation of your victory has come to you from another
quarter than mine, and your regret at your undertaking shows that you rather believe that the event
has fulfilled my wishes than that my wishes have
anticipated the event, I feel called upon to maintain
not the expediency of carrying on the war which
all admit to be necessary, if with your safety and
liberty you would also retain your former glory,
but the lawfulness of carrying it on after the ratification of this treaty (such as it is) on both sides.
For I see many perplexed about the empty names
of faith and treaty, and deliberating not so much
what they desire to do as what they ought to do—as
though some unadvised words mutually banded in
hope and fear could have the name and sanctity
of a treaty; when that alone is rightfully a treaty
which is entered upon by those who have a right
to treat, and is ratified, not by a mere pledge of

words, but by a fulfilment of its stipulations. This, however, has neither authority in the consenting parties nor the subsequent execution of the articles agreed on, but merely boasts the name and ceremonies of a treaty which do not become holy and binding until they are loyally carried out on both sides.

" To begin, then, with what seems to be the origin of this agreement. It was competent to the king to negotiate for truces and for peace with the Turks so long as he carried on the war with the strength and success of this illustrious kingdom; so long as, without external aid, and at the risk of his own kingdom, and with his own resources alone, he preserved the safety and dignity of Christendom. But when he was pleased to communicate with other Christian princes the plans and object of his warfare, he ought to suspend it only with the consent of those with whose resources and under whose auspices it is undertaken and carried on. But supposing that the whole affair had been the king's alone, as it was before his alliance with the other princes, even then it was not competent to him to have any correspondence with such a race of men, far less to conclude a treaty with them; nay, such a treaty is not itself binding without the consent of the pope. Add to this, that the conditions stipulated by the enemy have not been in any way fulfilled, for which reason, even if there were no other, all which is alleged to have been said or done is made void. Furthermore, since the faith of the stipulation, nullified, as it is, by themselves, has not established the sanctity and obligation of the treaty, we must conclude not only that the king is released from his bond (if there were ever any), but that all the propositions and acts of the orators who came to us to ask for peace were deceitful and fictitious.

" If the enemy had desired to conclude a treaty which should be firm and solid,—if his desire and pledge had been altogether free from deceit—had he no other man to send than one foreign to him in language, race, habits, and (except his pretended religion) in the whole object of his life?—one who, on the behalf of the Turks, could promise nothing, nor, on the other hand, could stipulate anything for them truly, honestly, religiously, but every one of whose promises and agreements it would be free for them to reject or to disavow without dishonour, if it should be expedient to them to do so. For it would be dishonourable even to them to simulate such an act of submission as this in the person of one of their own nation. And they would guard, for very shame, against any act of submission of their own people, any act which should fall below the popular estimate of their magnanimity and prowess ; they would not that the king should be able to boast that a Turk had ever been a suppliant to him.

" Besides, as the whole action required much duplicity, it was thought that no one could better succeed in deceiving us than one who, but a little before, had been our co-religionist; that what could not of itself command our belief might, under the veil of religion, find an easy access to our minds. If he could obtain such stipulations as pleased him, the enemy would stand by his agreement; if not, he would by the pretence of a treaty obtain at least the advantage of being able in the meantime to plan the course of a future campaign. That this is indeed the case, the fruitless issue of all the stipulations which he ought to have fulfilled plainly indicates. I know that the despot and Hunyiades in a special degree have so much knowledge, and have had so great experience in matters of warfare, that it were a sin to deny that everything is as they have persuaded themselves.

"But the ardent desire of regaining his children, and of receiving again his lost honours and fortune, have, as I believe, constrained the one—while the distrust in the immediate assistance of the allies has induced the other—to apply their minds but lightly to the subject, and not at once to discover the insincerity which is hidden under these gracious assurances. Yet, surely, neither the fear nor the authority of any man ought to influence your minds more than truth, seeing as you do that no one can be bound by such a treaty, whether regarded as concluded without competent authority, or as dissolved through the fraud of the enemy, which has left its conditions unfulfilled.

"But supposing that all has been lawfully done by the king, and nothing insidiously by the enemy, even

then you are bound to remember that your fidelity to
the Christians, whom you invited and admitted to a
participation in the war, has a prior obligation to that
which you pledged to the Turks. And since your
decision is reduced to such narrow limits, that you
cannot keep faith with both, and one or the other
must be relinquished, no one can doubt for a moment
that you ought to select that one who is bound to you
by the stronger tie. What then, I ask further, have
you in common with an enemy like this, from whom
you are separated by your profession, habits, and whole
course and principle of life? What, on the other
hand, have you with Christians, which is not of the
highest obligation? For to pass by the beginnings
of an eternal life, which you had in common—temples,
sacrifices, sepulchres, ceremonies, and holy rites, by
which your minds are bound together by a far closer
tie than that of nature and of a common parentage—
is it not these, I ask, who but a short while ago sent
their fleet into the Hellespont for your safety, for your
glory, adding their strength to yours, and taking up
with you the prosecution of the war, and thus laying
you under such an indissoluble bond of obligation
as cannot be broken without the eternal stain and
infamy of ingratitude?

"Since, therefore, on the one hand, you have men
who, besides having everything human and divine in
common with you, have added the benefit of an
assistance so lately rendered, and who touch you so

closely in every human and divine relation, as to pre-
clude every other alliance; while on the other hand
you have an enemy—cruel, perfidious—opposed to
you not only in war, but in faith and worship;
despising as profane all that you hold sacred, and
violating it when he is able; one to whom faith cannot be given without grave criminality, and with
whom even when given it cannot be kept without still
graver error; there can hardly be much hesitation in
deciding with whom our stipulations ought to be
carried out. If you persevere in the peace you have
taken up, not only will you have been deluded by the
frustration of the conditions on the other side, but
stained with inexpiable guilt, and with the loss of
the glory you acquired in the former war; you will
drag on an infamous life under the daily execration of
all good men. But if, repudiating that impious alliance which even in itself is vain and null, you enter
true to yourselves into that danger into which you
have yourselves led the way, not only will you possess
your own thenceforth in safety, but will regain with
everlasting glory not only those places of which mention is made in the treaty, but everything else which
that dreadful race possesses in Europe.

"Of the ease with which this may be done I
might proceed to speak, were it not for the consideration that the Greek emperor and the Cardinal
Francis (Condolmieri) have sufficiently convinced you
of this by their letters. And their authority ought to

have the greater weight inasmuch as they are nearer
to the enemy, and judge from what is immediately
before them. The fear of the enemy, moreover, greater
than his orator could well dissemble, ought far more
than any address of mine to stimulate you to seize
the present opportunity as your own; which if you
pass by, you will be compelled hereafter, despised and
deserted by all, and with as much disgrace as dan-·
ger, to accept a contest within your own boundaries,
to which, by your very appeal for foreign aid, you have
professed yourself unequal."

To these arguments the cardinal added many others
from the pontifical law, which he prefaced with asser-
tions of the power and strength of the papacy; and
concluded by rescinding and abrogating in the name
of the pope the treaty, such as it was, and absolving
from the oath and pledge they had given to the Turks,
the king, and all who were involved in it.

It is difficult to detect, under this strange disguise,
the features of that enlightened mind which inspired
the decrees and directed the correspondence of the
Council of Basle. And yet there are subordinate
points of resemblance in the course and manner of
the argument to those of the celebrated letters of a
better period, while there are as striking points of
contrast in the nature of the reasons themselves.
The same tendency to accumulate arguments with
such profuseness as to weaken the separate force of
each of them is as apparent in this address as in

z

the appeals to Eugenius.    The same invocations of
Catholic feeling and sympathy which meet us in the
addresses to the Bohemians, meet us also here; the
same sophistical method of explaining away the
terms of a positive and inflexible law which cha-
racterises the speeches of Julian in the Council of
Florence, reappears in his endeavour to escape the
obligations of the most solemnly ratified treaty which
the Christian world has ever witnessed.   Yet the
very versatility of the legate in his arguments for
resuming the war, not only proves that he had but
little confidence in any of them, but that they are
simply introduced to hide the deformity of that single
argument which underlies them all, the anticipated
prohibition of the papacy in every case of a compact
with heretics, and the dispensing power as the sole
remedy for its infraction.

It is hard to suppose that Julian could have attached
any weight to the argument that the non-delivery of
the fortresses by the day appointed was a sufficient
ground to overthrow the treaty when he had contended with energy and even indignation against
Eugenius' advisers, who had attempted to invalidate
the Council of Basle on the ground of a similar delay
in its inauguration.   The specious argument, that "to
whom faith cannot be given without criminality, to
him it cannot be kept without still heavier guilt," is
the only one on which the cardinal really relied, and it
was one that his great patron, Martin V., had too well

taught him, in his letter to the Duke of Lithuania, where he writes: "Know that you cannot give faith to heretics, and that you sin mortally if you keep it to them." *

The true position, which (however repulsive it must be in any form) has never been fairly put by the adversaries of the Church of Rome, is not "that faith is not to be *kept* with heretics," but that "it is not to be *given* to them." Every member of that Church is supposed to be in the position of a precontracted person, whose paramount obligation to the Church can never yield to any subsequent compact, however sacred it may appear to be. "*Juramentum non tollit obligationem priorem*," is the rule of one of our own casuists ;† and the Court of Rome having unhappily undertaken to make the *ecclesiastica utilitas* ‡ the measure of this obligation, has found it easy to annul the most sacred engagements if they interfered with her temporal policy.

It is refreshing to be able to fall back upon one great and bright example even in this day of con-secrated faithlessness and treachery. Gregory de Sanocenis, Bishop of Leopolis, stood alone at this fatal juncture as the representative of the unchanged fidelity of the Polish clergy and people, and raised his voice in loud and energetic protest against a breach of faith which has few parallels in history. The sanguine

* Cochlœi Hist. Hussit.p. 212.
† Sanderson 'De Juramenti Obligatione,' p. 32.
‡ Decret. Gregor. de Jurejurando, l. 2, tit. 24.

temper of the legate, irritated by this unforeseen
resistance, knew no control, and even burst forth in
expressions unworthy of his station and character, and
singularly contrasted with the habits of his earlier and
better days. He scrupled not to call his enlightened
opponent a rustic, a fanatic, ignorant of divine and
human laws, an enemy of religion, and an obstacle to
the extermination of infidels—even venturing to add
menaces to insult. The sturdy Pole, undaunted by
the onslaught of the cardinal, maintained that even
if it were wrong to conclude treaties with infidels, it
was a duty to observe them when made, declaring
that GOD would never sanction an act of treachery
nor suffer it to prosper. With this noble reclamation,
worthy to stand beside the silent protest of the Chancellor Caspar Schlick when he withdrew from the
Council of Constance in the day of the condemnation
of Jerome of Prague, the illustrious representative of
the clergy of Poland left the assembly.*

The address of the legate met, however, with an
eager response from all the other leaders of the
crusade. Even Hunyiades and the Despot of Servia
withdrew their resistance: the one too easily con-
verted by his military ardour, the other bribed, as it

---

* The life of Gregory de Sanocenis, written by the same Callimachus who is the historian of the battle of Varna, is extant in MS.
in the library of the University of Cracow. It is cited in the "History of Polish Literature" of Wiszniewski, published at Cracow, in
the Polish language. I am indebted to my late friend, the lamented
Count Valerian Krasinski, for this important incident in the last
scene of the life of Julian.

is affirmed, by the promise of the crown of Bulgaria, in the event of the expected victory. With a fatal unanimity, the peace which had been accepted was declared void, and the renewal of the war determined on. Emissaries were sent with the news of this sudden change of counsel to Cardinal Condolmieri, who commanded the fleet in the Hellespont, to the Eastern Emperor, and to all the princes who, as they had been made parties to an inglorious peace without their knowledge, were now involved in a far more inglorious warfare, without their consent being even asked.

The more distant allies appear to have viewed the alternative with very little interest or anxiety; but to the Poles, harassed by a civil war, which the presence of their king could alone terminate, it was one of life and death. As soon as the news of the determination of the allies reached them, they assembled the States of the kingdom at Piotrkow, and resolved to send their representatives to Wladislas to entreat him to remain faithful to the treaty, and to hasten without delay in order to save the country from utter anarchy.

But the too eager prince had anticipated the messengers of peace by sending deputies to Piotrkow to explain his reasons for reopening the war, and to prove that he could not recede from his position without the sacrifice of his own honour. In the meantime the proceedings of the fatal day of the renunciation of the treaty had been closed by a

solemn absolution of the Polish king from its obligations, and the publication of an instrument in
which he bound himself to the legate and to the
allies to reopen the war with the Turks without
delay.   This document was signed at Szegedin, on
the fourth of August, 1444.   Among the witnesses
to this paper are to be found the names of Robert de
Thur, Bani of Macedonia, and Sylvester de Thruma,
count of the same: titles, observes a Hungarian
writer, which, as they occur nowhere else, must have
been bestowed by Wladislas, in the sanguine hope of
reconquering from the infidel the country from which
they were assumed.*

Before his departure with the army, Cardinal
Julian took a final and affecting leave of all his
household, in sad presentiment that they should
meet no more, and commended himself to the for-
giveness and to the prayers of all around him.   The
discordant features of his character seem grouped
in stronger and wilder contrast as he drew near to
the closing scene of his life—the attributes of the
warrior and the ecclesiastic exhibiting themselves in
strange and unexampled combinations.   In his twofold
character of priest and general, the legate celebrated
mass daily before his crusaders.   The labours of the
day of warfare were opened with prayer and supplication as regularly as in the more spiritual, though
perhaps scarcely more peaceful, labours of the

* Georgii Pray Annales Regum Hungariæ (Viennæ, 1766).

Councils of Basle or Florence. Well might he have said in his last hours with one who was nearly his cotemporary, "O Lord, Thou knowest that my times have been rather a confusion than a life."* He had, from the first, endeavoured to reconcile in his own person the conflicting characters of the divine, the pastor, the legislator, the negotiator, and the warrior, and now they stood forth altogether, in their closest and last combination.

Breaking up their encampment at Szegedin, the allies moved on to Orschowa, on the banks of the Danube, which they crossed at that place and advanced to Widin. In the meantime, the surrender by the Turks of the places they had agreed to restore came like a last warning and reproach upon the Christian camp : a surrender made the more complete by the restitution of all the captives, including the sons of the Despot of Servia. The mind of the king seems at this moment to have again faltered; but the sanguine eloquence of Julian soon restored it to its former resoluteness. The plan of the campaign was to effect a junction with the naval forces under Cardinal Condolmieri, the Pope's nephew, at Gallipoli; and in order to succeed in this, it was found necessary to take the longer of the two routes which presented themselves, and to pass through the plain country of Bulgaria, along which the war-chariots could be most easily conveyed. Arrived at the suburbs of Nicopolis,

* S. Laurentii Justiniani (Vita).

the soldiers could no longer be restrained from the
work of rapine and plunder. After robbing and
destroying the dwellings in the environs they attacked
the town itself, which was so strenuously defended by
the inhabitants, that they were compelled to relinquish
their expected prey, and to content themselves with
spending two or three fruitless days in a neighbourhood whose opulence had so fatally tempted their
rapacity.

Here, as the king was marshalling his troops, and
preparing them for the more formidable conflict which
awaited them, he was met by the Walachian Prince,
Wladislas Dracula, a man who is described as " never
to be named without the title of a great and most
gallant commander." The ruler of a thinly peopled
and mountainous district, he had already decided that
the attempt to cope with the vast power of the Turks
must end in the extermination of his people. He had
accepted therefore such terms of peace as, while they
left him in possession of his religious and civil rights,
enabled him to reserve his strength for that more
critical moment, whose approach he foresaw, when
not only his liberty, but his honour, and even his
faith itself might be endangered.

When he saw how unequal the forces of the king
were to the great enterprise he had in view, he
entreated him in the most energetic terms to change
his fatal resolve, assuring him from his own knowledge that the Turks were able to bring into the

hunting-field a stronger force than he was leading into the field of battle. He conjured him to refrain from so rash and even insane an attack, and to reserve it for a better day. Even if the chances had been more equal in the battle-field, the near approach of winter must soon render warfare impracticable. To this faithful monitor, the majority listened as though he were uttering not his own sentiments, but those which his compact with the enemy had forced upon him. Not a few, however, acknowledged the wisdom and prudence of the advice, as well as the sincerity of the adviser.

Again, however, the influence of the legate rose above every other, and his sanguine mind once more conjured up before the king the image of the former campaign, and from every feature of the highly coloured picture drew promises and pledges of a higher and a final success. "The surprise would come upon the enemy before he could draw the sword; every place would be undefended. Amurath, on the other side of the Hellespont, could hardly sustain the attack of his adversaries there; and even if his hands were free, would be precluded by the Venetians and Burgundians, and by the pontifical fleet, from succouring those on this side. Moreover the Greeks, in no inconsiderable force, would meet them at the foot of the mountains. The friendly offices of Dracula might well be accepted by all as a proof of his affection to the cause; but no marvel that he should despair of its success, unaware as he was of the preparations and supports on which they relied. Never could he have said to the king what he did had he known how great and how well equipped a fleet—how many thousands of allies, Italians, Burgundians, Greeks, both horse and foot, were now awaiting them. Neither the king, nor those with him, were so wildly rash as to provoke a battle they were unable to engage in. Let the king then be of good courage. As far as regarded strength, all had been sufficiently foreseen and provided for; and as to their success, GOD whose cause it was, and who had already given it them, would Himself secure it to them again."

Addressing himself to the king once more: "Since fortune," said the Walachian chief, "which has never forsaken your highest daring, or the hope of foreign aid—which I trust may indeed be fulfilled—or the secret influence of fate carries you to another conclusion than mine; I will at least assist your plan, which my advice cannot alter, as far as the suddenness of the opportunity permits." He added, accordingly, four thousand cavalry, under the command of his own son, to the forces of the king, and enhanced this welcome gift by assigning two young men as his guides through the country, whose knowledge of its roads and paths was unsurpassed; presenting him at the same time with two horses of the greatest courage and fleetness, if (as he earnestly deprecated) misfortune in battle should compel him to fall back upon this last resource.

Whether inspired by the military ardour of the king, or fascinated by the treacherous eloquence of Julian, the brave Walachian was on the eve of himself joining the crusading hosts, and the religious motive would soon have overborne the moral restraints which his treaty with the Turks had laid upon him, had not the deeper influence of superstition held him back. An old Bulgarian fortune-teller, of whom he had inquired the day before his arrival in the camp, had prophesied the defeat of the Christian army in this campaign, and that the scattered hosts of the king after their defeat would obtain a better success, and a more hopeful future, than a victory at the present time could secure them. In this instance at least, the superstition which dissuaded a breach of faith stood on a higher ground than the religious sentiment which enjoined it.

Passing on through the country parts of Thrace, the Christian army arrived at the river Pamisus, where they destroyed a number of small craft, suspecting them to have been built by the Turks, in order to harass the river districts of Hungary. At this point the king began his preparations for crossing the mountain chain of Hæmus, by sending on Hunyiades with the Walachian auxiliaries, and three thousand Hungarians; the main body of the army following at a considerable interval, and the war-chariots being placed in the midst. As they advanced, they destroyed all the towns which lay along their route, in order to prevent their being fortified, so as to endanger them from behind. Their progress thus became one of desolation and plunder, carried to so barbarous an excess that neither the churches nor homes of the unfortunate Bulgarians and Greeks, through whose country they were passing, escaped profanation or destruction. Wladislas in vain attempted to restrain the marauders, whom he had gathered together for this unholy war, though he gave some restitution in the case of those whose religion had been so wantonly outraged.

In order to hold out an inducement to the Turks to surrender whatever fortresses they still held, they were offered freedom to go wherever they liked, or to enlist in the army of the king. By this offer immediate possession was obtained of many places which before had been strenuously defended. The fastnesses of Sumi and Pesech, whose natural position rendered them almost inaccessible, formed the only exceptions to this ready surrender. These, as they covered the path of his return, the king determined to invest with all his force. The undaunted courage of the assailants soon carried both places, at a loss to the enemy of nearly five thousand men.

At this juncture, when the prospect of success seemed opening out in all its brilliancy, the fatal intelligence arrived from the Cardinal Admiral Con-

dolmieri, that Amurath, eluding the blockade of the
Asiatic coast by the Christian fleet, had conveyed a
vast army into Europe, which had already effected a
junction with that assembled in the Thracian Cher-
sonesus. The Genoese, more mercantile than patriotic,
were believed to have assisted in this masterly movement; but the culpable negligence of Condolmieri
could alone have made their work of treachery successful. From letters of Julian himself, referred to by
Æneas Sylvius,* it appears that the fleet was badly
provisioned; and hence the probability arises that
Amurath seized the moment when the Cardinal
Admiral had put in for provisions to effect a landing
in Europe. In one important point the cotemporary
historians are at variance, Æneas Sylvius charging
Condolmieri with neglecting to announce this fatal
passage of the Turkish army to the leaders of the
Christian hosts,† while Callimachus affirms that the
news came immediately from him to the king and his
allies.‡ It is certainly hardly credible, that the nephew
of the Pope could have been guilty of positive conni-
vance in an act so suicidal as this. His previous
history rather indicates his neglect to have proceeded
from that reckless folly and incapacity of which he
gave such early and convincing proofs.

The crisis was now desperate. Some counselled a
retreat, others were for holding to the mountain passes

* Æneæ Sylvii Europa, c. v.      † Id. Ep. lii.
‡ Callimach. de Morte Vladislai, &c. l. 3.

and fortified places; but the king, blinded by an infatuation which seemed rapidly forming itself into a destiny, descended from the fastnesses into the plain. Here town after town surrendered to the Christian forces without a struggle; Macropolis, Callacrium, Galata, and Varna, the closing scene of this disastrous expedition.

At this place the mountain chain of Hæmus, approaching the coast, loses its former elevation, and sinks gradually into gentle hills and slopes, inclosing valleys of a fertile and picturesque appearance. Two promontories extend into the sea on either side of the town, the land on the south being hilly and cultivated, and that on the north opening into an extensive marsh, which renders the access to the town difficult on this side. The advantages which Varna presented to an army fatigued with so long a march were doubly welcome at this critical moment, as the king was suffering from a tumour which required medical treatment and a rest of at least some days.

In the meantime, the Turkish army had reached Adrianople, and by the seventh day the watchfires behind the nearest chain of hills announced the approach of the enemy to within a few miles of the Christian camp. Presently, as the moon rose, the outline of the vast hosts which were arrayed against them revealed itself to the eyes of the crusaders.

No time was now to be lost; and doubling the watches, and ordering all to be under arms, the

generals hastily assembled together in the quarters of
the king, and consulted on a plan of defence.  Julian
was for putting off any offensive operation until the
strength of the Turkish force was fully known, and
till then fortifying the camp with chariots and other
munitions.  He still clung to the hope of support
from the fleet, which already must have entered the
Black Sea, and, as the blockade was now useless,
might with its whole force co-operate with the Christian army.  The same view was urged by the Bishop
of Agria, the Bani of Slavonia, and other of the
generals; the king maintaining rather an attitude of
acquiescence than of approval.

But Hunyiades and the Despot of Servia denounced
the proposition of the legate in the strongest terms—
" To be shut up in their own camp was rather the
last refuge of the conquered than the honourable position of the invaders.  In everything, and in war above
all, success depended on the first step.  The first encounter would be the measure of the whole war—as
the one was vigorous or feeble on either side, so would
the other be—no sign of fear ought therefore to be
given either to their own men or to the enemy.  All
their safety lay in rapidity of action.  By doing and
daring, and not by scheming, such an adversary as
this was to be kept in awe.  What was to become of
them if the Turks surrounded them while inclosed in
their munitions of war, and gave them no opportunity
to fight?  For they were wholly unprepared for such

a siege as this. And as to the naval forces, what had been said was utterly absurd. For where, in all the world, was such a thing seen or heard of as a land fight carried on with soldiers from a fleet, who could be of no more use on land than cavalry on the sea?" After enlarging on the folly of this hope of naval co-operation, "Let us dismiss," he continued, "so vain an expectation, and go forth in battle array against an enemy whom we have over and over again routed and destroyed this last year—whose timidity and confusion makes him break off every undertaking he begins; now betaking himself to Asia, and now to Europe, rashly hastening hither and thither, anxious and alarmed at the sound of the lightest rumour.

"Let us not ask how many are coming against us, but with what spirit and boldness they come. However countless they may be, they will bring nothing but the memories and the fears of the conquered. Soldiers should never be accustomed to defend themselves in intrenchments, which are the defences of those who distrust their arms, and who ought to obviate the necessity of such defences by attacking the enemy without delay instead of shutting themselves up, like the unwarlike multitude, in fortified places and intrenchments. Base it were, indeed, for brave men to believe that they could find a better protection in chariots and trenches than in their arms."

The words of Hunyiades, spoken in the full consciousness that he was standing in the presence of an inevitable and overwhelming danger, and yet with the resolution to perish rather than to shrink from the perils he had himself invoked, found an echo in the heart of the courageous king, and an eager response from all but the legate and those who had seconded his more prudent but less spirited counsels. The enemy was already preparing for the attack, and an hour's delay might be fatal. The arrangement of the defence was at once entrusted to the great Hungarian. The other generals rushed to their posts. Every one prepared for a conflict of life and death.

After an anxious survey of every point which was open either to a direct attack or a subtle approach, Hunyiades brought together the chariots in the gorge between the valley and the marshes, so that he might with the least possible danger fall back upon them in case of a repulse, while, with the other munitions of war, they might form a protection against any attack from behind. The defence of the middle of the valley he assigned to the king and the royal troops of Poland and Hungary. Towards the marsh, where the natural defence was greatest, he placed only five regiments of Hungarians, concentrating his greatest strength on that side of the valley which skirted the town of Varna. The fortunes of the day would be plainly determined at this point; and here, accordingly, he fixed the great standard of Hungary, defended by the Bani of Slavonia and the Bishop of Agria, to whose forces he added those of the Despot of Servia, and the crusaders under Cardinal Julian. In the rear, and under cover of the chariots and instruments of war, he stationed the Bishop of Waradin, to whom was confided the Standard of St. Wladislas, with an additional guard of Poles, under the command of Lesco Bobricius, a leader whose reputation of vigour and boldness made him a fit protector of so sacred a trophy. To himself and the Walachians the great Hungarian assigned no special place, holding himself ready to rush to the critical point wherever assistance was most needed, or danger was most imminent.

Amurath, in the meantime, had sent forth six thousand cavalry rather to take a complete view of the position of the Christian host than to precipitate an attack. But, either from the irresistible desire to open the battle with their old adversary, or from the conviction that the Christian forces were this time, at least, unequal to the conflict they had provoked, the Turkish horsemen harrassed the enemy with their darts, and it was with difficulty that the Ban and the Bishop of Agria restrained their men from rushing on to the charge.

Their prudent forbearance, however, was mistaken for fear, and the Turks at once began the attack. After a vigorous repulse they were pursued by the troops under the Bishop of Waradin, who, " more skilled in sacred than in warlike arts," believed that the victory was already won. The Despot and the Bishop of Agria followed the perilous example of their clerical colleague, and presently found themselves confronting the close ranks of the enemy in the further part of the valley. From this extremity of danger the Despot found a path of escape, while the Bishop of Waradin, thinking to escape towards the mountains, perished in the treacherous swamp between. The Bishop of Agria, after a desperate effort to make for Galata, returned to the attack, and was never heard of more.

The tide of victory now carried on the Turks as far as the standard of St. Wladislas, for the Despot, the Bani, and Julian, were already driven back by an overwhelming force. There the fight was close, and with varied success, until the death of the brave Lesco, who had hitherto been the very soul of the battle, gave the decided preponderance to the Turks, who rushed against the chariots, as well as the soldiery, and by the violence of their charge overthrew several of them. The king and Hunyiades hastened to save from destruction their last means of refuge in case of a defeat, and their appearance again turned the stream of battle. The Turks took to flight, and were pursued to some distance by the ardent king, who was eagerly recalled by Hunyiades to the more important task of supporting the Bani and Julian, who were now hard pressed by the enemy. Here the energy of the battle revived, and the Christian host rang with shouts of encouragement and earnest mutual appeals. Nor were the Turks wanting in the

most vigorous efforts to animate and inspire one
another against those who had shown that nothing
would satisfy them but the utter destruction of their
faith and race.

The carnage was frightful on both sides, and the
places of the slain were filled and filled again with
unyielding obstinacy.    At length the Turks gave
way; but the temptation to fall upon the prey rendered their flight more perilous to the Christian host
than their most resolute attack.  Hunyiades, whose
mission had carried him from one point to the other
of this battle-field, was now compelled to fly to the
succour of the king, who was engaged in a hand-to-
hand fight with the Janisaries, who surrounded him.
Cut off by a too rash advance from his own people,
they had already believed him to be slain, and scarcely
had the Turks taken to flight, when the troops of the
king fell into a confusion no less fatal.    Before
the great Hungarian could rescue the young prince,
the horse upon which he was mounted was pierced
with a spear, and fell, and Wladislas in an instant was
added to the heap of the slain.    Hunyiades rushed
into the midst of the enemy with his faithful Walachians to snatch from the hands of the Infidels the
body of a prince now become no less the martyr of
the Christian cause, than the model of the Christian
warrior.    But even the last energies of despair were
fruitless; and the flight of all around him compelled the brave Hungarian to save the remnant of

his men by flight. Already the Despot of Servia and Julian had retreated towards the dense forests which lay beyond the hills, and which they reached at nightfall, followed by hundreds of fugitives, all alike ignorant of the extent of their defeat, or of the calamity which had deprived them of their chivalrous but too daring leader.

The closing scenes of this day of confusion and dismay have never been cleared up, and the fate of Julian is among its last and most affecting mysteries. Between the hour of his retreat from the field of battle, and that in which he was found lying naked and wounded in the wild mountain pass, which he had entered on that fatal night, there is a void which only the conjectures of his cotemporaries can fill up. " There is a report," writes Æneas Sylvius to the Grand Duke of Milan, " that the most eloquent and most prudent man of our age, Julian, the Cardinal of St. Angelo, has fallen in this battle, and has given forth in death that noble spirit which was so divinely fitted for every work he undertook to fulfil. Some allege that he fled with John the Vaivode of Tran- sylvania . . . . which I should have rather hoped, but his death is more probable, for he was never fortunate in war." * A little later, the rumour passes on into an admitted fact :—" Wounded in the battle, and fainting in his flight through loss of blood, he was slain near a marsh by the impious hands of the

* Æneas Sylv. Ep. 52.

Hungarians, not at the instigation of the nobility, but through the rage of the populace; and thus breathed forth that glorious spirit which once with its sweet discourse swayed at will the assembled fathers at Basle." * These words were written in the very year of this fatal conflict. In his history of Europe, written some time after, the cardinal is said to have perished through the perfidy of the Hungarians, who slew him while watering his horse, for the sake of plunder, rather than for revenge.† But though the conjecture here assumes the bold front of a historical fact, the cloud must still remain. Few had escaped to tell the tale of that dreadful night, and who of that few could authenticate it? We can but faintly track the path of Julian through the wood into which he escaped, to the verge of the fatal marsh where, plundered and wounded, the victim rather of avarice than of revenge, he sank down alone and friendless to die.

It is impossible for those who have followed him through a life so marked by the strange rapidity of its vicissitudes to pass hastily over a scene like this. The hero of Bohemia, the moderator of divines at Basle, the religious diplomatist at Florence, the counsellor of princes and diets, the negotiator of the peace of Europe, was now lying naked and wounded in a wild and desolate mountain-pass of Thrace; the pillar of the Roman Church in the court and in the camp,

---

* Æneas Sylv. Ep. 81.          † Europa, cap. v.

the undoubted successor to the papal throne, had he
survived Eugenius, whose rival he had so nobly
refused to become, was left to perish without a
mourner, and without a friend; leaving the history
of his fate to the conflicting rumours of the battle-
day, and commending his soul to God, amid a tumult
of wild recollections, a death-dream of wars and fears
confused and fitful, yet not undisturbed from without,
or freed from the terrible realities of which it was the
lingering shadow; for there rode up one to his side in
this moment of agonising conflict, whom, if the power
of recognition was not entirely lost, he might have dis-
cerned to be Gregory de Sanocenis, the only protesting member of the council-chamber of the fallen
prince. The cruel reproaches of this relentless ecclesiastic sank deep into the ears of the dying man. He
reviled him for his breach of faith to God and man,
and charged him with all the slaughter and misery
of that fatal day. " 'Tis just," he exclaimed over the
all but lifeless body which was stretched at his feet,
" 'tis just that you should perish thus—you, who
made the apostolic see perjure itself, and taught
mankind that God sanctions treachery and infidelity;
to him you shall now answer for your motives, as for
your words." Thus cruelly avenging himself for the
insults which he had received in the council, and the
losses he had experienced on the battle-field, he left
him to die.*

* See the MS. life of Gregory de Sanocenis, by his cotemporary

Strangely was the almost prophetic wish which Julian uttered from Basle fulfilled in this eventful hour in both alternatives—" If any one seek my death let him send me to Prague or to the Saracens, where I shall die as a Catholic ;" for it was in warfare with the Saracens that he fell, while from the hands of his own followers, if not of Prague, at least of Christian Europe, he received the fatal blow. Nay, a doubt might even arise whether the immediate cause of his death be not still balanced between the crusaders of his own ranks and the infidels who were his proper adversaries ; for the accounts even of cotemporary historians are too confused and conjectural to enable us to determine with certainty on which side the fatal scale preponderates.

But the eventful history of the defeat of Varna, so abruptly succeeding the account of the victories and triumphs of the Christian confederates, and resting upon the rumours of a battle-field deserted under circumstances of such strange perplexity, received at first but little credit in Europe. Hopes and conjectures, the most wild and groundless, were everywhere entertained, and the unquenchable valour of Waldislas and Julian seemed to give them in the imagination of the eager multitude a kind of immortality.*

Callimachus, preserved in the library of the University of Cracow, and referred to by Wiszniewski, whose work was cited above, and also the close of the narrative of Callimachus, " De Clade Varnensi."

* "Diu post mors Vladislai et Juliani incredita fuerat, quidam

The suspense which they encouraged and prolonged prepared them for the reception, or rather gave occasion for the fabrication of a story which is too singular to be passed over in silence, and which was related by a person professing himself to have been an attendant of Cardinal Julian, to Gilles Charlier, Dean of Cambray.* "Concerning this most reverend father," are the words of the Dean, "one of his household related to me in the French language the triumph of his most glorious martyrdom, in the month of February, 1447. When, for the punishment of our sins, the Turks had gained a victory over the Christians, many of the faithful being slain, and others betaking themselves to flight, this most reverend Father was taken and placed before the Turkish Emperor. The doctors of his execrable law are produced, who contend with him on the faith, seeking to subvert him, and turn him to their impious sect. But when they are by no means able to do this, they ply his holy mind alternately with promises and threats of punishment to turn him from his good resolve. For the tyrant promises him, if he consent, to make him high-priest of his law, but if he consent not, to try him with sundry tortures; but when this most reverend Father acquiesced not for a moment, but professed with constancy the Lord Jesus Christ, there approached torturers and physicians. In

namque ut invictæ virtutis illos sciebant, sic et immortales esse rebantur" (Æneæ Sylvii, Ep. 81).

* V. Baluzii Miscellaneorum. l. 3, vol. iii. (Ed. 1680, p. 301.)

the middle street of the city, in the presence of the
tyrant, a venerable bishop and many Christian captives
standing near, he is placed upon a ladder and flayed
by the torturers, the flesh being lanced with iron
spikes.   When he had been wearied out with this
martyrdom he was again asked to give up the Christian
law, and come over to their sect.   If he will do this
the physicians promise to heal his wounds.   But
neither ambition of their honours, nor the promised
blessing of health, could injure the holy man, but,
persevering in the faith of Christ, he is again tormented
as before.   His end now approaching, turning to the
bishop who was present, he says, 'Behold, venerable
Father, I go to Christ; to thee I commend my flock,
that is, the Christian people; be a brave warrior of
Christ, and confirm it in the faith;' and thus triumphant he migrated to the Lord.

"This," proceeds the Dean of Cambray, "the aforesaid domestic related to me in Cambray, having been,
as he affirmed, himself present at the time, and seen
him alive and dead.   He added that the tyrant
ordered the body to be burnt, and the ashes placed
in a gold or silver case, in token of the victory he had
gained over the Christians.   Whether this be true (he
concludes) or not, I know not."   We, however, can
have no doubt on the matter, the evident and glaring
absurdities of the whole narrative being more than
enough to condemn it if it were even reconcilable with
more authentic facts.

The circumstances which it alleges were not only utterly unknown to Æneas Sylvius, Callimachus, Cochlaeus, Michovius, Bonfinius, and all the earlier historians of this period, but are incompatible with the facts which they relate. The cruelties imputed to Amurath are equally inconsistent with his historical character; and were they not so, the folly of aggravating the Christian world by a display of them when he might have gained so much by the ransom of the Christian prisoners, would render them incredible. Nor is it very likely that Amurath would have believed in the sincerity of the conversion of one who claimed the power of absolving a whole nation even from the most solemn and voluntary obligation.

The ignorance of the narrator in supposing that there was a high-priest of Mahomedanism corresponding to the Roman pontiffs in the Christian hierarchy, the absurdity of the cardinal commending to one under the same condemnation as himself the care of the Christian people, and so far recovering from the deadly wounds he had received in the battle (and which Gregory de Sanocenis himself witnessed) as to be capable of being made the subject of the tortures here detailed—all this, and much more that will occur to the most casual observer, compels us to reject the statement recorded by the Dean of Cambray as altogether absurd and fictitious. And when it is further considered, that the relation was made to a stranger by an anonymous person at a great distance of place and

time, and probably to obtain sympathy and assistance
for himself by ministering to the known passion of the
ecclesiastics of the Roman Church to make martyrs of
their eminent men, we cannot fail to transfer it from
the severer page of history to that of fiction and
romance. We hold it, therefore, to be indisputable
that the fatal day which witnessed the defeat and dispersion of the Christian host at Varna was the last
which dawned upon Cardinal Julian, and that he died
as a soldier rather than as a martyr, the victim either
of the avarice of his own followers, or of those who
pursued him from the field of battle. His life
belonged to the close of that chivalrous age in which
the characters of the warrior and of the priest were
too strangely mixed up and confounded together to
enable us in every case to separate the self-devotion of
the one from the martyrdom of the other; but his un-
disguised predilection for the camp leads us to expect
that the sacerdotal character would be found to the
very last subordinate to that of the warrior, in which,
though never fortunate, he was ever most distinguished.

"In this place," (we may continue in the words of
his cotemporary Vespasiano Fiorentino) " before we go
further it appears right to say somewhat of those of
his virtues which were known to me out of that infinite
number which he possessed.

"In the first place, it was the firm opinion at the
Court of Rome, and wherever else he was, that he

was of perfect chastity. He slept always wrapped in a woollen shirt; he fasted every Friday on bread and water; he fasted, as was the custom, on all the vigils, and the forty days of Advent as well as in Lent; he said the matin service regularly: rising at night, and calling his chaplain to say it with him; often by night he said it in the Church de Servi, near which he lived; and had had a staircase made which went into that part of the Church where the body of Christ is now kept. He went forth from his chamber and along the passage above the cloister, and entered the Church by the stairs already mentioned, where he said matins, and prime and terce.

He had in his house a most pious priest and attendant, old and tried, a German by birth; to him he confessed every morning, and said mass every morning, nor did they neglect to confess every day. He had by nature an unheard of liberality, in giving all that he had to God, and more than he was able; no one ever went to him without bringing away what he desired, and going away from him contented. One day, when certain brothers of a religious order, having obtained the alms they sought, were departing, I happening to be there with a chamberlain of his, who was like his patron, he said to me, " If you were to see my lord some day go to the palace without a cloak, do not be astonished at it, for he gives to God what he has, and what he has not;" and in this manner he assisted all the necessitous.

Having been a student himself and experienced the need mentioned previously, he had pity for poor scholars, and used to inquire whether in the Court of Rome or at Florence, where there was an excellent seminary, there were any poor youth and of good ability, who could not pursue his studies from poverty, and having sent for him, kept him in his house for two or three months, to see if he was apt in learning, and to watch his life and habits. Having done this, if he discovered him to be good and of good habits, he procured him the body of the civil law, and then sent him to the college, either of Perugia, or Bologna, or Siena, whichever the student preferred, for seven years, giving him the text of the civil or canon law, whichever course he chose, and a sufficient sum of money for his maintenance; finally, he clothed him suitably to the college which he was to enter, and having done this, would call him and say: "Come hither, my son, I have done for you what was not done for me, only in order that you may become a good man. Above all, love God and fear him, and doing thus all will be well with you. While I live, trust me, nothing shall be wanting to you that you may stand in need of." These are the truest and best alms, and this every good man who has the means should do; he who reads this life bearing in mind that the Cardinal had no other income than that of his hat and of the bishopric of Grosseto, and sought for no other.

He lived at home very sparingly, without any display, and was naturally a stranger to every kind of pomp. He did not cause the dishes to be fore-tasted when he dined; he used to have but one dish; sometimes he dined alone in his chamber. As soon as that which he had to eat was brought he washed his hands without wishing that anyone should kneel to him; only two held the towel and one simply held the bason in his hands; as soon as he had taken his seat at table, he desired every one, except two or three attendants who remained to wait upon him, to go to have their dinner. When he took wine he put only enough into his glass to cover the bottom of it, and filled it up with water, so that the water was merely coloured, and such as it astonishes me to reflect on.

It happened the first summer that he spent in Flo-rence,* that all or the greater part of his family were taken ill, to whom he exhibited this unheard-of charity. First, he arranged that every one in his service should be visited by the physician twice daily, in the evening and in the morning, and ordered him to give them all that they required. He desired them to have a care also of their souls, and to confess immediately they fell sick. I will mention here his amazing humility, and exceeding charity; every day he went twice to visit all these sick persons in the morning

* Probably we should read Ferrara instead of Florence, as it seems to have been the plague which raged at the former place that attacked the cardinal's household.

and in the evening, to see that nothing was wanting to them; nay even, when the servant of his groom fell sick, the humblest of all the servants of his household, he visited him like the rest. Oh! unspeakable love, Oh! immense charity! I am struck with amazement at that which his lordship bestowed, and at that which he bestows on most people.

Let us come now to those who were at the point of death, and who needed spiritual assistance in the extremity of their life. I saw in the Cardinal's house his secretary, a Lombard, by name Messer Bartolomeo Battiferro,* at the very point of death. The cardinal stood over beside him, and in the very hour of his departure I saw him sitting at the bedside with his face on the pillow, close to that of his secretary, comforting him without ceasing in his parting moments, and anxious that he should expire in his arms; he never left his side, and desired to remain alone with him. Let every one mark the ardent charity of this lord cardinal—how wondrous and worthy of imitation. I will say thus much in this place: I have known many saintly men, but of all these admirable characters I never knew the like of the Cardinal of St. Angelo.

*     *     *     *     *

The alms which he gave and the succour which he afforded to the poor were derived, when his means were not sufficient to supply them, from the sale of

---

* This Bartolomeo the reader will remember as the successful purloiner of the seal of the Council of Basle.

books which he possessed : often have I seen him sell books, duplicates, and those which he did not require, entirely to make up these alms. He ordered his household in the most admirable manner, and there were in it many worthy persons and of good and laudable habits. It consisted of thirty persons, of whom fifteen were servants, the rest being chaplains and other persons of consideration.

Pomp, as I have already said, was foreign to him, for he had so many virtues that they were his ornaments. He kept eighteen or twenty mules, and when he went to the palace, as is customary with the cardinals, his attendants, when the pope had entered, went to take a walk ; and, because the cardinal set so much value on time, when he alighted, if he saw that there was nothing to do, or that the pope was engaged, he returned home. And it happened many times that wishing to go home, there were only his chaplains to be found, yet he did not care to be without his train, but mounted with his chaplains and went in that manner from Santa Maria Novella to the Servi where he lived.

He was of a most patient disposition, and a great lover of good men, nor did he cease to strengthen and exhort every one to do rightly, or to urge the Jews to come to the Christian religion. There was living in Florence in his time a Hebrew physician, learned in the Jewish law, named Maestro Giovanni Angelo, a Spaniard by birth. It displeased the cardinal that he was a Jew, and every day he ceased not to urge him to become a Christian, and he succeeded so completely as to prevail upon him to be baptized. Messer Gianozzo Manetti, who had great skill in the Hebrew language, co-operated with the cardinal to bring about this agreement. He wished the baptism to take place on a feast day in the church of San Giovanni, and desired Messer Agnolo Acciaiolo, and Messer Gianozzo Manetti, together with his lordship, to be his sponsors; and they made in the church of San Giovanni, over the great font, a fair preparation of coverings of cloth, and there the cardinal baptized him with his own hand, and performed all the ceremonies of baptism. When he was baptized, the cardinal had him clothed anew in a garment of rose-coloured stuff, and leaving with the above named citizens, and with the baptized Jew, returned to the Servi, and there held a fair entertainment to celebrate his success in conducting him to the true light of our faith. He desired him to remain in his house and always to eat at his table, and paid him an extreme honour. He gave up to him one of his principal chambers, and assigned him a servant and two horses, and wished him from thenceforth to dwell in his house, and treated him no otherwise than if he had been his own son. These are the fruits which prelates ought to produce in the Church of God.

There was, and is still, a society in the hospital of (nello Spedale di Lemmo), called that of San Girolamo, which met, and still meet, every Saturday evening, and say a certain office, after which they discipline themselves, which was a devout object, and specially at a time when there were so many men of exalted character and admirable habits. Having heard of its fame, the cardinal used to go most Saturdays accompanied by two or three of his household, and after he had entered he permitted those who had accompanied him to leave him and to return at an appointed time. When he had entered the chapel and offered his devotions, he placed himself beside the head of the company and desired the others to stand at his side, while he stood during the whole service and disciplined himself like the rest.

There were, at the time that they arrived at this discipline, so many tears and groans, and such astonishing devotion, that no heart could be so hard as to remain unmoved, and chiefly when Bartolomeo di Ser Benedetto was speaking, at whose words, as he was a man most excellent and most devout, and had an omnipotent tongue, no one could be hard enough to resist the deepest emotion. The cardinal exhibited the greatest devotion in this society, as we have said before. When I was young, and went one day to his lordship, he asked me if I belonged to any company of young men. I answered that I did not. See the unheard of charity of my lord, who said to me, I wish you to enter that of Ser Antonio di Mariano, I will go to him myself upon it. And thus he did, for he was careful not only of the greatest but the least things that affected the salvation of his neighbour. He asked me further if I wished to be a priest, adding that if I did, he would assist me in pursuing my studies and in obtaining a benefice afterwards. He told me to take fifteen days to consider it, and at the end of that time asked me what I wished to do? I answered that I did not desire to be a priest. He rejoined that he could not do better for me than he had done; there was in him nothing but charity and love.

He wished his family to be most well-conducted, and that at the Ave Maria every one should be in the house; at that time he used to go in person to lock the gate, and had the key deposited in his chamber. It happened one day, that one of his servants, having occasionally passed by the door of a citizen on the other side of the Arno, that citizen came to complain of it to the cardinal, who, as soon as he heard it, caused the servant to be called into his presence, and ordered him not only not to pass before that door, but not to go to the other side of the Arno where that citizen's house was, and whenever he did so to be ready to quit his service. It happened that that servant did not pass over the Arno, but he used to go to a place which was opposite the citizen's house, but at a great distance, and this he did more out of spite than anything else. The citizen came again and told the cardinal what the servant had done. As soon as he heard it he caused the servant to be called into his presence, and said to him, " My son, depart from my service, for I require you no longer in the house; since you wish to live in your own way and as it seems fit to you, and I wish you to live in such a manner as is without offence both to God and men," and immediately he desired him to quit.   His lordship ever busied himself in ordering things that required arrangements, and chiefly those things which involved the honour of God.

It appearing to him that in the Servi they did not live with that honour of God which he desired, and wishing that all religious fraternities should be bound to the observation of their rule, as he was often with Pope Eugenius, he arranged with his holiness to re-form this order and make it one of observance.   He dismissed accordingly all the brothers that were there, so that not one remained, and introduced a becoming observation into the same order, and formed the house anew into a house of religion; and all the time he was in Florence he preserved it thus, so that at that period there were two well-conducted monasteries there, the one in question and that of Saint Mark. The cardinal endeavoured to do all that he could for the salvation of those souls whom he could prevail upon by his authority to be diligent in good works.

He used often to go to the chambers of his servants, and chiefly at hours in which they did not expect him, and ask them familiarly what they were doing.   One day he entered the chamber of one of his secretaries, who had in his hand a book called the Hermaphrodite, written by Panormita. Immediately he saw the cardinal he threw the book which he had in his hand behind a chest, but not so cunningly as to escape his observation. The cardinal having entered the chamber of this secretary asked him what he was reading. He blushed and was unable to answer. The cardinal smiling, for he was of a cheerful nature, said, " You have cast the book behind that chest," and he confessed that it was true. Then he took it, and overwhelmed with shame showed it to the cardinal, who gently received it, telling him that it was not well to read it, seeing that there was a papal excommunication against those who read it published by Pope Eugenius. Then he bade him take it and destroy it, and when he had done so, and it was destroyed, he smiled and said, " If you had known how to answer me, peradventure you would not have destroyed it; the reply you should have made me is, that you were hunting for a precious stone in a dunghill." He adopted this mildness that the young man might not be alarmed, or think that the cardinal had accused him from having a bad opinion of him.

Of such gentleness he gave frequent instances. It happened one day, that as he was going to the palace, one of his servants through carelessness or neglect lost a mule which he valued; when it was lost and the cardinal had returned home, he called the servant and asked him how the loss had occurred. When he heard it, he remained some time silent before he replied; then he turned to him and merely desired him to use all diligence to find it if it was to be found, if not, he added, we must have patience; then he dismissed him. There were in the room some who wondered at so great patience. The cardinal, to clear up the minds of all, said, "You are surprised at my having abstained from replying, but I did so for this reason; I wished, before I replied, for my reason to return to its place; when it was returned I made my answer." After this manner did the sages of old who did not suffer themselves to be ruffled for any cause whatever. The cardinal was of a sanguine temperament, which was readily excited to anger, but which he moderated in the manner described above; in all his conduct he manifested his virtue."

From the private habits of the cardinal we are led to take a last survey of his public life, the more prominent parts of which have formed the subject of our narrative. The great objects which engaged his attention throughout, and in the pursuit of which he manifested a boldness and decision which amounted almost to recklessness, were the reformation and the union of the Church. These co-ordinate objects, whose necessity was the theme of the discourses of all the great ecclesiastics of the age, and the means of effecting which were so anxiously devised but so feebly executed, maintain, in the life of Julian, an unceasing conflict for priority.

His ardent mind, which at Basle had so boldly endeavoured to effect the union of the Church by means of its reformation, and had forced Eugenius into union that he might not arrest the progress of reform, speedily discovered that it was attempting an impossibility. A divided body has not the power over its own members, even if it has the desire, to effect those reformations whose tendency is to reunite it; while a body which is only externally and superficially united shrinks from that work of reformation which would betray its real and deep divisions. The one of these truths was proved at Basle, while the experience of the council of Constance had firmly established the other. In the former the Church, weakened and divided between the Eugenian and the synodical factions, not less than by the Hussites, and other open adversaries, vainly attempted to reform its distracted body. However admirable its canons and plans of reformation, they were utterly ineffective; and that council, whose laws we admire as a perfect model of ecclesiastical wisdom, was unable to enforce the very least of them—unable even to reform a single convent of nuns within the city of Basle itself.*

In the council of Constance, on the other hand, an artificial and political union had been effected, which its constructors were too well aware could not endure the work of reformation, which was the second great task assigned them. Unwilling, therefore, to discover

* Joannis Nyder Formicarius, lib. i. c. viii.

the weakness of their structure, they transferred their
office to a future council, and separated as soon as
they had completed the settlement of the papal
monarchy. Julian, taught by a long and trying
experience the impossibility of carrying on the work of
reformation with so shattered and strained an instrument as the council of Basle, through its many factions,
had become, and finding that its remaining powers
were ready to be exercised for the destruction of all
that the preceding council had effected, was in a
manner compelled to make the union of the Church
the means of its reformation rather than its reformation the means of its union.

The opportunity of the reunion of the Eastern with
the Western Church was singularly adapted for this
change of plan, the execution of which was hastened
by the circumstances of danger and of difficulty
which multiplied around him. The sudden and premature termination of his eventful life prevents us
from deciding whether he abandoned altogether his
former position as a Church reformer, when he entered upon the labour of reuniting the divided body
in which he held so exalted a station. Perhaps he
might have returned to the task which was yet little
more than begun ; perhaps he might have been too
utterly disheartened by the practical rejection of all
that had been done to enter upon the reformation of
the Church anew, or at least to enter upon it in a
synodical manner. A successful effort, which he made

while at Florence, to reform, with the authority of Eugenius, a monastery there, gives some indication that he would have returned to the work of reformation, though along a more quiet and private path than that which he had trodden before; but the growing fear of reopening, by the attempt to reform, those schisms in the Church which the prudent policy of his first patron had so recently healed, renders it very improbable that he would have taken part in any public deliberations on this subject.

The greatest and the best minds in every branch of the Christian Church have been unable to overcome the obstacles which everywhere present themselves to its real reformation. The bishops Alamanni and Ippoliti, the predecessors of the celebrated Scipio de Ricci, Bishop of Pistoja and Prato, who had entered with an apostolic zeal upon this gigantic work, sank under it, and left it to their great successor fraught with increased dangers, and complicated with new difficulties. His long and useful life was spent in the fruitless endeavour to reform the religious orders, and to restore a simpler and more practicable form of government to the Roman body. There is, however, an undercurrent of influences flowing on steadily against the executive power in that Church, which has hitherto rendered the noblest efforts of the supreme government ineffectual; and these influences derive from the religious orders their chief strength and direction.

Even the council of Trent itself, whose labours for
the reformation of the Church have been very insuffi-
ciently recognised by the adversaries of the See of
Rome, found its efforts opposed in this direction by
practical difficulties which rendered them inoperative,
or at least, but partially effectual. The obstacles
which present themselves to every church which
addresses itself zealously to the work of its own
reformation, and which even in our own Church has
left disfigurements and abuses which equal those
developed during the great schism itself, lead us to
look with charity, and even sympathy on the difficulties that increased around the path of the reformer
of the Church in that earlier day, and to be very jealous of neglecting that work of personal reformation
which may be the means of ministering to the health
and vitality of the Church to which we belong. Many
of the best regulations of the council of Trent were
obsolete even in Italy in the days of Ricci; many of
the laws of our own Church have become a dead letter
in our own day from the same spirit of laxity and
negligence; and until we carry out, as far as we are
able, our whole ecclesiastical plan, adjusting it, as far
as possible, in all its distinctive features, to our own
state and to the present necessities of the Church, we
can have little hope to see its primitive vigour renewed,
or its full design accomplished. The fear of disturbing
a settled order of things will ever make men look
with suspicion, if not with abhorrence, on any plan of

reformation which acts upon the body from without,
and is formed upon new principles, or, at least, new
habits of thought from those which appear in the first
design. A strict adherence to the organic laws of the
Church is the best means of securing reformation, and
at the same time, of preventing innovation. "All
great mutations," in the words of Lord Faulkland,
" are dangerous even when what is introduced by that
mutation is such as would have been very profitable
upon a primary foundation." We must study well
the design and foundation of the building which we
propose to alter and to reform, or plans, however perfect in themselves, will be vain and impracticable.

The life of Cardinal Julian may supply the Church
reformer with many lessons and many warnings. His
prophecy of a violent reformation from without, if a
constitutional reformation should be delayed too long
from within, had not its last fulfilment in the Reformation of the sixteenth century, nor was the temporising
diplomacy of the empire at that great epoch the last
imitation of the Eugenian policy that the Church is
destined to witness. The worldly, but profitable,
"neutrality" which followed the dissolution of the
council of Basle has still too many advocates, and the
distraction of the Church itself in deciding between
the claims of reformation and of unity, of truth and of
peace, remains still. May the Spirit of truth and
peace suffer not His Church, while settling the prece-
dency of these great labours, to forget that the

night is at hand, in which no work may be done; that a conflict may be yet nearer, in which the powers which we are now permitted to exercise for our reformation, may be taken away from us to our destruction!

# APPENDICES.

# APPENDIX A.

*On the Theory of the Church, as propounded at Constance and Basle.*

THE confusion into which the great schism had thrown the entire Church had not only opened many invincible arguments against the theory of the decretalists on the universal monarchy of Rome, but proved the necessity of arriving at some more fixed principles on the derivation of ecclesiastical power, and the mutual relations of the several members of the ecclesiastical body. The greatest divines and jurisconsults of the age had been assembled in the Council of Constance to judge the claims of rival pontiffs, and to determine the great question whether and how they might be altogether deprived of their hitherto supreme office. The precepts of the decretal epistles were accordingly unceremoniously set aside even before their spuriousness had been discovered ; and though it was reserved for the age of the Reformation to explode the entire system of the pontifical law by discovering it to be but a pious fraud, or rather a successful forgery, the Council of Constance, less critical, though not less enlightened, claimed the honour of first repudiating and overruling the antiquated maxims of decretalism.

The great question discussed in the council, and by the celebrated Gerson, *de auferibilitate Papæ ab Ecclesia*, drew after it the whole theory of the Papacy, and disclosed its unsoundness. This illustrious doctor and Cardinal Pierre d'Ailly have left us

c c

most valuable treatises on the theory of ecclesiastical power as expounded at Constance; and as these were written in the Council, and read publicly in its open sessions, we may conclude that they fairly represent the sentiments of the entire body on this important subject. We shall endeavour therefore to point out some of their principal features to the reader in this place. " Ecclesiastical power (writes Gerson) is that power which Christ supernaturally and specially conferred upon His apostles and disciples, and their legitimate successors unto the end of time, for the edification of the militant Church, according to the laws of the Gospel, for the attainment of everlasting bliss." (Von der Hardt, tom. vi. p. 79.) In which definition he observes that Christ is the *causa efficiens*, the apostles the *causa subjectiva*, the Gospel the *causa formalis*, and the edification of the Church the *causa finalis*. He uses the word *specially* to separate those who are set apart for spiritual rule from the other members of the Church (*omnis viator*), to whom faith, hope, charity, prophecy, fear, piety, &c. are equally given. He then separates the *potestas ordinis* from the *potestas jurisdictionis*, both of which he makes twofold; the one being a power over Christ's real body (in the Eucharist), and over his mystical body, the other a power *in foro exteriori* and *in foro conscientiæ*.

From the fact that Judas received with the rest of the apostles the power of consecrating the body of Christ, he draws an argument that " ecclesiastical power is not necessarily founded in faith or grace, but in the baptismal character." This is aimed against the doctrine of Hus, who maintained the foundation of such power to be in the predestination to faith and good works, and who held that wicked bishops and priests were not properly bishops or priests. With respect to the power of order, he grants that there is none higher than the priesthood either in pope or bishop; but that the same power exists in all in different manners; and gives this rather ingenious illustration of his meaning : " Sicut exemplificant quod eadem est humanitas in

homine dum est puer et eadem dum factus est vir : vir nihilo-
minus generare potest sibi simile, puer nequaquam." (P. 85.)

He then passes from the distinction of the power of order in
bishops and priests to the power of a general council, which he
makes supreme in all acts of legislation, and which acts as
the whole Church in everything. The power of the keys he
maintains with St. Augustine to be given to the whole Church
(claves ecclesiæ datæ sunt universitati). The power of inflict-
ing punishment he asserts to belong to the Church only by the
permission and concession of the civil authority. Proceeding to
examine the foundations of ecclesiastical power, he shows first
the necessity of all its several parts, and yet the possibility of
the removal of any one of their representatives (even if it be
the pope for the time being), if it be by the authority of a
general council, which includes in it the papal power as well as
every other.

. The fact of Peter's bishopric at Antioch, and perhaps also the
recollection that so many of his alleged successors lived out of
Rome, leads him to assert the truth of the popular maxim at
that period, *ubi Papa ibi Roma:* But as it is manifest even upon
the most orthodox Roman view that the localising of the papal
power in Rome fixed its succession in the Roman bishopric ; it
cannot but appear that the dislodgment of the papacy for so
long a period, and its residence in Avignon, broke up the succession, or transferred it to Avignon, as St. Peter had transferred
it, according to the Roman legend, from Antioch. As the fact of
St. Peter's death in Rome is the principal argument for this
transfer of his authority, the deaths of so many pontiffs at
Avignon might give the inhabitants of that city as reasonable a
claim for the possession of the papal throne.

. The necessity of Reformation constitutes in the eye of Gerson
a sufficient cause for the "*auferibilitas Papæ ab Ecclesia.*" The
papal power is then more fully discussed, and is shown to consist
of a *plenitudo ecclesiasticæ potestatis* given by Christ to Peter

c c 2

and his successors. The origin of this monarchy he traces to
the greater convenience of consulting a single person than a
general council, refuting those who alleged the supreme power
to be derived "by an immutable divine right, and a primary
institution of Christ." The supremacy of a general council is
then laid down in the emphatic form so well known to those
who are conversant with the decrees of this council and of that
of Basle, and the assertion made that a general council can be
assembled without the pope, and to judge the pope, and that it
can decree laws to moderate and rule the *plenitudo potestatis* of
the papacy. (P. 107.)

After expressing an opinion that the council would exert this
controlling power as regarded the interpretation of its laws, he
lays down certain general maxims to this end. He then shows
the right of the council in electing a future pope, and passes
thence to the demolition of the decretalist theory of the dominion of the popes in the temporal affairs of the clergy and laity.
These are the principal points of interest in a work which,
when we consider the period of its composition, must be deemed
one of singular enlightenment ; and when we consider the
authority which it possessed, must be regarded as one of the
very last importance in determining the ecclesiastical opinions of
this remarkable period.

Of no less importance is the cotemporary work of Pierre
D'Ailly, *de Ecclesiasticâ Potestate*, written in and read publicly
before the Council of Constance, in 1416. He professes, in his
preface, to set it forth as the Catholic *via media*, avoiding at
once the doctrines of the Waldenses and of the Ultramontanists
of that day. The treatise begins by a definition of ecclesiastical
power similar to that of Gerson, and which he divides into the
power of ordaining, that of dispensing the sacraments, of preaching, of judicial sentence, of ecclesiastical arrangement (*i.e.* the
disposition of ecclesiastical persons and places), and of receiving
sustentation. The power of working miracles he holds to have

belonged only to the primitive Church, and not to be inherited by bishops and priests, "*quia jam non indiget fides miraculis confirmari;*" a notable passage from such a writer in the day when the visions and miracles of St. Catherine of Siena, St. Bridget, and so many modern claimants of supernatural power, were the deepest part of the popular belief. All the six powers, he enumerates, he pronounces to have been equal in all the apostles, except the fifth (the *potestas dispositionis ministrorum*), which he holds to have been specially given to Peter ; although even this he maintains to have been originally bestowed equally on all the apostles, and only centred in Peter from a foresight of the necessity of order that would arise subsequently. As the cardinal makes the *potestas ordinis* to be equal in every bishop, whether pope, cardinal, or simple prelate, and the *potestas jurisdictionis* to be alone unequal, the diametrical opposition in which he stands to the advocates of the papacy of a later age is conspicuously seen ; for these make the papacy the fountain of all power, and while to the pope as patriarch they consign a universal jurisdiction, from the pope as successor of St. Peter derive all spiritual power whatever. The sense in which St. Peter, and any of his successors, may be called the head of the Church, is thus declared : *potuit dici caput Ecclesiæ in quantum principalis est inter ministros.* The writer then goes into a long and elaborate examination of the steps by which the doctrine of the papal supremacy is reached, and enables us to discover that he is much better acquainted with the difficulties which beset the argument at every step than the advocates of the doctrine at the present day are, or profess to be. First, he alleges the election of the apostle to this universal jurisdiction ; then, that a power was given him of selecting a particular see as the centre of it.

Next, he admits that the apostle exercised this power by choosing as his see, Antioch, over which he presided seven years. After this period, Christ, it is asserted, appeared to him and revealed to him his will that he should transfer it to Rome; whence he affirms that there is in the Roman See the concurrence of a universal and a particular bishopric. Now, weak as this argument is in the facts which are brought forward to sustain it, it indicates how many are the *desiderata* of this complicated argument; how many points of attack it opens to its adversaries, how many points of danger it requires its defenders successfully to hold out, by the loss of any one of which all the rest must be surrendered. First, it must be proved that the power was originally granted; then that it was localised; then that it was transferred, and became what Milton would call a "dividual moveable;" then that it was made hereditary; then that the inheritance has been fairly transmitted to the present time, and according to the terms of the original grant. We may say of the papacy as of the Roman empire—

"Tantae molis erat Romanam condere gentem."

Cardinal Pierre d'Ailly is not, however, without some of that *esprit de corps* which Cesarini claimed even in his letters from Basle, in the words, "Numquid non ego sum membrum Ecclesiæ et curiæ Romanæ?" For he maintains the college of cardinals to represent the other apostles, as the pope represents St. Peter, and traces their office and dignity even into the pages of prophecy, and indicates (p. 26) that efforts were made in the Council of Constance to depress the power of this venerable body, and even to prove the possibility and lawfulness of its extinction.

The different forms of election which have obtained in the papacy are then described, and the suggestion put forth that the election which was then coming on should be made, not by the college alone, or by the council alone, but by both united. It would appear from this, that the object of those who depressed the cardinalitial dignity in the council was to confer the right of election on the council alone. He then passes on to the consideration of the temporalities of the clergy, and their right in them ; and after a defence of annates against the attacks of the representatives of the French nation in the council, proceeds to establish the supremacy of a general council, and the subjection of the papal authority thereto. Such are the principal features of this remarkable treatise, and if the account here given of it lead the reader to examine it more closely, he will easily forgive the length of these observations which have introduced him to it.

One passage, among many others which deserve a separate notice, may be here produced before we turn from the subject before us, inasmuch as it vindicates the doctrine of our own Church, which requires even a general council to found its laws in and to govern its decisions according to the Scriptures; and does not hesitate to aver that some councils, when too regardless of this principle, have erred both in ancient and modern times : "Ex quibus patet quod judicium concilii præferendum est judicio Papæ cum ipse in his quæ fidei sunt possit errare, sicut et Petrus, de quo dicit Paulus (Galat. ii. cap.) quod ei restitit in faciem quia reprehensibilis erat non recte ambulans ad veritatem evangelii, &c. Tamen secundum aliquos hoc est speciale privilegium universalis Ecclesiæ, quod non possit errare in fide. Licet hoc idem pie credatur de concilio generali, scilicet *quando innititur divinæ scripturæ* vel auctoritati quæ a Spiritu Sancto conspirata est. Alias sæpe errasse legitur." (Von der Hardt, tom. vi. pp. 72, 73.)

The theory of ecclesiastical unity of the age of the Councils of Pisa, Constance, and Basle, is so clearly laid down in the four following propositions, which were written at the time of the first of these bodies, and are given at the end of the "Acts of the Councils of Pisa and Siena," printed at Paris in 1612, that no apology is needed for introducing them here :—

"I. Prima : in unitate capitis Christi plena ac perfecta consistit unitas corporis mystici totius Ecclesiæ Christianæ, juxta illud apostoli *Christus est caput Ecclesiæ*, et illud *omnes unum corpus sumus in Christo*.

" II. Secunda : licet Papa in quantum Christi Vicarius quodam-
modo possit dici caput Ecclesiæ, tamen Ecclesiæ unitas non
necessarie dependet aut originatur ab unitate Papæ, patet ex
prima parte : et etiam quia nullo existente Papa semper Ecclesia remanet una, juxta illud in Canticis *Una est columba mea*, et
illud Symboli *Unam Sanctam et Apostolicam Ecclesiam.*

" III. Tertia : a Christo capite ejus, corpus mysticum quod est
Ecclesia, originaliter et immediate potestatem habet et auctoritatem, ut ad suam unitatem conservandam rite valeat seipsum
ad generale concilium ipsam representans, congregare, patet ex
illo verbo Christi, *Ubi duo vel tres*, &c.   Ubi animadverten-
dum est quod non dicit *in nomine Petri* vel *in nomine Papæ*
sed *in nomine Meo*, dans intelligere quod ubicumque et a quo-
cumque congregentur fideles, dum tamen hoc fiat in nomine suo,
hoc est in Christi fide et pro Ecclesiæ suæ salute, ipse assistit eis
tanquam ductor et infallibilis rector.

" IV. Non solum auctoritate Christi sed etiam communi jure
naturali præmissam auctoritatem habet corpus mysticum Ecclesiæ Dei, patet, quia quodlibet corpus naturale naturaliter resistit
suæ divisioni et detractioni, et si sit corpus animatum naturaliter congregat omnia membra, omnesque vires suas ad conservandam suam unitatem et repellendam suam divisionem : simili
quoque modo est, quodlibet corpus civile seu civilis communitas
vel politia rite ordinata ; ideoque corpus spirituale seu mysticum
Ecclesiæ Christianæ quod ordinatissime compositum est, propter
quod ecclesiastica politia in Canticis describitur velut *Castrorum
acies ordinata*, simili jure uti poterit ad suam unitatem conservandam et quamlibet schismaticam divisionem repellendam,
tanquam suæ ordinatæ compositionis destructivam."

# APPENDIX B.

## On the Former Letter of Julian from Basle.

I HAD prepared a very long defence of the authenticity of the former letter of Julian to Eugenius, against the groundless attack of Spondanus, but found the whole of the historians of this period of every party so perfectly decided on this subject that it would be needless to lay before the reader a tedious or elaborate examination of it. Even Spondanus, when it suits his purpose (as at an. 1431, sec. 8), refers to it as a genuine document, and is irresistibly compelled to own the authenticity of the second letter, which is found in most of the MSS. of the Council of Basle, including that of the College of Navarre, written by the very hand of a person there present, and that in the Harleian collection, numbered 826. I will, therefore, merely recapitulate here the grounds of the argument which I intended to offer in vindication of this remarkable letter.

I. Its existence in MS. in the public libraries of Basle and Vienna, and incorporation from the beginning into the works of Æneas Sylvius, as appended by him to his history of the council. His object in this was to justify himself in the eye of the world, as appears from his words to Eugenius when recanting his former opinions, " Erravi, quis neget? sed neque cum paucis neque cum parvis hominibus. *Julianum Sancti Angeli Cardinalem,* Nicolaum Archiepiscopum Panormitanum, Ludovicum Pontanum tuæ sedis notarium sum secutus."* Now, the opinions of the two latter are given by Æneas, embodied in their own

* *Vide* Gobellin. Vit. Pii II.

speeches. But, as his history begins after Julian's secession from the council, he could avail himself of the cardinal's authority only by appending to his work these celebrated letters, which accordingly he did. And with these he intimates, in his Bull of Retractations, that he pressed the cardinal so hard in argument as nearly to overcome him.

II. The second argument for the former letter was derived from the admitted authenticity of the latter one. The parallelism between the two is so close, and sometimes even verbal, as to convince an unprejudiced mind that they proceeded from the same pen.

III. Another argument was founded upon the parallelism, also often verbal, between the disputed letter and the synodical epistle which Julian dictated in the council, dated September, 1432, and beginning, " *Cogitanti huic Sanctæ Synodo.*" This is even a more remarkable coincidence than the former, but it is difficult in either case, from the singular resemblance of style and idea in all these documents throughout, to select separate proofs and instances of it.

IV. The fourth argument sprang from the comparison of the statements of Æneas Sylvius (in his letters and Bohemian history) with the facts contained in the letter in question. So exact is the identity between them that it plainly indicates this letter to be the source of the historian's information, while it proves at the same time the credit and authority he attached to this source.

V. A very strong argument (and one to which the reader needs only to be referred to be immediately put in possession of) is, that both in style and historical fact the latter letter implies the former. So much is this the case that the one would be imperfect without the other, and almost unintelligible. Even if the former epistle were not extant, we might discover from the second that it must have existed. The abruptness with which it opens, the manner in which it takes for granted Eugenius' know-le̦l̦ c of tho events detailed in the preceding letter—these, and a multitude of similar circumstances, indicate that a letter had been sent before, and that the document we possess is a faithful copy of that letter.

VI. Another argument may be derived from the fact that these letters were indispensably called forth by the request of Eugenius, in a letter to Julian, in which he writes :—" Circa vero negotium concilii generalis, quia in pluribus mutationem esse factam sentimus *omnia quœ emerserint vel ad notitiam tuam pervenerint* celeriter nobis scribas, cum consilio tuo qualiter in talibus providendum et agendum esse videatur." (Concil. t. xii. p. 934, ed. Labbe.)

Both the letters were published from authentic MSS. existing at Basle, not a century after they were written, and from that original and extremely rare edition (a copy of which is in my possession) they were transferred by Ortuinus Gratius to his *Fasciculus rerum expetendarum et fugiendarum ;* which, after several editions, was finally re-edited in London by Brown. All the historians and divines of the Roman communion admit them without hesitation, with the exception of Spondanus, who, when it suits his purpose, does so also. The learned Abate Vertua di Soresina, in his recent work, " *La scienza teologica, l' eminente scienza di Gesù Cristo*," after quoting copiously from Julian's former letter, concludes—" Cosi parlava quel grande prelato che non avea in vista che la verita e gl' interessi della chiesa." (Tom. xi. part ii. p. 80.) Some apology is due to the reader for appearing to balance the unsupported assertion of a single writer against the testimony of the learned of every subsequent age; but the extreme importance of the letter I have endeavoured to establish urged me to vindicate it even from the suspicion of inauthenticity.

# APPENDIX C.

## *On the Addition of the " Filioque."*

THE period and the occasion of this addition to the creed on the part of the Western Church are involved in much obscurity. It appears, however, admitted by both parties in the controversy that Spain was the place of its origin, and its object the desire to fence the creed from the dangers of Arianism, which there maintained a long conflict with the doctrines of orthodoxy. It is not improbable that the attempt to revive a species of Nestorianism in Spain and the south of France, by Felix Urgelitanus and Elipandus of Toledo, promoted, if it did not even occasion, the adoption of this change. The earliest writer who countenances and even prepares the way for the doctrine of the double procession, is St. Cyril of Alexandria, in the ninth of his celebrated *anathematismi*, or doctrinal canons, drawn up against Nestorius. The doctrine of all the rest of the early fathers, without exception, had been that the Holy Ghost proceeds from the Father alone, which is the clear statement of the Scriptures on this mysterious subject. Indeed, the pertinacity with which the Provincial, in the Council of Florence, clung to a single passage of St. Basil, proves how very limited was the ground of the Latins on this subject in the field of antiquity.

The addition which was introduced in Spain was so openly discountenanced by the Roman Church that Pope Leo III., to whom it was referred, not only prohibited it, but caused the creed, without the addition, to be engraved on two silver plates, that they might be preserved in the Church of Rome for ever, " amore et cautelâ orthodoxæ religionis." These were seen in the eleventh century by Petrus Damiani, Cardinal Bishop of Ostia.*

The addition thus repudiated was readily entertained by Nicholas, the successor of Leo, and a controversy between the missionaries sent by that Pope to convert the Bulgarians, and those sent by the Eastern Church, carried the dispute from the centre of the West into the daily increasing debateable ground which lay between the Eastern and Western Churches. For the papal missionaries, like Anastasius and Photius of old, had introduced to their converts the interpolated creed, but were furiously and successfully encountered by another and a far greater Photius, the celebrated Patriarch of Constantinople, in learning and vigour of mind the prodigy of his age. In an encyclical letter to the patriarchs of the West, as well as in a letter to the Prince of Bulgaria, he challenged the orthodoxy of the Roman Church, and exposed the innovating spirit which has from the beginning so fatally characterised her rulers.

The schism grew more inveterate and irremediable as the controversy advanced, and every effort to unite increased, by the violence of the reaction it produced, the distance of the severed members of the Church. And, as some of these efforts were forcibly and others surreptitiously made (those of Innocent III. being of the former, and that of the Council of Lyons of the latter kind), they not only left the former causes of disunion unremoved, but added others. Neither the domination of the Latins at Constantinople, nor the zeal for union which Michael Palæologus displayed when the seat of the Eastern Empire was recovered by its ancient possessors, effected anything towards this great object.

The Council of Lyons, the result of this prince's zeal and bad faith—for the signatures to its decrees on the part of the Greeks were forged throughout with the most unblushing effrontery†—

* P. Damiani in Opusculo xxxviii. de Processione Sp. S. c. 2.
† Pachymeris, l. vi. cc. 17, 18, &c.

was never even acknowledged by the Eastern Church, and the Latins ventured not to found upon it any of their Florentine decrees, far less to assume that it had settled any of the controversies which it proposed and professed to resolve.

Though boasted of at the time as a Roman triumph, it soon fell into such oblivion as to be unable to retain its place even among the advocates of the Roman See as an Œcumenical Council. The authentic acts of the Council of Florence,* Cardinal Bessarion,† Cardinal Pole,‡ and all the Eastern authorities, by giving to the Florentine Council the title of the eighth general council, disallow the claim of that of Lyons most effectually. Between these two councils the controversy, though occasionally awakened by the zealots of either Church, sank slowly to rest, and the natural and political separation of the Eastern and Western world tended to produce an ignorance of the grounds on which the doctrine was received on the one side, and rejected on the other.

So complete was this in the time of Aquinas that in his writings on the errors of the Greeks he does not touch the real root of the controversy, the prohibition of the Council of Ephesus ; and, when that argument came upon the Latins at Florence, the students of Aquinas, and such writers, were as confounded as their master would have been had he been suddenly met in his metaphysical speculations on the doctrine itself, by the stern and unbending decree of the Ephesian fathers.

In the corrupted pages of the canon law the only two proofs of this doctrine adduced from antiquity are an alleged extract from the decrees of the Council of Ephesus, which is properly, however, a fragment from the synodical letter of St. Cyril of

---

* In the preface, in which it is plainly stated that there were only seven general councils before that of Florence.

† Concil. Florent. ed. Justiniani, p. 425.

‡ Reginaldi Poli, De Reform. Angliæ Decret. II.

Alexandria, and a passage of Didymus on the Holy Ghost, a
writer who flourished more than four centuries before the controversy began.  This latter passage is so corrupted and mutilated, that Didymus, who makes mention of the procession as
from the Father only, is made to propound a doctrine which
nearly approaches the Roman standard.  The corrupted and
genuine text of Didymus runs thus :—

| GRATIAN. l. iv. dist. v. c. 40. | DIDYMI DE SP. S. l. ii. |
|---|---|
|  | Dehinc in consequentibus de Spiritu veritatis *qui a Patre mittatur* et fit paracletus, |
| " Salvator qui est veritas, ait [non enim loquetur a semetipso : hoc est non sine me, et sine meo et patris arbitrio, quia inseparabilis a mea et patris est voluntate, &c.] " | salvator qui est veritas ait, non enim loquatur a semetipso, &c. |

Where the reader will observe the suppression of the most
important part of the words of Didymus, words which qualify
all that follows.

Of the controversy itself we may observe further, that had
the word procession been taken in that plain and simple sense,
which the original ἐκπόρευσις alone can bear—had it been taken
in the sense of a temporal mission for the sanctification of the
creature, and not as an eternal procession implying origin, this
fatal controversy would have never arisen.

The former was the meaning which the Fathers of the Latin
Church, down to the very time of the opening of this controversy, uniformly gave it.  Isidore of Seville,[*] in the seventh,
and Anastasius Bibliothecarius in the ninth century, thus understood it, the words of the latter being these, "Sicut procedit ex
Patre ita cum procedere fateamur ex Filio, missionem nimirum
processionem intelligentes."[†]   Jansenius, Michaëlis, and almost

* Isidor. Hispalensis Epistola.
† Anastas. Biblioth. Ep. ad Joannem Diaconum, tom. v. Concil. (Labbe) p. 1,771.

all modern critics, have held the word ἐκπόρευσις (John xv. 26)
to relate thus to a temporary mission only.*   Peter Lombard
appears to be the first who discovered that this procession was
of a twofold kind, eternal and temporary.†   Of the former he
asserts that "between the generation of the Son and the procession of the Holy Ghost, we are unable while we live here
to distinguish." ‡   The latter he defines to be "that whereby
the Holy Ghost proceeds from the Father and the Son to sanc-
tify the creature." §

The scholastic divines, when they had so fertile a field open
to their speculations as that of the eternal procession, failed not
to cultivate it with diligence ; and Aquinas, outrunning his
fellow-labourers in the boldness of his conclusions, presents us
in his work " Against the Errors of the Greeks," with some of
the most startling and perilous deductions that can be conceived to be derivable from it.   Let the reader take these as
an example :—

1. That the Son originates (*deoriginat*) the Holy Ghost.
2. That the Son is the Author of the Holy Ghost.
3. That the Son is the principle of the Holy Ghost.
4. That the Son is the fount of the Holy Ghost.‖

And after all these theses, he betrays his own mis-apprehension
of the original term ἐκπόρευσις, by saying that the word *processio*
is of all words *which relate to origin* the most general, and the
least determining the manner of that origin.¶   Had the Roman
Church never insisted on the doctrine of the procession in a
sense so fraught with danger, the Eastern Church would have

---

* V. Theophan. Procopowicz de Processione Sp. S. p. 25.

† Sentent. l. i. dist. 14, A.

‡ Id. ibid. dist. 13, C.          § L. i. dist. 14, A.

‖ Aquinas, "Contra errores Græcorum," Opusc. I. (Opuscula Insigniora
Aquinatis.  Duaci, 1609.)

¶ "Verbum enim processionis inter omnia quæ ad originem pertinent
magis invenitur esse commune et minus modum originis determinare."—
Opusc. tom. i. p. 45.

never been aroused to that strong and just resistance to it which has severed these Churches so fatally and effectually.

In the other meaning, the strongest advocates of the latter communion do not hesitate to admit the double procession ; even Phranza himself, who clung to the old paths with the strictest orthodoxy and most determined zeal, recognising the Procession from the Father and the Son in this sense, while he summarily rejects the doctrine for which the Roman Church contends. In a declaration of his faith, at the close of his history, he affirms :—

Ὁμολογῶ βεβαίως τὸ πνεῦμα τὸ ἅγιον οὐκ ἐκ τοῦ Πατρὸς καὶ ἐκ τοῦ Υἱοῦ ἐκπορεύεσθαι ὡς κατὰ τοὺς Ἰτάλους ἀλλ' ἐξ αὐτῆς τῆς ὑποστάσεως τοῦ πατρὸς ἐνικῶς . . . . πέμπεσθαι παρὰ τοῦ πατρὸς καὶ τοῦ Υἱοῦ τὸ πνεῦμα οἶον αὐτὴ ἡ χάρις καὶ ἡ δωρεὰ αὐτοῦ δίδωσι.


# APPENDIX D.

*On the Principle of Developments, as rejected in the Council of Florence, &c.*

THE theory of developments in Christian doctrine introduced by Möhler, and developed by Dr. Newman, has awakened attention rather from its supposed novelty than from the solidity or consistency of the arguments upon which it rests. To those, however, who have watched the controversial diplomacy of the Church of Rome, which, like her external policy, has its regular cycles and revolutions bringing back the same phenomena of doctrine and argument in almost invariable succession since the day when her theology was systematized at Trent, it will not be able to offer even the charm of novelty. Among the parallels to the present course of Roman advocacy, which will occur to such observers, the line of defence adopted by the Latins in the Council of Florence, on the question of the *Filioque*, must obtain a distinguished prominence. And as this addition to the ancient creed by the Roman Church was first introduced as a development, a new discovery, a *profectus fidei*,* we might expect to see it defended on this new ground. Accordingly we find the theory of developments asserted by the Latin Archbishop of Rhodes, in the sixth session of the Florentine Council, and eagerly patronized by Cardinal Julian, who even in the strict letter of the decree of the Council of Ephesus, prohibiting every addition to the creed, discovered a latent power of development. Like Dr. Newman, who urges the capabilities of the text of St. Ignatius for the process of subsequent development, the Cardinal fixes on the words οὐδὲν προστιθέντες ἢ ἀφαιροῦντες ἀλλὰ διασαφοῦντες, κ.τ.λ., as giving this power to explain and develop; the Archbishop maintaining further that the *Filioque* as an explanation was not properly an addition. In proof of this, he applied to it all those tests of a true development which Dr. Newman has defined in his treatise, and applied to the more modern additions of the Church of Rome.

I. The first test, that of the preservation of the type, or idea of the system, which is characterised as "too obvious and close upon demonstration to be of easy application in particular cases," (Essay, p. 65), is alleged for the *Filioque* by the Bishop of Forli, who came to the assistance of the Archbishop of Rhodes in the tenth session; and he describes it in like manner as being one of those truths which are *propinquissimæ suis principiis*, and are to be inferred from them *syllogismo imperceptibili*.

II. The second test, continuity of principles, is applied to the *Filioque* by the Archbishop of Rhodes, in the seventh session, who subjects the creed to the philosophical rule which permits

* Baronii Annal. ad an. 809. The words of the deputies of the Council of Aquisgranum addressed to Pope Leo III. openly admit the doctrine to be a development. "Quia hæc quæstio," they say, "diu a quærentibus jacebat indiscussa, voluit Omnipotens Deus in eandem suscitare corda pastorum, ut negligentiæ torpore sublata, exercitationis sanctæ brachio cœlestem valeant perfodere thesaurum."

the conclusions to be varied and modified so long as the principles remain the same. "You affirmed," said his opponent, Bessarion, Archbishop of Nice, and afterwards Cardinal, "that the principles and primary propositions of every science contained in them virtually all that came after them, and you undertook to show us from principles and first propositions that the dogma is true according to the principles of faith." In other words, "continuity of principles" was asserted for the *Filioque* as the token of its fidelity as a development.

III. The third test, that of "the power of assimilation" possessed by a true development, enters rather singularly into the controversy between Bessarion and the Archbishop of Rhodes. The former contends that the *Filioque* being extrinsically taken, is, according to Aristotle, a proper addition ; the latter, that as it is internally produced it is not extrinsically taken, and therefore is an explanation and not a proper addition. From the assertion of Aristotle that there must be a power of assimilation between the body which is nourished and the nourishment (the very illustration produced by Dr. Newman, p. 74), Bessarion draws the conclusion that the *Filioque*, however assimilated to the doctrines to which it is added, is properly an addition, and so comes within the terms of the prohibition of Ephesus, which forbids all addition. His adversary, from the assertion of the same philosopher that all nourishment is externally derived, contends that the internal production of the *Filioque* frees it from the charge of addition, and makes it only an explanation, as such saving it from the prohibition of the canon. It is notable that the Eastern advocate lays down as a distinctive mark of addition from without, that which Dr. Newman makes a principal token of development from within. Whether a doctrine so well contested by one of the greatest philosophers and divines of the Eastern Church (for such Bessarion undoubtedly was), and rejected by him even after he had become the advocate of Rome, and a prince of the Roman Church, can become a safe test of truth, let the reader judge. And that he did reject, not only this mark of development, but the entire theory, is proved by his letter to Alexius Lascharis, in which he writes that until the speech of Cardinal Julian (in which the argument from development was abandoned for one derived from the circumstances of the prohibition), nothing worthy of the subject or to the purpose had been produced by the Latins,—adding what so learned and modest a writer would not but from a strong conviction have professed,—"Quando (etsi absque arrogantiâ dictum) potiores ad hanc rem ex parte nostrâ productæ rationes a me et inventæ et dictæ fuerunt, testes sunt qui adfuerunt."* So much for the judgment passed upon the theory of Dr. Newman, in its most reasonable and least offensive form, by the Florentine Council, and even by the most illustrious convert to the Latin views,—one who may be said to express the judgment both of the Eastern and the Western Church in this matter, and who at one time was very nearly elected to fill the papal throne.

The remaining tests of (IV.) "early and definite anticipation," (V.) "logical sequence," (VII.) "preservation of former truth," and (VII.) "chronic continuance," were all alleged for the *Filioque* by the Archbishop of Rhodes; for he produced many early and definite anticipations of the addition from Basil, Epiphanius, Cyril of Alexandria, and Maximus; he dwelt upon the logical sequence it exhibited by means of the trite argument, the Holy Ghost proceeds from the Father; all that the Father hath the Son hath also; therefore the Holy Ghost proceeds from the Son. He urged, moreover, not only its capability to preserve, but its necessity for preserving prior truths, and he showed on many occasions its "chronic continuance" in the Western Church. In the tenth session the Bishop of Forli took up a more general argument on the subject, urging again that the *Filioque* was not an addition but rather the evolution of a complicated subject; *complicatæ rei evolutio impliciti explicatio et indeterminati deter-*

* Acta Concil. Florent. (Horatii Justiniani), p. 399.

*minatio*—in other words, that it was a true development made by an authority competent to explain and develop.

From the saying of St. Augustine, "Tempóra variata sunt, non fides," he derives an argument for a gradual evolution of the truths of Christianity from their first principles, while the comparison of the Old and New Testament with the original and subsequent creed, furnishes him with an argument similar to that of Dr. Newman, who alleges the New Testament to be the development of the Old. And here he quotes from St. Augustine a passage which, in its plain signification, defeats his assertion, " Christus non venit legem solvere sed adimplere ; non ut adderentur legi quæ deerant sed ut scripta fierent : quod ejus verbis confirmatur. Neque enim dixit iota unum aut unum apicem non transiturum de lege donec addantur quæ desunt ; sed donec, inquit, omnia fiant."*

But for all this the Eastern Church resolutely resisted the principle thus introduced and defended, and on the same ground upon which we still resist it, viz. the unchangeableness of Christian truth. "All sacred doctrines," affirmed Bessarion, "and which form the foundations and principles of our faith, we derive from the sources of Holy Scripture, and nothing has been added to them or can be added by us, while we are sane, or by any other Christians. And it follows necessarily that nothing ought to be added to the creed, since it has, in the Church, the nature of a first principle." (Sess. VIII.) Marcus Ephesius up to the very last maintained this great principle, and opened the twenty-third session with the memorable confession, " Our faith had not its origin from man, or through man, but through our Lord Jesus Christ himself, who himself imparted it to his disciples. Wherefore, laying aside ambiguous expressions, let us recur to that authority whence the rule of determining even these is to be drawn." Georgius Scholarius (or Gennadius), in defending the Latin views on this controversy, takes the same

* Contra Faustum, l. xviii.

ground. After making the Scriptures the first principle and rule
of faith and controversy, he examines first their direct or implied
meaning, next the interpretations given to the passages alleged
from them by the Fathers, and lastly the conclusions to which
these ancient expositors arrive from the comparison of these
passages ; and he labours, as Ephesius did throughout, not to
show that they were developers of doctrine, but rather "pious
and prudent hearers of the Scriptures."* Nay, he affirms that
the Scriptures explain all those passages which are not clearly
expressed by others which are ; and bids us reconcile whatever
doubts should remain after such a collation of Scriptures by
"taking notice of diversities of times, customs, senses, and the
like," and alleges that in this manner the Fathers of the Council
of Nice deduced from the Scriptures the true belief touching
the Son of God.

A late primate of the Russian Church nobly vindicated the
truth that the Scriptures contain the full and final development
of Christian doctrine, in a learned treatise, "On the Procession
of the Holy Ghost," which great controversy he opens thus :
"Recal, I pray you, all that I have said at length in my book of
prolegomena on the principles of divine theology, where I have
shown that we cannot know anything which is properly theological from any other source than from the word of God ; wherefore," he adds shortly after, "I could never sufficiently express
my amazement at the incredible levity of many who deem it
sufficient to allege in their own defence, or to hear as the defence
of their opponents, the single saying of some Father which seems
to favour our side or that of the Latins, and then think that the
argument is completed.   But if for the resolution of so difficult
a question, the clearest and most consistent words were produced
from all the Fathers of every age, and nothing could be alleged
from Scripture, they would be of no moment whatever."†   The

* Oratio III. de Pace, &c.

† Theophanis Propocowicz Archiepiscopi Novogrod. de Processione Spiritus Sancti, c. ii. sect. 24, 25.

truth that all necessary doctrine is fully unfolded in the Scriptures could not be more clearly expressed. Not only the doctrine of developments, but the supposition that the Scriptures are only a partial revelation of divine truth, is set aside by this unqualified appeal to the Scriptures as the depositories of Christian doctrine. The Council of Florence, by its abandonment of the ground taken by the Latin advocates in defence of the addition made by the Church of Rome to the creed which the Council of Ephesus had made unchangeable and inviolable, tacitly but most effectually condemned the theory of developments. The doctrine was not even introduced but after a desperate effort to prove that the addition had existed from the first, or had at least obtained from its antiquity a kind of *quod semper* existence. Cardinal Julian accordingly produced, in the fifth session, a Latin MS. in which the word was to be found, and eagerly wrote to the Prior of the Camaldules for a Greek copy of the same, from which he affirmed the disputed word to be *evidenter et ad oculum abrasa.** Cardinal Humbertus a Sylvâ Candida, in the eleventh century, had boldly affirmed that the Greeks had erased the word from the creed. But an allegation which might serve to prop up a bad cause in the darkness that succeeded the separation of the East and West, was vain at the period of learning and intelligence in which the reunion of the Churches was attempted at Florence ; and it failed accordingly. Upon its failure recourse was had to the principle advanced by Dr. Newman, as we have already seen ; and upon the failure of this argument also, the field of controversy was first extended and then changed. From the legal question the Council passed to the doctrinal one, and though here the theory of development might have been most successfully propounded, the very weakest possible argument from tradition was put forth instead, and for a whole year the Fathers were occupied upon a single passage of St. Basil and a few statements of St. Epiphanius and other Fathers,

* Ambrosii Traversarii Epist. p. 976.

all of ambiguous meaning and all of doubtful authenticity. Finally, a temporary union was effected on the faith and in the terms of a doubtful passage of St. Maximus ; and the labours of this otherwise fruitless Council terminated by proving that the weakest possible form of the *quod semper* argument was stronger and more satisfactory than the best argument that could be derived from the right of explaining and developing revealed truths assumed by the Church of Rome. And it is a singular parallel to the ancient course of Roman advocacy, that after the rejection of the *quod semper* argument by Dr. Newman, in his introduction, he falls back upon it under the cover of ambiguous expressions on almost every occasion of doctrinal examination. At the close of his treatise he actually returns into the beaten track of tradition, and submits himself once more to its inflexible rule. Thus, to give one example among many, he admits that certain Catholic doctrines are found in the Epistles of St. Ignatius, "in a definite, complete, and dogmatic form" (p. 369), —he holds that as these Epistles prove certain doctrines, other writings as ancient may be discovered to prove all the rest (p. 146), and asserts that silence is a proof not that the doctrine was not held, but that it was not questioned (p. 370). From these admissions the conclusion inevitably follows that he believes Romanism to have existed in all its parts and in their fullest growth in the apostolic age, fully developed though not fully defined. Thus his entire theory is destroyed by his own hand, unless what St. Ambrose said of one of the mysteries of Christianity be true of the whole body of Roman doctrine, *sunt quæ erant et in aliud commutantur.**

* See an article in the "Christian's Monthly Magazine" (May, 1846), "On the self-refuting tendency of Mr. Newman's treatise."

R. CLAY, SON, AND TAYLOR, PRINTERS, BREAD STREET HILL.